Angel Of Anglonia
Legend of Anara
Book: 1

Elston Latimer Errol Taylor

ISBN: 9798498028835

DEDICATION

This book is a dedication to what you can do when handling struggles that seem unsurmountable. That being said, to everybody that was patient with me in writing and sitting on this project all this time, I can only say thank you from the bottom of my heart.

To Kalen, I have no words. You and I both know that this does not get written without you. Thank you for thinking I was great and believing I could be better. This story is dedicated to you.
Prochnost Brother!

ACKNOWLEDGMENTS

Before jumping into this story, I must forewarn you, this is not traditional fantasy. All I can say is that it's a view of how I saw the world at the time I wrote it and how I see the world now. This book is also a celebration of everything I am and love. This is why Martial Arts, and its principles are at the heart of this story. By the end of this book, you will know me better than most.

To call this a labour of love would be an understatement, not because you couldn't fathom how much I loved this. I wouldn't be so condescending. It's an understatement because, I wrote this with more than love, I hated this, I was fatigued, I was healed by this and it caused me unimaginable pain. I celebrated it's grown while writing it and mourned its loss when I finished it. So, I couldn't let it go, and for years this has sat idle, edited, and dormant until I could.

Now it's time to raise the curtain.
Showtime!

1 THE REAL CELESTINE

It was the last night of spring and the warmth of the encroaching summer battled with the chill of night. Thunder clouds hung ominously above. Tonight was not the night to go sailing. Nevertheless, the crew of the Aduantas did just that. The nose of the ship nodded with the eagerness of a starving man offered bread and honey. They were in deep water. Nothing but ocean and horizon on every side. Despite the perils and omens that faced them, the crew powered on regardless. Gipsies, also known as Travellers, never took such warnings from neither man nor nature. Their will to sail was too strong, their need to see the emerald isles of their homeland, Eireann, too great.

On deck, the crew and passengers danced and sang along with each other. They had become accustomed to falling on their arse repeatedly because they had not stopped drinking since the night before. Be it Nordic mead, Anglo ale, or strongwine the world over, they drank it all. Strongwine was the most abundant of the beverages because it was the easiest to make and the most potent of the lot. It was a concentrated spirit made through fermentation and distillation. Strongwine could be made with nearly anything. The Celtish people, however, were partial to a grain-based strongwine they called Scottsdrink. This would not stop them from sampling every other kind available. The Celtish were renowned for their drinking, and this was surely an occasion to do so. The late King Lochlyn McMahon led the Celtish to independence thirty-one years ago. There had been a celebration across the entire country every year since then, The Festival of King Loch.

The Aduantas set sail to gather food and drinks for the oncoming festival. Although Zorrodon was to the south in, Kings Anglonia, just half a day's sail there and back, by no means would a Celt go to King's Anglonia to make trade. They sailed north to Nordic Deutschland to the port of Jurden-Tove. They had better strongwine anyway, none of that prissy juniper nonsense. It was on that little excursion where they acquired their two unexpected passengers. Celestine of King's Anglonia, and Luke Chef of Caledonia.

Celestine was not Celtish, but Luke Chef was, which was a great selling point when bartering to get onto the ship. However, so was a small bag of gold. They were both aboard the ship and their difference in nationality was highlighted in their whereabouts. Luke was on deck with his kinsman, slathered in alcohol and singing his merry heart away. He was welcomed into this group without question. Luke was from the Shetlands of Caledonia, and the Gipsies from Eireann, the principal states of Celtish Anglonia. Often, the two had an amicable rivalry like that of siblings. Throughout the year, members of each side would volley banter back and forth, asserting that they were the premier state of Celtish Anglonia. Despite the rivalry between them, both sides knew what was fought for and lost in their fight for independence. So, drinking ensued and singing of folk legends like Finn the Brave, and Sheamus the Nasty, began.

'He's a McMahon!' Said Luke, slamming the base of his mug onto the wooden table. He was enthralled in a heated debate about the marquee attraction of the upcoming festival, Finn II. Finn II was the first-born son of Finn The Brave, the greatest Celtish Legend in the country's short history. Legend had it, that he was singlehandedly responsible for winning the battle for independence for the Celtish, becoming their first champion in doing so.

The festival had a tradition of having the land's champion defend their title on the Proving Ground, where they had clinched their independence. Finn II had earned his way to an opportunity to bring the championship back to his family and restore their name. This was still a point of fierce contention, as this was the topic of the debate at hand.

'A McMahon? That little twat? Not in my country.' Said one of the travellers.

'That little twat's father is the reason you even have a country to call your own.' Luke looked around to see if anybody could or would rebuke his point. Nobody did. Of all the drawbacks that drinking brought upon men, honesty and pragmatism were one of the few virtues bestowed on the inebriated. It wasn't like Finn the Brave was disliked; the population would rather just forget about him. He brought disgrace and shame upon the country in his final defeat, in a time they could ill afford any loss in credibility. He died as the champion of Celtish Anglonia, but the word that came out of Zorrodon was that he - Died a coward. Finn II, on the other hand, he proved a polarising figure. Where the Celtish were quiet, he was loud, where they were humble, he was arrogant, and he had a grudge to settle with the people and the royal family. He went as far as to say that this fight would be his revenge against the nation of Celtish Anglonia. That stirred the people the wrong way and the majority of those in attendance at the Proving Grounds would be pulling for current champion Michael, in spite of Finn II lineage.

'Aye you have a point, but Michael is a tough, tough man. That little gobshite, don't even reach his shoulders, and weighs about as much as my right leg.' Said the traveller.

'All I am saying is, I only back winners.' Luke smirked confidently.

'Is that right?'

Luke nodded. The traveller beckoned his cohort that were half-listening to pay full attention now.

'The Caledonian has just told me he only backs winners?' He said to his flankers. 'Right, how about a wager then?'

'A wager? On Finn? Alright, how much?' answered Luke. He was not assured without reason. Celestine had endorsed Finn II as one to watch. Luke had always disagreed with how Finn II and his family were treated anyway, and supported him in his quest to redeem his name. Celestine was one of the cleverest minds Luke knew when it came to fighting, his word was law on the matter.

'No mate…' Said the traveller. 'a fight on this ship. Seven gold pieces for you to, back a winner, as you say.'

'Can I pick anybody I like?'

'After me of course, but plenty of good men here outside of who I choose.' He said with someone already in mind.

'In that case, I'll bet you double.'

As the party went on upon the deck, Celestine was in his small cabin dreaming of home. The room was lit with oil lamps that burned a warm orange. He rested laying sprawled on his back with the third edition of, The Legend of Kastielle, stories open on his face. He was on his eighth time of reading this book, and still, he found it compelling enough to keep reading until the second he fell asleep.

This edition followed the series' central character Kastielle Neriah, on his return home from the Arrow Island after earning the powers of the Children of Nature and world makers. Celestine loved the stories since he was a young boy, barely old enough to read himself. The grand adventure and narrative were marvellous, but Kastielle Neriah was a real person, the most famous person in history. He was the last King of Anara and personal friend of Celestine's Uncle Talion. Talion was Kastielle's champion when he was king and he was present when Anara fell. Talion gifted Celestine the series of books when he discovered Celestine reading the seventh book in the series in his bedroom. "The Story of King Kastielle and Emperor Wukong" a relatively recent story in the cannon of the narrative. Talion, of course, prefaced this as a work of fiction for children. Although some events were real, they were greatly exaggerated. Seeing as this came from the last living companion of King Kastielle, and therefore the foremost authority on the man himself, Celestine was inclined to believe him. It did not make the books less interesting though. Now Twenty-Seven years of age, Celestine had read the entire series many times over. Now he picked some of his favourites to re-read at his leisure.

The cabin was just about big enough to house, two bunks one above the other, a coat hanger on the door, and a table at the foot of the beds. Celestine and Luke's bags were stored underneath the bottom bunk. They packed lightly for a long journey. A journey that was coming to an end. Inspired by his stories, as well as his uncle, who had seen the world a dozen times over in his own right, Celestine decided it was time to do the same with his best friend.

Both Celestine and Luke lived on Sakura Farm in the south of King's Anglonia with Talion and the many other workers there. They were reared and educated there, and now, they worked there in adulthood. Their life had been dedicated to the small community of people under Talion's employ. The farm was large enough and there were enough faces, old and new, to keep things fresh, but Celestine yearned for more. He had travelled before, but he wanted to explore, go on an adventure. There was only so much wonder he could get from his ten-thousandth trip to Zorrodon market. So, at the beginning of the journey, Celestine could only think of the places he was set to go to next. Now, as time went by, he started thinking of home, then missing home, now he dreamt of it almost every night. Finally, after half a year, he and Luke were on their way back.

Celestine snored lightly as the tips of his golden locks flitted on his forehead. His leg hung off the side of his bed and the leg of his long johns rolled halfway up his calf. He was dreaming of sitting in the Big House, Sakura Farm's residential quarters, with a banquet prepared by Luke's sister, Samantha Chef. Celestine missed her food. He had tried the best cuisines the world had to offer on his travels, and they were delicious, but Samantha was special. She did not earn the name Chef for being mediocre at cooking. Only excellence could define a person and their family. Celestine often fantasised about coming home and fixing himself a bowl of Samantha's famous pumpkin soup. His lips smacked and spittle slithered from the corners of this mouth as his dream returned him to that very fantasy. He could smell it, feel the vaporous warmth, and see the cubed cutlets of orange laying in the hot bath of liquid the same colour.

Then, abrupt knocking.

Celestine opened his eyes.

The knocking proved to be a redundant exercise seconds later as Luke barged in and Celestine was now fully awake with no hope of recapturing that moment of sweet pumpkin spice radiating from a deep spoon. He was also a little disappointed it was not real in the first place. Celestine sat up with a great sigh. He rubbed his eyes and blinked away the grogginess. Luke was drunk beyond belief. It took a lot to get him drunk, but once he was, he was a self-admitted arsehole.

'Get up bawbag!' yelled Luke. It was the middle of the night, or the early hours of the morning, dependent on one's perspective. Celestine was exhausted, the last few days were packed with activities and drama, compounded with being on the final leg of a half year adventure. All Celestine wanted was time to rest before they reached the port of Fearon in the morning. When he expressed this to Luke earlier, in his misguided sobriety, Luke had respected his wishes. He dismissed him rather tamely by calling him a "Tosspot". Now, there was only five hours until port and Celestine cursed his optimism in believing the sober intent of the self-admitted arsehole, forgetting the inevitable outcome once strongwine was brought into the equation.

'Good morning Luke.' Said Celestine. 'Is it even morning?' There was no way to tell with the absence of windows to see out to the sky. He wrestled his long hair to tame it from the exploded mess that it was. Then, he coughed his throat clear and peered up. Luke rocked like he and the ship were one, adjusting his imbalance to go with the flow of the violent waves. Celestine wondered how many times he had fallen over before he mastered that little trick. When Luke stumbled and slammed into the wall, he realised that he was one or two shy of enough.

He studied Luke's face and he knew he couldn't be angry. Behind the shaggy beard and curly hair, which looked like a shower cap that a granny would wear in this light, he could see the little boy he knew as a child. He was excited, almost bouncing with excitement. The Festival of King Loch was a special occasion for him; it was the celebration of his nation's independence. Celestine could not fathom how proud he must be of that, but he understood why Luke went to Celtish Anglonia every year for it. It was a countrywide celebration of drinking, singing, dancing, and much more drinking, bringing the country together to remind them of their shared endeavour to call the land their own. Celestine could not be angry at Luke, not for embracing his culture. It was a major time in its short history. King Loch was a legend akin to how he saw the late King Kastielle in his books, but there were no celebrations for Kastielle. In fact, most people did not even talk about him outside of the context of the children's books and case studies. His past was grand but gradually became more troubled. It was easier to forget him than relive the years of strife that plagued the latter of his rule.

'Mate!' Said Luke, much too loud considering the distance between the two. 'Ah have made a wee bet in which I require your skills.' He maintained the same volume in an accent thicker than Miss Nonna's porridge back home on the farm. Celestine rang his ears and shook his head.

'And what may that be?' he said.

'Promise ye won't get angry?' Luke asked.

'I absolutely will not.'

'Good! I bet about, thirteen gold pieces that you could take on the biggest, baddest, man on this ship.'

'You did what!' Celestine jumped to his feet.

Luke cowered like a child. 'You promised you wouldn't get angry.' His voice dwindled to a whisper.

'I did no such thing! I said I wouldn't promise not to get angry!'

'Oh, well honest mistake. Maybe be a little bit clearer next time?' Said Luke, slowly losing his tenuous grip on his balance. 'So, about the fight...'

'There is no sodding fight!' Snapped Celestine.

'Shhhhhhhhhhhhhh....' Luke pushed his finger to his lips as the sound slipped from the corners of his mouth. Now he had lost his footing completely dropping to his bottom blinking as he slumped against the door. 'No need to be that loud.' he whispered like he was hiding some unknown secret from heaven knows who.

'You are a bloody idiot sometimes!' Said Celestine. Red anger was drawn on his face. There was embracing culture and there was being a reckless fool, Luke was doing the latter. The only redeeming factor of this whole situation was that Luke freely admitted his foolishness when drunk. His eyes stabbed at him with a malicious stare that could only be accompanied with a growl or a hiss. Celestine opted for dead silence instead. Although thirteen gold pieces was a lot of money, enough to by a three-horse carriage and the horses to go along with it, and way too much to bet with. Celestine was angrier at Luke for once again forcing him into a situation he did not want to be in.

Luke looked up, first obliviously, then gleefully. 'That's it!' He yelped excitedly and hopping to his feet. He wrapped his arm around Celestine's back and kissed him on the cheek so aggressively that it could have been mistaken for a headbutt. The old Caledonian Kiss. 'If you use that anger there, he won't stand a chance.' Before Celestine knew it, Luke had ushered him out of the door to his cabin.

'Wait!' Said Celestine repeating himself quickly to deaf ears. The door slammed behind him and before he knew it he was locked outside of the room he was sleeping in minutes before. The joys of Luke Chef's friendship.

'Alright mate, you'll be fine! I'm knackered now I'm getting some kip. Big day tomorrow.' Said Luke from behind the door.

'Oi!! I'm not even dressed!' yelled Celestine. He was only dressed in a pair of long johns that did not leave much to the imagination. They were nightwear after all.

'Are you Celestine?' a man said from behind. Celestine cringed and slowly turned around. There were three burly travellers, drenched in a strange concoction of ale, strongwine, and sweat, all of which pooled at the top of their round bellies amongst a nest of crumbs and torn cooked carcass. The smell hadn't reached Celestine yet, but it was foul.

'It depends…' He said timidly. 'If it's about a fight, my name is Luke Chef.' Surprisingly, the men looked perplexed, and Celestine believed his ruse successful.

'My name is Luke Chef!' yelled Luke from behind. 'That's my name. Who's using the same name as me?'

'Oh for The Heavens' sake.' Celestine sighed. The Heavens was a less formal name for The Spiritual Court or the Children of Mother Nature.

'I know which one of yous is Luke Chef. Question is, what's your name?' The middle traveller said. He was the one that Luke had made the bet with and he was considerably more invested than the other blank-faced men at his flank.

'Luke Chef?' Said Celestine as more of a question than a statement. He smiled awkwardly at the men who were beginning to piece things together. 'Common name hey?' he shrugged and chuckled praying that this would work. The men lurched forward groping at Celestine like he was the key to life itself. Celestine backed up to the cabin door. 'You know what isn't a common name? Celestine, if I find him, I'll be sure to let you know.' Said Celestine in a last-ditch effort, but these men were unfortunately not as stupid as they looked. The door swung open suddenly and Celestine stumbled back into his cabin. Luke stood half-naked and very cross.

'Will you please, keep it down! I'm tryna get some kip!' He said. His potbelly hung over the waistband of his loose white shorts and a blossom of black hair spread across his belly and chest, looking like an abstract charcoal drawing of a willow tree.

'Grab em both lads! We have a wager Mr Chef.' The burly man in the middle shouted, then Luke and Celestine were hauled to the deck.

The onset of the rain that had ominously foreshadowed its arrival, was an unwelcome addition to the situation that Luke and Celestine found themselves in. The deck was awry with rowdy travellers. They chanted and yelled louder and more ferociously than the battering of the raindrops and the howling of the wind. Luke and Celestine were thrown to the middle of the crowd. The cold set in and their teeth chattered, and they clutched their arms to hold on to their warmth. They were soaking wet in seconds.

Amid the gargles and burbs, trumps and retches, the crowd managed to utter a coherent name through the ruckus. That name was Alec. They yelled over and over, and they parted forming a disorganised drunken honour guard for their interim champion that led to the bewildered stowaways. Ahead of them all was a man who towered over all the others around him by close to a foot. A king amongst them. He was large not just in height. His belly hung like a lead weight. He was broad of shoulder and his thighs looked as big as boulders. He had an ale mug in each hand, one of which was full.

The other one was placed to his lips as he guzzled down the ale inside. He lowered it revealing his round chin and a thick moustache. He strode forward confidently licking the beer from his whiskers and snatched another from the crowd.

Once he reached Luke and Celestine, he looked down on them and laughed. Then, he swilled another ale until finished with impressive speed, without spilling a drop. The crowd cheered even that. At this point, drinking wasn't really anything to write home about, but Alec was an exception. Everything he did granted a reaction from the eager audience.

'Which one of you is Celestine?' said Alec. Luke pointed immediately at Celestine and Celestine nodded. There was no point in pretending now. If one of them had to fight, there was no question it would go much better if it were him and there was no escaping this fight. Without a word, Alec swilled his other ale and stooped to get eye to eye with his opponent. He unleashed an unearthly belch which was as forceful as it was pungent. The type of belch that was teetering on the edge of projectile vomit. Celestine did not move, not even a flinch. That was a challenge and a statement from Alec there was no turning back. These were fighting words. He no longer had the luxury of being conscious of how much his long johns would reveal when wet, or ashamed of the recklessness of this exercise, what people would think. He had a task ahead of him, and he did not need to overthink it. He was free to be in the moment. Luke could see it in his eyes, this was the real Celestine.

Celestine exhaled and the smell hit him.

'That's disgusting.' He said. It was a struggle not to gag. All he could do was hold it in. He pushed Luke gently aside and stood front and centre. 'If I must Luke, I guess I have to beat some manners into this fool.' Luke jumped giddily clapping. Celestine was not only the nephew of Talion, but he was also trained by him from the moment he could stand and there had not been a champion like Talion ever. Everything that Talion knew as a champion was passed on to his nephew. There was no question of his pedigree; Luke had watched Celestine train and seen him fight. It was a spectacle. He thought Celestine could beat any champion of any land, he just needed to believe it himself, or at least, allow himself to believe it. He put champions on a pedestal they deserved, but, was ultimately unrealistic.

'Oh manners? Manners?! You must be a Princess.' Alec said. 'We have a Princess amongst us!' he continued now addressing the crowd. Princess was what Celtish Anglonians called King's Anglonians. It was an expression of their disdain for the people of their sibling country. The bitterness and hatred that the Celtish had for their southern former kinsmen bordered on violent. With all that was going on, the festivities, the occasion, Celtish independence, the battle they won to get it, the crowd erupted in an emotive retort. They threw their ale's in the air and screamed profanities at Celestine. He was calm, he felt at home in the chaos.

'You, a fellow Celt, back this man to be the winner against me?' Said Alec disgusted by the betrayal. Luke patted Celestine on the shoulder.

'I do. You can back out now if you like.' He said.

'I'll give you this, you have balls the size of melons you do. You are definitely a Celt. But, you aren't too smart.'

'Is your fight with him or me?' interjected Celestine. Alec went red with shock at the affront. It then became amusing to him, how this small man could act so bold before him. He smiled coyly.

'I'm happy with either. A bet's a bet and muney's muney.' Said Alec.

'Let's get on with it then.'

Luke fell back into the crowd and said. 'Don't say I didn't warn you.'

Alec dropped his mugs with a clang against the wooden deck and without hesitation, he tackled Celestine before he could assume a fighting stance. He wasted no time.

Alec drove him into the mast of the ship. He was strong, and quick for his size. Celestine was not a small man. He stood a hair above six-foot-three, and he appeared much taller when his hair was tied up and not sagging against his face. He looked slight but boasted an above-average weight. He weighed eighty-seven kilograms on average, although he didn't look it. As Alec drove his shoulder into Celestine's midriff, he felt the strength of his slender frame. There was no surplus mass on him; he was solid as a rock. The crowd cheered him on and chanted for the Celtishman to prevail against the "Princess" from King's Anglonia.

Celestine clobbered Alec's back, every strike slapping with the base of his forearm absent any effect. Celestine anticipated as much. The crowd laughed at the meagre attempt, and Luke smugly rolled his eyes. The mass of fat that covered Alec's back proved to be a shield in this circumstance. What he lacked in skill and training he made up for in experience and size, and experience with that size. The hot pies that Alec's granny had forced him to eat as a child were finally paying off. Despite both children and adults alike teasing him for his weight, he was about to win a hefty sum of money for using that weight to his advantage. He barely felt the strikes from above and relished every single second helping he ever got from granny. The heat of battle convinced him that it was this very moment that his glutenous youth led to. He didn't take into account the numbing effect of the alcohol in his system.

Celestine knew the alcohol would be a factor that could benefit his opponent. Brute strength wouldn't work, but there were other avenues to exploit. Celestine adjusted his plan. Alec rammed his shoulder into Celestine's body. That would have winded any other man, but Celestine was tougher than his fair looks would have people think. He had endured worse in training at home. Celestine hooked his arms underneath Alec to gain control of him. It was easy to manipulate opponents from this position. It was a struggle, but he managed to slip it under with the aid of the rain, as well as a little bit of wriggling. As soon as his arms were hooked under, Celestine shoved with great force to pivot out and away from the mast. Now it was his fight. The momentum carried Alec headfirst into the solid wood of the mast. The dull *"Thonk"* was muted by the static sound of shattering raindrops on the wooden deck. Alec stumbled backwards and dropped to one knee whipping his head up to see Celestine, fists up and waiting.

Celestine brushed his hair from his eyes, then beckoned Alec to attack again.

Alec rushed in. Celestine avoided damage with a combination of blocks and dodges. Luke knew Celestine's style, it was very defensive and relied on counters, the other travellers didn't, and the onslaught Alec was unleashing gave the impression that he was winning. They clapped and banged and stamped to encourage him. From Alec's perspective, that meant nothing. He was trying his utmost to hit Celestine and could not even get close. Celestine was so elusive, it felt like if he chose to, he could evade even the raindrops in the sky. Celestine spun out of the line of fire then countered with two quick jabs to his eye. They sounded like quick slaps, but they stung. Alec recovered and blocked his face by crossing his arms. Celestine slipped his fist under the guard with an uppercut to the chin jarring Alec bolt upright. Stunned and sluggish, Alec was unable to defend as Celestine dug left hook into his unprotected liver.

'Ohh thah's gotta hurt!' Luke shouted from his front-row vantage point.

Alec gasped unable to hear him. A liver punch was one of the most debilitating blows in hand-to-hand combat if done right. It sobered Alec up. Now the hits that he didn't feel before crept out in dull aches and throbs. The colour ran from his face, and he stood as if petrified to stone. He wanted to grunt or yell but he could not muster the air. All he could do was howl silently and try to hold on to the sea of booze in his belly. Celestine danced away, bouncing on the balls of his feet. Watching him move, as well as recent experience, it dawned on him that Celestine was not a typical type of fighter. He moved quickly and slowly at the same time. Alec was in over his head, but, a gipsy never quits. Celestine waited as the spectators jeered him. He found Luke in the crowd with an I told you so look on his face. Celestine could not deny that his friend had a point. He was having fun.

Alec struggled upright again.

'You should have finished me when you had the chance.' said Alec.

'I intend to. Don't worry.' Celestine winked at Luke. With a hand behind his back, he used to other to beckon Alec to him, in an outlandish show of disrespect.

Alec screamed launching a straight punch with killer intent, frenzied by the embarrassment. Celestine skipped back grabbing the ham-fisted blow by the wrist. He landed with Alec's wayward wrist ensnared in his grip. He bounced back up to lift a kick into his armpit. It was a sensitive part of the body and not a comfortable place to be hit. Alec flinched but had no time for further reaction. Celestine launched another kick into his ribs, and another, and another. Alec grimaced but did not scream. He would die before losing face in front of his people. Celestine could feel the laboured cadence of Alec's breathing through his wrist. When he listened in, he could hear it clearly over the ruckus. Alec was wheezing and gasping for air. Alec was a tough man, but fatigue made cowards of all. An old lesson from old Talion. Alec's breathing told a fine story.

Celestine capitalised on the opportunity to move him again. He brought Alec to his knees by twisting and putting pressure on his wrist and shoulder joints. Celestine skipped over to synch in a vice-like choke. He put Alec's head under his arm and pressed the blade of his forearm hard against his Adam's apple.

'Yield!' Celestine shouted. The once rowdy crowd fell silent, even the rain stopped. Only the waves could be heard.

Alec did not reply. Celestine clasped his palms together and wrenched the choke simultaneously thrusting his hips forward for leverage. Alec grew tense and squawked trying to suck air into his constricted airway. His arms flailed as he reached for options.

'Yield!' Shouted Celestine again. Then remorse set in. He felt the wash of shame covering him. 'Please... just... I don't want to.' He pleaded with him. Celestine loosened his grip knowing he could not finish this fight. He was about to yield himself when Alec tapped quickly and loudly on Celestine's back symbolising that he had given up.

Celestine had won. He raised his arms in confused celebration. Alec dropped to the floor limply. When Celestine looked back, Alec was moving again. He sucked in air and struggled back to his feet. When they locked eyes, they understood for vastly different reasons that they had earned each other's respect. Alec raised Celestine's arm again in victory.

'Get this nutter a drink will ye!!! He's earned it!' He shouted to the crowd hoarsely.

'And don't forget to pay me!' said Luke scurrying towards the two combatants. Mugs of mead and ale were hurried their way. Their drinks clinked and their festival began early.

There was no sleeping to be done tonight.

2 THE BALLAD OF TALION

Vida- Chrono- 1- 1827

While Luke and Celestine travelled across the Celtish half of their homeland, their home to the south, Sakura Farm, celebrated a successful spring. It was the first day of summer, according to the calendar King Kastielle devised during his rule. The month of Life, the day of Time, and the first day of the month. There were ten days in a week, and ten months of forty days in a year, all of which were named after the divines of The Spiritual Court. Today was – Vida- Chrono- 1.

Talion Ulrich Schultz, the famed champion that had reared and trained Celestine, awoke moments before the sunrise. He laid still in bed, anticipating the rigidity and stiffness of his weary bones and muscles, a constant reminder of his advancing years. He creaked and clicked like an oil-thirsty hinge, and the dull ache within him reminded him that he was no longer the champion he once was. Those days had long since passed. Removed from his past in combat, Talion became an elder statesman of King's Anglonia. The fame and fortune of his youth brought him favour and opportunities that not many others had in this country, especially considering that he was an outsider of the nation.

Talion was not Anglonian, nor had he any heritage linking him to the land. Nor was he from the Deutschlands, Norse or Baltic, contrary to what his name suggested. Talion was born and raised in the heart of the Earth, Anara. Commonly known as the Bosom of Mother Nature, Anara was the birthplace of all life. It was where the first men lived amongst the Children of Nature, as the legends told. That lineage alone would make him a remarkable person amongst non-Anarian natives. Talion had fame and intrigue that stretched beyond where he was born.

Talion was very coy about giving details of his time in Anara, however, some details were simply inescapable, seeing as he spent the vast majority of his life there. His storied reign as Anara's champion was at a time where the title of champion meant something much different to what it meant at present. Champions were originally billed as the finest warriors in their land; they were sent to settle international disputes in the stead of armies, sparing countless lives. The role of a champion was to fight for their country to avoid war but, times had changed, war had changed.

The creaking symphony of percussive popping joints and clicking bones, followed by the harmonic groans of the weary old man that they pained, ended with Talion sitting on the edge of his bed massaging his legs. Age was but a number to an extent, then age was a mean old hag that only wanted to inflict pain. Talion shook his head trying to deny the sensation, seeing as waiting for it to stop was not working. He palmed for his cane and hobbled over to his window upon finding it. His back was hunched, and his movements were slow like each motion was a decision or risk. He poked the hook of his cane between the curtains and spread them apart. Sunrise was about to begin, and the brush of daylight was going to paint his home bright again. The vision of his legacy anew, Sakura Farm.

Sakura was the name of Talion's late wife, she was also King Kastielle's sister. His love for her caused a rift between him and Kastielle that would only be reconciled after she died before the invasion and fall Anara. Talion built this farm in her honour, but the pain of her loss was still fresh. The sun scaled the ladder to the sky, spreading the glowing orange of its light like the tide coming out. The dark blue, black, and greys that covered the visage of the landscape came alive. The dewy grass shimmered and waved in the morning breeze. The light revealed shining silver linings that spread over the acreage making the fields appear like the bed of a calm emerald sea. The trees of the forest on the far side shook themselves bright and awake in the quick sunrise. The land stretched to the oceanic blend of the sea and sky that formed the horizon. Talion watched the sunrise with a smile on his face, saying a quiet prayer. He had nothing to say to the Children of Nature or Mother Nature herself. His prayer was to his beloved Sakura, as it was every morning.

At sunrise's conclusion, the pain returned sharply to Talion's legs. Most mornings he could stand at the window without aid, but his body was becoming temperamental as of late. He felt like he was ageing a year each day. Talion was a very old man now, no matter how coy he was about his exact age. Talion revealed his years to nobody, not even his own nephew Celestine. He eased himself onto the rocking chair beside him and watched out of the window from a sitting vantage point. As the pain screamed, it did not matter how old he was anymore. He was deteriorating. The stories of Kastielle, in which he was featured in most, recounted stories of a man that lived a hundred lifetimes, but Talion's opinions on the series remained consistent. They were just stories.

Age was knocking on the doors of his worn joints and wary muscles and no legend or hyperbole could save him from that even if he believed it. Aches and pains would find new places to settle around his body and this morning it was his leg that assumed the role of the sacrificial limb.

He rocked in the chair to ease his mind. The pain relented. The chair was a gift crafted by Celestine. It was fine craftwork and Talion used that chair to read by his window. Since Celestine had left, he could not bring himself to do much in that chair but look upon the cottage where his nephew stayed. The cottage that was half a year empty. He took solace that his boy would be back in a matter of days. He left in Autumn and was gone all of Winter and Spring. His return would make for a fine Summer indeed.

The sun was high in the sky now, the great eye of Time himself warming and gazing upon all. The rooster was yet to call and Talion managed to spot Staphros sprinting across the field to the outhouse after his daily run to Zorrodon. Staphros trained with every spare minute he had. The run to Zorrodon was thirteen miles there, and thirteen miles back. Staphros always challenged himself to be able to get back before the rooster called. He swung the door open and slipped inside the red and white wood building he called home. Talion smiled. The moment Staphros's door closed, the rooster called as if it were waiting for the giant to get home before it could begin the day.

The cry of the rooster faded into the daylight and the first day of Summer was official.

The outhouse was where Staphros, lived, trained, and managed the farm. It was a large barn-like structure, painted red and trimmed white, assembled with thick Mayan Ebony Ashwood, one of the strongest woods in the world. The interior was accommodating for an eight-foot giant, a high ceiling, big doors, and custom handmade furniture, most of which were fashioned by the man himself. Only he and Celestine were entitled to their own living quarters. Although Talion didn't adopt Staphros as his nephew, Staphros was family to Talion as much as Celestine was. Talion felt responsible for him, and Staphros was loyal to Talion without falter or question.

Staphros began life in Anglonia as a refugee fleeing Anara, lined up and on sale as a slave on the docks of Zorrodon. Staphros, although not eight-foot-tall yet, would still command a tremendous price as a slave. To this day, twenty-seven years later, he could still see Talion, a fellow refugee, negotiating with the slavers to buy him, and then sitting with him to set him free immediately after.

Staphros owed Talion his life and pledged it to him from that day on. Together they found the cliffside in the south-east of Zorrodon, purchased it, and built Sakura Farm on top. Just him, Talion and Celestine.

He was relieved to get back to the outhouse before the rooster called. He wiped his head dry with a cloth and got undressed. Staphros trained in trunks and weighted chest plate armour, not really suitable attire for managing a farm. He filled his iron bathtub with water and warmed it by lighting a fire underneath. He took a cup of the steaming water and tossed it on top of the coal and charred wood once it was hot enough. He gingerly eased in, letting the heat penetrate deep into his muscles and took a deep breath.

His runs to Zorrodon troubled him as of late. Zorrodon was the crown jewel of the west, and its people were amongst the most charming King's Anglonia had to offer, especially in the village. In recent months, he had seen a marked transition of its people and their downturn into struggle. The children were skinnier playing with sunken faces and bloated tummies. With each day that he visited, more children were on the streets, but less were playing and even fewer smiled. There was an unsettling desperation in the people's tone when he heard them. Even when attempting to coax customers into visiting their stalls, their sales pitches sounded like meagre attempts at ebullience. The spirit of Zorrodon was a candle burning with a wet wick. Things were wrong in Zorrodon, and it began with the appointment of Mayor Magnus.

Staphros had altered his run in the morning to include the outskirts of the docks. He heard tell of a journal that was being scribed in the docks by a faction of men called the Hondos. They aimed to inform as many as possible of what was truly going on. Staphros had become an avid purchaser of the weekly journals, now finally understanding the full extent of the city's struggle. If there was one saving grace in Zorrodon, a beacon of hope, it was that the people of the docks appeared to be organised.

Staphros wanted so much to be able to do more but did not know what he could do. He cleared his mind of it, as it only served to anger him. He let his muscles relax in the healing waters listening to the farmhands head to work outside.

Clicks, clacks, and kerchunks all reverberated in a quick sequence at the large door to The Big House. The Big House was what the workers called their living quarters. Talion lived in the Big House too, in his private chamber of course. The golden doorknob jittered and jostled and finally twisted, then an outpour of fresh faces, young and old, emerged from the great hall and out to their stations. Some to the stables and pens, others to the fields, and a few to the garden enclosure that surrounded the Big House.

Talion was a man of habit and the workers of Sakura Farm knew that he would be at the window that they called The Eye. They all looked up, one by one, to meet his gentle gaze and wave him good morning. Talion returned it with a smile. With the labourers at work, it was time to begin his day. His working day started slightly later on, alongside the more vocational workers he lived with, the teachers, doctors, and housekeeping.

Talion buttoned his black blouse and fastened his brown slacks which were prepared and laid out by his handmaids the night before. He roughly brushed his rapidly thinning hair and shaved his oddly thickening beard. He used a chromium razor with an ivory handle, a razor that he had from his younger days as the champion of Anara. With master strokes, he sliced away his whiskers on his cheeks as a scythe cut through the wheat and grass. He lifted his chin to shave his neck. He brushed up once revealing the pale skin of his exposed neck. Each stroke was like the row of an oar bringing him closer to home. He froze mid-stroke, the edge of the blade against his Adam's apple. It appeared a beacon in the mirror, singing a siren song in its reflection. The blade would not move. The razor sank just deep enough to part a thin layer of skin at his neck, nothing more than if he were to make a mistake shaving. A mist fell over his eyes, as once again his internal struggle was coming to a head, the pain was good. These moments seldom came, but they did happen. Talion's hands trembled as the blade remained at his neck with blood trickling from the piercing. Sin could not be erased, just hidden.

Kastielle's descent into madness caused shockwaves that changed his immediate vicinity at first, then eventually the world as they knew it. In the end, a collaboration of the most powerful nations around the world conspired to invade Anara and kill him. That invasion ended with the entire country burning and two ships, out of a whole nation, able to escape. The memory of losing his friend to mania and the loss of his country was too painful to think about, but it followed him every day. Talion was loyal to Kastielle, not only as his champion but as his friend, and carried out his orders and requests, no matter how questionable. It wasn't until the moment that he watched the results of Kastielle's wrath, that he realised his part in it all. His hands were not clean, but no other eyes could see the bloodstains on his palms but him. Talion had a history with the world. He was not always kind to her, nor she to him. Sailing to sanctuary in the west, Talion knew all he could do was forge a new legacy, one that overshadowed his past. That was proving difficult at present. Everything in him was telling him to push the blade in and end his guilt. Nothing was telling him to take the blade away.

Talion jolted out of his trance when the door knocked. It frightened him as an immediate layer of sweat instantly lined his frail skin.

'C...come in!' He called out panting. The door arched open. Hanabi emerged from the slowly opening door. She entered.

'Breakfast is ready Talion san' She said. Talion looked over to see her, inadvertently revealing the distress in his face. The tears in his eyes had not fallen but hadn't yet found a place to go.

'Arigatou, Hana, I'll be down in a minute.' He said, as calmly as he could. Hanabi knew something was amiss, but she didn't pry. She was a very young lady, but she and Talion had become very fast friends. She knew him well in the year that she had been here. They shared ideas about philosophy, culture, and the world as a whole. Talion had lived in the Wukong Empire, in the province of Nippon which was where Hanabi was from. She lived there almost all of her life, up until a year ago.

'Hai.' She said in her mother tongue as she slipped back behind the door.

'Oh Hanabi!' Talion called abruptly. The door closed; Hana didn't hear. Talion grabbed his cane and hobbled over to the door as quickly as possible with the soap suds drying on his neck. He swung the door open. 'Hana, chotto matte!' he said begging her to wait a second. Hanabi stopped. 'A favour if you wouldn't mind.'

Staphros rested in the tub drifting in and out of a meditative state. The steam of the piping hot bath cobbed a spray of beads of sweat on his bald head. His full beard was also sodden with the bottom wisps of the facial hair dipping into the hot water. There was a sudden knock on the door and Staphros knew who it was. He had assigned a project to a young boy that had recently withdrawn from schooling on the farm, and now was training as a blacksmith. After months of work, he heard that he was nearly finished. The boy's name was Archie.

Staphros hoisted himself from the iron tub, dripping wet, and he grabbed a towel to wrap around his waist. He pulled the door open. Archie was standing there proud and smiling. He had a spray of orange freckles across his nose and cheeks, and a head of onyx black hair. Staphros was the one that recommended that Archie be removed from his academic schooling because it was not working for him. Archie had dreams of becoming a blacksmith and school never pertained directly with that skill, so he lost interest. Over the last few months, Archie had been working on his assignment from Staphros, a steel axe.

'H…here you go sir.' Said Archie. The first thing Staphros noticed was that the weapon Archie had constructed had to be pulled by a wagon, such was the size. He couldn't see the axe, but it was very big indeed, built for him no question. Archie studied Staphros's stunned expression and giggled as he pulled away from the white cloth cover. The weapon was well crafted, the edge was a crescent that mimicked the Earth in its seamless curve. The butt was flat, not quite shaped to be a hammer, but the broadness of the steel backing meant that it could be used as one. The shaft of the large axe was a smoothed long branch of wood. It lacked the detail of the head but was symmetrical and well balanced. Staphros stepped by and reached into the wagon to pick it up, utterly impressed.

'Well done boy.' He said. Archie shook with excitement at the sound of hearing the praise. He idolised the giant. He was massive and strong, but also incredibly wise and good to him. As a child, Archie was hyperactive and could be disruptive in his schooling. He was taken in by Talion at seven years old as an orphaned slave. Talion naturally enrolled him in his education program and signed as his guardian, the closest equivalent to freeing an orphaned slave. Where teachers had trouble with the boisterous young boy, Staphros had a way with him, like a mentor. They had spent a lot of time together speaking about what made him tick. Where his teachers thought he needed discipline, or structure, what Archie really needed was a role model.

Staphros handed the axe back to him. 'Firstly, you need to finish the shaft, I can tell you spent much more time on the head, but the shaft is just as important. I need to be able to grip the axe and know it won't slide.' He said.

Archie bowed his head disheartened.

'Look at me!' Commanded Staphros. Archie stood on attention and looked directly up to Staphros's hard eyes. 'This is an incredible first attempt at smithing, but it is not perfect, and it never was going to be. You will earn the Smith name very quickly if you continue to work hard. And if you spend as much time on the woodwork as well as the steel craft, you will have made a fine weapon.' Staphros placed the axe back into the wagon and headed back inside.

'One more thing sir.' Archie called out.

Staphros stopped. 'Training?'

Archie nodded shyly. Staphros stopped to think, nodding once the idea came to his head.

'I want you to report to me, how many press-ups you can do in an hour. Once you can get to a thousand, then we learn something else.' Said Staphros. Archie's face lit up and a grin stretched from cheek to cheek on his face. He looked up at Staphros with grateful inquisitive eyes. Staphros nodded, confirming what he said, and closed the outhouse door.

He headed to the desk where he placed the journal, he had picked up this week. He then pulled the frayed brown rope to release it. The parchment roll expanded into its broadsheet form revealing the top headline.

"Zorrodon To Raise Tax Again for Golden Guard Uniform"

Staphros couldn't bear to read beyond the headline. He thought of the malnourished and dirty children that he passed on the streets of Zorrodon, even that morning. There was something amiss in that city and he was getting tired of being a spectator. He had to ask Talion, he would know what to do.

With the final upward stroke of the blade, Hanabi had finally finished shaving Talion. He had his eyes closed throughout the process, and Hanabi noticed his peculiarly deliberate breathing pattern. Talion was acting unusual, but he was an unusual man. He had never asked her to shave him before and she could not understand why he asked now. Something was wrong, but she could not figure what, and it wasn't her place to ask. She had warmed some water over the woodstove in the corner of the bedroom. She checked it. It was just about cool enough to handle. With that, she removed the small tin basin from the stovetop and submerged a rag beneath the water's surface. Talion opened his eyes to see Hana returning with the steaming wet towel then placed it over his face. The warm wet soothed the now raw skin on his chin before she removed it. Talion felt at peace again, and the dark thoughts had disappeared for now. He could be the man those around him knew him to be.

Hanabi cleaned up here and there. There was not much of a mess but, this was Talion's room after all. Talion got up with great effort and hobbled over to her forgetting his cane.

'Hana,' He said now remembering it as the pain in his legs sang at a glass-shattering pitch. 'Arigato gozaimasu' He said wincing.

'You're welcome' Hanabi replied.

Talion screamed as his knees buckled and he fell into Hanabi, gripping her shoulder tightly to stay upright. Frustration had now overridden his feelings of pain and gratitude as the once champion and protector of Anara found it a chore to stand upright without aid. Although frail, Talion was not the smallest of men and Hanabi was not blessed with physical strength. She too was struggling to hold him up.

The door opened.

As Staphros dipped his head underneath the rim of the doorway, he rushed to help when he saw Talion's predicament.

'Are you alright sir?' He said placing his hand on Talion's back for support. Staphros's hand was solid as a rock and covered his whole back and he guided him to his reading chair. The pain was etched on Talion's face and redness spread like a rash of wildfire from his neck upwards. Quietly, Hanabi slipped out of the room, knowing this was not a state that Talion would want her to see him in. They were close, but Talion was above the frailties of normal men, at least in her mind he was. This was a vulnerability that she wasn't used to, and she wasn't sure he was used to showing it. As much for her sake as his, she decided to no longer spectate.

Staphros knelt beside him with grim concern, but not surprise. He had seen him like this before.

'Is it your legs again?' He asked. As soon as the door closed, Talion's quivering hand massaged his thigh, which wept silently as only a muscle can, speaking in a language that was loud and clear to only one in the room.

Talion nodded.

'It's something new every day.' Said Staphros.

'I know…' Talion paused for breath, sucking in the air through his gritted teeth 'it's like my body is decaying while I'm still alive.' With a fierce determination that could only make a champion, Talion exhaled to regulate the agony.

'How bad is it this time?'

'Worse!' Talion replied in a laboured bark with tears in his eyes. 'Staph, I don't know how long I have left of this life.'

'Do not talk like that ever! You have always said, "If something is broken, we fix it. If something is hurt, heal it." No more of that nonsense. No more at all.' Staphros had seen the bad times, but Talion hadn't spoken like this before, at least not to his face.

Talion nodded 'Alright, alright, the pain should subside in a moment.'

'How do we fix this?'

'A cup of tea wouldn't go amiss.' Said Talion cheekily, trying his best for a smirk. Staphros was eased by the attempt at humour, and he was more than happy to make the tea.

Staphros relit the half-burned wood at the foot of the stove and set the iron pot to boil. The pain was starting to ease as Talion assumed it would. He relaxed in his chair watching his ward tend to him. Many things kept his thoughts peaceful on the farm, this day's challenges could not take those away. Staphros was every bit his own man, but he was still proud of him, even as old as he was now. The dark thoughts that beckoned the blade to slit his neck, could not compete with the facts presented before him today. Like that, a great deal of the pain alleviated itself from Talion.

'What brought you up here anyway, it's not like you to visit in the mornings.' Asked Talion. The unstrained tone in his voice lifted Staphros.

'Aah yes, I almost forgot.' Staphros left the stove and delivered the local news to Talion. He read the headline. 'I didn't think it could wait until our evening chat.'

'Of that, you are correct.' Said Talion examining the headline. Staphros was passionate about what was going on in Zorrodon and spoke with Talion at length about it. Talion had experience and wisdom that Staphros found both insightful and calming.

'When we went to Zorrodon last, it was bad. The people in the village could barely live with the tax as it was. And I wonder, who will this raise in tax apply to?'

'It was certainly bad, there isn't much more we can do to help them either. At this point, any money we give them may end up going to the people that don't need it.' Talion studied the article further. Staphros handed the freshly brewed tea to Talion, who gladly took it. He smelt and sipped his tea. Nettle and ginger was his personal favourite type of tea and Staphros had learned how to brew it perfectly.

'This is a damned shame.' Said Talion when he finished the journal.

'Does it get worse?'

Talion shook his head. 'No, but it seems like the story is more about the outrageous circumstance and not the people it's affecting. Instead of cultivating a love for those who are suffering, it is inciting hatred for the cause. Not a great many people will act out of hatred because they are scared of what they might do, but when people do act in such a way, things only get worse.' Said Talion.

'But if people stand against Mayor Magnus and fight back if enough people do it, won't it make a difference?'

'Maybe in the immediate, but something worse will come. Hatred cannot create lasting peace, only love can. If we act out of love for the affected, and not hate for the affecter, lasting change will come. My teacher Eros taught me that.'

Staphros nodded. He knew Talion was right if there was ever an instance of acting out of hatred it was the fall of Anara. Millions died there and in the end with Kastielle gone, every world government wanted to occupy the void the most powerful King the world ever knew had left. Talion knew this was not the way, because he had lived it before.

'Besides, Mayor Magnus seems to be a man that you do not want to cross. His power seems to run deeper than the mayoral office.' Said Talion grimly.

'How so?'

'I'm not quite sure, but there are stop gaps usually to prevent tax rates from going as high as they are. He seems to be able to do as he pleases, in the nation's capital of all places. An independent state yes, but there are rules. I have been reading about this man for the last four months and he has the look of a man with absolute power, the kind a tyrant wields. I don't know how he had managed it, and I don't wish to find out. But if I can burden you with an old man's advice…'

'Of course, sir.' Said Staphros.

'Stay out of his way.'

3 A CHAMPION OF ZORRODON

Vida- Labor- 2- 1827

Zorrodon Docks was a busy place. Their work was intense from morning to night. With Zorrodon being the most desirable destination for more traditional travellers, not Gypsies, their work guiding ships and assisting with the porting process was always intense. Anglonia's weather was always temperate and stayed at an even keel year-round, with temperatures not getting too hot or cold, so traffic was steady all year round.

Ships rolled in and out of Zorrodon docks that morning from the crack of dawn. With each ship that arrived, the working men pulled and tied ropes that ripped their skin. The rough calluses on their hands contrasted with the softness of their dark skin. The foreman of the docks was an elder gentleman by the name of Hendry. The crown of hair on his head was thick and knotted like wet black cotton. He, like most of the other people that lived and worked on the docks, was from West Akoku. They had a melodic manner of speaking, and sometimes slipped into a wholly different dialect they called Patois.

Hendry was bemused by the length of time it took for a ship on Dock Four to be set. Dock Four was where the younger men were starting to work, mistakes were expected, but not like this. He rushed down with intent and purpose; they could ill afford any dip in their service, they survived on donations from a job well done. The porting charge went to the government. Dock Four had done well historically but they had caused some issues as of the last few days. As he expected, the captain did not leave a donation and went as far to query the porting charge too. This was the fourth time in three days that this had happened. Hendry interjected the conversation.

'Wha'appn?' Asked Hendry, speaking naturally. The captain was incredulous at first at the relaxed and common way his distress was addressed.

'I beg your pardon.' Asked the captain.

'Mi name, Hendry, I run dis ting here-so. What seem fi be de problem?' Still, it took a moment for the captain to decipher the codex that was Patois, but finally, he understood. Hendry, like many others from West Akoku, was used to the long pauses after he spoke.

'Oh. Well, your men took forty minutes to dock my ship and had the blasted gall to ask for a charitable donation, on top of this extortionate porting charge.' Said the Captain.

Hendry put his hand on his heart. 'Mi sorry for dat, h'an for the likkle iidiyat bwoy asking for money h'afta a poor job, but dis porting charge me can't change. Come from boss man up top.'

'Well then let me speak with him.'

'Gwarn-no, mi can't speak wid him. If you can reach him, talk wid him.'

'How do I find him? Do you have any details?'

'You can find him, in parliament. He's the Mayor, Magnus.' Hendry delivered the information as a matter of fact. Neither respectful nor disrespectful. The captain's face dropped as he silently placed one gold and two silver pieces in the secure box and moved along.

Hendry marched over to the group working on Dock Four. Nine out of the expected ten were present. Kojo was missing. Kojo had been distracted recently when he got ideas about joining Lion and the Hondos faction. Still, he always showed up to work every day and provided for his family. This was the third consecutive day he had been absent. The crew looked at him with tired but fearful eyes. They knew how important those donations were. On top of that, Hendry was an elder of the docks and they knew to respect him. Hendry was confused and then concerned. It wasn't the boys' fault, and he was beginning to think it wasn't Kojo's either.

'Mi hav fi go find him madda.' He said before leaving the boys and going back to the slums, where the dock folk lived.

Hendry knocked on the door and Kojo's mother, Olive, was already crying when she answered. He was apologetic and pained by the thought of Kojo being hurt or worse and his mother's sadness was confirming something bad. She sat down on a rickety chair next to a rickety table. Hendry remained standing.

'Olive, where is your son?' asked Hendry.

Olive, broke down into uncontrollable sobs. 'Mi no know!' She held her face in her palms and shook as she wept into them. Hendry walked by and hugged her. The docks were a community, one person's pain hurt everyone.

'When you see him last?' asked Hendry.

'Laas week. Harmon, Mortis.'

'De tirty-ninth? Dat was the laas day him was in work.'

'Mi know, mi know, he want fi blow off steam, inna de village. Mi told him not fi go and chat bout Hondos, cause all him want fi chat bout is dat man, Lion. He love him.'

'So him went to de village? Him have a drink wid fren?'

'No man, him want fi be alone wid him thought him said. He no like living like dis, it pain him. Dat's why him love Lion, cause he stan up for us onna de docks.'

'Den let him stan up for your bwoy. Mi have fi tell him.' Said Hendry. He kissed Olive on the cheek and took her hand. 'Don't worry. Lion will find your bwoy.'

Lion took his men to the village immediately after learning of Kojo's potential disappearance. The culture of togetherness was heavily inherent in the people of the docks but was enforced through the leadership and guidance of Lion himself. He always walked with his back straight and his head high. Anybody who took the time to observe the man walking would intuitively know where he was heading. He had a piercing stare that was unbreakable, never deviating from his destination, such was the man's focus. The problems in his periphery did not concern him; distractions didn't catch his eye. He appeared unstoppable.

He dressed humbly, sack bottoms and an open vest that exposed his arms and abdomen. He walked slowly, bopping rhythmically like he was privy to a song that played silently to all but him. He was different from most. He was light-skinned, a hybrid of Anglonia and West Akoku meaning his skin was not the colour of wood, which was how many described his people, but the colour of sand. The docks were his home, but still, he was different. Being a hybrid, or half breed, as many called him growing up, proved challenging because he was different everywhere he went. The dock folk were just nicer about it. He had a crown of dreadlocks on the top of his head, which fell just between his shoulder blades. He inherited his light eyes from his father, who was also a half-breed of Anglonia and Akoku. His father had very pale skin and despite his mother being quite dark, Lion inherited that fair skin of his father, being only a few shades darker than he was. He inherited his effeminate features from his mother. A long face, high cheekbones, and big eyes. Lion's appeal extended beyond his quality of leadership; he looked the part too.

His men flanked him, five on each side. The people in the village gave the group a wide birth, stopping what they were doing to look at them. The villagers working in the market were always busy and rarely stopped for anything, but the crunch of twenty-two feet stepping in unison, eleven at a time against a dry dirt path, seemed to be the only sound worth listening to - *The people of the docks were of no concern unless they pose a threat* – This was posted on the local bulletins and yelled by the town crier consistently. They posed a threat, at least one of them did. The one in the middle, Lion, moved differently. It wasn't arrogance or assuredness, it was power, a power that threatened to challenge everything that the villagers thought about those on the docks.

He took his men into the village knowing how they would be viewed, but at least the people would see them. Each of the onlookers watched the group march in like an invading force, ready to claim the land as their own. They were ignorant to the fact that these men regularly visited the village. They were customers to some of them. The truth was, every single one of Lion's men were born in and residents of Zorrodon. They weren't recognised, because they weren't acknowledged. They only appeared like outsiders because they looked different to every onlooker there.

The group marched through the path of the market to the central hub, the statue of Mother Nature, at least it was an idol of what they assumed she looked like. She had a thin curved nose, her hair was straight and flowing, and thin lips. She was everything Lion and his men were not. Lion examined the structure that stood above all who looked upon it and then read the plaque at its bed. – *Mother Nature- The Mother of All Creation* -

'Yes-I.' Said Lion under his breath. He turned to address the people behind him that still shot quizzical looks at the strange group of dark men.

'Do you see us now?' he said in the melodic tone of his mother tongue but not the dialect. He needed these people to understand him clearly. 'For those of you who do not know me… They call me Lion, and this is my faction, The Hondos. We don't come as a threat, we're here because one of our own is missing. His name's Kojo, and he's gone. He may appear a man to your eyes, but he's a boy to me. He's seventeen. I'm not asking for you to know where he is, I am aware of what you think of me and my people. You call us Ebonies.' There was a weight in the atmosphere as he let the words hang in the air a moment longer than the rest. Ebony was a word to describe the colour of their skin, Ebony being a famously dark wood. Though the word described their colour, it was only reserved for the people of Akoku or of Akolese heritage. It had deep-rooted demeaning contexts. Lion was a learned and well-read man and believed the only true way to predict the future was to study the past. By his own logic, he should have been a clairvoyant, because of the extent of his historical studies.

'We do not exist to you, what would be classed as untouchable in the nations of Bharat and Arabia. I understand. I'm not asking you to change that or reshape your views. I'm just asking you to see us, so you can notice when you see him.' Lion continued. Out of the blacksmiths came a small round man. He was balding and very greasy, hissing and sneering at the group that had interrupted the day.

'Listen yeah, you and your lot need to move along. I've had enough of this nonsense, talking about what we call yous. I ain't never called no Ebony an Ebony.' He said from a fair distance down the street. 'If your mate is missing, it's not our problem. It's a docks problem. We have our problems here and we don't need you causing any more, bringin old Mags down. So, just piss off back where you came from.' He said. The blacksmith's outburst started to break loose the silence that befell the street and rumblings amongst the people. The dark-skinned men were no threat, Lion had said as much. The blacksmith's challenge proved it. Now, the group was drifting into the nothing that anybody from the village and beyond perceived them to be.

Lion's men looked to each other confused and angry. Lion remained calm. He took a step forward and as the volume rose, he took another step. He would not be ignored. People knew of him because Magnus knew who he was. Magnus was an Ebony just like them, but he was not invisible, neither was Lion. The villagers just weren't aware of that yet. At the moment that the enforced ignorance of the villagers could erase Lion and his men, Lion commanded their attention by walking into the centre unafraid. He moved differently; it captivated the eye. He was someone important, someone, with power. He waited and the crowd quieted. His piercing gaze looked at every person in the marketplace, ensuring he had their attention. He owned the area even the blacksmith. Then his gaze turned to the idol of Mother Nature.

'Look at her! Truly, look at her. This is Mother Nature, as you know, the daughter of Time and mother to all creation. She is our mother, which makes us bredrin! As much as you know about her, have any of you read a single word written about her?' Lion looked about the place and the sea of ashamed faces proved his point. 'Don't let this statue fool you. The texts from the ancient times, times when the divines of The Spiritual Court walked amongst man, she walked with man too. And she did not look like that. This is common knowledge.' Lion grabbed his dreadlocks. 'Mother Nature had black hair like thick wool and a wide nose.' Lion held up his fist and his men followed suit in a proud display of their skin. 'She had skin the colour of the Earth at our feet. You stand on Mother Nature, you feed on Mother Nature, you breathe Mother Nature, but now, are you going to tell me you don't see Mother Nature? Because she, is an Ebony by all accounts, by your own definition. Don't let the work of a sculptor with an agenda, skew your sense of what is important. Don't let it separate us. Kojo being missing is not a Docks problem! It is our problem! So I'd appreciate it if you would at least have a watchful eye for him because he's one of us, you and we.' Lion returned to his men to a chorus of ponderous silence. He needed them to hear, he needed them to help. Zorrodon Village Market was the busiest place and it saw many people come and go. If half the shop keepers and tradesmen cared enough to ask their patrons about it, Kojo would have a chance.

Magnus stood at his window up on high, looking down on the land and the people that he governed. He was dressed in pure white linen robes and shining golden jewellery. His slender frame made him appear taller than he was, like a tower or Olympic column. He was elected as mayor the previous summer after promises of a sea of gold and record-high profits, promises he did deliver on. Zorrodon was thriving, monetarily. The people, on the other hand, were not. The trickle-down effect of the economic wealth had pooled at the top, and the people that had earned that money were not seeing any of it back. He was coming to completing the first year of his term in his mayoral office. He had found that looking out of the window was a calming refuge from the stresses of rule.

Outside the window, he had all four quadrants of Zorrodon in his sights: The governmental complex, Zorrodon City, Zorrodon Village, and Zorrodon Docks. Separating the city and the village, was one of the great wonders of the world, The White Wall of Zorrodon. If the charm of the residents, the history of the nation, and abundance of culture, was not enough of an attraction for tourists, the White Wall would be. It was so tall, it looked like it touched the sky when looked at from the ground. It was made of solid stone, smooth with no visible brickwork, curving around the city like a perfect enclosure. It was a symbol of excellence and a reminder of what was capable when Anglonian's joined together in common cause and unity. Yet from that window, Magnus saw the wonderous structure for something completely different. He saw a symbol of division, a physical manifestation of his scheme to conquer the most powerful city in the west, and then dominate its people by dividing them.

Zorrodon City saw great returns on the promised "sea of gold", but that was where the flow stopped. The wall acted as a dam to ensure that nothing beyond what was necessary would go to the village. Class divides created conflict when visible, but when hidden, in this case behind a great wall, it set a standard because nobody could understand why it was happening. Their only option was to accept it.

Magnus's deputy mayor, Fredrickson, slipped into the room. His nose was what poked in first, like a mouse sniffing for both cheese and danger, then he slithered in. He was a short and stout old man. He had pale skin and expensive clothes. He was a worm, spineless, slimy, and weak, but he had the protection of an eagle in Magnus.

'The boy is ready sir.' He said.

'Has he said anything of Lion?' asked Magnus.

'Not yet. He hasn't said a word to anybody.'

'He doesn't trust himself.'

'How so?'

'He's not allowing himself to talk, because he's afraid of what he'll say. He knows something. Something we can use.' Magnus turned from the window smirking.

'Ah yes sir, very good.'

'Send in Butch to have a word.' Magnus sat behind his desk fumbling with bills and mandates that he had let accumulate staring out of his window.

'I'm not aware of a Butch on our guard ranks.' Asked Fredrickson timidly. It was never a good idea not to know things around Magnus. His heart was beating, and he awaited his wrath, but the only thing worse than not knowing something, was doing something wrong. Magnus looked up and shook his head.

'Butch isn't a guard. He's one of our… Volunteers.'

The search of Kojo was proving fruitless for Lion and the Hondos. After his showing in the centre of the market, people were more receptive to their questions, even looking at them when they talked. Sadly, none of them could recall seeing Kojo. Lion persisted alone to the north in the direction of the city and the wall. There was a spectrum of smells so strong they were almost visible. The streets weren't clean. Animal excrement littered the streets and was left to dry in the sun. The emaciated children, that ran indiscriminately between everyone, were slick with muck. Their faces were black like they were a perverse imitation of Lion and his people. The way they smelt confirmed that it was no imitation, the children were just dirty, and the adults weren't much better. Lion usually unfazed by the harshest of conditions, had to hold his nose at times making sure to be subtle. He didn't want to offend. They called the docks the slums, but the people knew to wash. Their houses were smaller and breaking down, but their streets were clean. Lion had been to the village many times before, but his senses were engaged while looking for Kojo. The villagers were not the only ones waking up to the strife of a separate class. Life was as hard if not worse on the docks, Magnus took just as much money away from the people there and afforded them half of the opportunity, but they knew how to live. It pained him to know that he had missed this before and thought about what he could do to fix it.

He arrived at the gate to the city and the White Wall. Lion saw the wall as the symbol of togetherness that it was meant to be, and it inspired him to go on. He was exhausting all his options in the village, but down the curved street to the left, Kings Avenue was his last hope. He marched on.

Lion knocked on the door at the end of the road. He bypassed all the houses and businesses on the street. If anything happened there, he knew that Temina would know. She ran a florists and botanicals shop with her mother Marina. Marina was a resident healer in her part of town and knew almost everyone there. When Marina had died in the Winter, that responsibility was been passed onto Temina. She and Lion were close. If something happened to Kojo, she would know. Temina answered the door and her eyes brightened after seeing him. She leapt and hugged him and Lion smiled.

'It's so good to see you, Lion.' Said Temina.

'And how are you, young Lady?' asked Lion. 'You've grown.'

'Come on Lion. I'm twenty-five now. I think my growing days are years over.' She said. Lion meant what he had said; Temina had grown. Last winter, she was timid and unsure of herself. Her mother protected her, and she remained the delicate flower that her mother treated her as. No good came from the loss of Marina, but Temina had blossomed into a strong young woman. Lion didn't care to explain all that and simply nodded.

'What brings you here?' Asked Temina.

'I want to talk to you, about a boy.'

'Setting me up to be courted, are we?' Said Temina impishly.

Lion laughed. 'No sah!' He said slipping into his Patois roots for a second. 'The boy's name is Kojo. He's seventeen, dark skin, strong-looking boy.'

'I know who you mean, came here after having a little too much to drink and got into a fight. Just a nosebleed and split lip, but he was quite angry about it all.'

'Do you know where he went?'

Temina shrugged. 'Couldn't be sure, but he was with a woman. She's a comfort girl, she works at a brothel in the city called, The Pickering, I think. What's happened?'

'When was that?' Asked Lion.

'Not sure, two-three days ago?'

'The thirty-ninth?' Lion pressed.

Temina thought about it first, then nodded. 'What's going on?' She asked.

'The boy has been missing, since then. You're the only person I've asked that's seen him in the village.'

'Oh, my Heavens. I'll pray to Time and Nature that you find him quickly.' Said Temina as she placed her hand on the signet of Nature that hung on her neck. 'Oh, and if you go to the Pickering, ask for Nero. He won't be at the door, but he's always there. He owns it.'

'Thanks, and bless.' Said Lion as he headed out and towards the city.

The Pickering was quiet. The middle of the day on the day of Work and Labour meant the comfort had to come later. Lion stepped in and the hostess approached. She rubbed his arms with the base of her palm. She had chestnut brown hair and big eyes.

'Ooh look at your muscles.' She said. 'Are you looking for some comfort today?'

Lion shook his head. 'I'm looking for Nero.'

'That is a wonderful accent you have there love. Where is it from?'

'My homeland. Where's Nero?'

'I'm sorry love, Nero leaves the calls to us ladies.' She quipped.

'I need to talk to him. I'll wait if I have to.' He said. 'Got any Canewine?'

He said heading to the bar.

Nero came out eventually, and Lion didn't need to wait long at all. He was a Roman fellow, and his features made it obvious too. Straight dark hair, strong nose and steely eyes. He hustled to the bar but stopped in his tracks when he recognised that it was Lion waiting for him. His pace slowed then. Lion was hunched over the small varnished bar top. He nursed his drink in his clay mug, sipping slowly and deliberately.

Canewine was a favourite strongwine of Lion's and his people because it came from their land. Only Akoku or the Mayan Islands could organically grow sugar cane, which was the titular ingredient in the drink. It tasted smooth.

Nero appeared with the bottle and another small mug. Then he topped Lion up and poured himself one.

'One-love, thanks.' He said. He slipped a few silver pieces to him.

'It's complementary. I'm a fan of your work.' Said Nero.

'That's kind of you bredda, but I'm buying more than a drink.' Lion placed the mug on the table and looked Nero in the eye.

'Here then fine have another one for your trouble then.' Nero poured another. 'What do you need?'

'I'm looking for a girl.' Said Lion.

'That's funny because Cassandra over there said you weren't.'

'Not like that, I'm plenty comfortable. One of your girls spent the night with a friend of mine a few days ago.'

Nero dropped his head and slid the money back. 'You might as well take that, cause I don't have much for you if you're after information.'

'At least tell me what you know.' Said Lion quickly draining his drink.

'I assume you're asking about the young Ebony man from the other night…'

'His name's Kojo.' Lion interrupted, annoyed about the Ebony slur.

'Yeah him. I know he was respectful when he came in although a little hyperactive, but the girls took to him. He spent the night with Annaliese, my best girl.'

'Then what?'

'You don't know yet? It's all over the city.' Said Nero. 'Kojo was arrested for raping Annalise. Guard dragged him out of here in the middle of the night. That's all I know.'

'How you mean?! Wha' did she say happened?'

'She said that he beat her and wouldn't let her leave the room, so she waited until he was asleep and got the guardsmen.'

'You believe her?' Asked Lion.

'Why wouldn't I?'

'Because, seventeen-year-old Ebonies, as unuh like fi call dem, know better dan fi h'act like dat to Anglonian women.' Lion slammed his mug to the bar top, spitting his venom in the fire of his Patois. 'Dat a man you chat bout, my people dem. Him naa some iidyat bwoy a come rape pon woman. Him know de consequence of what would h'appn. Dat bwoy had a good heart.'

'I don't know that.' Said Nero.

'No.' Said Lion. 'You wouldn't know.' Inside Nero felt there was something wrong with it all but his loyalty was with his girl, Annaliese. She wouldn't lie. She wouldn't send an innocent man to the gallows, so the truth made sense because it had to. Lion finished his drink and slid the mug back to Nero. He made for the door, there wasn't much else to get from here.

'Keep the money. An apology for losing my temper.' Said Lion. He pushed open the door.

'You know, I do admire you. Standing against the government like you are. Zorrodon needs more people like you.' Nero called. Lion stopped in his tracks.

'Zorrodon has people like me. They just have to be willin to stan when it matters.'

4 THE FESTIVAL OF KING LOCH

Sunrise had come behind the cover of the heavens. As the morning progressed, the summer sun melted the vaporous vanguard that shielded it. It broke through the storm clouds that threatened lightning which never came. Celestine and Luke made it safely to Fearon in one piece, if not a little worse for wear. After he defeated Alec, Celestine guzzled buckets of ale until he passed out against the mast where his battle began. When they ported, they were in no shape to travel on to Elgin. They set some silver aside and stayed the night in the coastal town.

Their first day home, the first day of summer, was spent mostly asleep.

Vida- Labor- 2- 1827

They hired a stagecoach to take them across Eireann to Elgin in Caledonia the following day. Luke was bouncing with excitement even before the stagecoach stopped. The driver shot frustrated looks behind because the incessant bouncing was distressing the horses. It was distressing Celestine too, the motion of the stagecoach on the dirt paths was enough to irritate the lingering hangover he still nursed. He sighed knowing the trip would be over soon. They got there after sunset, but the festivities hadn't slowed in Elgin. Lanterns of fire lit the streets, and songs filled the few open spaces there were. Luke was swept up once more; he loved this time of year. Although he lived in Anglonia, he was a proud Celtishman. He and his sister Samantha were taken to settle a gold dispute with their parents, a dispute that ended up killing them regardless. Talion took them in, in Anglonia, but it did not change his blood. The same pride flowed through him. Luke jumped off the bed of the stagecoach, what was indeed a rare show of athleticism by him, however at this point Celestine wouldn't have been surprised if he somersaulted off of the coach. Celestine dragged Luke to the Grazing Cow Inn and bartered two days stay. Luke was like a big puppy pulling at the lead so he could run and play. He hated the administrative bother of travelling, even at the best of times. There was very little that could stop Luke from having a good time.

Despite many warnings from Celestine, Luke scurried into tavern after tavern from the moment they left the Inn.

Celestine tried to make him behave, but there was no stopping him now. He had had his fill and now drank to overflow. In Elgin, Luke looked overjoyed and Celestine did not want to stop that. Luke was outwardly bullish, tactless, and somewhat overconfident, but there were a few things that he kept to himself, secrets. Luke did not cry in front of people, he did not dance, and he never sang. He chanted along with folk songs, of course, but he did not truly sing. One could be mistaken into thinking Luke could not sing and his hapless, out of tune chants of songs about Celtish legends was the extent of his vocal abilities, however, Celestine knew in his heart that that was not true. As he sat back in the crowded tavern and watched his best friend dance with his brethren, he listened in. He was not chanting with them; he was singing, and it was beautiful. The men around him were too lost to hear it, but Celestine did for the first time in their friendship. It was their little secret.

Luke was too happy to be an arsehole, but just in case, Celestine left quietly. He had his fair share of fighting. He trusted Luke would find his way to the Grazing Cow Inn, and they could wake up bright and early, to head to the big fight.

Celestine snuggled in his bed. His fantasies once again commandeered his dreams. Dreams of home, friends, his animals, and a girl. A girl with fair pink lips and pale Arabian skin. He saw her in his mind with flowers in her long shimmering black hair, the last gaze from afar before going to Zorrodon Docks to start his adventure. Celestine's mind was a beautiful place, which was why he always slept like a baby.

Vida - Amor- 3- 1827

A scent coaxed Celestine out of his deep slumber in the morning. He blinked his eyes open to see Luke's hairy arm, which was peculiarly moist and draped over his face. The abhorrent snoring of the Celtishman kerranged against the drums of Celestine's waking ears. The haze was departing from his clouded mind, and it took a minute or so for him to realise that Luke had gotten into the wrong bed whilst blind drunk. Then enlightenment hit him, and Celestine rolled suddenly. He had been pushed to the edge of the bed in the night by Luke's beer bloated belly and curled knees. He had no place to roll but down. He landed face first with a splat on the wooden floor. There was something underneath him and he did not want to know what, though he had his suspicions. The sour smell crept out from the sides of his wetted abdomen. The thought was too much, and he leapt to his feet with the speed of a surprised feline, wiping away the chunks of the modest heaving that Luke had left on the side of the bed. He seethed at his friend who slept peacefully and ignorant. Celestine rounded the bed and picked up a pillow. He looked at Luke, then the pillow, and back to Luke, then he beat him with it until the duck feathers burst from their seal.

'Wake up you daft bastard!' Screamed Celestine. Luke woke up sharply with a gasp and protected himself to no avail. He then rolled away from the beating and suffered the same fate as Celestine before him, landing face-first with a slap on the wooden floor.

'What on Earth are you doing lad!' Said Luke.

'Do you not find it strange that you're in that bed?'

Luke blinked blankly. 'Not really.'

'It's my bed! And you got in it with me.' Said Celestine throwing the pillow at Luke. Luke wondered a second trying to recall the haze of the night before.

'Oh aye!' Said Luke. 'I remember getting in the bed now and finding it strange that you were in it, but we're all friends here. I didn't think it would be an issue.'

Celestine rested his face against his palm and shook his head. Half of the time, Luke had his head in the clouds. His intentions were always simple and never malicious. When he removed his palm from his face, the subtle cling of his fingertips reminded him of Luke's second trespass.

'And what on Earth is this?' Said Celestine pointing to his lower torso.

'Well, it's a very impressive abdomen.'

Celestine flushed with a strange concoction of frustration, rage, and flattery. He did work hard on his abdomen. Luke knew every combination of words that would get him in and out of a problematic situation. He took a deep breath in through his nose, and a heavier breath out of his mouth. Then, he tossed Luke a pile of his cleaner clothes and said.

'For that, we're heading to the fight for when I said.' Celestine liked to get places early and Luke did not. Luke wanted to get to places just in time, or late if he could help it. It had been a topic of much debate over the last five months. Now, Celestine was leveraging his anger to his advantage.

'Alright, fine.' Said Luke, pulling on his clean clothes.

'Oh no, no, no.' Interrupted Celestine. 'Bathhouse first.'

The streets of Elgin looked like a desolate wasteland. It was early in the morning and the dusty roads and cobbled streets were empty. They did not need to be awake for another few hours, and if the last few days were any metric, they were glad of it. The bathhouse was a short walk from the Grazing Cow Inn. Celestine remained in his long johns but wore his coat to cover himself.

'How are you wearing that in this heat?' Asked Luke. It was a nice coat, a gift from Talion and Staphros for his twenty-seventh birthday. It was white and blue, with golden stitching. But this was one of the rare occasions when it was not required to wear a coat in Celtish Anglonia.

Celestine shrugged. 'I like it.' He said, 'Is that such a problem?'

'Oh no, you're very pretty.' Luke winked at him. Celestine was tall fair and handsome, and by Luke's admission had a very impressive abdomen. Luke, on the other hand, was short mucky and a little pudgy, but it was their differences that brought them together. Luke, out of jealousy or admiration, would exclaim that Celestine looked like a prince, and that was the reason why he could never get a girl with him around. Celestine patted Luke on the shoulder.

'Thanks, but you're not my type.' Said Celestine.

'Oh, very funny! I'll have you know you could do much worse than me, you cheeky shite!'

'Could do a lot better as well.' Said Celestine. 'You know, somebody that doesn't have to sneak into bed with me?'

'Honest mistake is all.' Luke placed his hand on his heart. 'Promise.'

'Yeah, yeah.'

'All I'm saying is I never feel the need to doll myself up. I'm happy the way I am.' Luke slipped into his thick Shetland accent when he was exacerbated. More times than not, his accent was so mild that people often forgot that he was Celtish at times. Alcohol and anger often served as a worthy, albeit unwelcome, reminder. 'I don't know why I need to have a bath to go to a fight. I've been to these fight's before, it's not an occasion to dress up.'

Celestine stopped outside of the bathhouse. 'Luke we both have sick on us that needs washing off.'

'Come on, it's only a little sick, it's barely worth talking about. We've wiped it off.'

'You're a little sick if you think I'm going a whole day without washing your vomit from my chest.' Said Celestine. Luke blinked and checked his mind to counter and found none.

'Well fine! You go in and I'll wait in the pub.' He said.

'But, mate... You stink.' Said Celestine half-joking if the joke was one of those that was funny because it was true.

'And so will you, by the day's end.' Said Luke stubbornly.

'And then, I will wash and change again.' Celestine patted Luke on the cheek, heading to the entrance to the bathhouse. It was called The Chancery.

'Celestine, I fear you'll never change.' Celestine laughed pushing the door to The Chancery half open then stopping.

'Not on your life my friend...' He said as Luke approached the door. 'Not on your life.'

Celestine and Luke were washed and cleaned thoroughly. Luke ended up enjoying himself once Celestine paid for him to have an attendee help him wash. This was not so much the show of altruism that Luke perceived it, he just wanted him to be clean. Their clothes had been prepared and scented with perfumes. The Chancery was one of the better bathhouses that they had come across on their travels.

Celestine and Luke arrived early to the Proving Grounds, the arena where the contest would take place. Being among the first few people in the arena, they were able to choose where they wanted to view the fight from, opting for front and centre directly opposite to the king's podium reserved for King Lochlyn II, son of the famed King Loch.

'Why on Earth are we here so early?' Said Luke.

'To take it all in. This may be one in many visits for you, but this is the first time seeing this for me. I can't believe that this patch of land was the exact place where the Celtish won their independence.' Said Celestine leaning on the waist-high stone wall that formed the barricade. 'Do you not feel that? The history of this land began here.' The sun beamed down upon the large grass pitch where the battles would be taking place and it glistened in the morning light. The wind blew and echoed against the ashy stone of the arena walls, it sounded like the whispers of the dead.

'Okay. You may have a point.' Said Luke truly seeing what was before him. As contentious as he was, how set he was on being late, his Celtish pride could not deny that the Proving Ground had spirit. In their solitude, they could hear the land speak to them.

The numbers trickled into the arena, a few at first then a cavalcade of spectators rushed in. Celestine and Luke spent the last hours sitting with stretched legs on extruded stone steps that they mistook for benches. They were for people to stand on. In the times Luke had attended the fights before, he had always arrived too late to even be able to see a vantage this close, however, the front of the arena was as cramped if not more so than what Luke had remembered at the summits of the stands. The droves flocked in and Luke's previous statement was being proven correct, the men in attendance made no effort to dress up. Most of them smelt like cooked meat and ale, their beards saturated with remnants of the two, but that was still better than how Luke smelt that morning.

There was no room to move, and no space to be created. Every solitary gap in the audience stands were filled to the brim. Much like Celestine and Luke, everybody privileged enough to get the vantage at the front of the barrier were pressed against it by the people behind them. With the sun beating down and the mass of the bodies in proximity, it became very sweaty very quickly. Celestine felt a nudge at his side and decided to ignore it. Not only was it not worth the trouble, but it was a bother to turn and investigate where it came from. He was nudged again, this time harder, he sighed annoyed.

'Oi bawbag!' Said Luke. Celestine craned his head to look upon his friend. They were scrunched shoulder to shoulder. Ashamedly for Celestine, this was not the closest the two had been. A twenty-two-year-old friendship with Luke boded for plenty of strange and uncomfortable circumstances. Luke had his arm hanging over the stone barrier with a metal flask in hand.

Celestine said nothing.

'Ere, have this.' Said Luke.

'What is it?' Asked Celestine. He too had to hunch over the edge of the barrier to manoeuvre his arms. He took the flask and smelt it. The smell was uninviting and sharp, but unmistakably Scottsdrink.

'Shut up and get it down you!' Luke exclaimed. Celestine always found it funny, the more Luke was drunk, the more Celtish be became. He was sounding like every other person there. Celestine grabbed the bottle and took a hearty gulp. It was a good one, Oakwood and Barley, not that Celestine's pallet was educated enough to distinguish that. But he knew it was good because the good ones were incredibly strong. He wiped his mouth and breathed fire out of his stinging lips, handing the flask back.

'What you playing at?' Said Luke. 'Finish it!' Luke was an irresistible force so there was no point arguing. It was, drink now or later, and if Luke could embrace his culture, so could Celestine. He put mouth to bottle once more and guzzled the whole thing. The thin fiery liquid slithered into his stomach a flaming snake searching for its resting hovel underground.

The Festival of King Loch was a grand occasion, culminated with a fight to decide the nation's champion for the year. However, this was not the only battle that took place at the famed Proving Grounds. There had been years when the reigning champion, Finn the Brave, Finn II's father, would dispatch his challenger in less than a minute. Most occasions saw the fighting in the arena take far less time than filling it. It sometimes was underwhelming. After his father passed, one of the first decrees by King Lochlyn II was to introduce supplementary fights to build to the final fight. He called it the Undercard. The Undercard was not a wholly original idea by the young king, Olympia and Roma had similar structures, but Lochlyn II did not believe in slaves or their prolonged slaughter for the entertainment of the public. The undercard would be reserved for volunteers in non-lethal combat and often fanned the Eireann and Caledonian rivalry by pitting nation against nation. Luckily, this year Finn II was of Eireann and Michael was of Caledonia.

The undercard was underway. The fighters were stationed at opposite sides of the arena beneath the stands. The roar of the crowd shook the cellar which housed Finn and the other Eireann fighters. The cellar was dark, only lit with few torches. Rays of daylight leaked in at the sandy stone stairway.

Wood pillars were stationed all around for a strong foundation and stone-paved the floors. The fighters communed, before and after their fights. There was a tension in the room, most of the men there were entering the Proving Ground for the first time. It was hallowed soil, the birthplace of Celtish Anglonia. Some fighters dealt with that pressure by pacing around and slinging banter between their fellow competitors. Others dealt with it by drinking and smoking. What was unilateral was that they did whatever they needed to together. Finn II, however, did not.

Finn II was sat on a wooden stool bolt upright. He had his eyes closed, and he breathed deeply and deliberately. His chest rose and fell as his hands were placed on his knees. The chorus of laughter, singing, and swearing of his fellow Eireish fighters, was muffled to his ears as he visualised his upcoming fight in his mind. The only thing he let in and allowed his senses to register was the sound of the crowd's roar and the feeling of their vibrations. It gave him energy and steeled his resolve. He had cut his fair hair short and slicked it back with duck grease. His eyes, when open, were hazel and sharp. He hadn't yet put on his armour, sitting in just his riding bottoms for now.

One by one the undercard fights ended. With every climactic cheer, Finn II's fight drew nearer. He blinked his eyes open. The dim lighting helped his long-shut eyes. By his estimations, he was next. He saw several of the competitors look at him oddly. He understood that his methods were rather unorthodox in Celtish Anglonia. He shot a wink back at his onlookers. Most of them turned away, except for one, an older gentleman sat in a darker corner of the room. He and Finn II's eyes met. The older man approached him, and he extended his hand.

'Name's John. John the Angry.' He said. The firelight revealed his broken nose and dried blood on his chin. He gently held his side like it was injured, a broken rib perhaps. 'Do you mind?'

Finn II pondered and then nodded. 'So, John the Angry, did you win?'

'Does it look like I won?'

'No.' Said Finn II.

John laughed and rocked to soothe the onset of pain that his injury caused. 'You should see the other fella then.'

Finn II smiled. 'If he looks worse than you, I'd rather not.'

Their laughter faded almost as soon as it came. The roar of the crowd, the climactic roar, meant that Finn II was to be called up very soon. They looked to each other and John seemed more afraid than Finn II.

'Here it comes, the big one.' Said John.

Finn II nodded.

'You know, no matter how loud that crowd gets, you have all our support from us down here. What they did to your family was wrong. Go and take it back.'

Finn II stood. He circled to where his leather armour was placed. He held it in his hands and thumbed the embossed McMahon crest on the chest piece. His gaze lingered and his head looked like it carried a weight with it that nobody would understand. It was the first chip in Finn II's unwavering focus.

'You know? This armour was my father's.' Said Finn II. He held the chest plate and pointed at the embossed M in the centre. 'This is the McMahon crest for my family. It was on our banners, on our walls, on everything, because it was father's name. It was a name my father earned and was given to him by King Loch. My father… my family deserves better.'

'Aye lad, they do.' Said John. The final undercard competitor was carried into the cellar. Finn II and the others watched as he groaned in pain. His nose was bleeding and some of his teeth were missing. The stewards hustled him in and laid him on an empty bench. The group tracked his entry in, but once he was left and groaning on the bench, they could not bear to watch. Finn II gulped hard. That man had returned from non-lethal combat. Finn II's championship fight was not. Killing was not only encouraged anymore; now it was allowed. With all that Finn had said, he knew his life was in danger. He stroked the crest on the chest of his armour once more, steeled his nerves, and remembered what he was fighting for.

'Do you mind?' Asked Finn II handing over the armour to a sitting John.

John nodded and gingerly got up and hobbled over to the title challenger. 'Not sure how much help I'll be.'

'You'll be enough.' Said Finn II. John fumbled with the straps and strings to tether the armour to Finn II's body. It was slow but he was getting the job done. First the chest, then the shoulders and arms.

'So, what's the plan? Go out there win the title and get your name back?' John asked fastening the last few straps on Finn II.

Finn looked off to the stairs, 'Something like that.' He was all done and ready to go out. He marched towards the stairs.

'Good luck with your fight.' Said John.

'Not a fight old man… Revenge.' Finn II winked and climbed the stairs to his destiny.

5 FINN II "THE REVENGE"

The groundskeepers prepared the battle area. Its rich emerald grass was trimmed with care and precision. Chunks of wood were cleared as best as possible, but the show must run quickly and smoothly. Finn II hastened proceedings by emerging onto the Proving Grounds early. He strolled on casually like he owned the whole of Elgin. The crowd slowly spotted him one by one and their reaction was visceral. They hurled abuse and anger towards him. A chorus of boos formed a dome of sound above the Eireish challenger. Finn II smirked as he did not acknowledge them but fed off their energy. The groundskeepers scrambled out of the area once they saw him. They were not going to get in the way of this fight starting.

The king's stand still did not have the king in it but had a perplexed master of ceremony in. He was an older man, hosting the event since its inception. This was his twenty-ninth year of service to the role. Before he could salvage any semblance of control of the situation, Michael emerged from his cellar at the opposite side of the arena visibly annoyed. He wore leather armour too but had a pale arm exposed. He was slightly bigger than Finn II, both in height and general mass. Finn II was slight, not a man that would typically appear in a championship fight, but he had earned his way there like any other man. He declared himself a contender amongst a long list of men before him and travelled to build a legacy with word of his aptitude in combat returning home. That was the only way to be considered: travel the world fighting and hope that word returned home of your victories. It took him two years to be called to fight after declaring himself for contention. This was an utterly uncanny turnaround from contender to champion. From complete anonymity to jumping past all other contenders that were in the pool before him, was unprecedented. It may have been because of his name, many thought it was, but he was about to find out if he belonged, if he was worthy to be called champion.

Now the crowd was cheering Michael and booing Finn II. The noise was palpable, and the atmosphere felt like it was about to burst.

There was no exchange, no conversation. They knew the routine, Michael having done it the year before and Finn II had studied it for most of his life. They circled the outer rim of the grass pitch to the weapon rack. Now they could choose their weapons. Finn II remained stoic and as Michael was overtly confident, projecting to his challenger that he was not threatened. Michael picked a short sword and shield, and Finn II picked a spear. It was a strange weapon for him to pick, the Celtish were not typical spear wielders, but Finn II had a plan. When he looked over to Michael, he saw his gaze linger quizzically on his weapon choice. He was concerned. Finn had won the first battle.

Now their gazes met as they both stood by the weapons rack. It was time.

They stepped slowly at first then quicker until they were in a full sprint. The roar of the crowd spurred them on to run faster, then they met in the middle. Finn II jabbed with his spear twice. He thrust to Michael's stomach first, missing. He retracted the first blow and thrust upward to Michael's face. Michael parried. The parry pulled Finn II off balance. He twirled the spear above his head and planted his feet to stableise. The blunt end of the spear hit his opponent flush in his cheek. He staggered back, spitting out a glob of blood and chipped molar. Blood trickled down his chin and he smiled brightly. As soon as Michael looked back at him, Finn II had his spear held like a javelin and launched it at the champion. The whistling projectile carved through the air, narrowly being dodged by the Caledonian champion.

Finn II ran toward the off-balance Michael to capitalise. He rolled underneath a desperate horizontal swipe of Michael's sword. He heard the howl of the air as the blade barely missed him. His roll did not take him close enough to his weapon and he was exposed. Michael ran into the path between Finn II and the spear, he brandished his sword and invited him to attack. He was closing in and Finn II appeared defenseless.

Michael was close enough to launch an attack. He began with three strikes. Finn II ducked the thrust to the head and then slipped the diagonal slash by stepping out. He had to jump back from the final horizontal slash at his stomach. The tip of the blade scratched his leather armour. Finn II breathed a sigh of relief but was immediately hit in the face with the broadside of Michael's shield. He flew and crashed on his back, nose bleeding. Now he and John would have matching noses. He coughed as his nasal passage was blocked and he resisted the urge to blow his nose. It was definitely broken.

He caught sight of Michael aiming to land a downward lunge at his prone body. He rolled sideways evading it. Michael committed to the attack and his blade was deep in the grass. Finn II's fingers dug deep into the field and unearthed a large chunk of mud and grass. As Michael wrestled his sword from the ground, Finn II charged and slammed the hunk of mud in Michael's face. He didn't see it coming. He freed his sword and swung it blindly and Finn II caught the blow under his arm. Michael was trapped and Finn II aimed to return the favour with a Caledonian Kiss to Michael's nose. The arch of his forehead collided with the cartilage and Michael yelped and tried to escape Finn II's grip. He held on tight and unleashed a barrage of punches body, then head, then the body, then the head, over and over. He slung a stunned Michael to the floor and sprinted for his spear.

The two stood off and the crowd exploded with appreciation. Michael took a second to take it in while Finn II remained stoic and focused.

As the fight got back underway, Celestine was completely in tune with the action. He was now unconcerned and unaware of the jostling that went on at his back. While all those around him cheered, screamed, and yelled profanity, Celestine was silent in his appreciation.

'What a fight ey?' Said Luke gleefully.

Celestine nodded. He was engrossed as his fighting mind analysed what was going on before him. Finn II was blocking more than he was before, his movement had slowed. Losing his ability to breathe through his nose was slowing him down. Michael suffered the same deficit, but his style required much less oxygen to be inhaled. Finn II was trying to parry the attacks on the broadside of Michael's sword, but the wood of the spear was chipping slowly.

'It could go either way. You seemed so sure about this one, but it's close.' Said Luke.

'It's close, but Finn will win.' Replied Celestine.

'How can you be sure?'

'Because technique beats power, and timing beats speed. Look at how Finn is moving, he is leading the dance with his technique, and timing Michael's attacks to choose where he goes next. He has this under control.'

'I dunno, it looks like he's running away.'

Celestine shook his head. 'He's waiting for an opening dummy. I said he'd win, I never said it would be easy.'

The crowd were wild screaming and shouting for the action. Finn II's arrogance was proving not to be misplaced and some members were warming to him. They chanted his name or the name of his father. Either way, they were coming to his side. This did not do much for Finn II, but it royally pissed Michael off.

Horns blew and the two stopped fighting. Up across from Celestine, at the king's stand, King Lochlyn McMahon II made his entrance. The arena bowed, including Michael, who had completely forgotten that he was in a fight. Finn II, however, did not bow he stood bolt upright and stared intensely at the king. Memories flooded his mind of him being dragged from his estate as a child and flung into the slums of Collister Mere, on that man's order. Every evening he starved, every time his mother cried, his sisters begged, none of them understanding why the King would do this to their most famed champion's family. He walked towards the king's stand. With each step his rage got deeper, hearing everything they said about his father, fraud, pretender, false champion. Finn II grimaced and King Lochlyn II caught his gaze.

'You took my father's name!' Shouted Finn II. 'It was not yours to take. It was the dying decree of your father, the real King Loch!' Such a show of disrespect to the king turned the crowd against him once more.

The kingsguard drew their bows and aimed for Finn II. Finn II did not move; he was ready to die for this. King Lochlyn II urged his guard to withdraw.

'We mustn't interfere with the outcome of the fight.' He said.

'But sir.'

'No. Let him speak.' The kingsguard withdrew their bows and obliged to the order of their King. Michael was not so calm in the face of Finn II's disrespect.

He volleyed four ferocious strikes with his sword; Finn II blocked them all. The final one jolted on withdrawal as it dislodged from the wood of the spear. Finn II tried to focus back on the fight, but his gaze kept returning to the king upon high. He was getting hit with blow after blow.

'It doesn'ee look like Finn is in control now?' Said Luke

'That's because he isn't.' Said Celestine.

'Wait, I have a reputation to uphold, I only back winners. Your man is about to make a fool out of me.'

'You don't need Finn for that. Besides, it's not over yet.' Said Celestine intensely.

Finn II blocked another horizontal strike, the blade of the sword lodging itself once more. He was then sent to one knee with a stunning front kick to his stomach. He was trying to gulp all the air that had left him. Michael swung down a straight slash and Finn II blocked it by holding his spear horizontally at arm's length above his head.

SNAP

The blade cut through the spear. The wood could not hold up to the barrage of strikes from the blade. Michael immediately followed up with a killing blow, a forward thrust of his sword to Finn II's belly. Finn II jumped back grabbing Michael by the wrist and pushing the blunt shattered point of the split spear at Michael's shoulder. The move saved his life. As Finn II pushed for survival they were in a stalemate. Blood gushed from the wound that the blade carved. Finn II tried to stand strong, but as the pain set in and the blood oozed out, his legs gave way and dropped to a knee. It was only a flesh wound and Finn II holding the stick against Michael's shoulder was ensuring that it remained that way.

The crowd fell silent. Michael volleyed a knee to Finn II's face that knocked him to his back. Finn II was motionless on the floor. The crowd erupted. Michael celebrated his victorious defence by spreading his arms wide and walking towards the king's stand to soak in the praise. The cheers of the crowd washed over him and it felt like a drug.

'Oh see! Your man just made me a liar to all those gipsies on the Aduantas! I'll never be able to show my face again.' Said Luke.

'Shut up!' Snapped Celestine. 'It's not over yet.'

Celestine watched intensely as Finn II rolled to his knees holding the bleeding wound. The pain of the stab was going numb. His vision was blurred either through blood loss or the concussive knee to the face. He saw Michael pandering to the king, but soon it faded with everything else.

Instead, he saw his father standing on the very field he was on, refusing to die. Against insurmountable odds, he led the charge against the King's Anglonians and pushed them back. His father's legend could not die here, because he refused to die on this field. Tears rolled down his face and he wept with his head to the ground.

Celestine stared intensely at Finn II while he wept, encouraging him on. 'Use it.' He said.

Finn gripped the grass, forming a fist, slamming it against the floor.

'Use it!' Said Celestine. Luke shot a confused look at his friend.

'What you on about?' Luke asked.

Celestine ignored him.

Finn II posted himself up fighting to get upright, the crippling pain grounded him again. His face slammed against the grass. The stream of his tears wet the soil to sod as he sobbed in mourning. For the first time, he mourned. He punched the grass. Images of his father rushed through his mind, not the champion but the man. Finn II punched the grass again.

Memories of his father running and playing with him and cradling his sisters as babies and kissing his mother. Finn II punched the grass.

He remembered his father teaching him how to throw a punch and wield a sword. Finn II punched the grass again.

He remembered crying as he watched his father leave for Zorrodon on invite by King Peter IV to defend his country's honour, the McMahon crest on his cloak. Finn II punched the grass again.

The memories faded and Finn II lifted his head to look for his father, but he was not there. All he saw was the crowd cheering for Michael. All of them but one person.

'Use it!' Celestine screamed. That caught Finn II's attention through the noise and they locked eyes. He looked familiar but he couldn't remember where from, like a face he saw in passing but had never interacted with. Celestine looked at Finn II like he knew what he was feeling, understood every complexity of what he was going through.

'It's okay. Use it.' Said Celestine. Finn read his lips and it unlocked something within him that he had locked away all of his life.

Finn II summoned a cry from the depths of his soul. It was a yell so loud that his lone voice shook the arena to silence. The cry went on for what was like an eternity as Finn II let out everything he could. He never had the chance to mourn his father, everything he felt was locked away to achieve his mission, to exact his revenge. He shook with adrenaline as clarity returned to his vision, his numbness disappeared. He fought to his feet, every time the pain stopped him, instead of hitting the floor he beat the wound and fought on. The crowd watched in amazement as Finn II fought to his feet screaming and hitting his wound until his knuckles were bloody.

'On the stormy hills of Elgin! Ole Finn lifted his sword...' Finn II chanted as loud as he could muster. He banged the M on his chest for percussion.

'And he faced the south'ner's power! And he sent those fuckers home!' The crowd stomped and clapped in unison along with him. It shook the entire arena and surrounding area. *'Oh Finn the Brave!'* a subtle crack in his voice crept through as he sang his father's song. Michael watched in pure shock at Finn II's resolve. Before he could struggle the words that choked in his throat. The crowd chanted it for him.

'FINLAY! FINLAY! FINLAY! Oh! Finn the Brave! FINLAY! FINLAY! FINLAY!' The crowd stamped their feet over and over and continued to sing. Finn II was showing the resolve it took to win Celtish independence, they were seeing history repeat before their eyes. The sins of the father were being absolved by the son. The earth shook beneath their feet. Their voices could be heard throughout Elgin and beyond. Finn II looked around tears running down his cheeks. He never knew why his father fought so hard before, but he knew now. The song of his nation, the song of his father rained over him and galvanised his spirit. This fight was not over. He picked up his split ends of the spear, one short stick and a shorter spearhead. Michael was stricken afraid by the showing of the crowd. Finn II was fighting for something bigger and Michael felt it.

He spread his arm wide and screamed the battle cry that his father won the war with.

'Eireann!' and the crowd repeated. 'Eireann!' He shouted again and the crowd repeated. 'EIREANN!' As the crowd mimicked his call again, he charged.

Michael slashed and Finn II dodged to his right and sprung to a roll back the way he came before any follow up. Michael's empty attacks left him vulnerable. Finn II spang to his feet and span out with a backhand slamming the snapped stick of his spear against Michael's face. Michael staggered but recovered quickly and met Finn II's follow up. Horizontal slashes were met in quick succession and the blunt half of Finn II's weapon was now quartered. He caught a piece before it fell and slung it as he jumped backwards. The wood caught Michael hard in the neck, but it only angered him. Michael jumped forward and came down with all of his force. The blade cut through the sharp half of Finn II's spear. Before a follow up could come, he rolled out of the way. The crowd cheered and Michael grimaced. Finn II flung the point of the spear and it lodged itself in Michael's side. Michael doubled over and Finn II ran and jumped into a two-footed kick to Michael's face. Michael's sword was flung in the air as he fell to his back. Finn II sprang to his feet catching Michael's sword as he did. He pointed the tip of the blade at Michael's throat.

It was surrender or die. Finn II had won.

As a bloody and broken Michael was on the ground motionless, Finn II unleashed a wild scream again like a phoenix reborn. He dropped to his knees and wept into his palms. King Lochlyn II approached the edge of his stand and applauded the new champion. Finn II looked up at him.

'You!' He screamed, pointing to the king. Suddenly the entirety of the kingsguard drew their swords or aimed their bows directly at the brash warrior. Finn II was undeterred, he had to say what was on his mind. His heart pumped hard and fast, his body was tense and aching, and it was a struggle to stand. 'Do you not remember why this country was built, what we fought for? Your father built this country based on loyalty, loyalty to the people that did right by us. We refused to turn on King Kastielle because we were loyal. He fought our war because we refused to turn on that man as the southerners did. Now, look at you. You sit up there looking down on me, condemning me for the things I said. Without my father, we'd still be serving those gobshites down south.' The crowd clapped for him, even in the face of disrespecting the King. Finn II was not approaching this as a contender, he wasn't arrogant, finally, he was speaking as a man who was wronged. The Celtish people understood that. 'My father fought for this country because he loved it, and I know he would have died for it a hundred timed over. My daa died for Celtish Anglonia and you disgraced him, based on the word of the very bastards that we're fighting against. It wasn't right then, and it's not right now. Do with me what you want, I don't care. But please learn from the past, learn from your father, and right the wrongs done to my family.' The impassioned speech silenced even the winds, and Finn II stood accountable for addressing the King in such a manner. Everyone waited, some unsure if Finn II would live to see his championship reign last more than a few minutes. The company of the kingsguard still had their weapons trained on him.

The king lurched over the balcony and leered at the young man who had challenged his judgement. He ordered the guards to lower their weapons, then he clapped again, and the crowd applauded with him.

Finn II finally had a chance to look upon his king without spite, and he did not see a villain. He saw a man not much more than a decade older than him. He would have been younger than him and not long a king when he made the decision that caused such suffering. Now looking at him, he understood that King Lochlyn II was remorseful, he was also human. Their roads were parallel, they both had to live in their father's shadows, just for different reasons and under different circumstances.

'Finlay of Collister Mere the second, you have done me a great service. You have given me the opportunity to right one of my greatest wrongs in my young reign as king of this land. You have displayed the determination that the Celtish people are known the world over for. It was a mistake for me to treat you and your family in such a way, and you have my deepest apologies and sympathy. In my youth and naivete, I was blindly taken a fool by the south and to save this young country I dealt it its most devastating blow.' He said. It was rare to see a king show such vulnerability, but that was the difference between the Celtish and the rest of the world. There was no need to appear tough, being Celtish already meant that you were. 'Take this token as my gift to you. You and your family will no longer be nameless, I shall restore your McMahon name and your honour with it.' The king waved his hand to conclude his statement and the crowd jumped to their feet screaming for Finlay McMahon II, as he was known once more.

Beer was flung in the air and the thudding shook the entire town. Songs of Finn II's father, Finn the Brave, filled the arena. It was a moment that was significant to the country, not only the McMahon family. Since Finn the Brave, there had not been a hero of the same stature, there had not been a Celtish legend. Finn II became only the second man in Anglonian history to be ordained with the King family name. Finn II was a legend reborn to the Celtish people, however, with the same gesture as the king, Finn II silenced the crowd.

'Thank you for restoring my family name, but…' The crowd leant in anxiously. 'I do not wish to take it.' Finn II said. The spectators gasped at the rejection of the king's offer.

'Have a care when denying a king Sir Finlay.' King Lochlyn II said. The sun travelled behind the stand that housed him and his shadow extended over Finn II. It cloaked him in the darkness, but Finn II stood strong.

'My father was Finlay McMahon, and he served the King, your father. I don't wish to serve just you, but all the people of this fine land that stood by me when we needed it most. I want to be the people's champion. So, I want to take the people's name, my people's name. Name me after the Emerald Isles as Finlay Eireann first of my name and any others.' Finn II dropped to one knee finally showing the due respect to the ever-courteous King Lochlyn II. The king nodded, however his expression seemed impatient and irritated.

'As you wish.' He said before leaving out of the back of his stand, led, followed and flanked by his kingsguard.

When Finn II rose, he was no longer second of his name. He was Finn

Eireann the people's champion. He embraced the crowd with one more throaty cry, leading them in the loudest of celebrations. With more to come, Finn decided to make his exit, stepping out of the shadow of the King's stand, and the shadow of his father.

High in the tower of Zorrodon, word reached Magnus of Finn's victory that night. Magnus smirked, licking his lips.

'Perfect. Maybe it's time we extend an invite to the son, that we did the father all those years ago.' Said Magnus.

'A fine idea sir.' Said Fredrickson 'A fine idea indeed.'

6 THOSE WHO DON'T LEARN FROM HISTORY

Vida- Ego- 4- 1827

In the cover of night, Fredrickson ambled the cobbled paths of Zorrodon's Governmental Complex to the courier he had lying in wait. The courier was a rugged man with calloused greasy fingers. He smiled a crooked toothy grin at his instructions and mounted his saddle. He was gifted a slender brown horse, bred for long journeys. He had a delivery to make for the next day, which meant the horse must have the stamina to race through the night.

Many roads ran through King's Anglonia like veins on a human body. The major roads connected the regions and smaller paths spread like a rash across villages, towns, and cities. Boyd's Walk was the spine of King's Anglonia; it connected all roads. All major journeys had to go through the iconic pathway. It was also the only road that connected King's Anglonia and Celtish Anglonia, with all other connecting land separated by Loch's Trench dug during the war. The beating hoofs of the courier's horse thudded into the darkness of the flanking trees and foliage. Curious glowing nocturnal eyes peeped from their seclusion confused by the man riding at the absurd hour. It was only when he emerged from the shroud of the covering forestation that the courier realised that he had ridden through the night because the sun was shining on Celtish Anglonia.

Celestine was in the comfort of the Grazing Cow Inn, he rested through the night and fell into a dreamless sleep. Now, he lay stationary in bed, arms behind his head like he was relaxing. It was truly a wonder how relaxing it could be to wake up without a smelly Celtish imbecile cuddling him. Honestly, he felt guilty for not appreciating this creature comfort when he had it; yesterday morning opened his eyes. As he did yesterday morning, he heard the abhorrent snoring that he had grown accustomed to, this time it from the other side of the room. As much as he complained about the noise, amongst other things over the last half-year, there was nobody else he would have preferred on this trip. Luke saw him for who he was, and he didn't need to be anybody else. Luke knew Celestine better than he knew himself. All Celestine saw when he looked in the mirror was a product of his Uncle. He always saw what was expected of him, and constantly he fell short of it. There was no way he could be anything else. This trip around the world was to discover who he was so he could see himself in his reflection and not his uncle. Today was the last day of that venture. They would be home tomorrow, whether he found himself or not.

He took a moment to stare at the wooden ceiling and ponder his journey home. He missed it. Being home gave him a feeling of belonging and safety like steady ground.

He sighed.

When he rolled over to check on Luke, Luke was paralysed on his mattress. He was sprawled on his duvet with one foot hanging from the bed and his forearm draped over his eyes. There was a pool of drying vomit on the floor beside his bed and some appeared to get in his loose ginger curls. Disgusted, Celestine decided to rise for the morning.

'Not again man.' he said quietly.

When he stood, he staggered a little. He dragged his feet to his clothes and roughly pulled his hair into a ponytail. He took his light luggage and left instructions for Luke on the table of where to meet him. He then slammed the door; Luke didn't even stir.

The streets of Elgin appeared a ghost town once more. The likely reason being everyone sleeping as deeply as Luke was back at the inn. A few of them having the same liquid surprise waiting on or by their beds. Celestine couldn't bear the thought. Though the smell escaped him, the sight made him feel like he needed a bath. He was heading back to the bathhouse he and Luke went yesterday. There was no hope of getting Luke to have baths on consecutive days, and Celestine hadn't the patience to try. The Chancery was close to the southside border and close to a tavern that served good food and ale. It wasn't long before he was there once more for another cleansing. In the distance, he spotted a man on a slender brown horse headed south. His greasy fingers gripped the reigns as his crooked teeth mutely cackled into the horizon.

Celestine purchased a hot bath with the first-class service, the same service he purchased for Luke, but not himself. A lovely young lady would come to bathe him, and he could relax with his thoughts. The weight of returning home pressed heavily on his mind. Celestine needed not a functional bath to just cleanse his body, but a relaxing one to cleanse his mind. The bath did not disappoint. Even in the summer heat, the bath had produced a tremendous amount of steam in the beach wood room. Without hesitation, he disrobed and slipped in. His mind screamed while his mouth hissed at the heat, it was just the way he liked it. Cobbs of sweat barreled down his forehead and neck. He splashed the hot water on his face and poured some over his head. He then laid back and allowed his water cradle to comfort his weary body and mind. A little shy of five minutes later and young female attendee entered the room.

She was small and shapely, she had rich maroon hair and strikingly light blue eyes. Her smile put Celestine at further ease. Her skin was smooth like cream marble, unlike those from the Highlands of Celtish Anglonia who were prone to freckles. She was a dark-haired beauty of Eireann. When she came in, Celestine imagined the girl in Zorrodon with flowers in her hair. The steam of his bath imaging a mirage of her shining onyx hair and large eyes. It eased his troubling mind to know he would see her soon. Celestine was still stricken by his attendee's beauty but was disappointed that his impossible mirage was confirmed untrue.

The attendee began with placing the bar of soap on Celestine's shoulders and then lathered his back and neck. With her soft hands, she rubbed her lather in, simultaneously massaging the tension he carried into the room. He closed his eyes not sleepy or tired, but so relaxed that it seemed like the right thing to do. The attendee's hands ached as she wrestled with each muscle on Celestine's back to relax. His body, although supple, was very dense and solid.

She rubbed his chest and stomach with soap and unintentionally slowed hanging on each muscle. She was of the mindset that the good-looking ones usually were rather unimpressive when it came to physique. Real male specimens were not pretty, or handsome, at least not until him. Beguiled by his long golden hair and strong jaw, she became one of the many who believed that Celestine looked like a prince. Somehow, Celestine could feel that her energy had changed as she rubbed his back and washed his hair. She took meticulous care when washing his locks. They shone even in the steamy dullness of the room. She lathered, rinsed, and combed them gently. The teeth of her comb glided through like a spoon through heavy cream.

'Would you like to me to do your legs when I'm finished here?' She asked.

Celestine shook his head politely declining. His instincts sensed the connotation behind her words and that just was not something he did.

'Well then, I think I'm done here.' She said with one final stroke of the comb.

'That was great, thank you.' Replied Celestine. 'What's your name? So, I can leave some gold for you when I go. I'd give it to you now but I seem to have misplaced my trousers.' He continued.

She blushed and giggled. 'Lizbeth, my name is Lizbeth.' She said.

'It's a pleasure to meet you, Lizbeth.' Said Celestine. Lizbeth stood and left the room quietly still smiling when the door closed behind her. Celestine dried himself and wrapped a towel around his body to head to the steam bath.

It was nearly impossible for Celestine to see an arm's length in front of him in the steam bath. The room was large and dark, especially considering that there were several windows to the outside and the beautiful summer morning. The steam had all but blocked what light could leak into the room. The sun's rays broke and bent in the swirling darkness like the ripples of water. Gingerly, Celestine edged into the room. The floor was paved with wooden slats where the steam permeated from below. It was a struggle not to slip on the floor because the steam made the smooth wood slick. He shuffled straight with his arms out in hopes he would find an end.

He wanted to sit in the hot fog and clear his senses, breathe in the vapour, and emerge fresh from the womb of his adventure a new man. He had found himself on his travels, the trouble was keeping him around. Now he was a day away from home and he was getting scared. Celestine pondered the possibility of him inadvertently going in circles as the room went on almost forever. That would be foolish, to navigate the entire world but get lost in a big room with steam in it. He pushed on, disregarding the nonsense notion. A few steps later, his hands did not find anything, but his feet did. As he stepped out clumsily, his heel landed on foreign toes. Celestine yelped and hopped backwards.

'Oh, I am so sorry.' Said Celestine.

'Not a problem friend.' The other said. His voice was familiarly unfamiliar. 'You can't see anything in this room.' Celestine could not place the voice.

'I should have been more mindful, I'm sorry. Are you ok?' he said bowing to a man who couldn't see or appreciate the gesture.

'Listen, if I can't handle another man stepping on my foot, I wouldn't be much of a man myself.' The other said. 'I mean, after all, I am the Champion of Celtish Anglonia.'

Luke headed into town on Celestine's instruction, not before cleaning the bedroom and leaving a few extra gold pieces for the inconvenience. Luke rolled his eyes as he did it.

As he spryly strode down the street, he watched on as his countrymen crawled out onto the streets like wounded soldiers. It was like there was another civil war. In Luke's experience, there hadn't been a festival like this one; it felt special like it was a marker in history. Finn's victory in battle was the correction that the country needed, reuniting the nation once more. The resulting chaos and debauchery were an example of what a united nation did to celebrate, however now, the effects of that celebration were being felt by all. Well, almost all. Luke did not suffer hangovers. Celestine thought that Luke's uncanny ability was part of a practical joke by Mother Nature or her divine children, but at least that gift was not squandered. He saw the

Chancery Bath House and the tavern that he was instructed to meet Celestine in across the way.

Luke approached reading the sign outside.

"The Stagg and Bull Tavern"

"We do not accept Copper or Brass at this establishment. We do however accept, bronze and fair trade."

No mention of gold often meant that the place was cheap. Luke liked cheap because it meant more drink. He pushed the doors open with a small pouch of gold and silver in his hand.

'Barkeep, your finest ale please!' He said.

'Finn?' Said Celestine. He stared and blinked through the blinding steam. With the aid of his words and thin swirling sunlight, Celestine could identify Finn's features. He was staring, however.

'Well, are you gonna sit or what?' Said Finn friendlily.

'Oh yes, and sorry about the foot again.' Said Celestine crouching and pawing for a seat.

'Enough of that, bygones mate!' Finn tapped Celestine with a soft backhand on his shoulder. 'Do you apologise for that much for every mistake you make?'

Celestine shrugged and pondered a second. 'Pretty much yes.'

Finn howled laughing 'I mean skies above. If I apologised for that much for every mistake I'd made, I'd still be at me ma's back in Collister! Cause let me tell you, I was a proper twat for a good few years in my teens. I swear to The Court!'

'I never thought of it that way.' Said Celestine laughing. Finn draped his arm around Celestine as if sharing a secret.

'Listen, friend, sometimes learning from a mistake is apology enough. Take it from an old veteran.'

Celestine nodded ignoring the fact that he was likely older than the Celtish champion.

'Wait…' Said Finn blankly. 'I recognise you. You were at me fight yesterday!'

Celestine shook his head. 'No… I mean I was, but you've probably got me mistaken with someone else.'

'No mate, I know a face. You were next to a chubby fella, opposite the king's stand.' Finn was intense and there was no escaping for Celestine. He didn't know why he wanted to escape in the first place, there was shyness or a humility that didn't want a champion of Finn's stature to recognise him. Finn was on a pedestal now.

Celestine nodded his head before he could think of a reasonable alibi.

'Listen yeah, I owe you a great many thanks. You were the only one who was spurring me on when I was down. I don't know what it was, but whatever you said or did made me fight on.'

'I didn't do a thing. That was all you.'

The two rested back and closed their eyes and the room was silent, save the sound of their breathing. Celestine could feel everything becoming looser in his body and the thoughts of home became much less anxious. He had so much to tell his uncle about his adventure. This time was the greatest endeavour he had embarked upon. Half a year travelling around the world with Luke, they explored the plains of Arabia, visited the shrines of The Wukong Empire, and scaled the mountains of the Deutschlands. It paled in comparison to the storied travels of the great Talion Schultz, but he could add one more experience to his diary. He was now sitting next to a champion, one of Talion's kin. It was special because it reminded him of his ambitions as a youngster, to one day assume that title for his home of King's Anglonia. He never attained that status because he never attempted to grasp it. Talion had been a champion and refused to allow either Celestine or Staphros to become one.

"Being Champion has an ugliness to it that you cannot fathom until it's too late. You are a weapon as much to destroy as to defend. It is a fate that I would not wish on my enemy, never mind my boys." Talion would say. There were few things that Talion was adamant on and that was one of them. Celestine understood, but it broke his heart that he never had the chance to try.

Celestine awoke with a jolt. He blinked himself back awake after drifting asleep. Finn was up ducking, and weaving, and shadowboxing. He was very fast and precise despite the damage he sustained the day before. The steam had let up slightly and the room was much easier to see in. Finn had a type of focus on his face which was reminiscent of his fight the day prior. He was light on his feet and moved very well. The movement he displayed the day before required constant practice, and now it was clear how Finn could do it. He looked over to a blinking Celestine rubbing his eyes.

'I thought I'd lost you there for a second.' He said still sparring.

'I must have drifted off.' Said Celestine pulling his soaking hair away from his face. He stretched and his bones silently clicked themselves awake. He felt revitalised.

'Good dream?' Asked Finn still throwing punches.

'Can't remember.' He grew perplexed as his mind cleared. 'Wait, didn't you fight yesterday? Why are you training?'

'Always time to improve I say.'

'Fair, but it takes real confidence to know when to rest.' Said Celestine. 'At least, that's what my uncle says.'

'Your uncle seems like a wise man, but…' Finn paused. He deliberately halted his chain of thought, and it was visibly clear that he struggled with the thought. 'Ahh bollocks to it! I got a letter through this mornin from those Princesses down south. No offence.'

'None taken.' Said Celestine quickly.

'They have issued a challenge to me for in a week. They said it'll be in their new arena in Zorrodon City because they want to expose me as the fraud my father was to the public. I say bring it on!'

'Maybe, but your father was baited the same way was he not?'

'Aye, but I am not my father.'

'You're not, but you are his son.' Said Celestine. The room went quiet as Finn stopped boxing and turned to Celestine's face.

'Then what? I turn and run away?' Said Finn. 'Might be something you do where you're from, but not here. Not the Celtish!'

'What do you have to prove? You are Champion of Celtish Anglonia; isn't that good enough?'

'No, my country is a joke because of them. My family lived for nearly two decades in shame because of them. I have to prove the Celtish have real champions, like Talion of Anara!'

Celestine laughed suddenly and uncontrollably.

'The fook you laughing at?' Said Finn angrily. 'I told you, this isn't a joke!'

'I'm not laughing at you.' Said Celestine apologetically, yet still smiling. 'It's just funny that you mention Talion.' He continued.

'Why? You think I'm dreaming too big? Listen yeah…'

'A man can dream as big as he likes.' Interrupted Celestine. 'No, it's just, Talion is my uncle.' Finn examined Celestine. He had no lies or delusion behind his words. Finn was a logical man and had a keen eye for what made a man tick. He was very good at reading people. It dawned on him suddenly, that moment they shook hands he knew had met someone of great importance. The confidence that he exuded, the strength in his physical greeting. His mouth spoke a humility that his body could not replicate. The familiarity from the arena returned to him, but this time he could remember where he saw his face. They had shaken hands before, in the Wukong Empire. Celestine was an honoured guest master at the dojo where Finn had trained his spear technique. They met in passing, only seconds, but there was an unspoken conversation between them even then. Now Finn knew why.

'You're his nephew then?' Said Finn. 'Talion's nephew?' he wanted to be sure, but he knew already. It was exciting to hear that a member of the greatest champion in history's family was sat before him ten days before the fight of his life.

Celestine confirmed it with a nod.

'So, did he… you know?'

'Train me? Almost every day since I was around three.' Celestine said knowing the question that was to come. He had been asked it countless times. Most of the time, the people asking were either trying to get him to fight or get him to bed. He obliged to neither.

'And that was why you were at the Jun Bo Academy in Wukong.'
Celestine nodded.

'Listen, I know you're not him, but I'm honoured to meet even you!'
Said Finn in the humblest display he had shown in the brief time Celestine
had seen him. He was showing Celestine more respect than he did his own
king. Celestine stood waving it off.

'Don't be.'

Finn shook his head. 'You don't understand, being a champion is my
life! There was nothing else for me coming up, you know.' He said. 'Your
Uncle was my greatest hero after me Daa.' he pointed at Celestine's chest.

'I understand, but I have nothing to do with that. I don't even like
bringing it up because people treat me differently. To have a history of your
predecessor follow you is hard, I know you understand that.' Said Celestine.

Finn nodded. He knew exactly what Celestine was talking about,
positive or negative Finn would never escape his Father's shadow. That was
partly why he had to change his name.

'I know you don't have much time, but if you need to train before the
fight you can train at my uncle's farm. My Uncle would love to meet you, and
it's not far from Zorrodon at all. Besides, between me and Staph we've learnt
everything Talion knows' Celestine waited eagerly for a reply. Talion was
always enamoured with helping others, and Staphros could not tolerate
injustice. Celestine knew that both would help without hesitation.

Finn pondered a moment. His hands were on his hips and his sharp
eyes were directed right to the floor. After a few bobs of the head, he finally
nodded clearly. He had made his decision.

'I'll do it. I'll need to arrange a few things, but I'll meet you there in a
few days. Just mark a map for me, I'll find it.' Said Finn. They shook hands
again.

A shimmer of light gleamed in Celestine's eyes and he smirked. He had
a princely charm that was often overshadowed by the overwhelming
meekness that he projected. At this moment, his body reacted. His true self
devoid of social control shone through.

'Just be aware champ.' He said brushing his hair away. 'I'll not be
holding back.' He winked and released his grip.

Finn stared intensely and nodded. He liked what he saw and now, his
want to get to Sakura Farm, was now a need.

7 OLD FRIENDS AND NEW SELVES

Vida- Ego- 4- 1827

Luke's obnoxious entry into the Stagg and Bull Tavern went over as well as one could imagine. The tired patrons were not impressed with the blatant yob that had interrupted their breakfast. Most of them were the elderly residents of Elgin that celebrated the Festival, like any other Celtishman, but not in the same way. They absorbed the atmosphere and embraced the quiet beauty of the nation's unity. Luke's words met unamused blank silence and he flushed red with embarrassment and shuffled inside to the bar. The barkeep that Luke so loudly addressed was a barmaid. She had a plump jolly face and a nest of fiery ginger hair that appeared ungroomed, however, in reality, it was more uncooperative. Her face too was unimpressed as she polished a mug.

'What can I do you for?' She asked. Although the bar was in Elgin, the heart of Caledonia her accent was from Eireann, a very regional accent at that. Luke couldn't place it.

'Glass of ale please.' He asked timidly.

'Make that a child's cider.' Celestine said from behind. Celestine looked fresher and more confident than ever. His hair glistened and was tied in his traditional high ponytail and the waves below his crown flowed down his back. He wore his coat again, but his face was different than normal, closer to the man that fought on the Aduantas. Luke was immediately elated at seeing this side of him appear freely, therefore he let the order of a child's cider pass. Child's Cider was unfermented warm cider. It was very sweet, which was something Luke liked, but it had no alcoholic content whatsoever, which he hated.

'Good, cause I wasn't going to serve him an ale anyway.' The barmaid said. 'What can I get you lovely?' She flashed a smile at Celestine, and he blushed.

'Oh, a mug of milk if you have it?' He asked. Before he could take out his money to pay, an older gentleman interjected.

'Ay, lass! Put that on my tab and gizza nother one!' he said holding the mug that contained his Scottsdrink. He was balding and pale and his face was round, full, and red. He was mostly beardless aside from the grey whiskers that formed a patchy stubble at varying levels of darkness. He rummaged in his pocket and placed a silver piece in the barmaid's hand. 'That's for you sweetheart.' He said winking. 'Safe keepin.'

The barmaid blushed as she poured Luke and Celestine's drinks. The old man bounded towards Celestine and Luke with arms wide and a familial grin from cheek to cheek. He shook Luke's hand first cordially, then he grabbed Celestine's hand he stared at him intensely without saying a word, he smiled like he was waiting for something back. Feeling awkward, Celestine broke the silence.

'It's a pleasure to meet you and thank you.' He said while lifting his drink with his free hand. The old man gurgled a peal of gravelly laughter from his throat.

'You don't remember me do ye?' He said. Celestine looked around uncomfortably trying unsuccessfully to find an answer.

'Should I?' He said.

'You are Talion's wee lad aren't ye?' Said the old man.

Celestine nodded.

'Oh aye, ye would have been quite young when I last seen ye.' He said. 'But I did teach ye how to ride a horse.' The old man smiled a shaggy grin. Celestine pondered a moment before the memory returned to him. His eyes glimmered as he remembered the old man, who had aged considerably since their last meeting, but his smile made him young again for that moment. The flash of the golden tooth in his smile would always cheer an infant Celestine up when he got discouraged or afraid.

'Eulis?' asked Celestine.

Luke's eyes lit up. 'Bloody Nora it is Eulis! Com'ere ye old bastard ye!' He dived after the old man and hugged him.

'No way that's Luke Chef there!' Said Eulis.

'Aye, the one and only.'

'Ye've grown haven't ye! The both of ye.'

'Aye, I should hope so. I was maybe five last I saw ye.'

'You were five, I was seven.' Said Celestine to Luke.

'Right, listen you two. Join me for breakfast and we can ave a right good catch up.' Said Eulis with such an authority that the two reverted to their infant mindset and did exactly what their elder said.

The two sat at the table with Eulis. It was in a quiet corner of the tavern by a window. Celestine briefed Eulis on the beginning of he and Luke's trip and Luke took care of recounting the latter parts. Eulis ordered drinks for the table, and Celestine's milk and Luke's child's cider turned into mugs of warm ale. Ale was the only beverage to accompany catching up.

The barmaid hurried over with three mugs of ale on a tray, Eulis paused the conversation to help steady the wobbly surface in which his drinks rested. He placed his hand underneath the barmaid's and they worked as a tandem to guide the precious cargo to its destination. He said goodbye with a cheeky wink and she blushed at his old charm.

'Still got it after all these years, ey lads?' Said Eulis gloating.

Celestine and Luke nodded. Eulis took up his mug of ale and slurped it. Its hearty taste sent satisfying shivers down his body.

'So...' Said Eulis. 'You were telling me about this Aduantas. The travellers aboard that vessel are the roughest of the lot. You didn't find yourself in trouble did you?'

'No not at all.' Said Luke. Celestine shot a glare at his friend. 'Well, maybe a little.'

'Luke had me fight someone, even made a bet.'

'Alright, it wasn't my finest moment, but we came away without any injuries and a decent sum of money.' Luke shyly took a sip of his ale, knowing that it was drinking like that, that got them into the situation on the Aduantas.

'Oh so ye won?!' Laughed Eulis. 'Who was it? I know that lot. Was it Fergal, Paddy?'

'Alec?' Said Celestine unsure if Eulis was familiar with the name.

Eulis's jaw dropped. 'You fought Alec and won?' he asked.

Luke nodded. 'Aye and?'

'Alec has been in the pool of contenders for six years. If it wasn't for young Finn, he would have fought against Michael yesterday to be champion. Many thought he would have won if he did.'

'Oh, well you should have seen him. Celestine didn't only win, he made quick work of the big bastard. Came out without a scratch.' Boasted Luke.

Celestine hit him.

Eulis looked upon Celestine with a new admiration as he fidgeted with Luke. He was still that child that he knew, but he was a little different too. Last he saw him, Celestine was just a sensitive skinny boy. Celestine suffered greatly in his childhood; he had an affliction that caused him to have terrible seizures. The only way that he would be granted any respite was if he was sedated, and it had to be strong. Talion sheltered him as much as he could, everybody protected him as best they could. He was fragile. It appeared now that he had beaten whatever illness troubled his childhood so, but Eulis would not be so tactless to ask about it. Today was an occasion to celebrate, but still, it was stunning to think that the little boy that cried in the stables because he believed himself so weak, grew to be so strong. The benefits of Talion's tutelage were wonderous evidently. He poked Celestine in the chest, unaware of the force he put into it.

'Your old man Talion seriously changed my life, ye ought to say hello from me when ye go back. Ye do still live there don't ye?'

Celestine nodded.

'That's grand! Oh, that farm has so many memories, good and bad. I remember one time when I was drunk, I challenged young Staphros to an arm wrestle. He was only fifteen and although he was big, I thought I could handle myself. That boy almost crushed my hand didn't he!' He slapped Luke on the arm with a backhand and the trio burst into laughter. 'I don't know if that's a good or a bad memory but it's bloody hilarious! The worst part was that it was about ten days after I see him bloody lifting horses.' Eulis laughed again along with Celestine. Luke stopped laughing.

'What do you mean lifting horses?' Asked Luke. Luke had a fearful quake in his voice. Staphros was already a man of infinite intimidating potential and Luke had not heard of the horse story, because it pre-dated his arrival on the farm by a year or so. Eulis looked to Celestine and Celestine to him.

'You tell it better.' Said Celestine to the old man. Luke leaned in in anticipation. There was a mystique that surrounded Staphros that many of the farm hands speculated about. Most of the speculation came from Luke's sister Samantha, who had a thing for the giant. Her speculative musings were the stuff of nightmares to his ears. His lips curved to a quivering nervous smile and he listened to Eulis tell the story.

'This was early days of the farm, only the old-timers were around then. Young Staph comes out with two of my horses Hessledon and Kuster to plough the fields. He attaches the harness and the plough and puts them to work. At this point, Kuster is close to knackered, but he was strong enough, or so I thought. Turns out halfway through the job, Kuster collapses and can't get back up. Now, remember, Staph is only fifteen. Over seven-foot mind, but still, only fifteen-years-old man! He lifts Kuster on one of his shoulders and guides Hessledon back to my stables. I'm watching the whole things with my jaw on the floor.'

'What?! He carried the horse back?' Said Luke in disbelief.

'He's not done.' Said Celestine.

'No, not at all. The big fella straps the harness onto his own back and drags the plough through the fields himself. The boy did the work of two horses and then went to finish his other duties. I never missed work after seeing that.' Eulis was awestruck by the story even when telling it. The colour ran from Luke's face and he stared blankly past Eulis and to the road leading home. Staphros and Luke had a tenuous relationship because of Luke's work ethic. He had none. Luke shirked duties, he was irresponsible, and on a lot of days would not turn up to do work. Eulis' story shed light as to why that may frustrate Staphros. Celestine giggled as he watched his friend. He and Staph had spoken about what Luke had to offer, and those feeling of frustration came out from time to time. Maybe hearing something like that would kick him up the arse.

'You know the oldies still talk about that to this day?' Said Celestine.

'It don't surprise me! How is the big bastard?' Eulis asked.

'He's managing the farm now; it was too much for Uncle Talion to do.'

'Never thought that old git would ever stop running that farm. Thought he'd just work until he dropped dead.'

'It took some convincing from both Staphros and me to make him, but he broke after some nagging on our side.' Said Celestine proudly.

'Ah... Well, it's good to see you are coming into your own there Celestine!' Eulis said.

'Thank you!' It was small, and something that was likely said in a passing gesture. But Eulis's words hit Celestine, affirming his goals for his adventure. He was becoming his own man, and people were recognising it.

Now it was time to test that theory back home.

8 GLORY

Vida- Hostil- 5- 1827

Sumera rocked in the back of her transport carriage. The trees that flanked the dirt path of Boyd's Walk stroked the walls of the interior with the ghostly fingers of their shadows. The morning was ending and the afternoon was taking form as the sun was at its highest. It wasn't the hottest of days and the sky was blanketed with a sheet of grey clouds that Anglonia was known for. Sumera's eyes showed she was afraid her breaths connoted concern. The lighter streaks on the caramel brown of her skin revealed that she had been crying. It was a secret best kept in the privacy of the dark, but when the tree's allowed the dulled sun to leak through the window of the carriage, the tracks of her tears were there for all to see.

She clutched her daughter in her arms, who was becoming a young woman in her own right, making a long trip to a place they didn't know. They were travelling from Leeburn Valley, a small town in the midlands of King's Anglonia and the site for frequent slave auctions. The slave trade was always closer to the north than the south. The farms, vineyards, mines, and castles were all towards the north, so the need for slaves was greater. All slaves that were bought were often transported south after serving their purpose in the north to serve as maids and cooks mostly.

Sumera had come to Anglonia at seventeen-years-old at the turn of the century when Anara fell. She escaped Anara as a refugee. The Anglonian policy was clear, if a refugee had no wealth or home, they would be sold into slavery. She along with nearly all Anara natives that had fled their homes were sold directly into slavery. She ended up on a vineyard on Tyne Hill County, where she spent twenty-seven years plucking grapes for her master. Sumera knew a life before the one she lived now, but Lilly, Sumera's daughter, was born into servitude and worked alongside her. When Sumera had significantly slowed in her output on the fields at the turn of her forty-fourth year of life, her masters knew it was time for her to make her way down south. Lilly was to go with her so they could attach a premium to her value. They were purchased and ushered into the carriage that they presently sat in.

The trees of Boyd's Walk had withdrawn as the carriage turned down another beaten path. Sumera and Lilly took deep breaths and their grips tightened. The road was bumpier than Boyd's Walk and the harshness knocked them off balance more than a few times. It soon levelled out and then they slowed to a stop. A bright light shone through the carriage window, but Sumera did not see it. She had her eyes closed awaiting her new fate. The trip down south for women her age was mostly safe, there were dangers from time to time, but those dangers were infinitely more prevalent for women Lilly's age. Lilly was fourteen and a virgin, a fact that the auctioneer advertised in Leeburn Valley, followed by a response from the buyers that was unnerving to say the least. Lilly was smart and lively, but, although rapidly approaching womanhood, she was a child at heart. She spent all her life as a slave, but she was not ready to be that kind of slave.

The carriage door opened but limited light shone through. The man that had opened the door was gigantic, bald-headed and stoic. Lilly could just about see the space over his shoulder, which revealed the shimmering emerald grass, sky, and coastline gradient in the distance. This was not like the place they were before; nothing was. They had travelled in carriages before and no slave carriage was this comfortable. Often they would be transferred in similar pens to the animals. This was different, much different. The giant man smiled.

'The master is waiting in the Big House for you.' He said.

The two stared at him blankly.

'Don't worry. You'll be okay.' He said.

The size of the giant man could not be truly appreciated until Sumera and Lilly walked by him. They stood a little above five feet tall, Lilly was now a little taller than her mother, but this man made them look and feel like children beside him. He ushered them to the door and invited them in.

Behind the door was a great hall of glossed brown wood, marble surfaces and purple ribbon. There was a large table draped in white cloth in the middle of the room. It had a spread of cakes, tea, bread, and fruit, on top. Sumera and Lilly were placed at the table as the giant man went to the other side of the room. He disappeared for a while, before returning with Talion Schultz at his back.

Being a native of Anara, Sumera knew the man's face as soon as she saw it and she couldn't help herself but cry. It was a mixture of being awestruck, nostalgic, and filled with hope. If she was to be a slave, she was proud to serve the Champion of Anara. She had thought he died at Anara Castle alongside his king, and aside from her fellow slaves, she thought her countrymen were all but gone. She was glad to know she was wrong. He looked different, he was significantly older and he hunched over a cane, but his fierce eyes showed the steel of the champion he once was. It was unmistakably Talion Schultz of Anara.

Talion took a seat across from Sumera and Lilly, alongside Staphros, or "the giant man" in the eyes of the newly occupied slaves of Sakura Farm. He had kindness in his aged face that Sumera hadn't seen in him before. King Kastielle was always the kinder of the two when faced with the public. Now, Talion was adopting the kinder side of his late king and friend. Lilly took her weeping mother's hand.

'You must be Sumera and Lilly, my name is Talion and this is Staphros. I'm sorry for the pantomime, I ask Staph to purchase all of my slaves nowadays. In my old age, I've grown weary of the whole thing, and I have developed a less than savoury reputation in those circles.'

Sumera and Lilly's ears perked with concern. For Talion to have a less than savoury reputation around slave masters and sellers was troubling. Staphros poured Talion some tea.

'Tea?' Asked Staphros to the two across from him.

They both shook their head bewildered.

'Well, just so you know. This food is meant for you, made fresh this morning.'

Sumera and Lilly looked at each other now more perplexed than ever. Still, it wasn't their place to ask questions. Talion noticed.

'Please, allow me to clear a few things up.' He said. He dug into his jacket pocket and took out the papers of ownership for both Sumera and Lilly and placed them on the table. Not just in Sumera's case, but no slave would ever see their papers of ownership. Although slaves were not important enough to consider their feelings, it was perceived as taboo to flaunt such things to their face. The folded pieces of parchment rested half uncurled on the white tablecloth. As Sumera looked upon the document that took her humanity away from her for the first time, it looked small and inconsequential. The longer she looked at it, it became heavier and larger. It was now the only thing in the room as everything else faded to black. She could feel her heartbeat so prevalently it drummed in her ears. Her fingers became cold and stiff, as everything insider herself was telling her to take it and tear it to pieces even if it meant her death, but she couldn't. Talion watched her, as he watched the hundreds of other slaves that he bought in his time. He knew what was in their mind and he knew how they felt in their heart.

'Pick them up.' He commanded.

Sumera picked both up and handed over the one that pertained to Lilly. Talion rummaged in his pocket again and unearthed an envelope within.

'Now please could you take those papers and burn them?' he asked pointing to the fireplace in the corner of the room, clicking and burning quietly. 'I say please because you do not have to do so if you don't want to.'

'I beg your pardon mas...' Stuttered Sumera, utterly dumbfounded. She almost called him master, which she couldn't call him, but it didn't feel right to call him Talion. She didn't know what to call him.

'I see, it can be a little confusing all of this. The contents of this envelope is a signed and sealed decree as your owner, that I do henceforth set you free from the shackles of slavery. Which means, you needn't listen to a word I say. At this point burning those papers of ownership would be redundant because of this envelope, but I'd recommend it for the satisfaction.' Said Talion.

'He's not wrong.' Added Staphros.

Sumera and Lilly looked to each other and then to the two men across from them and then back to each other. Lilly burst in an uncontrolled eruption of incredulous laugher and quickly silenced herself, but then it came and again, and again. Tears barrelled down her cheeks as the new sensation of freedom made her feel physically lighter. It was new, something that was unheard and forbidden to be spoken. Every time Sumera closed her eyes to blink, she would see through eyes that had remained shut for over twenty-seven years. For the first time since her home was burnt down in Anara, she saw the world with hopeful and free eyes. She curled her weary hand to a fist, trying to grab this moment, this feeling, but she couldn't. She daren't pinch herself in case this was a dream, she just wanted to stay. She didn't want to have to wake up and pluck the grapes from the vineyard any more. Her eyes remained shut and she savoured her most vivid memory of home since leaving it, unable to bear thinking about it when the memories were fresh and unable to remember when they had faded. Now with renewed hope, dream or no, her memory of Anara had returned. She was there again, she could even smell it, and the great Talion Schultz was still her savour. Glistening tears rolled down her caramel skin leaving streaks lined with gold. Lilly clung to her mother, begging for her to confirm it. Sumera looked to her opening her eyes and accepting this was true, it was not a dream, for her daughter's sake. Lilly saw life in her mother's eyes for the first time and noticed that they were light brown almost yellow. She knew her mother was beautiful, but how she glowed with freedom and happiness made it so Lily saw Beauty, the daughter of Nature herself in her Sumera's face.

Sumera nodded. She had tried to say "It's true" but the words did not come out. She simply mouthed it like it was a clandestine plot to hide from eavesdropping ears. At the sight of those two silent words, Lilly and her mother embraced. They wept and wailed holding one and other.

Talion and Staphros had almost made a career out of doing this. With Talion's exurbanite wealth that he had earned in service to Anara, he had dedicated his life in Anglonia to give hope to the hopeless. He started with Staphros, but it grew into something more. The hundreds of people that worked on Sakura Farm past and present, were all slaves that Talion purchased. Slave owners didn't like that, and his reputation was that of a troublemaker to them, a disrupter of the system. Staphros came in handy on the many occasions where such harsh feelings came to a head. Talion remained undeterred, it was bigger than him. It was bigger than the slaves or the system as a whole in his eyes. He did this because that was what Sakura, would have wanted. When he was champion of Anara, he and Sakura would sit under a tree in a quiet field in Wildberry. Talion would promise the world to her, a fine castle and servants, a life for just the two of them. Although he shared that dream dozens of times with her, Sakura shared her idea just once.

'Why do we need servants? If we have the money to buy land, and a castle and the finest carriages and gowns, why couldn't we pay our slaves a fair wage? I don't need a castle, just a place to call our own. Somewhere where we can give people hope, and a chance at a new life.' Those words inspired Talion to build Sakura Farm in his wife's memory, but also do as she said. Sakura despised slavery and seeing a fifteen-year-old Staphros on the docks of Zorrodon reminded him of that. Once he saw Staphros's face when he freed him, it made him understand her. It was the same face that Sumera and her daughter were making.

Staphros watched the two former slaves intently. His face was hard and progressively hardening, almost looking like a frown. He leaned over to Talion.

'Excuse me' He whispered abruptly.

Talion nodded and without another word, Staphros left. He walked straight without looking back. To an onlooker, it appeared Staphros didn't care. Sumera and Lilly would later think similar, which in time would feed into the mystique of the giant. The stoic farm manager who's steadfast sense of duty hardened him to such human moments. He had work to do, and that was final. Only two others knew the real truth. Staphros had done this since the inception of Sakura Farm. He started because he pledged his life to Talion and wanted to help in any way he could. Staphros didn't leave because he wanted to, he left because he had to.

The door the Big House closed and Staphros marched quickly to his quarters. The farmhands saw the slaves go in and expected this march and were unsurprised when it came. Still, they had to stop and watch. Staphros had never noticed that they watched him, his focus was on the Outhouse. When he closed his door behind himself in the privacy of his quarters, he took time to reflect for the people he had freed, because he was one of them not so long ago.

Talion leaned forward, elbows on the table and rested his chin on his threaded fingers.

'Please excuse Staphros, he has many duties on the farm and ashamedly in my old age I work him too hard.' He said. 'So, would you like to burn your papers?'

Sumera and Lilly looked at the old champion and Sumera nodded for the two of them. They got up and gingerly shuffled towards the fireplace. Even though every desire within them wanted to run to the open flames and dash their parchment shackles in, every instinct that had been cultivated within them told them not to. Fulfilling desires was not a slave's prerogative, it was indeed the opposite, but they fought on. The mother and daughter held hands with each step feeding the other strength to take another, multiplying their resolve to become more than the sum of their parts. Talion unearthed one final surprise from his jacket and placed it on the table, leaving it there so he could stand and watch the moment of emancipation for the two. Sumera and Lilly stood in front of the fire, the heat pulsing against their faces. They held the papers reading them for the first time and seeing Talion's signature on them. Lilly looked to her mother for permission and Sumera kissed her on the head.

'It's okay. We'll do it together… One, two, three.'

Freedom at last.

9 MY BOY

Vida- Narce- 6- 1827

The stars were out in the south tonight as Celestine and Luke travelled on the road back home. The paint-brushed blackish-blue background was littered with flecks of shining silver, sparkling around a glowing moon. Most nights in King's Anglonia were unwelcoming even in the summer, there was always a moist chill in the air. This summer night was unique in its surprising warmth. The horse hooves sank into the soft soil bed, readymade for incoming horseshoes. The clip clap rhythm that started their journey on the stony roads of Elgin, was now replaced with a slow thudding percussion with the occasional splat and squelch. The vibrant whirring of the wooden wheels of the wagon and the soft and damp ground, made for a consistent overture to the percussive symphony entitled "A Long Journey with Horses".

The younger of the two horses that pulled the small wagon, started the journey full of life. Luke named him Sandy. The chestnut stallion to his side was yet to be named. He was more reserved in his vigour, but now with the end of the journey coming ever closer, the conservation of his energy was paying dividends. Celestine was directing the tandem of newly acquired horses to their new home in the south. Luke was laying in the back of the wagon; his head was resting on his bag and he stared at the sky, mesmerised by the stars.

Celestine left him one of his books to read on the journey home, he knew the trip would be long and would feel even longer because of the anticipation of coming home. It was no secret by either of them that they missed home towards the end of their adventure. Luke would be excited to see his sister Samantha and the old goats that did the gardening around the Big House. He was like a child when he was excited or bored, and the long trip would ensure he would be both, however, there was nothing like escapism to cure either. Celestine's weapon of choice to combat Luke's boredom was the first story of Kastielle's legendary series. Naturally, he encountered resistance when he offered Luke the book at first. They were children's books after all, flights of fancy for the underdeveloped mind. Luke was hardly able to articulate himself to such a degree, so he would often settle with calling Celestine a "soft bastard" whenever he caught him reading one. However, Celestine was a strategist in more than just battle, so he left the book in plain view and in Luke's reach. Hours into the trip, Luke's resolve waned, and he picked the story up.

It didn't take long for him to find that not only was this story invigorating but immensely educational. He was learning with every word. It began with the creation of the world, commonly known as "The Romance of Nature and Time". Nature was the daughter of Time and their romance was her tireless attempts to win his attention and love, resulting in the creation of the Sun and the Earth. The Sun was Time's vessel and the Earth was Nature's. When Nature's love was unrequited, she resolved herself to cultivate a love of her own by birthing her children, The Children of Nature. For each, she created a vessel, a star in the night's sky. Luke had the same reaction at twenty-five-years-old as Celestine did at six-years-old. It seemed the only appropriate thing to do was to look at the stars, knowing that the formers of the world and cosmos were looking upon you.

'Are you okay back there?' Asked Celestine.

'Oh aye, grand.' Replied Luke.

'It's just you went silent for a while. You weren't reading were you.' Celestine smirked trying not to giggle. He had peeked over his shoulder more than once to see Luke fully engrossed in what he was reading. He was so sucked in that his lips were mouthing the words as he read them. There were only two things Luke read that carefully, taxes and love letters.

Luke blushed. 'Aye, I was reading a little bit. I'll give you this, it's a good read.'

Celestine arched over again and nodded. 'It is yeah.' He turned back. 'You soft bastard.' He said under his breath.

'You what?' He knew Celestine had said something, but he didn't hear it, but he could have guessed.

'I was just saying that we're nearly home.' Luke didn't believe him, but the familiar paths showed that they were indeed very close to home.

Celestine was very weary and if they were farther away, he would have rested. In his tiredness, he noticed the difference in the horses too, not just physically but mentally. There was a conversation between the two. The chestnut stallion was guiding young Sandy and encouraging him along. There was a dynamic between them that Celestine could not understand but strangely could interpret.

They reached the fork in the road that signalled that they were minutes from home. It had a sign with an arrow pointed due east reading: "Zorrodon Twelve Miles Sakura Farm, one mile" The trip from Elgin to Sakura Farm was a tall order for an inexperienced horse, especially when dragging a wagon. They were a gift from Eulis, and a good-natured one, but it didn't take long to figure that they were not bred for such a long journey. Celestine took regular breaks with them, speaking with them and rubbing the stubbly fur on their faces. He was establishing a relationship with them, and he was doing it quickly. He always had a way with animals, like he could speak their language but had no earthly idea as to how. But now, in the final stretch of their long journey, the horses dug in deep to pull their master home, something that Celestine greatly appreciated.

The chimney of the Big House climbed the horizon like a beanstalk. The smoke emanating from the chimney looked like desperate fingertips reaching for the moon. The chimney of the Big House was the final sign.

They were home.

After a long half-year, two-hundred-six days to be exact, Celestine had finally returned home with a wagon and two new horses. He had made it home and it gave him a feeling that blended gratitude with immense achievement. It made him a boy again and it filled him with excitement. Returning home confirmed that he was an adventurer because the magic of adventure was not in the leaving but the navigating your way back. Celestine feared that the people on the farm only admired him because of his association with Talion. He did not see or would not allow himself to see the love they had for him already. He still needed to prove himself in his eyes. Coming home after adventuring alone, especially without Talion, felt like he achieved at least some of his goal.

Aside from winning the love of those who already adored him, Celestine's adventure was designed to equip him with the tools and confidence to win the love of someone who didn't even know his name. The man who froze in the village of Zorrodon at the sight of the girl with flowers in her hair had grown up. That day haunted him for a long time because he intended to speak with her before he left. He wanted to learn her name, hear her voice, hear what it sounded like when she spoke to him. He stopped in his tracks last time, but he would not make that mistake again. He had scaled mountains, fought gipsies, and offered to train the Champion of Celtish Anglonia. He was prepared enough now to ask this girl's name.

Luke and Celestine reached the gates of the farm.

The cover of the night meant that the fields were empty. It was long after sundown and about supper time. So far, the two absentee residents had returned without detection and Celestine craftily devised a plan. After hitching their new horses in the stables and storing the new wagon at the side, they made their way to the Big House. The flickers of the fireplace and a slew of candles lit a pulsating orange glow from behind the drawn curtains. Despite being alone and quite a ways away from the house, the two moved quietly towards the large grey building. Their muted movements were further hushed by the blare of crickets hidden in the tall grass.

The large door to the Big House, made with Staphros in mind, was pushed open soundlessly. The hall was filled with everyone sat sharing tea, bread, and cheese. The children were in their beds and the adults were enjoying their evening together. There were hushed murmurings amongst them. Celestine spotted his uncle on the other side of the room, sat by the very fireplace where he had freed Lilly and Sumera the day before. Celestine conspicuously walked through the crowd of weary workers that stood and chatted away not noticing him. Faces blended in after a while and familiarity formed the backbone of this small society. The best way to remain undetected here was to not try to be hidden. Talion was sat on a cushioned red chair; he had his pipe in his hand and a plate of cheese and bread on the table beside him.

Celestine flung himself in the adjacent chair unceremoniously. He then leaned forward and grabbed some cheese from Talion's plate. He used to do that to Talion when he was an adorable youngster; he had not yet learned that it was just irritating in adulthood.

'What a day...' Said Celestine. 'How was your day?' he bit and broke off half the cheese in his hand. Talion blinked and faced Celestine. His eyes were probably the only part of his body that was not failing him, but at this moment he believed that they were. He blinked again. The rough brown iris was swallowed by the dilated depths of his pupils the features of his nephew's face gulped into the blackness and digested in his slowing mind. The corners of his mouth quivered in stasis.

Then it clicked.

'My boy!' He screeched. The words crashed against the walls and high ceilings and echoed back. The uncanny cry of the old man caused concern amongst the occupiers of the great hall. The room stopped and saw Talion struggle from his chair to kiss Celestine on his cheek. Celestine met him halfway as his uncle beheld him. He appeared more of a man now. With the strength of his youth, Talion mustered a squeeze to give his nephew the warmest embrace he could. The wet of the old man's tears disappeared into Celestine's coat. Nobody else knew but him. The room came to move towards Celestine, extending their hands in greeting.

'Hi everyone.' Said Celestine waving awkwardly and quickly. The room laughed at the rather typical shyness displayed by Celestine. It was just part of his charm.

'I'm back too.' Said Luke from the back of the room. Suddenly, a tiny storm bundled through the crowd and tackled Luke with a powerful but amorous hug. Samantha hugged her brother tight then clipped him behind the ear.

'Hey, you wee gobshite! You cannae send your sister a letter.' She said. She always sounded more Celtish when addressing Luke and even more so when she was telling him off.

'Neither did Celestine.' Said Luke.

'I'm nae talkin' tae Celestine, I'm talkin tae you!' She said.

'Sorry Sam.' He slumped his head down.

'Go on eat summin. Looks like ye gone skinny!' Said Samantha. Luke did not have to hear that twice and went straight for the food which was on the table on the side. Celestine laughed. Luke and Samantha were always fun to watch. They were close enough to have a somewhat slapstick relationship. After spending some time in Celtish Anglonia, he understood why. They were very physical people, with unrivalled family values. Which reminded him...

'Uncle Talion...' He said. 'I met someone who wants to meet you.' Talion tutted to break the subject.

'Save that for later, tell me of your travels and let's eat!' Said Talion.

Celestine and Talion sat up all night in the great hall. They ate heartily and shared a cup of wine or two. It was nothing like the amounts that he was accustomed to drinking with Luke but far more than he had ever drank with his uncle before.

He spent the night recounting the events of his trip in much greater detail than what he and Luke collectively gave to Eulis in the Stagg and Bull Tavern. He did, however, redact certain events that involved fighting and drinking in excess. His story to Talion was fantastic, inspiring wanderlust and awe. He could feel the pride coming from his uncle with every word he spoke and more than a few times he had to pause to stop himself from getting emotional.

Talion looked and listened to every word Celestine said, reaching out occasionally to touch him on the arm to confirm he was real. He had the same look of incredulity on his face that Lily and Sumera had when he had freed them. Celestine had grown into one of the finest young men he could have asked for.

Celestine had described the climax of Finn's fight when Talion wiped an escaping tear. In the deep recesses of the night, they were alone with only the light of the wilting candle seeing the tear.

'You remind me so much of your father.' Said Talion. Celestine stopped in his tracks and sat bolt upright with a lump in his throat. This unsolicited mention of his father was a first for him. For as long as he could remember, he begged Talion to tell him of his parents. Only very rarely did Talion ever do it. Talion retreated in his thoughts like his outburst was unintentional but be it because of the drink, or the occasion, he had said it now. Talion rarely spoke of him, but he saw Celestine's father in him as he spoke. They had fought side by side to defend Anara during the invasion. He called Talion a brother.

'M…My Father?'

Talion nodded. 'I've watched you grow since you were a baby and seeing the man that you have become, I can't express how proud I am.' Talion sipped some more of his wine. He struggled with the truth on his lips, a truth that he had eluded for twenty-seven-years. Celestine was a man, and he deserved to know. 'Your father gave you to me as our nation burned to the ground…' Talion began to cry. 'and he entrusted your life to me with his dying words. That man served under me, he was in my squadron and he died on my watch. I'm so sorry I let that happen, Celestine, your father was a great man. I'm sorry I let that happen to him.' Celestine scrambled from his seat and kneeled at his uncle's side. He took his hand at first; it trembled in quaking emotion, brimmed and overflowing.

'It's okay…' Celestine hugged him. 'The war is over. Nothing that happened to my father was your fault, I know that.'

Talion wailed. 'I made a great many mistakes in my youth, sins that will haunt me forever. You are the only way I can make it right.'

'You've already done that. With me, this farm, everything. You have more than redeemed ten lifetimes of sins, I know that. My father knew you were the right man to take me in, which means he knew his death was not your fault.' Celestine gripped his uncle's hand tighter.

'I call you my nephew because you had a father back in Anara.' He sucked in a hesitant breath, trying to compose himself. He held the back of Celestine's head and rested his against it, forehead to forehead. 'But here Celestine, you are my son.'

Celestine and Talion hugged, sharing the last few tears in the privacy of night before retreating to bed.

Once Talion retired upstairs, Celestine quietly closed the door to the Big House. Sakura Farm in the night was almost as beautiful as it was in the day. The twilight sky beamed silver and gold on the pristine grass. The plentiful stars blazed a trail on the dark path to the bright edge of the world. The blaring of crickets, the hooting of owls, and the yapping of hidden foxes all harmonised to make the perfect sound of home.

Across the grassy field, the moon spared some of its silver glow to illuminate his cottage as it waited for the sun to rise. He made his way there. The cottage was the first building erected on this land. Celestine was too young to remember but at the very beginning of Sakura Farm's days, he,

Talion, and Staphros lived under that roof. It was small, slapdash, and drafty, but it was home.

Talion stood at his window as he did every morning, this time watching his nephew go where he belonged. After Celestine entered the cottage, Talion spoke his morning prayer before managing to get a few hours of rest. As he sat in bed, he noticed something peculiar and amazing all at once.

He had forgotten his cane downstairs.

10 GOOD SHEPHERDS

"Good shepherds make great leaders."

Celestine, like everyone else, had an assigned role on the farm. He was a shepherd. He took care of all the livestock when out on the fields grazing and he herded them from time to time. Celestine had a close relationship with the groundskeepers because between the grazing of the cows and sheep and the swinging of their scythes, the greenery was well kept. On top of that, they always loved to watch him work. With the aid of his two dogs, Porche and Mac, he orchestrated dozens of loose animals as if they shared a single consciousness… His.

They were the older lot of the farm, and most of them had watched Celestine grow up. Unlike Eulis, who was surprised that at the contrast of Celestine's adult and child selves, they were privy to see the remarkable transition happen in real-time. It was much more understandable, but not any less special.

When Celestine came of age at fifteen, he like every other child had the opportunity to pursue an occupation. Talion would have afforded him every opportunity to become a doctor, or teacher even assistant manager under Staphros, but his calling was to be with the animals. The job came naturally to him, so much so that it was instinctive. It was not easy and there were expectations to maintain. There were daily trials that he had to face, but he took each one in stride. What appealed to him more than anything about being a shepherd was that it was naturally a humble occupation. There was no such thing as a boastful shepherd who bragged about how great he was at herding sheep and cattle. He was free to feel confident, and capable, and not worry about how he was perceived. He also loved animals of all kinds and he loved his herd no matter what challenges he faced. The routine had to be consistent; he let out the livestock and herded them to their sections on the land. Then, he'd keep watch over them and keep them from getting into the crops or wandering off. Finally, and most importantly, he observed and maintained their health and wellbeing. He took the last duty very seriously.

Although his herd was like a family and he cared for them that way, he cared for his dogs more than anything. Porsche and Mac were Rottweilers from Nordic Deutschland. Rottweilers were good at herding horses, which were amongst the unruliest of the farm's livestock. If trained correctly, they would be able to keep any animal in check even better than the Anglonian Border-Collie.

Porche and Mac were gifted to Celestine as a present to aid him in his intended career path. They could sit on his palm back then, but they grew over the years. It wasn't long before his dogs were large enough to aid him. It had only been six years, but he couldn't remember or imagine a life without them. They filled his past and formed his future. They were part of him.

Being a shepherd on Sakura Farm returned to being a four-man job in Celestine's absence. Whereas when Celestine was at home, he could execute his duty alone. His instincts always served him very well. There was no doubt that Celestine was a good shepherd. And as Talion once said to a fifteen-year-old Celestine: "Good shepherds make great leaders."

It was well into the afternoon before Celestine had woken up; road weariness was a real phenomenon. His bedroom was just as he left it back in the autumn. The floor was immaculately carpeted, a large wardrobe painted white, and a study desk by the window. The white net curtains danced in a breeze that forced its way into the bedroom regardless if the window was open. The walls and ceiling were made from the same wood that built the cottage, sourced from the forest that flanked Sakura Farm.

Celestine ignored the temptation of slumber. Shunning the siren that sang her lullaby in his ear so she could have him all day. Her silent musings were subtle but paralysing. She made his quilt heavy and his mattress swallow him up, but Celestine blinked alert with a decision. He could no longer rest. He was home now and when he was home, he either worked or trained. He was much too tired to train but working could allow him an opportunity to reconnect with Porche and Mac. He rolled out of bed and staggered to the wardrobe to pull on some clothes. He groomed himself simply, pulling his golden locks into a bun and he got to work.

It was no surprise to see Luke was yet to emerge out onto the field. If left unchecked, Luke could sleep an entire day away and it would not faze him. Conversely, he could stay awake for days on end without trouble either.

Amongst his other observations, the chief among them was Everything.

There was nothing like a long absence that would make a man appreciate the small things. He took in a deep breath of the green glowing grass, and the wheat, and cornfields. Even the smells of the animal pens brought him joy. He knelt and palmed the ground. It was like there was distinguishable life within the soil as if the grounds of Sakura Farm had a different soul living in the roots of its foundation. He greeted it silently, somewhat unaware of his movements, and he stood back up like he had just reacquainted himself with an old friend. Come to think of it, it was time to go to the kennels.

The kennels were behind the Big House. It was an elongated building built with grey bricks. The front door was black and stout. When Celestine circled the Big House to see the grey kennels his heart jumped. He scanned the field for his dogs, but his instinct told him that they were in there. When Celestine reached the kennels, he anxiously pressed his hand against the black door, forcing it open.

The one thing that Celestine lamented about on his adventure was leaving them behind. If he could have, he would have taken them with him, but it was not feasible. He had gone away before and always returned to a mixed response. Mac was male, full of energy and playful love. He would bound to him, jumping and licking him. The longer he was gone, the more aggressive he was in his affection. Celestine expected to have to wrestle Mac. Porsche was different; she a bitch. She fiercely loved Celestine too but was too cool to show it so outwardly and excitedly. If there was ever a dog that could express disgust, it was Porsche when she watched Mac leap around like a giddy buffoon over their master. She found it much more appropriate to completely ignore him. She would even walk through him, knocking him over if the feeling took her. Celestine knew he was going to hurt them by leaving, and Porsche would take it the hardest. She always took it personally when he went on trips, and if ignoring him didn't communicate her displeasure effectively enough, she growled, snarled, and sometimes snapped at him. She never hurt him though. The snap was one that she would give a pup to correct his behaviour and leaving was indeed bad behaviour in her eyes.

Celestine creaked the door open and aggressive barking and snarling erupted from the doghouse on the far end. The kennel was empty aside from the two rottweilers. The growling sounded like Mac. Mac was a loving happy dog and Celestine had never heard him growl this way ever. There was no play in his tone, he was aggressive. It almost sounded like a roar. Mac's voice shook the shrouded darkness of the kennel's interior. In this dark room, only lit by the very small roof window and the slivers of light from the gaps in the wooden walls. Celestine he had heard it many a time from Porsche's mouth when she was warding off intruders.

Celestine's clammy palms inched the door closed behind him. He had never been gone this long before and he prayed to whatever child of Nature would listen, that his dogs hadn't forgotten him. Porsche was irritable around him after long absences. She and Celestines had a tumultuous relationship, but that was only because she was so attached to him. She loved him so much it allowed her to hate him at times.

Celestine inched forward, puckering his lips. Mac snapped a harsh bark and Celestine put his hands out and whistled. The growling stopped and out from the shadow of the kennel emerged the floppy ears and large head of the snarling canine. Though his eyes were still downturned and fierce, he saw his master through the protective rage. He skittishly trotted forward two steps and sniffed the air. The light revealed his soft dark eyes and the light brown patches on his face and legs. His legs looked like they had each stepped in a puddle of bronze that reached halfway up the leg. The tip of his piggish nose had a sprinkling of the same bronze to his eyes. That was Mac alright, no other dog had eyes that big. Mac retained his puppy-like features. His tongue waved and slapped his nose as it did when he was investigating, like he was tasting the air. Then, he was a dog transformed, as his mouth opened into was a wry smile. He clumsily bound toward Celestine, barking and howling. Celestine presented his open palm and Mac nestled underneath it after circling him three times. He jumped to his hind legs and wriggled in and out of Celestines embrace, licking everything as he did. He darted back and forth galloping like a terrified horse, still howling and barking frantically.

Celestine knelt and scratched his chin and ears. Mac plastered Celestine with his tongue on his face and hands.

'Good boy! You miss me?' Said Celestine.

Mac jumped away in circles with his tail wagging, charging back after a couple of revolutions. He sat in front of him.

'I missed you too buddy.' Said Celestine,

Mac placed his paw on Celestine's hand, pinning it onto his bent knee. Then, he licked his fingers over and over. It tickled. Celestine usually would make him stop, but this time he let it pass.

'Where's Porsche?' He asked.

Mac suddenly stopped. His eyes grew even wider and he boomed a powerful bark rearing on his hind legs once more. He began to dart back to the doghouse, stopping halfway to prompt Celestine to follow, which he did. Celestine reached the doghouse. He stood a bit taller than the top, but the roof was removable. He lifted the top to see his girl.

Porsche was lying there, and she was pregnant.

Mac sat at Celestine's side and stared at his reaction, his tail thumping the ground in anticipation. Porsche looked up at him lazily; her eyes darted for a split second. She too had beautiful big eyes. That was as much as she was going to give her absentee master, for now. Porsche was unique amongst rottweilers in the way that she was near entirely black fur. Aside from a tuft on her nose which was flecked with bronze, she was covered in a shimmering onyx coat. That little brown tuft wiggled as her nose betrayed her apparent indifference. She sniffed for her master until she succumbed. In the end, she had to lift her head. Celestine reached in anticipating her to growl at him in displeasure. This time, she just rested her head against his palm. At her touch he felt the vulnerability in her, too weak to be angry at him, too scared to want to be. This pregnancy was difficult for her and by all appearances, he had missed most of it. She was ready to burst and it wasn't long until the litter was to come.

'How are you doing girl?' He said. He stroked her cheek with his thumb. She didn't respond.

'I know, I know. I'm here now.' He said.

Porsche rolled her head and nibbled Celestine's sleeve until she had a firm grip. She pulled with what little strength she had to get him closer. He understood what she was saying, and he did not appreciate being called a buffoon.

Celestine got to his knees and crawled into the doghouse before turning to sit. His feet stuck out of the entryway and Mac could no longer fit inside. He placed Porsche's head on his lap. She closed her eyes as Mac rested at his feet.

Celestine was not going to work anymore today.

"Sometimes being a great leader, meant being a bad shepherd."

11 VICTIM BLAME

Vida- Innos- 7- 1827

It was another fruitless day in Lion's search for Kojo. He had tried to speak to the villagers, but many were too hard at work to give him much time. They were still frantic, having one single focus, survival. The tax rate was at the root of the problem. No matter how hard the people worked they could only manage to scrape an existence. There was anger in the village. Anger with their struggle, with the authority, even with each other. They blamed each other because it was easy, the streets were dirty because of the children, they smelt because of the horse riders, and every minor infraction was identified as the cause of their squalor. Although it wasn't wanted, Lion's visit and speech was the first time that the villagers were shown unity. It felt good and gradually that feeling resonated with more and more people. It made them feel empowered. Those people were looking out for Kojo and encouraging friends to do the same. Unfortunately, there was only so far they could see.

The docks may have been destitute, falling apart, and built upon a foundation of sand, but the people were strong. They were the foundation for their neglected society because the one they built it upon was designed for it to fall. It didn't matter that the government took their money and relegated them to the outskirts to battle the tide. They could and would endure because they knew how to struggle. Being from West Akoku meant that it was in their blood because they inherited a culture of togetherness that was unmatched. *"We are we"* was the phrase that was on their flag, it was their battle cry at times of war. It meant if one struggled everybody struggled; a shared load was never heavy. Lion united the dock folk with that ideology, and it ensured their survival.

Lion had been flanked by two of his Hondos bredrin, Roy and Cyrus. They had been part of his movement as soon as he started it and he trusted them with his life. He was happy to get back to the docks, the smell in the village served as a constant reminder of his failure to help the people there. Now he was home, he could smell the salty sea air and the menagerie of spices and flavours that filled it. Pots were on fires, and dinner was being prepared. Dinner time was always a festive occasion on the docks, few things could be classed as a win but having a meal to eat was one that could be celebrated every day. Although having much less opportunity and being taxed as much if not more than the village, villagers consistently went to bed hungry, while the people of the docks still managed to eat every day. *"We are we"*.

Sharing food was the easiest way to negate the deficit. Dinner was rarely served in the same house twice; they would throw on a big pot and cook enough to feed the twenty or thirty people that would come. Cow foot, fish tea, pea soup, and goat head soup, formed the steady diet on the docks. They could not dine on expensive cuts of meat, or fine vegetables, but they made what they had work. Olive, Kojo's mother, was making goat's head soup, or what they idiomatically called "Manish Water" for its benefits of strength and virility. Lion, Roy, and Cyrus were the guests of honour.

Olive's door was ajar when Lion arrived. The nattering and goings-on of the people inside seeped onto the terrace. The house was two small rooms. The main room was well lit with fires going and it was filled with people. A young couple was standing outside; they were smoking and holding hands. Lion approached and they recognised him immediately. The man was dark, and he had young features like he had just arrived at adulthood. The woman was small with lighter skin and looked slightly younger. It was clear their relationship was budding, their first adult relationship. The effects of the Manish Water was going to do nothing to enhance this man's virility. His girl and his youth had that covered. They broke their amorous soul gazing to greet the incoming Lion. The man shook his hand and Lion pulled him in for a hug, patting him on the back once. The young man had some power behind him. He was strong and he knew it. That made him a target for the city-dwelling guardsmen, Lion pondered that when embracing him. They were all targets. He hugged and kissed the woman on the cheek. She was going to be a target for many different and insidious reasons because of her youth and beauty. They had always been targets, but they were inconsequential before, invisible. Now, Lion was drawing an attention to them that they may not survive. He had lived a full life and understood his place in this, but it was the youth that would suffer if he went about his work the wrong way. Young people like Kojo. He had to wrestle with that every day.

Olive looked tired from the cooking when she greeted Lion. She looked like she hadn't cried today, nor did she look like she slept. She took his hands in a plea.

'Any word on mi baby?'

Lion shook his head. Her eyes filled with tears, but she steadied herself once she saw his guilt.

'It h'alright … It h'alright. Him was doing de work of de Spirits and our h'ancestor. Dem say him a come home soon.' She said.

Lion nodded. 'I will bring him home.' Olive dug into her cooking apron and handed Lion an envelope.

'Ere tek dis.' She said. She had a look of absolute trust on her face. It wasn't a matter to her of if Lion would bring her boy home, but when. She just wanted to do her part. 'It a journal like de one unuh bredrin write up. Mi wanted fi write sumting about me bwoy dem. Magnus and him bloodclart people dem ca'an tarnish my son.'

Lion nodded and opened the envelope in front of her. She waited in anticipation. Reading what she had said made him realise the toll it took on her as a parent. A boy missing could be perceived as a "Docks problem" as the misinformed blacksmith described, but Olive's words, her journal described a human issue, one people had to listen to.

Lion kissed Olive on the cheek again. 'Mi gaan get your son.'

He made his way back to Roy and Cyrus who were leaning on a wall with limited free space. They had a bowl of Manish Water in hand and were conversating about what most men of the docks spoke about… Women. They laughed and joked until they saw Lion approach with a grim expression.

'Wh'appn?' asked Roy.

Lion handed Olive's journal over to him. 'Mi want dis copied as many time as we can by next week pon de Chrono.'

'A wha dis?'

'A mudders love.' Lion left without eating. He had just remembered that he had to see someone in the City.

Magnus used the cover of night to travel to where he needed to go. He and Fredrickson were in the palatial estates far beyond Zorrodon. They were in a black carriage pulled by black horses. This was where the most powerful and influential men in the world lived. Throughout the trip, Magnus was visibly nervous because he was visiting the most powerful man of them all. Adan Thiago.

The carriage pulled to a stop outside the house that dwarfed the parliament building where Magnus stayed. He blinked and gulped hard, staring up and around the structure. He stepped cautiously towards the entrance and knocked. The large brown door boomed like it was reprimanding him for even touching it. Magnus lowered his clammy trembling hand. Moments later the door arched open with a dark-skinned slave woman pulling it. Magnus had an overt disdain for people of his complexion, he hated them at his heart. He looked at the woman with wide eyes and Fredrickson saw fear in them. Magnus slipped in and the slave woman closed the door behind him. The floor was stone and the ceiling was a sky of its own. There were pulsating fires everywhere that shone the white floor bright and made the gold skirtings shine.

'Master Thiago is waiting in the in his office, Magnus.' She said.

'It's Mayor...' Started Fredrickson before Magnus stopped him. He walked on to the back of the house and into a dark, low-lit room in the far corner. There he found Adan Thiago, staring out of his window, and wearing white robes and golden jewellery. He was the reflection of Magnus but with pale olive skin.

Magnus entered with his head bowed and closed the door before Fredrickson could come in. He didn't speak and waited to move after the door was shut.

'Sit.' Said Adan without turning around. Magnus sat on a red chair beside him quickly. 'Tell me of your preparations for Finn the Brave's son.' Adan's enunciated every word, ensuring that he was clear in what he said. Every syllable was deliberate. He never asked questions because he never asked for anything. He came from a family that took what they wanted by any means, which was their name. Thiago, meaning the supplanter.

'He has received and accepted our challenge to fight our champion on the fourteenth'

'And tell me what you plan to do next.'

'We will kill him there.' Said Magnus.

Adan turned and scowled, the dim flames revealed his black hair and thick goatee. His eyes were dark and soulless. He expected everything right away, including information. Magnus just didn't have the answers he was looking for.

'Fredrickson has it in hand.' Magnus said quickly.

'I didn't make Fredrickson mayor, I made you mayor and you're disappointing me.' Adan poured himself some wine in a glass. It was thick and red like irony blood. 'I need reasons boy!'

'O...of course... But the details are with Fredrickson. I have been occupied with another issue. A man from the docks by the name of Lion. He is uniting people and empowering them. My guards have been telling me that his influence is spreading into the city.'

'One man is inconsequential. Deal with it quickly.' Adan sipped from his glass.

'I will sir... I recently gained some leverage which will greatly work in my favour. He will be dealt with.' Adan circled his desk, placed his hands on the rests of Magnus's chair looming to get eye level with the mayor.

'Today.' He said.

'Of course, sir.' Said Magnus struggling to hold eye contact with the man. Adan patted Magnus on the cheek.

'Remember boy. I plucked you from nowhere. Nobody cares about you and your city hates you. Your life will not be much forfeit if you disappoint me.' He grabbed Magnus by the face. 'Sort it tonight! Go!' As soon as Adan stood Magnus scrambled for the door.

'Of course, sir. Tonight.' He said.

Adan finished his wine and unhooked his coat once Magnus had left.

Lion hummed to himself. He was sat on a wooden box alone dragging on the last of a smoke. He inhaled the fragrant burning herb and held in its asphyxiating gas while he stared at the night's sky. The stars looked back at him as he exhaled smoke from his nostrils like an ageing dragon. He hung his head after, still burdened with the responsibility of his people's wellbeing. He fought for them so they could have better lives and now people were starting to believe he was strong enough to win. The curtain of his dreadlocks hid the indecision in his eyes. He didn't know whether the fight was worth dragging the dock folk into it, and the choice was getting away from him.

He heard a carriage roll in from across the street at the gates of the Governmental Complex. It was a black carriage with black horses. He couldn't be certain, but his gut told him that it was Magnus. It was about the time they met.

Magnus waited silently for the gates to open once the carriage came to a stop. He was silent for the whole trip and he forbade Fredrickson from speaking too. Adan Thiago's threat was not to be taken lightly. He had until the morning to get some information on Lion and deal with him. Magnus jumped out of his skin when several sharp bangs rumbled the carriage door.

'What! Who dares…'

'It's Lion. Mi heard you want speak to me'

Magnus opened the door and came out with Fredrickson in tow. He looked like he was slithering, with the smooth and sudden way he moved. It was the first time they had met, but strangely they felt a sense of familiarity. They saw themselves in each other, not in their similarities but as one saw a reflection. It was a backwards image where everything was reversed, but it was their differences which made them feel connected. The Children of Nature were birthed in twos, each with an opposite of equal power and significance, connected forever. Lion and Magnus didn't know that this was them, but they sure felt it.

'It's a pleasure to finally meet you, Lion. I've been meaning to invite you to my complex.' Said Magnus presenting the tall buildings within the golden gates. Adan's warning rang in his head.

'Mi decline your invite. You want fi bring I in, charge me wid a crime.' Lion linked his wrists together presenting them for the shackles.

Magnus said nothing and did nothing. Lion was beginning to understand.

'Alright, dat's why you 'av Kojo inna deh.' He said pointing to the prison on the far end of the Government Complex. It hadn't made sense before. He knew that Kojo was arrested because of him, but he didn't know why. Magnus didn't have anything to implicate him and Kojo was his source of information.

Magnus smirked. 'Kojo was charged with the rape of a working girl named Annaliese and was found guilty of the crime. He's awaiting his sentence as we speak.'

'When him found guilty?'

'Just now.' Said Magnus through the gritted teeth of a frustrated smile. He wanted that to be Lion but there were some powers he could abuse and powers he could not. Levying a flagrant sentence on a criminal was doable, but what he really wanted to do was kill Lion on the street. Lion glared at the mayor; he was powerless to do anything. He knew the law, and Magnus had the power to do that. He searched for options.

'Where the gyal now?' he asked. 'The man from de Pickering said him naa seen her from laas week when unuh tek her in.'

'Well, you know how these things can be traumatic. I mean not only being raped but...' Magnus's lips cracked into a manic broken grin. 'but even being touched by such a dirty creature such as you people. Yuck.' He savoured every word. His slimy snake's tongue traced his lips to catch the taste the words left on them. Lion shot a look at Magnus that was at first angry then full of pity. He turned his back on him, pulling a smoke from his tattered trouser pocket and lighting it on the flame of a nearby lantern. He sucked in the fragrant herb and it calmed his nerves. Magnus wanted to spit on him, lash out, kill him on the spot. He was losing control because Lion was not getting hurt. He was bigger than the words spoken to him, and despite his position, Magnus was acutely aware that he wouldn't be. Lion turned back to Magnus and breathed out the smoke.

'You know, Mayor.' He said dropping the Patois. He had something to say and he wanted him to hear it. 'You are free to think of us the way you do, the way most of these people do. But they think the same way about you. You are just as dirty a creature as the rest of us.' Lion popped the smoke back in his mouth. 'Difference is, you're the only one proving them right. Goodnight gentlemen.' Lion started walking home.

Guards eased from the shadows from all sides and Magnus gave serious thought into giving the order. Adan's warning came back to him "Tonight". Magnus shook and grimaced. His hand twitched, with one signal Lion could be done for. Lion stopped.

'So you know bredrin, I have people who know where I am and expect me back. If you want me dead, get me in that building, if you want me in that building charge me of a crime. I have nothing to hide, and Kojo knows that. You can find him guilty, but I'll find him innocent. Believe me.' He said before disappearing into the city. Magnus had to quell his urge. Missing his deadline would disappoint Adan Thiago, but the complications of murdering a public figure would anger him. Nobody survived the wrath of a Thiago. Not even King Kastielle.

Kojo learned that he was found guilty and now awaited his sentence in the interrogation room of the courthouse. The room was a plain stone with a wooden table and chair in the middle. Kojo was chained to the chair. He kept a brave face in the low candlelight, but in the pit of his stomach, Kojo felt fear.

The door swung open vigorously slamming against the adjacent stone wall. The smack was loud enough to burst an eardrum. Magnus entered with three of his guards in tow. Two of his guards stood behind him on each side, the other loomed over Kojo like a vulture over a soon to be a carcass. His shadow stretched over him. Magnus had his fingers entwined in front of him.

'Kojo of Zorrodon, you have been found guilty of not only public indecency but the rape of a working girl. For that crime, I'd have to deem you a danger to society don't you think?' Said Magnus.

'I didn't do those crimes.' Said Kojo in protest.

'We conducted a thorough investigation and our findings were quite clear. As much as you can deny it, the facts are facts. I wished to levy your sentence personally because of the nature of your crime.'

Kojo remained silent, rolling his eyes.

'Before I do, I'd like to offer you a chance. I would like to know about your known associate, Lion.' Magnus was not met with an immediate response. Kojo avoided eye contact at first and Magnus waited. Kojo then looked intensely into the Mayor's eyes. The guards placed their hands on the butts of their swords.

Kojo smirked, then laughed. 'Don't know him. Is he famous or something?' He said coyly.

Magnus sighed. 'I need something, young man.'

'I said I don't know him. I don't even know who you're talking about.' The corners of Kojo's mouth quivered in a concoction of fear and humour. He was quickly discovering the fine line between the two.

'A danger to society cannot remain part of it, right now you are sentenced to slavery in the mines of the north-east. If you prove yourself useful maybe you can sway me, and I can allow you to go home.' Said Magnus.

Kojo's smirk disappeared.

'You have family, correct?' Asked Magnus.

Kojo nodded.

'They're worried about you right now. You know what, so is Lion. I've heard he's searching all over the city for a way to get you free. What you're doing for him here is very honourable, but I bet he'd be happier with you home. It's unnecessary, all I need is some information on his past, anything that could implicate him. If he were here, he would tell you to say something. Come on, let us get you home. Being a martyr does not serve him at all.'

'Well, Lion is not here to tell me that. So, you may as well send me away because I don't know him.' He said that like each word was a letter and he was spelling something out. This time Magnus smirked. A film of cold sweat coated Kojo's dark skin.

'You don't know him? I see what you're doing… you want to become a martyr. Well, martyrs are only such when given a platform. Some metal bars to cry their tears through. Inspirations for a battle cry against tyranny. Guess what! I am a tyrant and you do not know who you have just crossed!' Magnus slammed the table and the echo of his voice reverberated against the stone walls, bouncing back and forth.

Kojo shrugged, he had remained composed and now he was in control. He hadn't thought of it, but the people would hear his story and they would act. Magnus rolled his sleeve up.

'Look at this.' He said showing the brown skin on his arm. 'People don't see this, and they won't see you. They will forget about you when something else comes along. You won't even be missed. This is not the right hill to die on. Make the right choice young man, the alternative isn't worth it.' Kojo looked around the room and nodded smugly.

'This looks like a very nice hill.' He said. 'And if you can't see us then we're more dangerous than you think.'

'Very well. You are sentenced to a life of slavery in the Mines of Tyne Hills, for the crimes of rape and indecency.' Said Magnus calmly and as a matter of fact. He rolled down his sleeve and dusted himself off. He walked and opened the door and froze. On the other side was Adan Thiago and Annaliese.

He pushed past Magnus and Annaliese followed.

'Young lady please tell them what you just told me.' Said Adan.

Annaliese said nothing.

'It's okay, they won't do anything without my say so. Magnus works for me.' He said aiming a cruel look at Magnus.

'Um… I said I can't do this. Kojo is innocent. Magnus had his men pay me to say that he raped me so he could get information on Lion.' Annaliese looked at Kojo who was in disbelief, but he could not hide the betrayed rage in his glare back to her.

'How could you?' He said.

'I'm sorry, I thought they were going to kill me.' She said.

Adan turned to Magnus shocked. 'Is this true?'

Magnus said nothing. He just cowered like a scared puppy.

'Answer me!' Yelled Adan.

Magnus nodded vigorously. 'Yuh…yes sir it is.' Adan took the key to Kojo's shackles from Magnus and unlocked them. The metal slap on the wood was the song of freedom Kojo dreamt of all week.

'It's okay son. That must have been terrible to be falsely accused. I want you to die knowing that that crime won't go unpunished.'

'Wait what…' Before Kojo could ask anything, Adan stabbed him in the throat leaving the dagger in. Kojo gasped and pawed for his gushing neck, collapsing against the wood soon after. The blood trickled to a rapid dripping percussion against the stone floor. Adan slipped the knife from Kojo's lifeless husk and sauntered to Annaliese. He caressed her face with his bloody palm and fingers.

'Now normally, I don't like to ask questions so I'm just going to try and remember the gist of what you said. You felt bad for reporting a rape even though you hadn't been raped… correct?'

Annaliese looked away.

'I said correct.'

Annaliese nodded.

'I'm not deaf and you're not mute, so use your words girl.' He commanded. Annaliese shook and cried. Adan was cold. His eyes were like looking into the eyes of a tiger and much more dangerous.

'Yes sir.'

'I can fix that.' He said grabbing the door. 'Magnus come with me. And boys.' He looked to the guards then Annaliese. 'have some fun.'

The door slammed shut

12 MAN OF HIS WORD

Vida- Innos- 7- 1827

It was nice to have Celestine return to the evening catch-up in Talion's chamber again. He, Talion, and Staphros were sat together in comfortable chairs with cups of tea in their hands and matters to discuss. Talion and Staphros had missed the bright optimism and irrefutable logic that Celestine bought to their chats. It was presented to the others on Sakura Farm as a formal discussion between the three figureheads that ran the place day to day. In reality, it was nothing so formal. Occasionally, there may be a mention of current events or politics, but mostly the three just gossiped. Who likes whom on the farm, romantically or otherwise? Which people hated each other? Professionally, they would have to address such matters, but in the privacy of Talion's chamber, it was good to blow off steam. Being in the position that they were in, they never could natter like old women to other people, but in a society as small as Sakura Farm everybody was in everybody else's business.

Celestine had tried to mention this when he had arrived home at first, but the occasion of his return served as a distraction. He managed to bring up that he had offered to train Finn Eireann for his fight, and he was due to arrive any day now. Celestine was surprised to find out that Talion and Staphros knew of Finn's struggle with intimate detail. Piecing it together, it made sense seeing how the suspect events leading to Finn the Brave's demise happened but stone's throw away in Zorrodon. Celestine may have been too young to pay attention but if the two of them were anything like they were now back then, they would have followed it closely. It took no convincing at all to get the two onboard. In fact, the excited discussion and debate on a

89

training schedule almost took them past supper. Luckily, Staphros's belly was as big as everything else on him and he never missed mead nor meal.

The next morning, Celestine was up bright and early training. He had gotten up and ran down to the sandy shoreline at the foot of the forest and kept on running. When he got back, he stopped for breakfast, then kept on training.

He set up in his sitting room with a white towel splayed on the dark wood flooring as he did his press-ups for the day. He had adhered to his routine most days at the beginning of his trip, but towards the end, he had waned in his conditioning. His muscles squeezed and ached each time he extended his arm. The tension spread down his back like warm water on cloth, and he kept going. Now, the towel was soaked with a fresh batch of sweat that had rained from his forehead and drooping strands of hair. Finally, he reached one thousand, the Staphros benchmark. He collapsed with a flumping squelch on the towel, sprawled on his back and breathing heavily.

'Fifteen minutes?! Am I that out of shape?' he said between breaths looking at the hourglass he set to time himself. Now his body was sore, and he was slow, the thrills of neglecting training. He stayed on the floor, more because of his disappointment than fatigue. Familial paws and claws tapped their way into proximity until a shadow hung over Celestine and the warmth of a dog's breath breezed across his face. Mac was standing over his Master. He had puppy-like features on his face, but he did not have a puppy-sized head. Mac had a huge head with a big slobbering leathery tongue hanging out of his mouth.

'No…' Said Celestine, elongating the word to make his objection clear.

Mac licked his nose and grunted. His mind was made up.

'No!' Celestine said it sharper and snappy this time. He carefully lifted his hands. Mac bowed his head and licked Celestine's face before he could block it. Celestine wriggled underneath kicking and laughing.

'Okay… okay boy, stop.' Whilst sitting in the kennels with him and Porsche, he slipped into another siesta only to be woken up by the kennelmen, Jim. Jim was a long-time worker on Sakura Farm, part of the original cohort that involved Eulis and Doc. Before going to the evening discussion, Celestine asked Jim to help him get the pregnant Porsche to his cottage safely. His dogs lived with him now, and he didn't regret it for a second. Not even now while being assailed by his dog's tongue.

Mac darted off suddenly. Celestine thought that was way too easy to get him to stop. Mac although loyal and clever, was not consistently obedient. He only listened to Porsche. Celestine had forgotten Mac's uncanny ability to anticipate visitors. After a few taps of his excited paws, there were three sharp bangs on the cottage door. Celestine rushed to the door knowing it was

Staphros waiting for him, likely wanting to go over strategy for training again. He yanked the door open to find a very red-faced Hanabi. Celestine had only his blue training bottoms on and Hanabi hadn't a clue where to look.

'Oh my… I'm so sorry.' Said Celestine. 'I thought you were someone else.' He quickly pulled on a loose shirt and leaned casually on the doorway. Hana was exceptionally shy coming from a culture where that was not only encouraged but enforced in women. Celestine's awkwardness did not help matters whenever the two met. He could never get it right, and it just made her retreat further into herself. 'How can I help you, Hana?' He folded his arms trying to appear relaxed and sound helpful, but a mixture of his tension and fatigue made him sound quite perturbed and impatient.

'Oh, a Finn Eireann is waiting in the Big House for you. He said he was your guest.' Said Hanabi very quietly. Celestine could barely hear her, but he caught Finn Eireann and Big House and assumed the rest.

'I'll be right there.' He said smiling.

Hanabi turned and hurried away.

'And sorry about the shirt!' Celestine called. Hanabi didn't turn around, but everybody working on the fields did, and Celestine closed the door with his face reddening. 'This must be what Luke feels like on a daily basis.' He sighed.

Talion was already sitting with Finn when Celestine made it to the great hall. They were conversing and laughing together. There was an unspoken comradery between champions, at least champions of Talion's era. It wasn't an acknowledgement of ability but an acknowledgement of responsibility. A traditional champion had a nation on their shoulders. There was not a unit of measurement created nor a number available that could appropriately quantify the amount of pressure that responsibility put on an individual. One performance defined whether a land flourished or faltered. Talion lived with that pressure for decades, had met hundreds of others that dealt with it. He could see the signs when it was getting too much. Something in Finn's eyes showed that with each second, that pressure was coming closer and closer to breakthrough. Finn knew the stakes of what he had chosen to do. His reputation was at stake, his nation was at stake, his father's legacy was at stake, there was no way he could lose. This was a unique pressure, but one Talion still knew. The fact that Finn had accepted the challenge knowing what it meant, showed that he was cut from the same cloth as Talion. He liked him already. If Finn felt personally that there was no way he could lose, Talion was going to make sure that was certain.

Finn stood as soon as he spotted Celestine and they hugged. Finn still wore the scars of battle. He winced when they hugged and now up-close Celestine could see the bruising around his eyes from his nose injury. It didn't look like it was broken, or it was possible a clean break that was set very well.

'You know I can't believe you weren't having me on before! But Talion fookin Schultz is your bleedin uncle.' Said Finn.

'My middle name is actually Ulrich.' Said Talion struggling to his feet. 'How about we head over to Staphs? We have some great plans for you, young man.' Talion winked and led the way to the outhouse.

The outhouse door was open. This was not because Staphros did not value his privacy, quite the contrary, he protected his privacy so vehemently that everybody else knew better than to bother him. He was not mean or ill-tempered, but he hated being disturbed or distracted. His rule was, knock, wait, and leave if unanswered. Talion needn't know better and he let himself in. Celestine cringed behind his uncle as they walked in unannounced. Celestine's outward display of his nerves subsequently shook Finn's.

The overwhelming feeling inside Finn, outside of the fear by proxy after entering the giant's lair, was awe. Never in his life had he seen a training facility like it. It was segmented into stations, strength training, combat training, agility, flexibility, and mental. Finn had travelled the world and had seen certain aspects implemented in various places, so he was familiar with the equipment, but it had never all been under one roof. He never thought it had to be, but seeing it now he knew this was the image of how a champion would train in the future. He regretted that he didn't have the time to fully utilise the facility. Being injured and his fight being in six days, he knew he was going to be limited. The facility showed that they knew what they were doing. Finn couldn't believe that Talion and Celestine could walk through here and not be awestruck.

Staphros waited for them in the back room. Talion slowly poked open the thick wooden door and it creaked loudly on moving. Staphros beckoned them in. The wall behind him was covered in paper and parchment littered with notes and scribbles of every detail that pertained to the upcoming fight. It was a true goldmine of information. Staphros had spent the entire night collating the training ideas that he, Talion, and Celestine devised. The strategy was laid clearly on the wall and it was intricate to the finest detail. Finn's amazement struck him dumb when faced with the giant and the database of information in front of him. He didn't know where to begin, everywhere he looked, there was a new detail about his own fight that he didn't know. He was learning already, and the training hadn't begun. He started to feel drastically underprepared. He took a deep breath.

As they sat, Finn could not take his eyes from Celestine. Despite his awe-inspiring surroundings, a giant like Staphros, an encyclopaedia centred around his upcoming fight, and the greatest champion in history, Celestine was still all he could look at. Memories of them shaking hands ran through his mind and how it felt, the vibe he got from him.

'No wonder he's so bloody confident.' He said under his breath. He knew that outwardly Celestine was awkward and very shy. Even in the short time they had met in the steam bath, that was obvious, but there was something below his exterior that knew how good he was. Finn hoped to find out one day.

Staphros could not hide the wry smile of pride on his face; he did this type of research in his spare time. Champions meant something on Sakura Farm; they meant something to him. He was proud that a champion had travelled cross country to train with him. He knew he could do it well, but he still he felt a sense of accomplishment for the opportunity to train Finn. He knew the type of champion Finn's father was and Celestine description of him gave him strong indicators of the kind of champion Finn was going to be.

'Word was you had a big mouth, but you've nary said a word.' Joked Staphros. Finn's eyes sparked and there was a flash of the man that declared revenge on his nation again.

'Be careful, once I start talkin, I can't shut up.' He joked back.

'Good.' Staphros smiled and nodded, he was going to like him. He leaned over and extended his hand. 'Well, if they haven't told you, my name is Staphros. My friends call me Staph and any enemy of Magnus is a friend of mine.' Finn stared blankly.

'Is Magnus the twat that runs the show in Zorrodon?'

Staphros nodded.

'Then he's more than an enemy... I'll kill the filthy rat if I get chance.' Said Finn thinking about the words said about his father in the challenge given to him.

'Let's focus on one opponent at a time.' Talion said. 'Staphros, you have some details correct?'

Staphros had notes on Finn's potential opponent, but he didn't know what set of notes would apply on the day. When Finn received his challenge by Zorrodon City officials, Finn accepted without asking who his opponent was going to be. It wasn't stated on the challenge, which although it was an unwritten rule of engagement that went back centuries, it was not law. They wanted Finn to feel that it could be anybody so it was impossible to prepare fully. Whereas his opponent could prepare specifically for him. Their tactic revealed more than they bargained for to those who looked closely enough. The pool of potential contenders narrowed when factoring that the law was, they had to pit a champion against a champion and that there were only a select few nations corrupt enough to lend their men to the cause. The nations of the Anglo Latin Commonwealth fit the profile perfectly, narrowing the pool from anybody to just five men.

The Anglo Latin Commonwealth was formed when the Latin nations untied their forces to spearhead the invasion of Anara. Knowing their power was not enough, they had to recruit Anglonia to gain the influence to sway more nations to their cause. Anglonia was an ally of Anara and King Kastielle, but Anglonia's king, Peter IV, was not. He was convinced to betray Anara and form the Anglo Latin Commonwealth in turn, the epicenter of Anara's fall. The forming of the commonwealth symbolised the betrayal of King Kastielle, which sparked the conflict between the King's Anglonians and the Celtish Anglonians, which saw Finn's father dead. Everything linked; destiny was real. No matter who Finn faced on the fourteenth, it was going to be deeply personal.

The potential opponents were the champions of each nation in the commonwealth. Each had a page dedicated to them on the wall. It detailed everything about them, height, average weight, strengths, weaknesses, and traits. The most likely opponent was Drake of Anglonia. He was a skilled combatant, but he wasn't tough. He was a show pony, a typical Princess, as they'd say in the north. Finn felt he could beat him in his sleep even now as battered as he was. The other potential opponents were anomalies and could be inserted because Drake was the obvious choice. Orion of Olympus, Marcel of Roma, Axrotalus of Francais, and Hernan of Espania, Finn hadn't a clue about any of them. The information Staphros had curated about them was invaluable. Everything else on the wall was a little bit overwhelming. Finn saw a training schedule that was intense, running, weightlifting, studying, sparring. There were only six days until the fight and he still had to heal.

'We cannot be certain of who you're going to face, but I'm certain it will be one of these five men. We plan to prepare for them all.' Said Staphros. Celestine leaned forward.

'How is your sword and shield form?' He asked.

'It's good I guess.' Said Finn. Celestine and Staphros didn't pick up the encroaching unease about his Finn's voice, but Talion reached over and patted on the hand.

'That's good. Seeing as the sword and shield is the most diverse weapon set, it would be best to train with them.' Said Celestine. He stood beside Staphros against the wall of overwhelming information. 'Your strength and conditioning will be directed by Staph, and I will be directing your sparring.' Celestine's fingers traced the intricacies of what they had planned, and this would run a healthy man into the ground. It was impossible. Finn stood quickly and breathing heavily.

'I'm sorry, but the fight is in six days. I still need to heal, so I'm able to fight. I appreciate the work you've done, but I don't have time to prepare for five men. I only came here to sharpen my skills a bit.' He said. The room quieted and Talion placed his hand on Finn's back standing beside him.

'Son..' He said warmly. 'You're in good hands with my boys, trust me, we know what we're doing.' The pressure was mounting again. This was a risk that was getting riskier by the second.

'I really want to but…'

'Give us until the morning and if you still feel the same way, we'll do it your way.' Talion winked at him. 'I'll even teach you a few of my secrets.'

Finn nodded exhaling a sigh of moderate ease.

With three sharp bangs of his cane, Talion grabbed the room's attention.

'I think Finn has had enough for now, we can fill him in later. For now, let's just settle in. Finn, you'll be staying with Celestine in his cottage, he's recently moved his rottweilers in, so I hope you like dogs.'

Finn laughed. 'I fookin love em.'

'Good. I'll be sending our resident chef, Samantha over with some soup. She's been dying to meet you. Doc will stop by after that and redress that wound on your stomach. For now, head over there with Celestine and get settled.'

The soup had solid ingredients in it, but they were indistinguishable because everything was mashed. It resulted in an unappetising grey gloop that was presented to him. Luckily it didn't taste how it looked. Celestine had dealings with this soup for his entire life before Samantha became a chef. Back then, it tasted how it looked and smelt worse. Samantha managed to make it taste good, this above all else solidified Celestine's opinion that she was the best cook in the world. Talion had a selection of vegetables, seeds, herbs, and powders that were stewed in a broth of bone marrow and water. Finn was hesitant at first but remembered his promise to Talion to try it their way for the day and then see how he felt tomorrow. That encouraged him to taste it, and Samantha's skill did the rest. He wolfed the meal down and an inexplicable weight sat in his stomach. The bowl was small, and the soup didn't fill it, but it filled him up a treat. It was a struggle to finish it. He had to lay down.

He retired upstairs for a midday rest. He was staying in Staphros's old room. Even after all those years, Celestine hadn't changed the furniture which meant the bed was big enough to get lost in. The benefit was that it was comfortable, and Finn laid down on the mattress and sank in. The soup rested in his stomach and rumbled in his belly like water brought to a rolling boil. Finn rocked on the mattress as warmth spread throughout his body and he felt like he was melting. It wasn't like wax to a flame, but like ice on a warm day. He was giving himself to the sensation, but he hadn't a choice. Once the warmth rested on his head, his eyes began to give.

Doc entered the room without knocking, finding a dazed Finn gawking at her. She looked like she was between Talion and Staphros's age. Her hair was brown and greying and bobbed around her heart-shaped face. She had a nurturing look about her.

'Oh, you're awake?' She said. 'I thought the soup would have knocked you out by now.' Her voice was soft but decisive. Finn lay trying to fight the sleep that was taking him. He was gradually getting more dazed and his dreams were bleeding into his reality. When Doc stood next to the bed a concentrated Finn tried to muster words.

'Oh… you're a woman? That's good. I like women, my mother's a woman.' He said in a breathy trancelike voice of a man soon to lose grip on consciousness.

'That's nice.' She said. She then placed her palm over his eyes. 'Now sleep.'

Seconds later, Finn was snoring.

13 PULLING FOR THE UNDERDOG

The crickets were out again. They hummed loudly in the soft grass of the empty field. The world was asleep, and Time's great eye was closed behind the eyelids of night. Rain had passed, leaving as soon as it arrived. The only clue of its presence was the dew that softly saturated the soil and caused the greenery to glisten. The bright silver moon was hanging large in the night sky like a flawless pearl on a bed of black silk. Anglonian nights were windy, even in the summer. The gentle but consistent gusts pushed their way into the open window of the room where Finn slept.

Doc had tucked him in as any mother would to a child. She cared for the dozens that lived on Sakura Farm, adult or child, and had a maternal instinct within her from the beginning. She was a natural-born caregiver. Secured tightly in the thralls of slumber, Finn stirred to break free. He rocked like a boat on the bed of a gentle sea until suddenly he sat bolt upright. He took some sharp breaths before holding his head and the base of his clammy palms soaked by the dripping strands of his hair. He was covered in sweat from head to toe. His clothes were soaked through and were getting wetter. It was like he had been running in his sleep. The intrusive breeze through the window caused a chill to set in his bones through the moisture.

Celestine pushed the door open and Finn scrambled back on the large bed. He had been in the deepest sleep he remembered ever being in and waking up was taking longer than usual. Celestine's familiar face was restoring his dreary mind.

'What happened? How long have I been asleep.' Asked Finn.

'You've been asleep for a while, about fourteen hours.' Said Celestine. He noticed Finn's eyes widen. 'Don't worry, that was supposed to happen.'

'What do you mean supposed to happen?! I've lost a day's training.' Said Finn. A look of total disbelief, fear, and frustration crossed his face. He began to breathe heavily as the panic rose. As Celestine tried to say something, Finn raised a halting finger. 'Talion said, if I wasn't convinced, we could do things my way. Between the amount of ridiculous training and making me sleep through a whole day, I'm not convinced.' Celestine's face changed, and Finn noticed. It was that side of him again, the magnetic side that was self-assured without any question.

'You want to be convinced? Stand up.' He said. Finn did what Celestine said, not noticing it yet. Celestine reached out for the wound on Finn's stomach, Finn grabbed it immediately and awaited a twinge of pain that never came. He then allowed Celestine to thumb the precise location when Michael's sword entered, and still no pain even when pressed in. Once again Finn was gobsmacked lifting his shirt and examining the scar that had healed over. He felt around his recently broken nose, and still, there was no pain.

'Convinced yet?' Asked Celestine.

Finn gulped hard and nodded.

'I know Staph and I gave you a lot of information yesterday but trust us. The only limit you will need to be concerned with during our training will be your mental limits. If you can push and do exactly what we say, you can do everything that was planned on that wall yesterday and more. I believe in the strength of your mind, you have a purpose, Finn. If you can win your title with that wound fresh in your stomach, you can push yourself.' Celestine placed his hand on Finn's shoulder. 'With our help, you won't lose.'

'But how did you heal me? What did you do?' asked Finn.

'Let's just say, that grey sludge that my uncle calls soup has some healing properties. Without going into detail, it accelerates the body's healing and growth while sleeping tenfold. Old family recipe.'

'By the Court, he's as brilliant as the legends say.'

'More so... I just wish he was a legendary cook too. You're lucky you had Samantha's version. When Talion used to make it for me and Staph, it tasted worse than it looked, and it looked worse.' Said Celestine. Finn smirked as Celestine went to retrieve a pile of folded clothes at the corner of the room. 'The training is a lot, and it will hurt. Just know that we have thought about everything and we want you to win. If we stick to the plan you can do a week's worth of training per day and still be fresh. So, will you do it our way?' Celestine handed the clothes over the Finn.

'Only if you keep your promise not to hold back.'

Celestine nodded.

'Then you've got yourself a deal.'

'Good. Now get dressed because Staphros is waiting and he wants to leave soon.' Celestine ran for the door.

'Where are we going?'

'Well training start from now.' Said Celestine. 'We're running to Zorrodon and back.'

Twenty-six miles later, the sun was up and there was no rest in sight for the Celtish champion. Gasping and wheezing after the longest run he had ever done, he was pushed back into the outhouse for further strength and conditioning training. To his surprise, he was able to push himself further than ever already and he didn't know where the ceiling to it was. He pushed and pulled, squeezed and stretched until his muscles screamed with tension. When he couldn't lift anymore, he went straight to sparring. Celestine was able to mimic the styles of all of Finn's potential opponents except for Axrotalus. He was significantly bigger than Finn, and Staphros was better suited to copy him. For hours, Celestine and Staphros rotated fighting against Finn in the style of his opponents, until his movement was becoming second nature.

Finn's moves slowed and it was evident that it was becoming a struggle to stand. Finn hit his first limit just in time. It was time for a strategy meeting with Staphros. They retired to the backroom in the outhouse. It was just Staphros and Finn for this meeting and Finn learned that Staphros was much more than a big man. Staphros was the most intelligent man he had met. If there was a book or text, he had read it and understood it enough to apply all applicable information to any situation. Staphros was a mountain of a man, but a goldmine of information. Finn forgot about his fatigue but wished he could sit and talk with Staphros all day, but he knew he couldn't.

The next round of training began with agility training and tutorials on proper form with swords and shields followed by another round of sparring and strength and conditioning. Now the real limit was met. Finn managed to hobble back to the cottage on his own power but collapsed on Celestine's chair. Samantha brought the soup and volunteered to feed Finn because he was unable to lift his arms. Finally, Celestine helped him to bed and Talion visited him.

Talion knew he had a finite amount of time before the sedative effects of the soup would take hold and soothe Finn into a meditative state. Talion talked of the divines and shared philosophy on the Children of Nature, particularly Serendipity and Fate. Talion reminded him why he was fighting and that the Children of Nature were guiding him to victory. Soon meditation became sleep and a champion's resolve became divine purpose.

SMACK! SMACK! Staphros jumped out of bed. It was the middle of the night and he staggered to his door. *SMACK! SMACK!* The sound was coming from the training facility. Staphros stepped out to investigate what was going on.

He found Finn practising his swordplay on a training dummy. For the first time, Staphros was beaten to training. Divine Purpose.

By the end of the fourth day, Finn had completed the same amount of training that he would have done in a month. He managed to feed himself and climb the stairs to bed on his own, things that he took the granted more than three nights ago. He looked and felt different too. He was fuller and solid physically, but mentally he was transformed. His mind was iron. Failure was not an option when he arrived on Sakura Farm, four days later failure was not a possibility. He was at his peak and was happy to know that there were two days until the fight as of the next morning, and all he had to do was rest.

Celestine proved to be more than a great rival and trainer, he was a friend too. In the rare times when they had downtime, most often during meals, they talked. Well, he talked and Celestine listened. He grew up around people that didn't care what he had to say, didn't want to see him, disdained him, because of the slander levied against his family. Growing up on the streets and slums meant he was surrounded by some very bad people. People that would freely spit on him and his family, but wouldn't piss on them if they were on fire. Finn knew few good people in his life, but Celestine was one of them.

The bright morning sun beamed through the window to Finn's bedroom. The booming rooster cry brought him out of deep sleep. Finn was glad of it. It felt like a lifetime ago that sunrise or a rooster's cry were the things that woke him up. It was a welcome change to be woken up as Nature intended. He skipped out of bed, pulled on some clothes and jogged downstairs. Celestine wasn't there, which was strange. Finn paid it no more thought, Celestine was a busy man and was likely tending to affairs elsewhere. He poked his head in the sitting room where the dogs were. Mac was not there. Mac was not a busy man; all Mac did was sit by Porsche. Today, Porsche was at sat alone snoring with her eyes open. She often pretended to be asleep so people wouldn't bother her, but it was like she was aware of her snoring, but not aware that she closed her eyes when she slept. Needless to say, it was easy to tell when she was faking it.

Finn investigated further into the case of the missing Mac. When he opened the cottage door, he was happy to find Mac sitting on the grass next to Celestine and Staphros. They appeared to be waiting for him. Archie, the young blacksmith, squeezed past Finn without a word to get into the house. He wasn't meaning to be rude, but when Staphros gave him an order, that was the only thing on his mind. Finn could empathise.

'What's this?' Asked Finn.

'Training.' Said a grinning Celestine.

Finn wagged his finger in objection. 'Oh, no, no, no! I'm resting today.'

'Then call it a test if it makes you feel better.' Said Staphros. Finn had a lot of respect for Staphros; he spent an incredible amount of time picking his brain about any and everything not just fighting. Staphros was wise and Finn could not deny him if he asked him to do something. Finn's face twisted.

'Fine! What's this test then?' he asked. Staphros was holding back a smile and Finn knew they were up to something. Celestine hoisted a leash in the air and dramatically clipped it to Mac's collar.

'Simply take Mac for a walk.' He said.

Finn walked over and took the lead. 'This is hardly a test.' He said. He looked back to the house to see Archie peaking through the window. Finn felt Archie knew something he didn't, they all did. Celestine giggled and nudged Staphros.

'It will be when I do this.' Said Staphros. He pulled a bright red ball from his pocket and launched it clear past the cornfields and into the forest. Mac bolted after it, dragging Finn to an instant unprepared sprint. Celestine and Staphros clutched their sides laughing as they followed after them.

They eventually found Finn deep in the forest sitting on a log. Mac was content laying on the floor gnawing on the ball Staphros had launched. When he saw them, Finn couldn't help but laugh too. He knew to expect some sort of trick, but not that.

'How on Mother Earth can your dog pull like that?' Said Finn.

'Rottweilers my friend. Rottweilers. You're lucky Porsche wasn't on the leash, she could have Staph off his feet if she wanted.'

'I can't argue that.' Said Staphros corroborating Celestine's claim. Celestine unclipped Mac from his leash and let him roam the woods.

The forest was quiet and incredibly peaceful. It balanced the nerves and somehow made people feel closer to Mother Nature. Finn was now experiencing that. He could smell the soil and wood when the coastal winds delivered the scent to his nostrils. The sunlight broke through the overhanging leaves to shine in slivers on the wood, grass, and stone. Despite the way he got there, Finn was happy to be there. He had a jaded view of the world, a testament to the harshness of his upbringing. He didn't trust many people, so it was difficult to make or keep friends. Before today, his idea of fun would involve a drunken night with a woman who he would forget before the morning. It was empty. For the first time in a long time, Finn felt he had friends, had fun, had support. Not because of who his father was, but because of who he was. He felt whole.

Hurried footsteps rushed towards them and Mac returned to their side. The footsteps were Archie's, who emerged from between the trees panting.

'I've been looking for you all over.' He said doubled over.

'What's wrong? Has something happened to Porsche?' Asked Celestine. Celestine knew for Archie to break an order from Staphros, it must be serious. He was panicking.

'Erm, sort of. I don't know. Miss Hanabi told me to get you.' Archie said. 'She said Porsche was giving birth I think.' Mac bolted back home before any other.

He was going to be a dad.

14 PREPARATIONS

Vida- Amor- 13- 1827

Sakura Farm threw a banquet in the grand hall in celebration of the new arrivals. Samantha was on her best form, cooking chicken, a leg of mutton, and her famous pumpkin soup, the stuff of Celestine's dreams. Porsche had successfully given birth to a litter of seven healthy puppies. Maybe now, Mac would grow up a little bit, but nobody held their breath. Celestine cried like a proud father when the puppies were born, and the waterworks returned every time he thought of them. Finn was thrilled to be able to have something other than the grey soup that was designed more to fuel the body than pleasure the tongue. He could see now what Samantha Chef was about, and he was not disappointed.

The night was happy. The night was fun. The night was needed.

Finn slept his first night without the sedative aid of the grey soup or the guided meditation directed by Talion. He could confront the pressures that he dealt with in his dreams when he had access to those tools, but now, those pressures only served to keep him awake. Tomorrow, He, Talion, Staphros, and Celestine were heading into Zorrodon to get a feel for the crowd and see if they could be swayed to his side. He began to visualise how he became a champion, the voice of his people screaming his name and he was calming. He managed to guide himself into a state of bliss by repeating a mantra. The mantra reminded him why he fought; it was everything that Talion told him condensed into four words.

'Divine purpose. Nature's will.'

Vida- Ego- 14- 1827

Celestine rested on the porch of his cottage to watch the sunrise the

103

morning after. It was his routine to look upon his uncle's land, and it would speak to him every time. He, like Finn, had struggled to sleep the night before. He was nervous too, but for a different reason. Today was his chance; he was going to see her again, the girl who haunted his dreams for the last half-year. When he managed to muster sporadic slumber, he dreamt of her and their lips met for less than a second before he woke up. The perfect omen, he was ready. Mac plodded to his feet and collapsed wearily at his side. He was a welcome addition to his morning routine. Mac also had a reason to be nervous, being a new dad and all. This cottage was just filled with nervous men and new-borns. Porsche's paradise. The more Porsche and Mac stayed in by the cottage, the more Celestine realised that they never belonged in the kennels in the first place. The cool wind was warming as the morning matured. Celestine looked across the field to see Talion standing at the big eye saying his morning prayer. Celestine knew what or whom Talion spoke of and wondered if he would have the opportunity to pray for a similar purpose. He stared at the slowly sailing clouds and saw her face in their glimmering white canvass and he promised himself that he would learn her name today.

'Mr. Celestine?' Said Hanabi, snapping him out of his trance. 'Is Mr Finlay awake?'

'No not yet, I'd just wait, maybe have some breakfast. There's still some bread and milk from yesterday.' Said Celestine blinking back to reality. 'Also, stop calling me Mr Celestine, it's just Celestine.' He continued, trying to make things less formal between them. He didn't want it to come across as an order. Hanabi was teaching her philosophy class in the cottage today and she wanted to prepare her lesson. The cottage had an impressive library of historical texts and wonderful philosophy. With Celestine being out for the day, Talion offered her the opportunity to teach the texts. She was mindful that Finn was staying there, and she did not want to disrupt him as was the custom where she was from. She was always mild-mannered, and her head was perpetually bowed. She was particularly shy around Celestine and was discovering she was the same around Finn. They reminded her of her late brother Sarutobu because they were warriors of the highest order.

She loved and respected her brother greatly, and his prowess as a fighter was the centre-point of that respect. Though she hadn't seen either of them fight, she knew by the way they carried themselves that they too were of the same ilk. Sarutobu upheld traditional Nippon values. Young women were not to speak out of turn and were not allowed to interfere with the dealings of the men. He adhered to those values but was sure to exempt Hanabi from any enforcement of those traditions. That was up to their father to correct deviance from the marked path. She knew Celestine had no idea of those values and wouldn't dream of enforcing that upon her even if he did, but she could not help it.

She scuttled past Celestine into the house. Celestine watched her a minute as she sat perfectly still without touching the food he had offered. She looked troubled or sad, like a veil of doubt restricted her every move. He felt sympathy for her and an unwavering sense of confusion. Looking at her didn't seem to help, but he continued anyway. His gaze lingered and he found himself staring at her out of curiosity.

'Mate, she's out of your league.' Said Luke laughing and clapping Celestine on the back. Mac bounced to his feet and ran rings around the Celtishman, licking each hand as he passed. Mac loved Luke. They were like kindred spirits, both as silly as each other.

'Ok Luke, firstly, no she isn't, and secondly, I'm not even interested in Hana.' Celestine answered quickly.

'Ey, what's wrong with Hana?' Luke chuckled staring at her through the window. 'she a right bonny lass if you ask me.' He said waving at her.

Celestine rolled his eyes. 'I never said she wasn't a "bonnie lass" but she just isn't my type.'

'Oh aye, you fancy a bit of that florist from Zorrodon, I forgot.' Said Luke. Celestine had admitted his feelings for the girl in Zorrodon, after much pestering on their travels. 'So, Celestine, are you gonna ask her out or what?' Asked Luke prying.

Celestine ignored him and walked right by him avoiding him and the subject altogether. He had planned to ask her out eventually, but learning her name was the objective today. Any more would become overwhelming.

'I'm just saying all of the mad things we have done together, and you can't ask a girl out. I mean don't you call yourself an explorer?' Luke followed Celestine.

'That I do.' Said Celestine sarcastically.

'Well lad, I'm telling you this as your best friend in this entire world. You need to explore… her.' Luke flickered his tongue like a slimy lizard. The clap of his saliva-soaked tongue whipping about caused Celestine to shudder. The colour ran out of his face and a look of frozen bewilderment etched itself on his features. Luke burst into uncontrollable laughter the instant he saw the expression. Celestine was used to Luke's crudeness, but at times Luke could catch him off guard.

Luke looked Celestine up and down quickly. He didn't have a hair out of place. He put on a tight sleeveless black top, and loose brown slacks. Over it, all hung the very expensive white and blue cloak that wore in Elgin.

'Oh I remember now, you're going to Zorrodon aren't you?' He asked. Celestine flushed even more.

'Finn wanted to go, so I'm going with him. We're training partners after all.' Said Celestine. Luke screwed his face tightly and shot a very sceptical look at Celestine.

'Mate you shouldn't lie; it gives you spots.' Luke pointed at a bulging red pimple on his chin unabashedly. 'You see that? You won't be getting any florist girls with this on your face and this was from a wee tiny fib I told Sam.'

'I'll bear that in mind.' Said Celestine.

'You should and all. I've always been the wiser of the two of us. I couldn't in good faith allow you to go without a chaperone. I'm going with you.' Luke's eyes beamed at the prospect of going to Zorrodon. Zorrodon was a proverbial ocean of fine women, and unlike Celestine, Luke was not attached to just one. Celestine shrugged and laughed quietly.

'It's not up to me.' He said. Luke realised he was walking towards the outhouse.

'Oh shite.'

'Shite indeed my friend.' Celestine laughed. 'Shite indeed.'

As the manager of the farm and all of the staff on it, Staphros was ashamed to not have a close relationship with everyone on the farm. He was unlike Talion, who had an uncanny talent for remembering not only people but finite details about them, even if mentioned in passing. A staff member that he wished did not occupy space in his memory was Luke Chef. Luke was known as the coaster, shirker, and slacker extraordinaire. It was a real gift when you studied the lengths that he was willing to go to avoid work. The relationship between Luke and Staphros was that of a teacher and unruly child, a child Staphros had no intention of mentoring.

Luke's heart filled with dread as they approached the outhouse door. If there was one thing Luke tried to avoid as much as his duties it was Staphros himself. He was terrifying. More than his size and incredible frame, the most intimidating thing about Staphros was that he was a stoic Deutschman who suffered no fools. Luke was under no illusions that he was, in fact, a fool.

Celestine habitually knocked three times on the outhouse door. Slowly, the door creaked open revealing the mastodon before the two young men. The two arched their heads back to look Staphros in the eyes. He was sweating with a rag draped over his shoulder and they had appeared to have interrupted a morning exercise routine, his second of the day so far. He was wearing his black trucks and knee pads and his palms were covered in chalk.

'What's he doing here?' Asked Staphros. Luke erected his spine to a bolt upright rigidity sweating cold.

'Luke wants to ask you something.' Said Celestine. Luke fired a look of panicked disbelief at Celestine. Celestine winked and arched his head to Staphros urging Luke on.

'Hello.' Said Luke. 'You look like you've lost some weight.'

'And you look like you have found it.' Said Staphros. His tone was flat and neither Luke nor Celestine knew if he was serious or not. Nevertheless,

Celestine snorted in laughter until Luke scalded him with a glance.

'Well you know, sharing's caring.' Said Luke.

'Get on with it, I'm busy.' Staphros interrupted. Luke panicked and threw himself into a bow.

'I would like to come to Zorrodon with you all today please.' Luke closed his eyes even though it only shielded him from the sight of his quaking knees.

'No.' Said Staphros and abruptly closed the door in his face.

'Well… that's that then.' Said Celestine. 'See you when I get back.' Celestine walked away leaving Luke frozen.

Kojo's disappearance was silent in the city. He was gone without a trace. The dock folk were not quick to forget about the young man. The so-called ignored were beginning to make noise. They were not in a position to make demands or to stage a protest. They knew of the hierarchy in Zorrodon and they were insignificant long before the advent of Magnus's Parliament. They could, however, make contact with the next level up. The immense pressure of the looming government was beginning to break backs. The taxes continued to rise and so did the anguish of the people. This was not an unfamiliar feeling for those who resided in the docks. Lion assembled his delegates once again to take to the village and appeal to their emotions. The pain that segregated the peoples of Zorrodon was now forming a commonality amongst them. Olive's journal would further show that Kojo's disappearance was a human issue, rather than a "Docks Problem". It could even possibly prove to the people Kojo was framed.

Lion and his delegates were finding success in recent days. They knew Kojo hadn't been transferred yet. What was also certain was Lion was a government target and they were targeting any associates of the Hondos to get information on him. It was disturbing to find out and the revelation haunted Lion since that night. The spirit of his people lifted him and gave him the strength to carry on. They all were determined to retrieve Kojo by any means necessary.

Kojo's sentence and the verdict had been made public, even though it had been levied without a trial and they felt the squeeze of time at their backs. With the current success of their inquisitions and the new information from the city, the dock folk moved to investigate the night he was brought in, to find proof of foul play. They did not know yet of Kojo's fate.

Martyrdom was not a luxury that Magnus and Adan Thiago afforded Kojo in death, but the dock folk still stood for him even if they did not know why.

Lion set off in the morning to continue his investigation. His delegates all followed behind in tow. This time the village seemed different. It had slowed. This was the first time since his speech here that the village had willingly come to a standstill. There was a bustling mass forming in the centre of the street and an exacerbated voice booming from the statue of Mother Nature, much like Lion himself. Lion couldn't hear what was being said, but he could see the crowd reaction. Whoever was speaking must have been very important. The battle of nudges and elbows was ensuing at the back of the crowd. Lion wanted no part of the conflict, so he hung back. It was still difficult to hear what was being said and the struggle in front was clearly to gain a position to be able to hear it. Suddenly a powerful Celtish voice sang in a query,

'Will you stand with me tomorrow?' the hustle stopped and every fist in the mass of people launched into the air in resounding acceptance. The group parted as if like water with a pocket of air flying through to the top. When the partition reached Lion, he stood eye to eye with the centre of attention. He had never seen this man before, but he recognised his demeanour, it was the same as his. Lion was standing in front of Finlay Eireann the Champion of Celtish Anglonia. Finn walked boisterously with his arms flailing in a claim to the space around him. Lion stepped aside and watched this mysterious man walk past him without noticing he even existed. All the people, even Lion's delegates of the Hondos faction, had their eyes glued to Finn. He had a magnetic charisma that drew attention like gains of iron sand. Lion was always mindful to look where nobody else was, diverting his gaze to a carriage parked outside a café. There he saw an elderly gentleman, a young gentleman, and an extremely large gentleman watching on. Lion thought that this must be a testament to the attraction of this strange fellow's charisma, to draw attention from a man a great deal over seven feet tall. Lion fought through the crowd to get to the only three people, not in a starstruck frenzy.

Talion, Celestine, and Staphros welcomed Lion as he approached. Lion gave a grim upward nod to Staphros before addressing Talion, the clear leader of the group.

'Wha'appn, out towner? Dem call me Lion.' he said. Talion leaned forward on his beer barrel stool and shook Lion's hand firmly.

'Pleasure. I'm Talion and this is my nephew Celestine and my ward Staphros.' Staphros arched his stiff neck downwards to Talion. He hated being called his ward, he had surely outgrown that now. Talion looked up and winked at him. Celestine shook Lion's hand remembering his manners once Talion let go of his grip. Staphros did the same after Celestine.

'What goin on here so? Man look like him someone important?' Said Lion.

'That's the man who will be fighting tomorrow.' Said Talion.

'Fighting? Tomorrow?' Lion scratched his head and looked back to the crowd.

'You haven't heard?' Celestine spoke out of turn.

'No man, we don't get much news down inna de docks.' Lion spotted and plucked a leaflet that had been nailed into the stone wall behind Staphros. He squinted while he studied the scribbled words on the page. This leaflet was written by a slave that could not read but had to replicate what they saw. He shook his head.

'Will you be going? Finn could use the support.' Said Celestine.

'Who Finn? A him dat?' Said Lion. 'Him no look like a champion. Big man right here so look like a champion. Respeck.' Lion extended his fist to Staphros who obliged by placing his against it.

'I've read about you. Lion, leader of the Hondos Faction.' Said Staphros.

'Oh really? What you read about me?' Lion replied dubiously.

'You've been causing the government some headache.' Lion stepped back cautiously. The crowd was distracted and his delegates were swept in the occasions as well. He was alone.

'How you mean? I mind my own business and look h'after my people. Mi no trouble nothin.' Said Lion. Staphros stepped forward much to Lion's panic.

'People like you…' Said Staphros. He stooped forward and clenched his fist. Once he extended his arm his stoicism softened and he smiled. 'This city needs, people like you. Respect.' Lion relaxed immediately and stopped backtracking. He cracked into laughter of relief and sighed deeply. He gave a hearty pound to Staphros's fist and they shared smiles.

'T'hanks. Many, many t'hanks but dis place a have plenty plenty people like me. Dem jus need fi stan when it matters.' He said.

'Milton?' Said Talion.

'Good man bless up. Mi read h'all him work seb'n times h'over. Mi a paraphrase a likkle but unuh get de message.'

'Francis Milton was a famous revolutionary from Akoku. He liberated the country of Chinyerie from the Thiago Occupation. Above all of that, he was a fabulous writer.' Talion explained to the bewildered Celestine at his side, who was more into adventures than history.

'Yes-I. Mi tink readin him work serve me well. Zorrodon is a lot like Chinyerie if you follow.'

The three nodded.

'Big Man, you naa read bout a young man called Kojo av you?' Asked Lion hopefully.

Staphros shook his head.

'Teck dis. It a journal me and mi Hondos write each week pon de Chrono. The bwoy mudda write a likkle sumting for him.' Said Lion handing over the rolled parchment.

'I usually pick it up and leave a donation. I'm sorry, I was busy this week.' Said Staphros ashamedly and took the journal from Lion's hand.

'No worry big man! All love.'

'What's happened?' Celestine interjected.

'Him a fren. Got inna some trouble with the government. Now him been missing a few days now. Sent him for a slave for a crime him no do.' Lion placed his hand on his heart and grimaced. 'It a pain me. Keeps me up at night and mi ca'an stop tink bout it.'

'I'm sorry to hear that, really I am.' Said Celestine.

'Mi won't rest until I find him and deliver him to him mudder.' Lion vowed. He took a deep breath and shook his head.

'I'll pray to The Court for you.' Said Talion.

Lion nodded in appreciation. He stepped back looking down the road towards the docks. 'Mi gaan now, out towners, work fi do. But it was bless. One love until.'

'One second Lion.' Staphros called.

Lion turned.

'What was your friend's name again?' he asked.

'Kojo.' Said Lion.

'Kojo.' Staphros nodded. 'I'll remember that.' Lion walked down an alley to avoid the ruckus around Finn.

Staphros turned to Talion, but before he could speak Talion intervened.

'How long do you need?' Asked Talion.

'One or two hours just to ask some questions. If I find something, I'll leave the message somewhere for Lion.' Said Staphros.

'Don't rush, just be careful. Remember what I said about Magnus. He is not one to trifle with.'

Staphros nodded.

'I don't think Finn will be needing us for the time being how about we take a look around also Uncle Talion?' Said Celestine.

'Wonderful, I was meaning to buy some flowers anyway.' Talion smiled at his nephew and offered the same wink that he shared with Staphros.

15 RULES OF ENGAGEMENT

Vida- Ego- 14- 1827

The white wall of Zorrodon was a sight to behold. No matter how many times someone may have seen it, everyone stopped and stared at its tremendous size like it was the first time. It looked like it reached the sky and beyond, the beacon that summoned the world to see it. Now the three of them stared high at the wall with a different perspective. It brought the world to it but repelled the villagers who built it.

'They didn't have to go that far to keep you out.' Celestine jibed at the big man. Staphros chuckled as he led the group on. Suddenly, he stopped and grew tense. Two slimy looking men stood at the entrance to the city. They wore pants too short on their legs and jackets that were too small on their body. The smaller of them had features that appeared pinched like a rodent. The larger one had rounder features like a bloated fish. His belly globed from underneath his tight top and the undercarriage of his hairy belly sagged revealing his pale skin. They grinned as they emerged from seemingly nowhere like spiders on a wall.

'What's this?' Said Staphros.

'Travellers Tax fella! Now, pay up!' The smaller man said. Celestine came from behind Staphros.

'I could be wrong here, but you don't seem like public servants.' He said.

'Servants? Why would we be servants to the public? Not everybody is rich enough to have a servant you fool!' The smaller man said rolling his eyes. His large companion smiled idiotically as he let his accomplice speak.

Celestine sighed. 'No, a public servant is...'

'Don't bother, it'll be lost on them.' Staphros intervened. The smaller man heard and took immediate offence.

'You know what is not lost on me? You have to pay Traveller's Tax or you can't get into the city.' He said.

'I've never had to pay before, what's changed?'

'Zorrodon is under a new government, a lot has changed.' The small man's rodent-like features twitched in satisfaction as a crooked smile revealed the black gaps where teeth used to be.

'Out of curiosity, how much is this Tax?' Asked Celestine.

'Well, it's around…'

'It doesn't matter! I'm not paying them anything. They are the scum of society and aren't worth any more of our breath.' Staphros took a step forward. The two men drew their swords and the larger man now looked intensely at Staphros who still greatly dwarfed him.

'Now you've hurt my feelings, that's gonna cost you your mate's rates now.' He said. He was definitely northern, not just by his appearance and demeanor but his accent was thick.

'You draw a sword on us, it's going to hurt you.' Said Staphros gravely. He unclipped his cloak and removed it from his shoulders. One large hand eclipsing the other, he clicked his knuckles before Talion patted him on the back. Talion hobbled to the forefront and flicked a gold piece at the two grifters.

'That should suffice, now let him though.' Said Talion. The small man picked up the gold piece and examined it. A look of excitement hit his face once he authenticated it. Staphros walked through making sure he walked between the two men. They still had their swords drawn and their blades followed the giant as he walked past. He stopped and stared down the big one. The cold finger of fear tickled the big one's back. Staphros appeared a force of nature. Staphros grabbed the blade of the sword and with no effort, he snapped the steel blade in half and carried on through the gates.

'You can replace it with your stolen gold.' He said.

The gate closed behind him.

Talion and Celestine were now headed to the florists. Talion had asked Celestine if he knew any good ones, and Celestine was very coy in suggesting the one he had in mind. Talion always looked content, but no more so when he saw his boy's resolve when it came to this. Talion knew about Celestine's feelings for the florist girl even before Celestine did. Talion knew her mother and even then, when they were young, Celestine would stare and not understand why he couldn't not stare. His young mind was rampant with emotions that he was too young to feel. Celestine always said that adventure was his first love and he was right to an extent. That was only because he didn't know what love was when he first saw her.

They arrived outside. It was a quaint little village building, but the garden was magnificent, filled with flowers and plants that Anglonia has never seen grow before. Talion halted Celestine in his path.

'Listen son...' He said, placing his hand in Celestine's shoulder. 'You don't want me in there when you're talking to the nice young lady do you?'

Celestine shrugged. He couldn't bring himself to say yes even though that was exactly what he was feeling, but he didn't want to say no. Talion smirked and shook his head.

'This isn't a trick, you like this girl don't you?' Said Talion.

Celestine said nothing.

'Come on I'm practically your father, you don't think I notice things? I know you better than you do at times. Now just go in there and talk to her I'll be waiting out here.' He said. Celestine blushed at first but quickly calmed himself.

'Thanks, Uncle.' He said before going towards the florists.

'Oh yes, her name is Temina.' Talion shot a thumbs up. Celestine sent a trembling awkward thumbs up back and carried on. Words couldn't express how grateful he was that he could now put a name to the face of his dreams, but now he was going to speak with this person without a plan. Talion had taken away the one thing he wanted to take away from their conversation. Now he had to make it up as he went, but improvisation was more a Luke Chef special.

Celestine entered the florists soundlessly. The door opened without even a whimper and closed behind him with the guidance of his gentle push. The room was vibrant and lit by the summer sun which streamed through the abundance of open windows and waving white net curtains. The wood foundations of the building were made of large square pillars of golden ash wood, which reflected the light rays from its varnish. Between the ash wood skirtings, the ceiling and the walls were made of grey stone. The walls were barely visible through the curtain of plants and flowers that hung off them. The room was ablaze with many different colours, a still image that Celestine could have mistaken for an oil painting if he was not standing in it.

Temina had her back turned watering the plants on the other side of the room. She hadn't seen Celestine come in, and the beauty of her immaculately kept shop still paled in comparison to how she looked. Dreams often romanticised the image of a person, but in Celestine's case, they did her no justice. Her hair was longer and shone bronze in the sun, tied into a long singular plait that reached down to her hips. She had flowers in her hair again. His gaze lingered on her as the sun reached its gentle hand on her cheek and her skin glowed like the Children of Nature in a clear night's sky. She handled the flowers with extra care, almost caressing the vines as she moved them to pour the water on the soil. She moved slowly and deliberately like every move that she made had a purpose. The flow of her yellow sundress danced along with the net curtains in the wind, while still clinging to her waist.

Celestine waved knowing her attention to detail would not allow her to notice such a distraction. It would allow him another opportune a few seconds to see her at work. It had been a long time since he had seen her last. He had never spoken to her and never got this close to her. The heat got to him and he took off his coat and rested it on the hook by the door. He froze as he looked back, and she was still tending to her plants. Before coming in, he hoped that she would be dealing with a customer. He could have time to get used to being around her and buck up the courage to speak to her without having to initiate it. That hadn't happened and it was just the two of them. He was stalling and the courage was not coming to him as now he had spent too long in the shop to not say anything, and to be discovered now would result in an even more awkward conversation. His heart racing in his chest, Celestine closed his eyes and hoped that she would eventually notice him. In the darkness of his prayer, a flicker of light darted from him. He futilely reached after it to grab whatever it was, but he was too late. It hit her. Temina jumped as if pinched gently and she turned around.

Celestine panicked and sprinted into the wall slapping it with his cheek, body and palms. He let out a sudden *oof* as all the wind left him, and he clung to the wall to make the move look deliberate. He examined the lilies hanging in pots. They were yellow and in full bloom. Temina laughed at the odd man in her shop. He was nervous and appeared very strange, but the oceanic blue of his striking eyes put her at ease. She felt that he felt nervous, but he was pure in his intentions. She couldn't explain why, but that was how she felt.

'So, you like lilies then?' she asked. Celestine looked up face reddening and sweating.

'Oh, you know, lilies are good.' Celestine stammered. Temina smiled at that. Celestine detached himself from the wall and dusted himself off. He smiled back then laughed at himself for a second. 'I'll be honest, I have no idea about flowers. I'm basically assuming lilies are good, they may not be I've never really spoke to them.' He said. That made Temina laugh. He was charming when he didn't mean to be.

'I don't know, the way you looked at those flowers it seemed you knew them pretty well.' She said mocking the attentive way he stared at the flowers.

'It's like I said, I had never met them. I was curious.'

'Well?' Asked Temina. Celestine scratched his head stumped.

'Well, what?' he asked.

'What do you think?

'Oh yes, very nice, very nice.' He said. Temina placed her hands on her counter threading her fingers in front of her. Her large eyes playfully stared at him, but she could truly see him now. He was handsome, but many a handsome man had come into this shop before. There was something to this man, the way he stood, the way he smiled, or spoke. There was something within herself that pushed her towards him. She liked that he still had the soft features of a child but the strong jaw of a man. His face was shaved smooth and he was very well-kept. She also liked this game that had started. It had no rules, but there was a silent dialogue between them that they would figure out along the way.

They were both having fun though.

'I'm glad you like them. Now I have a business to run sir so I must ask, are you planning to make a purchase today?' She said.

Celestine nodded. 'I'd like to but I don't want to get this wrong.'

'The great thing about flowers is that you can never get it wrong. What are you buying them for?' She asked.

'Not what, whom?' Said Celestine impishly.

'Oh.' Temina looked down. It was small but a weight deflated her a little and she slumped. Celestine noticed. He had gotten swept up in the game.

'I mean they're for…' He paused.

Rule number one, "Don't reveal your hand too early."

'never mind.' He said.

'Okay,' Said Temina. She still felt the weight in her chest, she wasn't sure why or what it was but she couldn't help but feel it. She wanted to know who the flowers were for, but it was not her business.

Rule number two, "Mind your own business."

It went quiet in the room. Celestine spotted an open book on the counter next to Temina.

'What are you reading?' he asked pointing to it. Temina nodded embarrassed.

'You could have guessed.' She lifted the book. 'A botany book.'

'You could have given me one hundred guesses and I wouldn't have gotten that.' Said Celestine.

'Really? In a botany shop? The room full of flowers and plants?' Asked Temina.

'Yes, but until now in which I'd be making an educated guess, I didn't know what botany meant.' Said Celestine now embarrassed himself. Temina laughed and was back smiling again.

Rule number three, "Make her laugh."

Celestine enjoyed her laugh; it came through in bursts and small giggles and she blushed as if embarrassed. Temina enjoyed Celestine making her laugh because he looked so proud that he had done so. Part of her knew that it meant something to him. A larger part of her was not confident enough to believe it.

'I'd like to borrow your expertise in making a bouquet.' Said Celestine.

Temina felt the weight again but didn't show it. She now understood rule number one.

She nodded.

Celestine clapped in celebration. 'Thank you so much.'

'So, tell me about this girl. What does she like?' She said abruptly, trying to get his attention and regain her bearings. Rule number one was difficult to maintain. She walked around the counter and by Celestine. She smelt like vanilla and Celestine shivered. She had never been this close to him.

'I don't know' he replied perplexed.

'What about her favourite colour?' she asked.

'I'm not sure of that either.'

'Then what do you know about her?'

'Not much honestly, I just thought she would like flowers. I mean do you like flowers?' He said. A plan was hatching in his mind as they spoke.

Temina nodded, agreeing with his point 'I see, so you are looking for something general but special. Something that would speak to her.' she said.

He shrugged. 'You're the expert. Pick something you'd like, I'm sure you have good taste.' he said picking up her book.

'Good but misguided.' She said under her breath in reference to herself liking a clearly taken man.

Celestine's ears pricked. 'Pardon?' he asked.

'Oh, nothing.'

Rule number four "Play Coy."

They shared a laugh and their eyes met again the game had reached a certain point. The look was different, it seemed like both lost all senses and sensibilities. There was no sound, no smells, no taste, just a fleeting moment. The laughter stopped and so did the playfulness. They could both feel the electricity in their fingertips, and every urge pushing them closer together. They fought them for reasons unknown to them. Celestine stared at her lips, full and pink. This was not a dream and he knew if he acted now, he would not be turned away. He took a deep breath to find courage. Temina cleared her throat and the moment was gone.

She turned away quickly and shuffled into her garden outside her back door. Celestine watched from the window. He could hear her humming faintly to a tune he hadn't come across before. She rocked along as she picked an assortment of flowers. When she knelt to pick the final few to finish the bouquet, her long black plat fell over she shoulder and framed her cheeks. She was staring down at the flowers, picking each one with attention and care. It was like everything that she was feeling inside was allowed to come out in the privacy of the sunlight for the world to see. It was not for Celestine's eyes, but he looked anyway. He couldn't help it. She looked up with her big eyes and Celestine quickly turned away as to not look like he was staring. Her bouquet was finished and ready to be presented. She knew it was meant for someone else, but it was in some part meant for him. She didn't know why but, she wanted it to be nice for him so at least between the two of them, they knew something more than professional pride went into this assembly. Something neither of them would know what was.

'So, does this girl know you?' she asked handing the bouquet to Celestine. He did know something more went into this bouquet, but there was a small but significant part of him that made him doubt the thought.

'Not really, we've only met uhh, before, only in passing really.' He replied. 'I don't think she even knows my name.' he continued. Gladly, he took the bouquet and their fingertips touched. It was no accident on both sides. The laughed again.

'Oh okay.' She said.

'How much do I owe you?' Said Celestine rummaging in his pocket. Temina waved her hand.

'Don't worry, store policy. First one is for free.' She said.

'Wow, thanks. How long have you been doing that?'

'Let's say it's very new.' She said walking past him again behind the counter. The smell of vanilla hit his nostrils again and made him shiver. She placed her hands on the counter once more and propped herself to lean forward. She was enticing now. The purity in his feelings towards her now was warped by her shapely bosom and the slopes of her hips. He wanted more than to kiss her now. He could feel his heartbeat in his throat and once again his surroundings went mute. This time however he was alone, no longer swept up in the moment with her. His instincts pushed him towards her, and thoughts of them together ran through his mind. He wanted her then more than anything he had ever wanted before. He knew he wanted more than just the physical, but that was a big part of it. His next move was going to dictate how this went.

He stepped backwards.

This time the connection was severed and the game was over. That was the final play and the rules did not apply. Temina once again deflated and Celestine filled with nerves worse than when he first came in. He opened the shop door.

'Thank you.' He said stepping out.

'Wait!' She said. It was sudden and now that the game was over, she had forgotten to maintain herself. She had regained composure again. 'I didn't get your name.' Celestine fought off a wry grin and settled with a smile.

'It's Celestine.' He said.

'Nice to meet you, Celestine. I'm Temina.' She said.

'I know.'

Celestine left, forgetting his coat by the door.

16 PROCHNOST

Staphros was not one to dawdle. His conversation with Lion inspired him to act, an impulse that he had quelled for months on end. Every morning, he ran to Zorrodon and it was the same thing. The streets had the same paving, the walls were still tall, and the people never could rest. To an onlooker, everything seemed normal. It only took for someone not to look, but to pay attention. It was just shy of five months ago that Staphros began to purchase the Hondos journal from Lion and his men. He read their news each week and witnessed the narrative decline into darker and darker scenarios. This week's edition was the darkest of them all. Staphros read it as he walked. The words of a pained mother who had lost her son. Framed and convicted for rape by the government handing out the charges. The trajectory was falling long before Staphros noticed. With each story, he was filled with anger towards the authority that overlooked the white city. Ironically, he felt too small to make a difference.

Staphros passed the threshold into the city, which was littered with the culture and beauty that was boasted of all over the world. The people walked slower on this side of the wall and their smiles were not forced. They dressed in clean and fine clothing. Men strolled hand in hand with their wives and would pause to observe landmarks. He had been there before, but it wasn't until now that he understood the vast difference between the city and the village. Nothing but white stone separated the two areas, but they were worlds apart. Although it was better in the city than the desolate village on the other side, it was not thriving as much as it appeared to be. There was an intense show, a pantomime to play for the visitors and tourists. Zorrodon had to be cultured. They had to embody the finer things in life. With the added pressure of maintaining that image, their taxes were still high. They had the means to pay, but it was a struggle. The people who were beginning to look like they were struggling, were promptly moved from city to village. Walking the streets, Staphros could see through the façade to see a lost individual who didn't even know who they were themselves. They lived the lie forced upon them by governmental expectation, now they couldn't discern the truth for themselves. If they could not be honest with themselves, they surely wouldn't give Staphros a straight answer. Staphros didn't need to ask them anything to know that already. Honesty came at a too higher price.

The only place where Staphros felt he could surely find not only honest, but good information was in a pub. There was only one pub in the city that would be certain to be genuine. The King's Hideaway.

The King's Hideaway was King Kastielle's favourite place in Zorrodon. It was said that a big reason why Kastielle retained his bond with Angloina was because of this pub. Before his death, it had come to pass that Kastielle anticipated his demise more than people thought. He had left an undisclosed amount of wealth to the owner of the establishment, his friend with no name. The owner did have a name and it was common knowledge amongst the locals too. His relationship with Kastielle was built upon surpassing that moment where it would be polite to ask someone's name. It became anecdotal and Kastielle would laugh as he would tell his friends that he had known this barkeep for years and to this day hadn't learned his name. There was a bond formed between the two based on that simple and idiotic fact. The owner didn't want nor expect anything when the king passed, but Kastielle left him a sizable wealth which allowed him the privilege to stay in the fine city of Zorrodon without kowtowing to the whims of the government.

Staphros frequented the King's Hideaway when he was in the city for a spell. He would have a drink, or five, just to wet his beak. He liked the place, not just because of its ties with the fallen King Kastielle, but it suited him. Aside from the low lighting, subdued atmosphere, and sparse clientele, Staphros could always appreciate one thing The King's Hideaway had above all else, a high ceiling.

The pub was a quaint little building located in a more derelict area of the district. It had no sign outside, no banner, and no indication it was anything other than a standard building or a wall. It was somewhere that you would have to know how to find it, to find it, and that was how the owner liked it. No stragglers were stumbling in here. It was known as The King's Hideaway by design. King Kastielle would take his friends, associates and members of his council and drink the day away. Inexplicable things happened when Kastielle visited the pub. Kastielle would enter the pub and not appear to leave, however, days later there would be word from Anara that the King had been home for days still. Those stories combined with the unexplained wealth of the owner, caused the majority of Zorrodon to mark the Hideaway as a cursed building. Even though they didn't rightly know where it was. Staphros, on the other hand, didn't care for those things.

He was outside the thick wooden door, lowering his head as he walked in. He stood tall, looking up at the ceiling. He had always wondered why the ceiling was so high. Were King Kastielle's knights and champions that tall, or was the ceiling to accommodate the king's penchant for climbing things? Nevertheless, it was to Staphros's benefit. Like always, the pub was dark and quiet, and it had a good selection of ales and wines. Behind the bar stood the owner/barkeep he knew well. They spoke often, and they always got along, but unlike King Kastille, Staphros learned his name, Elias Belle.

He approached the bar whilst Elias polished a glass. This was one of the few places Staphros felt like he fit in. The bar was cornered by four stone columns, and stone carvings of King Kastielle's life rested above on a pyramid-shaped roof. The bar was in the centre of the room busy with tables and stages. The interior was designed with great detail. The walls of white stone and golden trim. Tapestries of the divines hung about the room and the tables had iron legs and solid tops. Staphros slapped down several silver pieces on the wooden counter.

'I'll take three big ones.' he said to Elias. He rummaged through his pouch for his money before Elias extended a staying hand.

'Looks like you had a bad day there. It's on the house.' He said pouring the first stein of frothy ale, one-litre capacity. The thick clay clicked against the table as Elias placed it down and slid it over to Staphros. Remnants of the erupting frothy head leaked over the lip of the mug, abseiling down to escape foreshadowing its eventual fate along Staphros's chin. Staphros looked up shocked at the kindness, he was a regular yes, but times in Zorrodon were not regular and kindness was a rarity.

'Thank you, sir.' He said, lifting the mug to his lips and taking a hearty gulp.

Elias waved it off. The head clung to Staphros's beard leaving white flecks of ale suds on the ends of his moustache. Then they soaked in to darken and saturate the sun-blushed fibres into a winter hue.

'Are you sure you can afford this? I can pay, I know times are hard.' Staphros took another sip of his ale. Elias nodded glumly before he looked back up with a smile.

'Don't worry about me, I'm sorted. The people out there, they need your worry and your prayers.' Elias pointed with the already tilted mug towards to the door, before placing it, now full, on the bar top.

'How bad is it out there?' Asked Staphros.

'Since Magnus became Mayor, really bad. I saw this coming since emancipation.' Said Elias.

'The emancipation?'

'Yeah, the vote for the people of Zorrodon to separate themselves from King's Anglonian rule. Zorrodon is a self-contained state. After the Anglonian Civil War, Zorrodon was the only place in the country that was still making money. King Peter IV was still pouring all the treasury funds into the invasion of Anara. Guess when you betray the most powerful man in the world you have to make sure he's dead, right? When Zorrodon got tired of paying for the war, the vote came about.'

'So, you voted for this? To be independent.' Asked Staphros.

'Neither I nor my father did. My family came from Alfheim in Nordic-Deutschland, who have a very similar system of government. A pearl of wisdom was passed down the generations that I believe to this day...' Said Elias topping the head on the final ale. 'Politicians lie.'

'I'll drink to that.' Said Staphros, draining his first mug and starting on his second. Elias slid the mug over to Staphros who immediately returned it. 'You deserve this as much as I. Come, drink with me.'

Elias shook his head and pushed it back. 'No, no, you asked for three ales, you drink three ales. But, I think I might just have a drink with you.' Elias got himself a very short glass and ported himself a Baltic-Root strongwine.

They raised their glasses in a common cause but for vastly different reasons, but too many to tell.

'So, what can you tell me about this Magnus?' Asked Staphros.

'I don't know much about him; word is that he's associated with some very bad people'

'How bad, like the thieves that are running the traveller's tax scam at the gate?'

'Not even close. Traveller's tax is the least of our problem, yes people like that somehow have free reign, but it's the people collecting the real tax Zorrodon must worry about.'

'And why's that?'

'Because taxes rise every day. As soon as the people have the means to pay, they ask for more. It's even worse on the other side of that wall, people are dying over there. They work non-stop and still their children starve. They live in the filth of the animals they sell because they cannot afford to stop and clean it.'

'Dying? Really? Why just not pay, take a stand or leave?' Said Staphros in disbelief. Elias finished his drink and quickly poured another.

'You need money to leave, to uproot your life and move away. I think that is the main reason why the tax keeps raising. If the people save enough to leave, there will be nobody left. The government cannot afford that, not when they have two million slaves working tirelessly to line their pockets.'

'How are you getting on?' Asked Staphros with newfound familiarity.

'I'm okay.'

'Have you ever thought of leaving?'

'I have, but I never would.' Said Elias looking around.

'Why not?'

'This tavern has been open for generations. My great grandfather opened it over a hundred years ago, and it has stayed in my family. Centuries of memories live within these walls.' Said Elias. He felt deep emotion, as memories of his late father streamed through his mind. He gulped down his second drink and poured another.

'But, what about the time when things are no longer okay? Won't you wish that you left when you could have?'

'It's like I said. It's the people out there that need your worry and your prayer.' Said Elias once again pointing out the door. 'Don't worry about me. I just wish there was more I could do.'

'There may be.' Said Staphros. 'I am the manager of Sakura Farm. We are known for taking in the wayward and disillusioned. Now I cannot take in an entire city, but if you see a particularly troubling case tell them to wait at Zorrodon's docks two hours before dawn, I will take them.' Said Staphros. Elias's eyes filled with tears. In these most irregular times, kindness was a rarity. This giant was kind, kinder than anybody really should be. Elias had heard of the famous, Sakura Farm, and had met Talion himself, although very young when he did. Talion's reputation for kindness spread to his associates and Elias now saw it was no myth. He grabbed Staphros's massive hand with both of his.

'Thank you.' He said bowing his head to rest on their grip.

'I do have a favour to ask in return.' Said Staphros, finishing his final ale.

'Anything.'

'A young man was arrested a few weeks ago, his crime was severe but unfounded. His name is Kojo and he has been in prison for a few days now.'

'Aah, I know of him. He was arrested for assaulting a prostitute. He was found guilty days ago apparently, but I haven't heard anything about it since.'

'Please, find out what you can about what happened to him. I would be in your debt.' Asked Staphros.

Elias nodded.

'Once you learn something, please relay that to Lion on the docks. You know of him?'

Elias nodded again.

'Thank you.' Said Staphros standing up. 'I guess that I should be taking my leave. Talion will be worried.' He shook Elias' hand.

Elias poured two small mug of the Baltic Root Starch Strongwine.

'One for the road?'

'Alright. One for the road.'

They smiled at one another and clicked their glasses, in common cause and common motive.

'Prochnost!' Said Staphros in his mother tongue.

'Prochnost.' Elias replied. His Deutsch heritage afforded him comprehension of the word. It meant strength, something Zorrodon sorely needed.

17 SHOWTIME

Celestine reminisced about his exchange with Temina earlier that day so much, that everything else passed him by in a haze. He didn't remember meeting back up with Talion, waiting for Finn and Staphros by the carriage or even going home. The only thing he remembered was the way she looked at him and how it made him feel. He missed Luke at dinner, as Luke opted to work through the evening. A joker and a slacker, he was, but he was serious about some things, and he knew missing the fight tomorrow was not an option. Luke worked the fields, shepherded the animals and took on extra kitchen duty. He needed to go tomorrow. Celestine did see him in passing when he rushed to Staphros's side to barter some arrangement to allow him to leave. A way into dinner time, it was clear that Staphros was having fun making Luke work for something for once in his life.

Celestine did not dine with the others that night. He and Finn had retreated to the cottage as he was still not allowed indulgent meals. So, while the fine people of the Big House stuffed themselves with bread, beer, and buttery beef, which would make a man sluggish even on the best of days, Celestine and Finn dined on corn and cauliflower. Although Celestine was not fighting, he wanted to show solidarity and support. Talion spoke of many times where doing such a small thing would mean the difference between winning and losing a battle. Most of all, they knew within themselves they would be fighting together tomorrow.

Vida- Hostil- 15- 1827

Finn had his head down as the muffled roar of the crowd shook the stone ceiling above him. Zorrodon had put together quite the show on short notice. The preliminary fights were assembled quickly, prisoners versus slaves both fighting for freedom. Several contests passed by each one bloodier than the last. The ten thousand strong assembly had their appetites wet. The sweet sight of blood on sand and staining steel blades caused a frenzy. Finn could hear it all, but he was not nervous, he was calm.

The underground cellar held all the fighters for the day's events. It was lit by wall-mounted torches and was made almost exclusively of sandstone. The cellar had an open design where all the fighters for the events would wait to fight or get medical treatment after. Finn was afforded a private chamber to get ready. He could hear the groans of agony on the other side of the thick wooden door that separated them. What haunted him the most was that it was the winners that were in agony; the losers were dead, forgotten failures flung into a shallow unmarked grave. The same fate that Finn's father was subjected to. He pondered that, lingered on the thought but still he was calm. He had an image of a lake in his head. The body of water was still. It didn't ripple in the breeze or splash in the rain it was always calm, always peaceful. Finn imagined that lake every time before a fight. He fixated on the image until he entered the image until he became the lake. His deep breaths flowed like the water, his chest bobbing up and down like a boat on its surface.

Celestine wrapped Finn's hands in bandages and fastened his leather wrist guards. Finn had been so focussed he had not noticed that Talion had smuggled a box into the room with him. Talion waited with a smile, as he saw the same look on Finn's face that he had seen within himself. He was ready, a wolf before the hunt. He saw a lot of himself in him, an assuredness that was often mistaken for arrogance. Sometimes it was the other way around too. There was not long until the fight and Celestine had just finished putting on the wrist guards. It was time to present Finn with the contents of the box.

Talion approached proudly with it in front of him. This was a substantial moment for him. For his lands and his wealth, he had his inheritors in Staphros and Celestine, but he didn't want the life of a champion for his boys. He saw his heir apparent in Finn, a champion to carry on his legacy. Divine Purpose, Nature's Will. Talion lifted the lid of the white box to reveal rich black leather. Finn snapped from his focus and gazed at the fine garment he was presented with.

'This was the leather armour I defended King Kastielle for many many years. This is the finest light armour man can make. Pick it up.' Said Talion. Finn gingerly reached into the box and slipped his hands underneath the garment like he was cradling the head of a baby. It was light to lift but it had the weight of history on it. Finn's arms trembled bearing it.

'I... I don't know what to say.' Finn stammered.

'No need. I had the seamstresses fit it to your measurements and make some adjustments to fit your unique combat style.' Said Talion. Slowly, Finn unfolded it sleeves first and lifted it by the shoulders to let it fall in front of him. The chest plate had removed the Neriah Emblem, the emblem for King Kastielle, and now appeared a clover and the embossed Celtish characters spelling, Eireann.

'Thank you.' Said Finn gasping back his pride. He stood and shook Talion's hand.

'You're a real champion now. You wear that proudly. It doesn't matter what happens, you are forever a champion.' Said Talion.

Finn nodded.

There was no turning back; it was real. This would be the revenge that would be spoken of for decades to come, the revenge that would redeem his country. The time was near. He put on his new armour. It was thick leather that felt hard to penetrate but supple like cotton. Celestine tightened the sides to be snug on his waist, where Finn wrapped his father's first championship belt. Finn put on his knee braces and shin pads himself and he was done. Finn moved around, kicking high and punching fast. He felt lighter in it and somehow stronger, something that he would put to the test in due time.

Talion nodded in approval. 'It looks good on you, young man.'

Finn blushed and bowed in gratitude. 'This is the finest gift I could have received. You honour me, sir.'

'Well then, do me the honour of doing your best out there.' Talion extended his hand in which Finn grabbed gratefully with both of his.

'Yes, sir.' He said. With that, they shook hands, and their backroom deal was agreed. Finn would fight to his last breath. With one more reason to win, he felt stronger. Talion left the room to get to the stands to watch the fight. Staphros followed.

'Good luck comrade.' He said to Finn, then he looked back to Celestine who shot him a wink.

The door closed.

'Tell me, Finn.' Said Celestine, 'How do you feel about facing an opponent you don't know?' He placed his hand in his shoulder. Finn turned with fire in his eyes.

'Bring on anybody they want. It will end the same way. Me bringing their head to King Loch back home, placing it on his table where we will proceed to drink strongwine and discuss our business.' He said.

'Do you feel ready?' Said Celestine. He knew he was, but it was always a good technique to eliminate doubts.

'Mate I've been ready since those bastards killed me Daa. This is the real revenge.' Said Finn assured.

'Well let's get you loosened up.' Celestine passed him a wooden sword. They stood in fighting stances across from each other and sparred with only minutes before showtime.

127

Celestine had left the room just before the bout. Finn's body was warm, his joints were limber and the Celtish champion was ready to redeem his country. He shook the rusty iron bars of the cellar and the heavily armoured guard opened up. The dank atmosphere and litter of broken bloodied criminals made this underground staging area look like a prison. Maybe it was and nobody knew until it was too late. The Zorrodon arena greatly dwarfed the proving grounds in Elgin. The large field was covered in sand and the ashy yellow stone that formed the building structure harkened to the Grand Colosseum in the capital of Roma. Talion was not too far from the cellar exit. He was positioned at the front and had a great view from a private stand. Talion avoided his past, but sometimes it had its perks. Celestine stepped out into the hot midday summer sun, shielding his eyes to find his uncle. The sheer numbers of the attendees distracted him for a moment. The capacity of the arena was ten thousand and it looked like it was holding twelve-thousand, barely. People piled upon one and other squeezing into what finite space they could. Finn II, as he was called still in the south, was a celebrity either in fame or infamy, but a champion always captivated the minds of the proletariat. No real champion was born of fine stock. No real champion was the beneficiary of a sheltered upbringing protected from the hardships of real life. Champions happened when the hardest of times bore down on the hardest of people. The pressure made diamonds, at least in the case of champions. There was no denying that Finn was one exceptional diamond.

Celestine's gaze dropped from the wild crowd and he spotted his uncle, with a sea of borderline rabid fans between them. He fought through each person, knowing he must get to his seat before the main event began, otherwise there was no chance. The stands behind were waiting to rush down the stairs to get a better position. They sat in the false civility, but they would discard it once the brutality began. He pushed past person to person pleading "Excuse me" as he passed each one until he encountered a white ribbon and a white dress. He slowed as he passed her, and she looked up and glowed with happiness. Caught in the shuffle, Temina was struggling with her basket of roses to make it through the crowd. Celestine stopped and came back to her.

'Imagine seeing you here!' He said, shouting over the crowd. He did imagine it too, but for it to happen was pretty ridiculous.

'What are you doing here?' Asked Temina.

'I'm here with my uncle. We have a stand over there.' He leaned close and his breath dampened her neck. It tickled and she quite liked it. 'How about you? I didn't peg you one for gratuitous violence.'

Temina shrugged. 'I'm full of surprises. Besides, I thought I could sell some of my flowers to throw at the winner.'

'How's that been?'

'I have underestimated how many people would be here. I can barely move never mind sell.' Said Temina wrestling with the onslaught of elbows and wayward limbs accosting her.

'Yeah, It's a little cramped.' He had forgotten about the crowd in speaking with Temina. 'I know! Come join me and my uncle in our stand. There's plenty of room.' He suggested. Temina tussled with the idea.

'I wouldn't want to impose. Besides, I still have flowers to sell.' She said.

'I'll buy them, all of them. Please, just sit with us it's no imposition at all.' Celestine insisted.

She nodded with a cheeky smirk that grew into a playful smile that crinkled the bridge of her nose. 'Okay.'

Celestine grabbed her hand and guided her through the crowd. The sea of people still refused to part, even though Celestine and Temina fought to get through. There was a dull flicker in Celestine's fingers, which generated a strange heat that tingled rather than burnt. It was too faint to notice and the people blocked the fleeting light at his fingertips.

When Celestine entered the stand with Temina in hand, Talion noticed immediately. Celestine noticed when Talion noticed and let go instantly. Talion stood on good manners, as did Staphros. Temina's jaw dropped at the size of the giant.

'Don't worry, I get that a lot.' Said Staphros.

'Oh sorry, I didn't mean to stare.' Said Temina quickly.

'It's nothing. Will you be joining us?' Asked Staphros.

'If that's okay. It's so cramped out there.'

Talion stood and took her hand. 'Don't be so silly. Come, sit.' He guided her to a spare seat. Celestine quickly followed and occupied the seat beside her. He didn't want to take any risks of Talion or Staphros taking the seat. She looked over at him and leaned to whisper.

'You didn't say your uncle was Talion Schultz unless it's the tall fellow?' she said. Celestine laughed.

'If I'm honest I never think it's that big a deal. I see him much differently than how everyone else sees him.' Said Celestine.

Temina nodded. 'My mother used to speak of him a lot. He used to come and buy flowers from her when she was alive.'

Celestine placed his hand on hers instinctively. 'I sorry to hear she passed.'

Temina nodded and her lips grew tight. The pain was fresh. Her eyes were wide and filled with stalled tears. Temina had lost her mother in the winter. Celestine could feel her pain, somehow, he knew it and felt it.

'Oh I'm sorry, sometimes I forget about it and it comes back unannounced.' She said trying to bring humour to it. She dabbed away at her eyes with her upturned thumb and examined the teardrops like rain on leaves.

Celestine stared, feeling a similar pain internally, but externally he could not help but appreciate her haunting vulnerability, and how beautiful it was. It was like a rich red rose surrounded by snow, sad and hauntingly beautiful.

He was staring.

'What?' Asked Temina blinking her now dried eyes.

'Oh, nothing.' Said Celestine adjusting in his seat to face ahead to the arena. Temina followed suit. Talion cleared his throat catching Celestine's attention. He gestured towards Temina with his eyes, almost making a pantomime out of it. Celestine took a deep breath and hardened his resolve.

'Temina.' He said.

Temina turned to face him.

'I... I... I think that yo...' The crowd burst in a deafening stone shaking frenzy as Finn emerged from the cellar below. He had a steel short-sword and shield. Both Celestine and Temina directed their attention towards the arena floor as Finn awaited his opponent.

The roar of the crowd, the smell of blood and sand in the air, his armour carrying the weight of history and his sword holding the weight of destiny. This was the moment that every moment in his life was leading to. Finn was armed with Divine Purpose and Nature's Will.

Showtime.

18 HISTORY AND DESTINY

Magnus perched himself upon high and separate from the masses. He was stood on the edge of his balcony, his white robe draped over his dark skin. He stared intensely at Finn, who paid him no mind nor respect. He was too busy staring at the opposite side of the proving ground in anticipation for his opponent. Magnus watched on standing as close to the edge of his perch as possible. The imposter champion fixed to be exposed. Magnus could not deny that the people loved Finn, even though he was not their countryman. Finn represented an antithesis of Magnus, and anything different to Magnus was a welcome change.

Luke had managed to gain leave to attend the event, but not to share the private stand with Talion, because he would irritate Staphros too much. He began chanting, urging the people around him to follow along.

'Oh Finn the Brave! Finlay! Finlay! Finlay! Oh, Finn the Brave! Finlay! Finlay! Finlay!' harkening back to a song to honour his father, Luke introduced the chorus to the south. One by one the chorus spread until almost every erratic voice harmonised in unison to appreciate the lone combatant on the sands of battle. The capacity crowd repeated the chorus over and over without signs of relenting. It encouraged Finn but his focus was still on the task at hand.

Magnus's eyes were wide at the defiance his citizens had shown him. He raised his hand to quiet them, but it made them louder. Magnus had Finn wait in the cellar longer than he needed, now it was him that had to wait for Finn's people, the common people, to allow him to commence affairs.

Magnus boiled with rage, and not even the screeching hot sun in the clear blue sky could match the intensity of his ire. The people took back the power he had stripped from them, even for a second. Hope was what fueled them and Finn represented that hope to them. Finn was their chosen champion to fight for their cause and he had them in his hands. For a second Magnus's wide eyes saw Lion and the power that he possessed on the docks. Adan Thiago's words rang in his head, telling him to get things under control. No matter what, Finn had to die today. One of them would be by day's end either way.

Finn took a moment to look at the crowd in its entirety then stepped forward towards Magnus, kissed both of his hands and spread his arms wide like a magician at the end of their trick. It was a gesture that suggested he had already won. He turned his palms upright in a staying gesture and the crowd quieted. He had a special kind of charisma. The power was in his hands.

There was a sudden blare of trumpets and the large wooden gates opened. In walked all five champions of the Anglo-Latin Commonwealth, Orion of Olympia, Marcel of Roma, Axrotalus of Francais, Hernan of Espania, and Drake of King's Anglonia. They walked together with a swagger that fraternities had. They lingered on every step, and their free arm swung nonchalantly while the other clinched an onyx steel great sword, the finest metal that could craft a blade. Their armour matched. As if rehearsed, they stopped as one and placed the tip of their swords into the sand, resting both hands at the hilt. Finn thought it was cute. Although he was expecting just one man to stand before him, he stood his ground, but his frustration crept up within him. His opponent stood before him, but he still had no clue who it was.

'You look confused!' Magnus gloated from upon high.

Finn looked up, snapping his neck to arch towards the mayor. His body was so tense that no other part moved.

'You see, I had such a hard time choosing your opponent and you seemed like such a formidable champion, I thought you deserved a challenge. The challenge being…' Magnus licked his lips as the smirk grew on his face. 'Run the gauntlet!' he said, mocking Finn's earlier gesture and spreading his arms wide. The crowd booed at the injustice. Like every other time hope reared its head in Zorrodon, Magnus was there to quash it. The gauntlet meant that Finn would have to face every one of the champions in front of him, one at a time.

Finn nodded accepting the challenge. 'I'll beat these pansies one by one, but I'm taking every head home with me!' He shouted, then he spread his arms and screamed to the crowd. 'Eireann!!' The spectators followed his lead and screamed his father's battle cry with him. He was the general and his supporters were his army. He slammed his sword against his shield to begin a percussive rhythm, a fraction slower than a heartbeat. The people clapped following him. Finn lifted his shield and pointed the tip of his sword at his opponents.

Drake of Anglonia stepped forward, as did Finn.

They met in the middle.

Silence.

Drake swung the sword sideways, and Finn blocked with his shield. The soles of Finn's leather boots skidded on the hot sand from the impact. Now on a stronger footing, Finn resisted the force of Drake's sword. They were entwined in a power struggle. Drake, the son of an aristocrat and trained by the finest swordsmen in the country, was going red with the strain against a poor Celtish peasant. His and Finn's eyes met, and they understood that they were matched in strength. Finn smirked.

'I wanted to face you.' He said. 'This little battle between us decides the real Champion of Anglonia don't you think?'

'You are no champion.' Drake said through stuttered breaths.

They broke from their struggle, both taking steps back. Drake took a second to recover but Finn went straight back on the attack throwing his shield at the Champion of Anglonia. Drake parried with the broad side of his sword. The shield landed on the sand and Finn jumped through the air spinning and chopping down and the lower part of Drake's blade. The impact disarmed him and forced a retreat, Finn pursued rolling through the attack and picking his shield back up. He jumped raising the shield above his head. The hard wood smacked against Drake's chin staggering him. Finn followed up by leaping forward into a front kick to Drake's chest dropping him to the ground.

The kick damaged more his ego than anything else, but Finn had floored him in quick time. It was unnerving. The crowd was cheering, chanting his name, his family name.

'Eireann! Eireann! Eireann!' Getting louder with each repetition. Drake struggled to his feet and Finn dropped his sword and shield. Drake was unarmed and he didn't want any excuses. He raised his fists.

'If you're man enough.' He said. Drake lunged forward swinging two haymakers, hoping to hit him with at least a trailing impact of his plate armour. Finn leant backwards and then ducked to evade the flurry. Drake's arm trailed and Finn slammed his fist into the armour plate. A loud gong wobbled from the plated steel and everyone's eyes were drawn to the sound, including Drake's. Finn was conditioned to be like a piece of iron, so hitting the armour didn't hurt him. He whipped a powerful uppercut into Drake's nose. Drake staggered holding the spewing crushed cartilage, but Finn did not relent, charging again. He led with a barrage of fast punches finishing with a powerful overhand left to Drake's right eye. Then another one, and another one, he kept on punching until Drake fell to the ground cowering. Finn mounted him and rained down precise blows. He had won the fight, now it was time for his revenge. One hit, three hits, seven hits later the spectators got louder with each blow. Drake tried to cover up but Finn was too precise. The end was near.

A sudden knee speared itself into the side of Finn's head. Finn was knocked off of Drake and rolled across the ground lying face first in the sand. For a second he lost consciousness, but he recovered quickly. The crowd went silent as Finn lay still for a second to regain his bearings until he stirred to stand again. Staphros and Celestine rushed to the edge of their stand.

'Come on Finn!' They shouted trembling in anger and adrenaline. Finn's vision cleared before the ringing in his ears stopped. Orion was helping Drake to his feet. Drake was once a relatively handsome man, but his broken nose and lacerated face changed things. He had bad intentions to get back at Finn for what he had done. Orion patted Drake on the back and the two commenced in surrounding the Celtish Champion. Finn backed to his sword and shield and picked them up quickly. He pointed it at Magnus.

'What the fook is this?' Said Finn, 'I've run gauntlets before, it's one at a time.'

Magnus licked his lips again. 'Not in Zorrodon it's not. In Zorrodon I make the rules.' He said.

'Shut the fook up about you make the rules. What kind of shit is this!?'

'It's a lesson, Mr Eireann. A lesson I personally had to teach your father.' Said Magnus.

'You killed my Da?' Said Finn. Magnus turned away. 'Did you kill my Da?! You filthy stinking rat!' Magnus had retired to his seat, comfortable in his victory. Finn's greatest strength was his focus, and he had broken it, now there was no more fun to be had.

Staphros shook frozen in his position at the edge of Talion's private stand. This was the first time he had seen the famed Mayor of Zorrodon, but this was not the first time that he had seen Magnus. His memory was faded, maybe with age or other means, but he could not pinpoint exactly where he saw Magnus. He just knew his face. Celestine sensed the distress in Staphros and comforted him, placing his hand on the giant.

'Finn will be fine. We've trained him through worse.' He said.

Staphros nodded. 'I know. I just get really into these things. You know that. I'm fine.' He said. He gestured to Temina. 'Go back to your guest. You don't want to be rude.' He ruffled Celestine's hair and tapped him on the bottom.

'Staph I already look enough like a child next to you without you doing that.' Said Celestine before heading back to Temina. Staphros remembered what Talion said about the power Magnus wielded, and that brought clarity to where he noticed his face from. It wasn't fully clear, he just knew that it was connected to the name Thiago. Thiago was a name that he knew very well, in association with his father. He was fixated on Magnus until the battle began again.

Orion dashed at Finn first from behind, just catching him as he dodged a fraction too late. The tough leather armour managed to withstand. Finn quickly parried a follow-up attack from Drake and kicked backwards into Orion's chest. He whirled his shield in a primal launch into Drake's throat sending him to one knee. Devoid of all technique he bared his sword like a wild man and turned to Orion. He screamed as he charged slashing at him from his waist. Orion dodged and countered as best he could, but Finn still had the wherewithal to slam the counters away with wild swings of his sword. Orion was being pushed back and in an unexpected move, he blocked a swing with his arm, as his armour would protect him, and slammed his shoulder into Finn. Before he could follow up, Finn span into a backslash which caught Orion's face. He had drawn blood again. This time, he wasn't emboldened by the sight, this time he was driven further into his rage.

In the private stand, Celestine returned to Temina as instructed. Their eyes were glued to the action. Talion was proud of the development that Finn had shown from the day he arrived on the farm to now. His movement was slick and there was no wasted motion. He clapped every time each crunching blow was landed, but he remained quiet. He didn't believe in shouting or yelling while spectating a fight. The combatants were artists, but their canvass was their body and their life, they could ill afford distractions. Staphros was of another school of thought, he leapt to his feet shaking his fist. He supported Finn with as much of his being as he could muster. Only if it were Celestine out there would he be able to give more support. He shook fist as he shouted instructions knowing that the critique would be ignored, not on purpose of course. Celestine sat and watched like his uncle, cheering and clapping. He was calm and very confident that Finn would prevail no matter what, even in the circumstance of a gauntlet. Finn was good.

Temina jumped in her seat and grabbed hold of Celestine's hand tight when Drake clattered Finn off guard. Her fingers threaded perfectly with his and a cold shiver slithered down his spine. He stared at the hand on top of his and then to her face. The moment had passed and Finn had gained the advantage again. Temina's hand did not move. Her large eyes fixed upon his, making it known that she acknowledged her hand was holding his and it was not her intent to let go. This was no game, she was making a move. It was now in Celestine's hands, literally.

He turned his hand to go palm to palm with hers and now their fingers clasped, and they spent the remainder of the fight holding hands. Celestine tried to hide it, but his heart was beating quicker and harder than ever. He had been in hour-long training sessions, sparring Staphros and had a slower heart rate. He knew that she could feel it because he could feel hers and it

135

was the same. Celestine could feel Temina flinch with every hit or throw. Finn was starting to dominate. He was utilising the swordplay and agility techniques he learnt in training. Small tells in Temina's fingers revealed to Celestine how she felt, she wanted Finn to win almost as much as he did. He could not think of anything else but her, he was missing the fight. He was focussed on Temina, she was fixated on the fight, and not him, concentrating in bated breath. Forgivably, she was not used to combat as he was. Celestine knew Finn had this under control.

Celestine felt the heat in his fingers again, not enough to burn but it tingled. A tidal wave of emotions crashed on him and he didn't know where it was coming from. The sensation came from everywhere and nowhere, fear, anger, betrayal, hope, revenge, love, everything. Finn fought harder urging the rising tide of hope to crash onto the sands. He remembered as a child a similar feeling, an empathic connection with the people around him, he still had it vaguely but it was so weak that he long doubted if it was real. This was too similar to be anything else though. The tingle in his fingers intensified.

Finn downed Drake and stalked Orion. Celestine felt that rage within him, he knew that this could be his downfall. Everybody's feelings were all over the place, the rules were changed, but Finn still dominated. It only fuelled his anger.

He threw his sword. The force of the throw carried the blade to penetrate through Orion's armour and lodge itself into his shoulder. The spectators cheered and Orion screamed in pain falling to his knees. He approached him unarmed, fear and pain were etched on Orion's face. His breathing was shallow, and he pleaded with Finn with his eyes. Finn checked back and Drake was still struggling to breathe but he was getting up. He parried an attack he saw in his periphery and slammed a punch into Marcel's face then he flipped Hernan onto his back. He tried to follow up with a punch, but he was ensnared in a chokehold from behind by the self-proclaimed giant, Axrotalus.

As the feelings intensified, not only within himself but everyone around him the heat rose to a burn in Celestine's entire palm. Temina turned to him.

'Are you okay?' She asked. Celestine now clutching his head said.

'I'm fine, just the sun in my eyes.' Temina noticed a slight glare coming from his eyes. They were a richer blue, but he closed them from a squint quickly after. Finn panicked as did everybody else, the panic was powerful because it was fuelled by the panic of others. Celestine was inundated with the panic of over ten thousand people. Through that sea of panic though, he could see a beacon of truth. He didn't know what had happened to him, but he believed it real. He believed the truth before him.

Magnus did not care to pretend for his citizens that this was going to be a contest, this was an assassination and a message to Celtish Anglonia.

Adan Thiago's plan to assassinate Finn to incite another civil war that would line his pockets was a resounding success. He looked to Finn, who squirmed in the chokehold and everything quieted in and out of his mind. He could feel Finn struggling for air. The way he looked to anyone or anything to get him out of this struggle. Each of his opponents drew small blades from their waists and approached him. Finn looked to the sky hopelessly, praying to a Spiritual Court he hadn't ever believed in.

'Help me.'

Celestine collapsed out of his chair onto the ground.

Celestine did not experience unconsciousness. Things didn't fade to black as he collapsed onto the floor. He was acutely aware that he was not in the same circumstance that he was in previously, and aware to the same degree that he lay convulsing on the floor. What was clear and apparent in front of him was the all-white void with a wooden door in front of him. The door stretched higher than the white wall of Zorrodon and was wider than Celestine's wingspan ten times over. The wood on the door was chipped worn and damaged. Areas were darkening as if damp. Celestine was intrigued reaching out in front of him to feel it, compelled by the urge to open it. He was motivated by his curiosity, but more so by his instincts. Something told him that what was behind the door was important and a necessity. He would need it eventually. It called to him silent and undeniable, unavoidable and inevitable.

'Help me.' Finn's voice echoed like a long-gone spirit trying to communicate with the living. Celestine turned around to see Finn on the floor. He rushed to his side helping him to his feet immediately. As soon as he came to, Finn grabbed for his throat and gasped for air only to realise that it was unnecessary. The two then saw Finn's predicament materialise beside them. He was still fighting, still ensnared in the chokehold. Axrotalus was making sure to keep Finn conscious. The other four champions were approaching with their knives drawn.

'The fook is goin on?' Finn spat in confusion. He fretted in a panic running his fingers through his hair. 'Am I dead?'

'No, you're not dead. I don't think you are.' Said Celestine. 'I think you're having an out of body experience.'

'Okay, why are you here then?' Asked Finn.

'I guess I'm having one too.' Celestine shrugged alongside his explanation. It did not add to its credibility.

'So, is this going on now?' Said Finn pointing to the image of him being choked and approached.

Celestine nodded. 'Probably.'

'This is it then. I'm shit out of luck.' The door banged hard and loudly.

Celestine trembled but Finn was unfazed like he couldn't hear, see, or feel it.

Celestine was struck with a sudden inexplicable idea. He stretched out his hand and offered it to Finn.

'What's this a goodbye?' Asked Finn.

'No, it's a lifeline.' Said Celestine. 'I can't explain it, but something in me is saying that if you take my hand and say yes I'll be able to help you.' Celestine looked back to the large damaged wooden door. Finn could not see it.

'How?' he asked incredulously.

'I can fight for you.'

'Fight for me? Even if that was possible, what could that do? It's an impossible situation.'

Celestine grabbed Finn's hand.

'What are you doing?' Finn initially tried to wrestle his hand away.

'That situation is not impossible for me. I have mastered the technique to get out of the chokehold.'

'What about the four other men?'

'I'll explain later! We have about five seconds to decide whether you want to live! Do you?'

'Do I what?'

'Do you want to live?!' Celestine screamed. Finn closed his eyes and gripped tight.

'YES!'

Finn kicked off Axrotalus's knee and hoisted his feet high into the air. He had made this attempt to escape before and failed. The other four champions stopped and watched in amusement, but this time was different. Finn arched his right leg and swung it backwards. His heel clattered against Axrotalus's testicles denting the steel armour in to apply constant pressure to the sensitive organs. The big man let go and Finn scrambled out dodging wayward disbelieving blows. Silence once more.

Finn caught his breath, then shrill, radical screams rang from every voice in the arena, all except Talion's stand who were tending to Celestine. The four champions turned in disbelief staring at Finn who remained on one knee smirking.

'A kick to the balls was your great technique?' Said Finn to Celestine. Finn was no longer in control of his body, in saying yes he diverted control to Celestine and now Celestine was fighting for him.

'You didn't think of it did you?' Said Celestine standing up. As he was in Finn's body, what Celestine said could be heard by everyone else and it confused his opponents. Finn no longer had a Celtish accent, and he was talking to himself presumably.

'It's dirty.' Finn protested.

'It's Krav Maga! Besides these idiots were literally going to kill you five on one.' Said Celestine pointing his sword towards the utterly perplexed men before him.

'Oi! Who are you calling an idiot?' Drake said, his nose was blocked with clotted blood so his tone did not come off as authoritative as he would have liked.

'Shhh… I'm talking.' Celestine lifted a staying finger.

'Fair. You don't actually plan to take all of these men on? Escaping a chokehold okay, but taking on five championship calibre opponents at once. No way.' Said Finn. Celestine took his fighting stance and the champions started to surround him. Axrotalus was still on the floor writhing in pain and wrestling the indented armour from his testicles.

'I know a lot of martial arts.' Said Celestine confidently.

'Knowing a lot of martial arts isn't going to help us.'

'When I say know a lot…' Said Celestine. There was that confidence again, only this time Finn felt it. 'I really mean, I've mastered them all!' Celestine charged after Drake.

Finn appeared a lot faster to Drake. He was already halfway to him before he could react, three quarters before anybody else could. Drake panicked and cowered, he had had enough of a beating from Finn, before he displayed superhuman speed and resilience. Celestine slapped Drake's staying hand away and fired ten rapid punches to the side of his armour. That was where the front and back plates met and exposed vulnerability. His punches dented the weaker edges of the plates causing them to dig into his sides. Celestine followed with a hook to his jaw and a palm strike to Drake's already broken nose. Drake gasped through his mouth and attempted though his nose, coughing up a clot of blood and spitting it on the ground. Celestine listened out and heard Drake blow his nose. He spread a wide grin on Finn's face.

As if he was dancing, the span behind Drake's concussed standing body dodging a blow that clattered against Drake's plate steel chest armour. Celestine poked his head to see that Hernan was the attacker. He jumped into a knee to the small of Drakes back jerking him to fall forward. Hernan caught Drake on his shoulder; Celestine pulled him back leaping to slam the butt of his sword into his cheekbone. Drake now faced the other way and looked to fall face first. Celestine grabbed his collar quickly to keep him upright, before following up with several undamaging but precise slices to Hernan's armour. The final hit knocked the sword from his hand. The strings that connected the armour snapped and the plates fell like low hanging fruit.

Orion and Marcel launched a simultaneous lateral attack. Celestine thrust two extruded knuckled into Hernan's sternum. He could feel his chest give into the impact, and he was done for the day.

He jumped back and sprang again into a spinning back kick, launching a dazed Drake into an oncoming Orion. Drake landed on top of Orion unconscious. Celestine sprang a third time into a jumping knee to Marcel's chin. Marcel dropped to the ground and Celestine followed quickly. He grabbed his arm and yanked hard, first with the left then with the right, dislocating them both. Marcel was finished too now.

Orion struggled to his feet reaching for his sword, Celestine kicked it away. He put up Finn's fists.

'C'mon!' he said. Orion stood and faced off against, what he presumed to be Finn. He was relatively fresh, unlike Drake, who's eyes swelled shut after blowing his broken nose, rookie mistake. Orion was surprised to see such diverse styles come from Finn, but he attributed that to adrenaline. He just needed to weather the storm. Orion raised his closed armoured fists.

Celestine faked low and Orion blocked. Then with pinpoint accuracy and breakneck speed, he slammed a spinning heel kick to Orion's jaw. He broke it on impact. Celestine immediately dropped to a knee.

'Oh my! Are you okay?' he said. He kicked too hard.

Orion didn't respond.

'Get up you daft bastard!' Finn screamed from inside.

'Sorry,' Said Celestine quickly standing back up. Then he slyly looked down and whispered. 'Sorry again.' He turned around and watched the crowd roar his name, or at least Finn's name. Way up in the stands, he spotted Luke in disbelief. Luke had recognised the way he fought but he couldn't put his finger on what yet. He sat confused. The people beside him, pulled him to his feet to lead the chorus again.

'Oh Finn the Brave! Finlay! Finlay! Finlay! Oh, Finn the Brave! Finlay! Finlay! Finlay!' Luke sang but did not take his eyes off of Finn.

In Talion's stand, Celestine's body was still convulsing violently. Staphros had to hold down his body with all his might. Temina still had her hand clasped with his.

'Is he going to be okay?!' She kissed his hand. 'Please be okay!' Her lips felt the heat emanating from his skin that her hand did not notice.

Talion nodded kneeling by his side in great pain 'He'll be fine dear, it's a seizure. He used to have when he was younger. It probably all this excitement.' Celestine's veins started glowing through his skin.

'Miss, I'd suggest letting go of his hand now. He's going to squeeze hard.' Said Staphros. Temina looked to Talion who nodded to concur. Still, she hesitated but the heat intensified while the glow brightened, and it burnt her. She yelped and let go immediately. Celestine's body arched its convulsing neck forward straining, eyes fully rolled to the back of his head.

'Help me! Help me! Help Me!' He screamed over and over.

'Help him please!' Temina screamed.

'Trust me we are!' Said Staphros now putting all of his weight on top of Celestine to keep him down. He looked to Talion grimly. 'It's never been this bad.'

Temina went back to Celestine and stroked his hair trying her best to comfort him as he screamed for help, or what they thought was a cry for help.

'It's going to be okay. Your uncle and the giant man are going to help you.' She said.

'Tilt his head back.' Said Talion.

'What?' Temina paused.

'Tilt his head back!' Talion repeated shouting. Talion pulled a vial from his bag and Temina did what she was told.

'What is that?' She asked.

'It's a tranquiliser.'

Celestine was still in control of Finn's body appreciating the crowd around him, but at the height of their adulation, they stopped suddenly. Axrotalus has managed to get back to his feet after stripping the indented armour from his groin. The pain was still great, but the anger was greater. Stripped of all protective clothing wearing only brown hide trunks, he lumbered towards Finn. Celestine poised himself to fight again until he heard a whisper.

'It's a tranquiliser.' He heard it faintly in his mind.

'Uncle Talion?' He said. He could taste it, the familiar taste that put him to sleep. 'Wait! No!'

Finn collapsed to the ground motionless and unconscious.

Axrotalus stopped in his tracks, wary of a trick. He studied Finn, but no conscious man would lay that still. The crowd was quiet. So quiet that every ear could hear the click of Magnus's footsteps on his balcony. He leaned over and observed the scene. Four of his champions lay completely decimated by one man, but one remained. This was a loss by any stretch of the imagination, but, there was still an opportunity to rectify the failure.

'Axrotalus!' Magnus boomed. Now the crowd hung on each of his words. A captive audience was all he wanted, for what was to come. 'As the last man standing, I could proclaim you the winner, but your victory would be granted and some could contest, not earned.'

Staphros looked to listen to Magnus now Celestine was calming. Magnus pointed at Finn's motionless body.

'Kill this man and assure your victory yourself. Leave no doubt!' he shouted. Axrotalus lifted his onyx steel greatsword and kicked Finn over to face upwards. He was completely motionless; his arms were splayed out wide and his breathing was shallow. He lifted the sword blade pointing down. Staphros screamed and leapt over the stand.

'NO!' he landed on the sand catching Axrotalus's attention. That was a real giant. He paused. Magnus looked on as the crowd silenced. This invader was strangely familiar. A man like Staphros was not the type to be just familiar, you either knew him or you didn't. There wasn't much room for confusion. He thought Finn the only threat that was in the arena and he was down, but Magnus was realising that there were many more threats that he could not anticipate in this capacity crowd. He didn't know what or who this giant was, but he felt like he should. He could be dangerous. Before he could speak, the realisation that this giant had inspired something, was catastrophically apparent.

19 ESCAPE

The sand danced and the ground rumbled at the stampede that was headed towards the sands. Axrotalus was stuck to his position like a man treading water that spotted a wave that would end him. Suddenly, feet slapped against the sands like the pattering of rain. Soon the entire the fighting area was full. Axrotalus pivoted in his position, now looking for an escape route. The wave was rising and getting ever closer. To his dismay, it was on course to crash on all sides. The spectators surrounded him, they cursed and spat at him as they wildly bore down on his position.

A tsunami crashed down as one by one each of the twelve thousand strong clambered to exact their retribution and violent justice. When the sands filled, the riot spread to the stands. Décor was ripped down. Anything that could be broken was broken. They directed their verbal hatred to Magnus in a slew of foul words and gestures at him. They were animals cornered until they needed to strike. The swarm charged and crashed into Axrotalus, who had no other option but to cover up. Whoever could reach, volleyed limbs towards the Francais champion until he crumbled to his knees, then they kicked and stamped on whatever they could. Mostly it was his head and body, but some especially malicious amongst them slammed their heels into his testicles. They were rabid with bloodlust. They even fought each other to get at him. The beating continued until he struggled no more. As the beating proceeded some picked Finn up and smuggled him to Staphros amidst the chaos. They cared for the Celtish champion and understood that he was a man marked for death. Magnus had shown his hand and failed. He wanted Finn dead and the citizens of Zorrodon would not allow it; it was the first thing he was denied by his people.

'Here you go, mate!' One of them said. Staphros swallowed and watched

143

the events unfold in disbelief. Was this the people of Zorrodon standing up? Was this what Lion had in mind? They attacked the downed champions and broke the wooden barriers. Projectiles soared towards the balcony upon high where Magnus was. They threw whatever they could find, broken rocks, pieces of wood, or clay, even weapons. When the throwing began, that was when the danger had become indiscriminate and now fellow spectators were getting injured. This had gone beyond an act of defiance, but a release of anger. Everything was a target. Staphros looked on powerless and Magnus had to retreat to safety with a company of guards protecting him. He hissed in anger as he scurried back into the confines of parliament, like the rat his contemporaries called him.

Staphros slung Finn on his shoulders and ran against the crowd to the exit. There was nothing he could do for these people. He heard his name shouted through the roars of the rioters. He turned to see Luke mid-way down the stairs but away from the crowd. Staphros gestured, signalling Luke to get Talion and meet him outside. Something told Luke that he needed to get to Celestine, he knew something was wrong, but he didn't know why. It was like Celestine was telling him himself. Luke reached the stand and saw Celestine unconscious on the floor. Talion and Temina were kneeling beside him.

'Is he alright?' Said Luke rushing to his side too.

Talion nodded. 'We need to get him out of here though.'

'Good idea, I think I saw Staph get out with Finn a second ago.' Said Luke. 'I'm Luke by the way.' He said offering his hand to Temina.

'Temina.' She said confused.

'I'm Celestine's best mate. You wouldn't happen to be a florist would y...'

'Luke! Now!' Talion shouted sternly.

'Oh, aye yeah.' Luke hoisted Celestine onto his shoulders. Talion prepared himself for a struggle as he pulled back the curtain to his stand. When the curtain was drawn back, the path was emptying. It looked like the riot in the area was spilling onto the streets. Talion led the way as Luke and Temina followed. They reached the exit to the city and Luke looked back to survey the damage. He suddenly had the feeling he was being watched. He spotted a hooded figure standing at the very top of the spectators seating area staring directly at him. They did not break their stare as Luke studied them. They had very dark skin and enchanting green eyes that almost shone through the shadows of their cloak. He lingered on trying to unlock the puzzle of who this interested party was, and more importantly what they wanted. Talion and Temina made it outside and noticed Luke lagged way behind. Talion yelled for him.

'Luke!' Luke immediately snapped out of his trance state and ambled on after them. The cloaked figure did not move.

Staphros was waiting with the carriage outside. He had loaded Finn already on the cot along the back of the cabin. He was sat on the driving seat, reigns in hand, hurrying the three along. Temina reached the carriage first. She sprinted ahead and opened the door for Talion. Talion hobbled on with the aid of his walking stick. Luke was the last to get on. He was not the strongest of men and Celestine weighed a lot more than he looked. He was dense. He struggled, sweating and huffing. He put Celestine on the bench where Temina sat, resting his head on her lap.

'Precious cargo. You look after him now.' Said Luke charmingly.

She nodded.

'Luke, come on!' Shouted Staphros. Luke scurried to the top of the carriage and sat next to the giant. Staphros hurried the horses along and the made their way through the city.

'Sorry I was late Staph, but…' Said Luke.

'Don't worry, you did a good job getting everybody out safe.' Staphros interrupted him. Luke was so confused that he stopped for a second and stared at Staphros. Staphros had very seldom praised Luke or said anything nice about him the entire time he knew him. It took him a moment to process what had been said.

'Errr, thanks.' Said Luke.

Staphros said nothing. He looked straight ahead with a stone-cold expression on his face.

'Are you okay?' Luke asked.

'Yes.' Said Staphros. A surge of guardsmen, clad in their newly minted golden armour, rushed from all directions towards the arena. Staphros pulled on the reins to halt the horses in their tracks as they passed. They all sprinted with anxiety about them. Some anxious through fear and others through excitement. They ran almost not even acknowledging the carriage in their way. Once the crowd had passed, Staphros urged the horses on a lot quicker this time. Things were going to get very serious very soon.

Talion and Temina both had the feeling they should hide when the rush of guards ran past the carriage. They stayed down until Staphros mushed the horses to move forward. When the two finally sat back up, Temina took a little longer. Her gaze remained where her face was, by Celestine's. He looked so peaceful in comparison to how he was in the arena. This close and with uninhibited time to look at him, he was beautiful. He had features of true, unusual beauty. His chin was rounded and his jaw slender and strong. His eyes were big behind the closed eyelids. His lips were thin and slightly opened as he slept, but they were curved into a contented smile. Temina hoped it was because she was near. The memory of her picking the flowers entered her mind. She picked the best ones she could find in the garden, carefully

145

selecting them like they were for the king himself.

Talion watched her as time was no concept to her; it appeared to have stopped in her mind. She was trapped in looking at him, a prison she did not want to be released from. Not back into the grim reality that life was now. It had been some minutes before she realised that time had not stopped. It was when the faintest sound could be heard from the distance. From the direction of the arena, they could hear screams. The faintness in volume made it all the more haunting; it sounded like the voices of the dead crying. Maybe that was true. The likelihood of that reality made Temina's blood run cold and a film of sweat colder than chilled metal covered her skin. She looked up to see Talion watching her.

'This must be hard.' He said.

'Don't worry, I'm a tough girl.' She said. Another distant scream caught her ear. 'What do you think that is?' She knew the answer but to deny it for a moment longer was a break from it. Talion waited to answer. He had come across questions like that before and asked a few himself in his time. These questions were not designed to be answered quickly.

'I think the guards have made it to the arena.' Talion had tried to put it in as gentle a way as possible.

Temina nodded accepting it as it was.

'If you would like you can accompany us to our farm. I believe the city and the village may be dangerous places to be, at least for tonight.' Said Talion.

'Oh, thank you for the offer, but I'll be better served at home. I specialise in medical botany, and a lot of the sick and injured come to my store for medicine. I expect many visits in the next few days if not tonight.' She said.

'Very noble. I knew of your expertise as a florist, but I see that spreads to all plant life.'

Temina nodded. 'My mother worshipped Mother Nature. She said by studying plants and understanding them, it was the best way to communicate with her.'

Talion smiled and nodded. 'I knew your mother well. She was a fine woman.'

'Thank you. That means a lot coming from you.'

The ride was quiet for a time. More distance was put between the arena and the carriage. Staphros weaved through the streets and side alleys as best he could. He wanted to get through unnoticed, especially as Finn was in the back. The route Staphros was taking was making the trip take longer than usual.

Temina stroked Celestine's head as he slept through the journey. Talion recognised the look in her eyes, it was unmistakable even from his perspective. It was the way Sakura looked at him on the plains of, Wildberry, in Anara sat in the shade of a willow. He'd pretend to nap on her lap, and she would pretend to read but she stroked his hair as Temina did Celestine. It didn't matter when, but every time he opened his eyes, she was looking down at him with that very same look. Her book was always on the same page as when she began.

'Tell me, young lady, do you love him?' Asked Talion. Temina stroked Celestine's hair a few seconds longer before the words soaked in and made meaning. She looked up.

'I don't follow.' Said Temina.

Talion laughed. 'You cannot hide from old eyes. The way you look at him betrays what your mouth says.' He said. 'You know what I mean.' Temina blushed and looked away.

'I only learnt his name a day ago. It would be silly to say I loved a man I know so little.' She said. Then, she looked at him again and her gaze lingered, and she couldn't help it. Watching him sleep seemed like something she could do forever, and she would be content.

'Who said love was sensible?' Asked Talion.

'You're right but...' Temina paused. 'He was buying flowers for someone when we met. He didn't say who, but he looked excited. The look of a man buying flowers for a woman he had feelings for. I couldn't get in-between that no matter what I feel.'

'So you think the flowers were for someone else?' Asked Talion. He got quiet towards the end of the sentence and Temina didn't quite hear. He surmised that it was not his place to intervene.

'What did you say?' Asked Temina.

Talion shook his head. 'It was nothing. You were saying?' Temina's eyes welled and she couldn't say why. For the same lack of reason, she couldn't look at Celestine without it getting worse and just crying.

'It doesn't matter how I feel. If I love him or not, I couldn't and shouldn't do anything about it.'

'And why's that?'

'Because stealing a man like him would make me the worst thief I know of.' She said. 'I can't do that.' She wiped a tear that had escaped from the corner of her eye. She was surprised to see, Talion chuckling. Talion thought it not his place, but he couldn't help but see the humour in it. The two of them were so modest that they refused to see the clear signs before them.

'Something the matter?' She asked trying to muster sternness but failing miserably.

Talion shook his head still chuckling. 'Just an old saying. *"Wisdom is wasted on the old and youth is wasted on the young."*'

Staphros was focussed on the road. He was trancelike mulling over and over his role in the chaos that had transpired. Luke was still getting over Staphros praising him. They spotted the wall coming in close. This was the signal that they were about the leave the city. They had been riding for nearly an hour. Zorrodon was not only the largest city in Anglonia in reputation but in size as well. As they approached the gate Staphros slowed the horses to a stop as he was met by a squad of men in a uniform he had not seen before. Talion peered out of the window.

'Is that the guards?' Asked Talion. Temina peered out of the window careful not to trouble Celestine.

'Worse, the army.' She said. Quickly, Talion drew a black curtain to the cot. He used it on most occasions when he wanted to sleep on long trips, but it worked well as a false back from time to time. The perfect hiding place for wanted champions.

The lieutenant in the squad stepped forward and examined Staphros at the helm of the carriage. He was properly dressed in his green and white uniform. His black hair slicked back to shining.

'Where are you coming from?' Asked The Lieutenant.

'We're fleeing the riots in the arena. I assume that is why you are here.' Said Staphros.

The lieutenant nodded. 'That's right, but it's just routine checks, nothing to be alarmed about. I will need to check the cabin though.'

'Wait, how come?' Asked Luke.

'Because there's a fugitive that has yet to be apprehended. The Celtish Champion Finn Eireann, you may know him as Finn II of Collister Mere. You wouldn't happen to know where he might be?' Asked The Lieutenant.

'Well… Oh, ah, ha, ha…' Luke stammered as Staphros gripped his thigh hard. His large paw wrapped around most of it.

Staphros shook his head. The lieutenant signalled and his men opened the carriage door. They found Talion apologetically bowing his head and gesturing to an unconscious Celestine.

'Please excuse us. My nephew was stricken with a wayward rock and has been knocked unconscious since. We must get him medical attention.' He said. Talion was mostly recognisable to the general public but to the military contingent, he was unmistakable. The other soldiers stepped off and huddled with their lieutenant. The lieutenant approached the open cabin door.

'Alright sir, I would say the nearest doctor would be about five minutes back where you came. An Olympic fella called Ulysses will take care of your nephew. The village also does have doctors, but they tend to be a little overwhelmed with emergencies and head trauma is best to be seen quickly.' He said.

Talion bowed in gratitude. 'I appreciate the advice, but I have a doctor on my farm estate who can take a look at him.'

148

'Farm? Unfortunately, the whole city is on lockdown, that includes the village and the docks. There is a perimeter that has been set up, nobody leaves until Finn is found.' Said The Lieutenant.

'Can't there be an exception?' Said Talion trying to leverage his status amongst the military.

'Sorry, the order comes from a ranking way above mine. Otherwise, I'd have let you go. There are some nice places you can stay in the city and some not so nice ones in the village. But the village is easier on the pocket.' The lieutenant backed off as if to end the conversation there. Talion grabbed his hand and shook it. He let go and the squadron saluted Talion. Talion saluted back and they marched back their position.

The cabin rocked as Staphros climbed off the driver's seat, as Temina emerged from the cabin. Luke stood next to Staphros folding his arms.

'What do we do now big man?' He asked familiarly slapping him on the arm. Staphros looked down and shook his head, forbidding Luke to ever think about doing that again.

'There's no way we can bring Finn to an inn. If he gets recognised, he will die. Magnus has made that abundantly clear.' Said Talion.

'We can't get him out with the city locked down. We're stuck.' Said Staphros. Luke looked up and nodded before looking back to Talion. He was once again, a spectator.

'He can stay with me.' Said Temina. 'I doubt that I'll be the first place they'll look. That will give me ample time to hide him.'

'We can't put you in that kind of danger young lady.' Talion objected against it, either through chivalrous instinct or ignorance to the level of Temina's experience and capability.

'When Finn wakes up, he could surely protect me. He just took down five champions.'

'On the contrary, he just fought five champions; he is in no condition to fight again. We couldn't put you in that position.'

'Sir, there is no other option.' Staphros intervened. Talion struggled with the idea, but no alternatives came. He had to concede.

'Okay fine! Luke, you go with Temina to help her get Finn in her house. Wait until sundown. I'll meet you at the wall's gate then to take you where Staphros and I find to stay.'

Luke nodded and climbed onto the carriage driver's seat. 'Staph.' He said. 'Look after him, would you. Please.'

Staphros nodded sincerely. Staphros hoisted Celestine on his shoulders and Luke went along with Temina through the wall.

20 MOONLIGHT

Staphros was unsure of whether he was being looked for. He had been the catalyst that incited the chaos when he jumped over the threshold and landed on the sands. For a moment, he and Magnus locked eyes. Magnus appeared to recognise him, or by any merit, note his appearance as one to remember. That sub-second exchange replayed in Staphros's mind as he carried Celestine through the alleyways of Zorrodon's cobbled city. He was paranoid at every pause someone took to look at him. A man his size could not go unnoticed for long. It was risky harbouring Finn in an inn for the night, but he too was an attraction to danger. Once the details of the riot's cause were divulged to the military, it was likely they would be looking for an eight-foot-tall giant. Unfortunately, Staphros was the only one he could think of in the area. Otherwise, he could have plausible deniability. "It wasn't me" didn't work for him in most cases.

These minor but very important details informed his decision of lodgings for the night. They had some distance between them and the arena, but the rioters could be heard, nonetheless. The combined sound of screams of both frustration and fear showed the difference between those who encountered the military and those who did not. Staphros decided to lead Talion to the aptly named King's Hideaway.

He didn't even know if it was an inn, but it was somewhere he could trust. The kind of pressure that this city was under did not breed trustworthy people and, Elias of the King's Hideaway, was trustworthy.

Elias rested on his bar top resting his cheek against his fist completely bored out of his mind. His business served its clients on a sort of invite-only basis. Most of the people in Zorrodon didn't know where the King's Hideaway was, despite its famed historical significance. This meant that most days were quiet, but the flow was always steady, a couple of people every few hours or so. It kept the day interesting. Elias had been staring at a pillar that had been chipped a few months ago. He had been looking to fix it and now he was simply looking at it. His mouth slipped open and he wasn't quite sure if he was asleep. Maybe this was the state somebody was in when they were going to sleep, but not quite arrived at sleep, he thought. The large entrance door cracked open as Staphros burst through them shoulder first; he had no time to be polite. Elias broke from his daydream, jumping out of his skin. His legs turned to jelly for a moment but hadn't yet recaptured the stability they once had.

'What are you doing here man!?' Said Elias startled.

'We need a place to stay.' Said Staphros. Elias looked at the young man in Staphros's arms and shook his head. Unconscious people usually brought trouble with them.

'Sorry, but this isn't an inn.' Said Elias. 'Is he drunk or something?' He asked referring to Celestine.

Staphros shook his head gravely. The open door let the in the sounds of screams and carnage from the streets that they had done such a good job of shielding. It was surreal to hear. This event, this level of violence, that was so audibly vivid, was inevitable. It was surreal because now that it was here, it seemed to have come too soon, like a birthday or turn of a new year. Elias didn't need to know the details, whatever happened to this young man had something to do with what was going on outside.

He nodded.

'Do you have guest rooms any bunks? I'll just need one, two at the most. I can sleep on the floor.'

'I have a guest room but...' Elias stopped his thought.

'But what?'

'It's the King's room.' Said Elias somewhat embarrassed.

'The King's room? As in Kastielle?' Said Staphros knowing the establishment's association with long-gone king. Bewildered and somewhat annoyed, Staphros shot a look of disbelief at Elias. Elias struggled with the logic too, but he had clear rules.

'Yes, and my father told me nobody was allowed in there. I'm not allowed in there.' He said. Talion poked his head out to get Elias's attention. Elias didn't even notice that someone else came in with the giant.

'Sorry to interject, would I be allowed in there?' He asked. 'I know I'm not Kastielle, but he and I were close friends. I'm...'

'Talion Schultz, the last champion of Anara. As I live and breathe!' Elias kneeled to honour him forgetting he was behind the bar. It just looked like he was hiding from where Staphros and Talion.

'Can we get the room or not?' Said Staphros.

'Yes of course.' Said Elias still kneeling. He jumped back to his feet and pointed to the back of the room. 'It's just up the stairs and the door right in front. It's not locked.' Staphros walked to the stairs.

'I'll take three beers while you're at it.'

'It'll cost you this time.' Elias shouted after him. Staphros stopped at the foot of the stairs.

'Talion pay the man my week's wages. I'm going need to drink quite a lot to forget this whole day.' He said.

He carried Celestine up the stairs.

Sundown.

Mayor Magnus took his normal position at his window, watching over his city. This time, he did not feel as assured as he had in the past. His hands were clasped behind his back tightly trying to grip onto what they could as the city was slipped through their fingers. The sun tinted red and it sank away into the orange quicksand clouds. He didn't blink, wishing not to miss a moment of what went on in the city. He had been there for hours, watching his private army quell the chaos. The military was instructed to use extreme force if necessary. He watched the droves of people, bloodied and beaten, be marched into the prisons. He stewed with squinted eyes and a clenched jaw; it was not satisfactory. Images of the people cursing at him and hurling things at him. He was supposed to be the authority; he was supposed to be the power. He slammed the windowpane and glared at the people. He relished in the sound of their screams bathing in their pain, but still, it was not enough. They deserved to suffer more. They embarrassed him. Furthermore, their efforts caused him to fail in his duty to Adan Thiago. His life would be forfeit if he could not rectify this quickly. The walls were closing in.

Three sharp bangs on the door. Magnus returned his hands behind his back.

'Come in.' Said Magnus not averting his gaze from the window view. The office door clicked open and creaked carefully while three men entered, two members of the private army, Captain Murphy and Commander Simmonds, and Magnus's advisor Vice Mayor Fredrickson.

'Good evening sir. We have managed to apprehend multiple rioters and the streets have calmed significantly. The city is still however on lockdown, including the village.' Said General Simmonds.

'I saw.' Said Magnus calmly. 'How many?' Simmonds looked to Captain Murphy.

'I believe the last count was three-hundred-twenty sir, but as you can see our men are still apprehending them.' Said Murphy.

'Good work.' Said Fredrickson.

'I don't think it's your place to say, what is a good job and what isn't.' Said Magnus, still statuesque starting from the window. 'As the man in charge of the guards and our city police, explain to me how this happened in MY city.'

'Sir I…'

'Those vermin even had the audacity to attack me, throwing things like the apes they are.' Finally, Magnus turned around. 'You let that happen Fredrickson.' He pointed angrily at his deputy.

'Sir…' Fredrickson tried. Magnus interrupted by grabbing his throat.

'No more excuses! If it wasn't for those men, who knows what would have happened, on your watch!' Fredrickson was starting to feel scared he knew the pressure was mounting on all sides. He lowered his head like a beaten dog, as the others looked away like bystanders to a crime they wanted no part of.

'I'm sorry sir.' He said.

'I don't want sorry. I want to know what you're going to do about it. How do I know this will not happen again?' Magnus walked right up to Fredrickson and pointed back to the window. 'More importantly, how will they know not to do it again.' Magnus loomed over his secondary, his eyes were pure white but filled with brilliant anger. He looked down on Fredrickson; he had the look of a man that had killed before, a man that had killed before and liked it. 'What will you do to prove that to me?' Magnus let the words hang for a while.

Nobody talked in the room. His words repeated silently in everyone's mind. Fredrickson felt true fear in that moment. Without a word, Fredrickson left the room determined to right his wrongs.

Magnus returned to the window ignoring the other two in the room.

'Sir.' Said Simmonds.

'That will be all. You've done this city a great service.' Said Magnus.

'What of the prisoners?'

'You caught them in the act of committing a crime, vandalism, assault, assaulting government officials, disturbing the peace, need I go on? It appears to me that there is no need for a trial.' Magnus's eyes turned manic and wide. 'Execute them all.'

'But there are children down there.' Murphy spoke out. Simmonds corrected him with a glare. Magnus neither noticed nor cared.

'Fredrickson has his preventative measures, and I have mine. Relay that order to the warden. We're done here.' Said Magnus.

'As you wish sir.'

Despite his carefree exterior, Luke was very concerned. Seeing Celestine in that state brought back long-forgotten memories. He saw Celestine in the hard times as a boy, being drafted to hold his friend's tongue so he wouldn't swallow it and choke. The howls that separated clouds. He remembered thinking that a little boy shouldn't be able to make such a noise, but he witnessed it, he felt it. The authoritative bellows by a titanic teenage Staphros. It was times like that which made him grow up fearing his command and direction. The image of Celestine's glowing pure white eyes burnt itself onto his retinas, so that even the comfort of closed eyes could not spare his disquiet mind. The image was disturbing, his infant friend convulsing and the genuine concern that he could see him die in his arms.

He was in the sitting room of Temina's home itching to go. Temina's home was behind the botany shop and garden. It was a quaint little cottage made of sturdy wood and painted daisy pollen yellow. Finn was resting in Temina's spare bedroom where she tended to his injuries. There weren't many signs of damage, but there were signs of severe strain. Temina could not figure out why, nor would she be likely to find the true answer as to what caused the damage. Finn's body was a vessel for two sets of consciousness, two souls. Combined with the exertion which forced him beyond his capabilities to reach Celestine's far superior threshold, it caused his muscles to burn and tear. He was fatigued beyond belief. Luke stared out of the window watching the sun linger in the sky, his knee bouncing anxiously. He felt trapped waiting for the sunset to be his que to meet Talion and see if his friend was okay. He was happy to help Temina, but he felt his work was done here, now all he had to do was wait. Waiting was an agony he struggled to bear. Temina placed a cup and saucer beside him on the wooden table. She had brewed some tea that he had never seen before.

'Oh, thanks.' Said Luke. He looked down and examined the rich purple liquid in the mug before the smell hit him. It was floral, but unlike the obtuse sweet smell of juniper strongwine. This was peaceful and subtle, it slowed things down and warmed the nerves to calm.

'Thought you could use one.' Said Temina. She sat beside him and sighed slumping forward like a chain attached to the world itself was wrapped around her neck. 'What a day.'

'Aye, you got that right.' Said Luke sipping the tea. He wasn't one for tea, but he didn't want to be rude. He would have gone for something stronger, but he didn't trust himself once he got started. Stress usually made him drink. Surprisingly, this tea wasn't half bad, and it calmed him more effectively than ale could have.

Temina nodded and watched to see his reaction to the tea. It was positive which she appreciated.

'What is this? Not like any tea I've ever had, other than it's hot.' Said Luke.

'It's Lavender and Camomile. It's a botanical remedy for anxiety and stress. I give it to some of the villagers who struggle to cope.'

'Job done. It's helping.' Luke took another sip.

'Glad to hear it.'

'You said that the people were struggling to cope. Is it really that bad? I see what's just gone on and I could feel how much they hate that Magnus guy.'

'I'd be lying if I said it was anything less than unbearable.' She answered, struggling with admitting the problem. Luke didn't believe her fully.

'If it is unbearable, why wouldn't people leave?' he asked.

'Can't afford to leave. It costs money to uproot your life and move. If your money is taken constantly, you'll never leave. Our only option is to pay the tax or die trying.' Said Temina.

'Has anyone yet?' Luke asked. 'You know, died trying?'

Quiet.

Temina leaned forward and poured herself a cup of the tea. She let the aromas slither up her nostrils before taking a sip.

'My mother did.' She said.

Silence.

Even the sounds of forcible apprehensions in the city were drowned out. The silence sounded like a heavy rumble in their ears. Temina took quiet deep breaths, the wound was still rather fresh, but she could ill afford to be distracted. Mourning was not a luxury afforded to the villagers of Zorrodon. She could not give her mother a funeral, she was cremated with a dozen others that died like her. After, her ashes were dumped off of the docks into the shallow sea to be washed out by the tide.

Luke shuffled in his chair as he checked the sun which, had gotten closer to the horizon. Still, it was not yet sundown. He muttered under his breath without knowing.

'So…' Said Temina abruptly. 'How long have you known him then?' she asked.

'Who Celestine?' Luke asked. There may as well have been a tattoo of Celestine's name on his forehead the way he stared out to the street. The city gate wasn't in plain view, but it was only behind a small terrace of houses.

Temina nudged him. 'Come on.'

'I've known Celestine since I was three, so about twenty-two/twenty-three years.' Said Luke like he was asking her.

'Have you been best friends that long?' She asked.

'If I'm honest, I don't remember a time when we weren't best friends. He's the kindest person I know, and I can't think of a time where he's made me think differently. I look up to him in my own silly way.' Luke laughed and sipped his tea again. Temina tried to hide her smile. She took the kind words for Celestine like they were made to her. 'You haven't got any biscuits, have you?' he asked.

Temina shook her head.

'Well that's shite, I'm starving.' He said.

'Any crazy stories about him? Girlfriends?' She asked. She had begun her inquisition to distract Luke from his stress, now she was serving a much more selfish purpose.

Luke shook his head. 'No girlfriends, all the mad stuff we do is usually my idea or my mistake. He's always there to get me out of trouble when I've needed him.' He looked back to the gate. Temina's curiosity was traded for sympathy because it was clear that Luke was struggling, and he didn't like showing it.

'You care about him, don't you?' She asked.

'He's my brother.' He said. 'I remember when we were kids and he got like that, watching Staphros restrain him and him screaming in so much pain. I couldn't understand what he was going through, but it felt like I felt it. And when he finally came to, he didn't remember a thing. It was like it was his illness, but we all suffered the symptoms. It bothers me because he's the strongest guy I know. Don't let the looks fool you, that man is tough.' Luke laughed when he said that. 'To see him weak in that way, to have to carry him after he's carried me for so long. It hurts. You know?' Luke dabbed his thumb under his left eye to catch a tear before it escaped down his cheek. 'I have no idea why I told you all that.' He said clearing his throat.

'Maybe because I was listening?' Said Temina. She got up and lit the candles around the room to add some light. The illumination of the candles enlightened them to the fact it was now sundown and Luke could go to meet Talion. Even on the other side of the wall Luke and Temina could hear the haunting sounds of the rioters being brutally apprehended over the last few hours. The madness had been going on forever, broken glass and screams were the most common of the dead echoes. When the sun went down, it went quiet, near-silent. It was like the cover of darkness had tamed the rabid populous. Little did he and Temina know, there was much more to it than that. Luke made a hasty exit shortly after the quiet fell.

True to his word, Talion was waiting on the other side and Luke pulled him up onto the passenger seat of the carriage before making their way to the King's Hideaway.

Midnight

Magnus was still in his office in the thick of midnight staring out of his window. The moon looked like it was in reaching distance and at the height of the tower, it may just have been. Magnus's face twisted as he cursed every person that lived in the city below him.

He looked to the courtyard below and an assembly was forming and growing by the second. Guards, policemen and soldiers, all heavily armed, formed ranks and formations. Each in the hundreds in number. Once the assembly was formed, they all looked up to Magnus's office and saluted him. The door knocked carefully. Fredrickson shuffled in, partly ashamed for his previous failure but emboldened by his imminent success.

'What's the meaning of this Fredrickson?' Said Magnus intrigued and smirking.

'The only way to train animals is with swift and strict correction.' Said Fredrickson.

'I'm listening.' Magnus had not looked away from the hundreds of men still holding their salute to their mayor.

'I've assembled all of our forces to deliver that correction, swiftly and justly.'

'How?'

'Our men are going to riot as they did. But instead of on the streets, they will invade their homes to take their possessions. I have told them that violence is not permitted...' A sick grin covered his face revealing sharp reptilian teeth. 'Unless necessary.'

'I like it. It harkens back to my time growing up amongst these savages. An eye for an eye.' Magnus stroked his chin ponderously. 'It's their law, tell your men to go enforce it.'

'They are waiting on your signal, Sir. As soon as you return their salute, they will unleash chaos.'

Magnus lifted his hand to his head and held it. He had spent the whole day cursing the city that had bitten him back, now he was smiling as a child did with only joy in his heart. He dropped the hand and the units scattered. Magnus had one more curse to give.

'Time to make the whole world blind.'

21 CELESTINE'S AWAKENING

The tranquilliser had worn off Celestine and he sat up with a great gasp. The room was only lit by the silvery shine of the super-moon in the sky. As his senses switched back on one by one, the agonising sound of Talion's snoring rattled his ears. Talion was laying next to him on the large bed in an unawakenable sleep. Talion was exceptional at sleeping through anything. Celestine surmised that his time as a soldier was likely the cause for it. He had no idea why he was where he was, but he didn't dwell on why very much. He was where he was, and he had to deal with it.

He could only remember parts of what happened that day. The day played out exactly how he expected, the cellar, the arena and even the skulduggery of the corrupt Magnus. Staphros had briefed him on the injustices that he had read about over the time he was away. He did not remember passing out, such was the case for most others who have experienced that. He had been dreaming for so long, some were vivid others were not. There was one involving Finn that seemed so real that he was not confident it was a dream. The only thing that made him believe that it was more dream than reality was that it was impossible. There was no use speculating about it now while sat in a dark room next to his snoring uncle.

The last thing he remembered was holding Temina's hand, his heart beating fast, and his head beginning to ache.

'Temina!' He said. He instantly regretted it and covered his mouth not wanting to wake Talion. Talion proved once more that he was a difficult man to wake up. Celestine's outburst only caused Talion to snore louder.

Celestine believed that it took him a while to decide to go and find Temina. There were bad omens about the whole thing. He was not staying in his own bed, he was sharing a bed with Talion, it was the middle of the night, and the inner city of Zorrodon, the largest city in the western world, was dead silent. Those were bad omens and Celestine believed that he pondered those omens deeply. In actual fact, Celestine sat for a total of five seconds before getting up to go and see Temina. He slung his legs off the bed and bunched his clothes before sneaking out of the room. He had no idea where he was. This place didn't look like an inn, it looked like somebody's home. The hall was quiet with a long rug that ran the length of it. Talion's snoring echoed from the closed door behind him. There were stairs in front of him, he looked left and right and the snuck down them.

He had made it to the bottom soundlessly, then pulled on his clothes at the foot of the stairs and snuck across the bar floor precisely and quietly. In the dark, it made it difficult to navigate this foreign environment. Celestine pawed his way into the void bumping into chairs and tables on his way. His escapade that began so very quietly was now becoming a clumsy affair. He tripped unexpectedly but managed to save the fall. When he looked back, the moonlight revealed the bar with feet sticking out from under the flappy door. Celestine went to look, there he found Luke sleeping with a strongwine bottle in his hand.

'Luke.' Whispered Celestine. Luke didn't stir. His head was turned to the side and he was smacking his lips dribbling into the pool on the floor that stuck to his scraggly hair. Celestine kicked his foot and Luke snorted like a pig loud enough to wake himself up.

'Wha...who's that!' Said Luke scrambling to his knees. He looked up and rubbed his eyes clear. He still had hold of the bottle of strongwine which dripped onto the floor. The bottle was practically empty.

'It's me, Luke.' Whispered Celestine again. Celestine grabbed his hand and pulled him to his feet. 'Fancy going for a walk.' Luke hugged Celestine tight burying his face in his shoulder.

'Celestine! I'm so glad you're alright!' he said.

'Shhh... Of course I am. Just needed a nap is all.' Celestine tried to make light of it, but he had seen it too many times as a child. He had scared them again. The way Luke was reacting, he knew that he took it very hard.

'I told you, you should have told Talion I was your supervisor. I should have been there for you.'

'Firstly, Staphros may have murdered you by the end of the fight. Besides you're there for me quite enough. I mean you've been hugging me an exceptionally long time for a starter.' Said Celestine unsure of what to do with his hands.

'So what.' Said Luke, still hugging.

'Don't you think it's getting a bit weird?'

Luke shook his head and said softly. 'Only if you get a stiffy.'

Celestine suddenly shoved him away and the two laughed. 'Stay away from me you pervert.' Celestine pointed a warning finger at his friend before dusting himself off. 'Anyway, about that walk.' He continued.

'It's the middle of the night, besides I need to catch you up on a few things before we go anywhere.' Said Luke,

'Do it on the way. Come on.' Said Celestine walking to the door. Luke grabbed his arm.

'This is serious mate. You had a seizure a bloody bad one, even if was safe out there you're not in any condition to go out.' He said.

'What do you mean safe?' Asked Celestine.

'There was a riot at the end of Finn's fight and Mayor Magnus called in the army in. The streets aren't safe. Talion think's Magnus will be on the warpath.'

'It doesn't sound like he's on the warpath. Nothing's going to happen tonight just come with me and we'll be back before Talion or Staph notice.' Celestine was pleading with him. Many a time the roles were reversed and Luke was the one urging Celestine into a bad idea. Neither of them knew how to handle the opposite position. Celestine was not convincing and Luke was not stern. The difference was the equity that Celestine had built over the time in either, rectifying or partaking in Luke's recklessness.

'You're going to see Temina aren't you?'

'Only if you go with me, I won't go if you don't.' Celestine was seeing reason, but his heart still held hope that Luke would help him. He felt fine, but he felt fine in the arena. He thought he passed out, but to know that he had a seizure scared him, but Temina was worth it. Although he was scared, he wanted to see her still and the look on his face was one of determination.

'You really like her, don't you?' Said Luke.

'I think I love her, and I think she likes me too, but I have to be sure. I have a bouquet in the carriage I was going to give her after the fight, but I couldn't. I'll know if she likes me when I give them to her.'

'Oh, she likes you.'

'How do you know?' Asked Celestine.

Luke brushed past Celestine and beckoned him to follow. 'I'll explain on the way.' He said.

The moment Celestine was tranquillised, Finn was not subject to the same fate. The tranquilliser had been synthesised specifically for Celestine's body to subdue his rather violent seizures. It was designed to not only bring the mind to sleep but to induce a light coma which lasted roughly twelve hours. When Celestine had fallen into that coma, he still had a grip on Finn's body like how a hand can seize to grip unintentionally. That meant that Finn's body was asleep, but his mind was not. Finn was trapped in a prison of complete darkness, with no form, no concept, nothing. It was like experiencing a cognisant death. There was no white light, no judgment, or forgiveness of sins, no closure. He couldn't move because there was nothing to move. He was trapped outside of existence. When he cried for help, he couldn't hear is own voice or process his thoughts. There was no way for him to know how long he was trapped in that state, all he knew was that he was awake once more and never wished to do that again.

The candle still burnt at this late hour, the warmth of a wooden bedroom lit by yellow flame. In his haze, he saw his family around him. His mother, sisters, and even his father were there. He didn't have the wherewithal to notice the peculiarity of his family's presence, especially his father's. He just knew they were there, watching him. He lay flat on the bed at first, forgetting how to tell his body to move. He had become used to the commands going unheeded. He had no control in the latter half of that fight. He still saw from the same perspective and he could see and hear what was going on, but he could not feel anything. It was like his whole body was numb, but instead of it being motionless it was moving on its own. When things happened, he commanded it to do one thing and something else happened entirely. It was surreal but sobering to see that he was a passenger to his glory. He closed his eyes and exhaled deliberately. No man had ever savoured the act of respiration more than Finn Eireann that night. He wiggled his fingers first, then tried to sit up. Sharp pain in his abdomen slammed him back to the bed. There was immense pressure in his stomach every fibre in his core felt like it was torn, but he embraced the pain. It was the first real thing he felt in a long time. There were times that in the darkness, that he thought he had died in Axrotalus's grasp and the exchange with Celestine was a fever dream, a final gasp at hope before passing away to the afterlife. However, his Celtish spirit did not allow him to think like that and as absurd as it may be, he assured himself that the events unfolded as he thought. Waking up, even in this unfamiliar setting proved that he was right.

Although excruciating, he forced himself to sit up. One by one more muscles cried out in pain. There was an immense strain that his body endured. Compression bandages were wrapped around areas where muscles were torn and bruised his skin purple, black, and yellow. The fresh pain caused the mirage of his family to disappear while convincing him that this was not the afterlife. He was alone now. With a deep breath, he swung his legs off the edge of the bed and managed to stand. This was, at least for the moment, the extent of what he could do for now. He was wearing only a pair of cloth bottoms; somebody had tended to his injuries and undressed him.

He had fought it, but he could not help but feel emasculated. Celtish tradition dictated that one of the greatest taboos a warrior could commit was to have another man fight for them. They were to leave a battle on their power and the only medical attention a warrior was to receive was from a mortician. He had broken all of the taboos in this one day. He came to Zorrodon to prove that he and his family were not frauds and cowards, by the last of his recollection he had done that in the eyes of the public. He realised that it was not them he wanted to convince; it was himself. In that respect, he had failed miserably.

He shuffled out of the room and peered out of the door. The wooden interior stretched out into the main area of the single floor home. Knitted tapestries of vibrant colours draped down the panel mahogany walls. The room was lit by candlelight, most of which was at the foot of a shrine to Mother Nature. Temina was kneeling in front of it, looking up to the heavens as she prayed. She had braided her hair into one stretching plait down to the small of her back. She was also dressed in a modest nightgown of blue linen. He wasn't sure if it was the candlelight or her beauty that made her face glow like that.

'Sorry to interrupt your prayers here, but I have a few questions?' Said Finn, gingerly walking into the sitting room where Temina prayed.

'You startled me.' Said Temina holding her heart. 'Of course, let me get some tea. Please sit.' She got to her feet without finishing her prayer to Mother Nature. A sin she had not committed before in her life until this very moment. She lit the stove and fed it a touch more firewood. Finn watched the curves of her body form against the drape of her gown and slinked deeper into the room. She inspired instinctual feelings in him, and this time his body was reacting. His mind was no longer in a one-way conversation; it was a tandem effort. Whether it was the hours in dark stasis or his damaged pride, it clouded his mind and the need to be validated was taking over.

'You got anything stronger than tea?' Asked Finn. His eyes were fixed upon her but darted about her body.

'Sorry I don't.' She said frantically. Her mother was the consummate hostess and she had inherited that compulsion. 'I do have some bread though now. I baked some just before. All this stress made me fidgety.' Finn sat down on the chair as Temina cut two slices and spread some butter over the top. She handed him the plate and Finn obliged by touching her hand as he took it. Her skin was soft and warm to the touch. He looked at her intensely as her human touch felt like a drug. Temina smiled and turned away. She thought it was strange, but he had been through a lot. She would explain everything once the tea was done. The sight of the bread made him realise how hungry he was. He scoffed the bread in a matter of seconds once Temina's back was turned. Now, she was working at the stove watching her teapot boil over the fire.

'So, I guess I owe you a thank you.' Said Finn struggling out of his chair. Temina turned around and Finn pointed to the bread on the countertop.

'Thanks for what?' She asked.

'Well, I assume it was you that tended to my injuries.' Said Finn walking slowly.

'Oh yeah. It's nothing I help who I can when I can. I'm a doctor.'

'No, I mean it, how could I repay you?' He asked stopping at the counter.

'Really, it's nothing. I meant to say sorry it was a bit ad-hock, but you hadn't sustained many external injuries so I could only add compression where I could. I'm brewing some pain suppression and anti-inflammatory herbs in your tea to help.' She said turning back to the pot.

'Oh, so like medicine?' He started moving past the counter, leaving the bread crusts behind. He was getting used to feeling again, and there was a force that magnetised himself to her. It felt real and his mind and body followed it.

'Sort of, it's herbal remedy but I'm not sure how effective they will be in your case, but it's worth a try.' She was nervous. Like many others struggling in the village, she was a fan of Finn's and admired him as a champion. Even though she wasn't a big a fan of fighting, she would be lying if she said she was not starstruck. This was Finn II, the most famous man in Celtish Anglonia.

Finn still slowly skulked forward towards her.

'Well I have something in mind that's always helped in the past.' He placed his hands on her hips and she froze. The thin linen layer between the palm of his hand and her naked skin proved a small barrier. His hand was cold and stiff like a corpse's. His fingers were rigid and bent at the knuckle. Cold streamed down her spine. His hands slithered back to feel her bottom and she slapped them away. He took a step back holding his hand. Initially stunned by the rejection, he began to smirk. He took it as playful, like a game of cat and mouse. She wanted to be chased and he was happy to pursue. He was beginning to find, he preferred it that way. He hadn't been rejected before. His status, fame and charm made him very successful with the fairer sex. This feeling wasn't only real, it was new.

He was still very close, and she could feel his faint breath on her neck. She cringed waiting for it to go away afraid to look at him and fuel this misguided advance. Finn needed to control something, he needed to own something. He grabbed her and turned her to face him Temina tried to push him away but Finn kissed her before she could do anything. Again, she froze. He could feel she was tense, but he mistook it for excitement. She didn't know what to do in reality. At first, she pushed gently, then a little harder. He didn't budge. She started to use a lot of her strength, he gripped tighter and slithered his tongue into her mouth. This was the reality and he once again felt like a man, this moment was real and the fighting only added to the truth. Everything, the taste of her lips, the smell of vanilla in her hair, the feel of her skin. He pushed his body against hers. His muscles ached against the resistance, but it felt good. His large firm hand slid from the base of her back to the side of her breast and a bubble of adrenaline burst from within her. With all of her might, she pushed him away. Finn had a crazed look on his face. His eyes were red as roses and absent thought, only driven by instinct. He smirked and stepped forward. Temina punched him in the jaw stunning him.

'The fook you do that for?!' Finn exclaimed holding his face.

'You stay away from me! There's more where that came from!' Temina backed against the very hot stove, but it was safer than what was in front of her. The star had struck her alright, and she struck back.

'I just thought…'

'Well, you thought wrong! I tried to push you away!'

'I was playing. I thought you were too.'

'Well, this isn't a game. Get out of my house!' She pointed to the door.

'Listen, lady, I just thought you were up for it is all. I don't need you spreadin rumours about me being a rapist or out!' Said Finn sternly. He was half pleading, but he had a tone in his voice that was not so apologetic.

She said nothing. Temina looked to the window as an impulse to look for help. No help was there, but peculiarly there was light coming from the shop window across the way. She stared out of the window confused, focussing on the light in her shop now. Finn still awaited her answer. He stepped forward carefully.

'Look, miss, I'm sorry.' He said. Now his tone was apologetic.

'Just leave.' She said pushing past him and running across to her shop.

Finn waited a moment and reflected on what he had done. He had lost himself, there was little to no chance to put things right. He had to try he didn't know what got into him. Seeing the fear and disgust in her eyes, made him feel dirty.

He left the house intent on speaking with Temina about what had just happened. When he stepped out onto the terrace, he heard his name spoken down the alleyway along with muffled voices. He followed the voices down the alley and out onto King's Avenue, the road that connected the gate of the white wall to the Temina's shop.

He looked out and saw Celestine confronted with three armed soldiers. Luke was stood behind him. The military shared a similar instinct that he did when he first saw Celestine, in that they knew that he was formidable just by looking at him. For that reason, they didn't take their eyes off of him.

'People around here say that they saw you arrive in the village with Finlay Eireann not but days ago.' The lead soldier said.

'I can't vouch for what they saw, but I don't know what you're talking about. I travelled to see this fight and I'm just out for an ale with my friend.' Said Celestine. 'I wanted the others to win. I was disappointed that five men couldn't beat one and I left.' He chuckled.

'I'd rather you not waste my time young man! Do you want to be arrested?' The soldier yelled. 'Finlay Eireann is wanted by the Zorrodon government, do not obstruct the course of justice.'

'You go first.' Said Celestine calmly.

Luke spotted Finn peering out from the alley and mouthed 'Go.' As the soldier spat curses in reply to Celestine's reckless albeit witty rebuke. Finn could sense anger in his voice like he was holding back a flood of emotions. Before he left a chorus of boots on the ground and flame torches curved around the corner as a large group of guards and soldiers alike marched into town. Luke shooed Finn away while everyone was distracted. Finn retreated managing a brisk walk as his muscles would not let him run yet. He stopped as he passed through Temina's garden. Temina was kneeling and crying, holding a bouquet. Although he was guilty, he could not risk her getting caught up in it.

Celestine yelled, 'What did you do!' It was followed by the sound of drawn swords and smashing glass.

Finn ran.

Temina learned that the bouquet in her hands was the one that Celestine bought when she saw the white and blue coat hanging by the door to her shop. She was looking around, using only the light of an abandoned carry lantern, by the door and on the floor. The waning light revealed the arrangement she made specifically for him. The slow glow pulsed and illuminated the coat hanging by the door and she remembered that day, the flowers she picked for him, which she thought were for someone else. He had been here, but now he was gone. She could almost feel his presence, absorb the remnant energy in the air and it told her with conviction that she was the one he was buying the flowers for. Why else would they be here now?

When the kettle whistled in her home, she knew why he was no longer here, and the flowers were on the floor. Her stove where Finn kissed her was in plain view from the window. He had seen it. He had seen it and left without knowing the truth, because the facts got in the way. She fell to her knees and cried.

The sound of a commotion on the street snapped her out of her depression. It was muffled but the harangue of steel impact pierced through the insulation. She looked out of the window and every place on the far end of the street was being raided. Fires were being set, doors kicked in, and windows smashed. It looked like the guards, the police force, and the military were all in a frenzy. Her heart sank as she watched men, women, and children alike dragged out on the street and beaten. She knew this was a reaction to what happened in the arena earlier that day. The flames intensified and smoke covered the sky. Afraid to stand, but ashamed to hide, she ran to the door. The open door let the sound of the destruction flood the silent atmosphere of the shop. The light from the flames and the glistening reflection of the bloodstains on the hard soil floor. She quaked in her place struggling to gasp. The smoke made the air thin. Her eyes darted all over, it was night but the fires made it bright as day. The street looked like fire itself. The ground was stained red, the walls were lit bright orange and the sky was blackened by smoke. The flames from behind the wall could be seen now too. A snowfall of ash danced to the ground. She looked to the street and saw a lone little girl wandering in the melee as the military exacted excessive force on the villagers. She stepped out to get her, then she was grabbed and pushed back into her shop.

'Hide!' Said Luke. Temina did what he said as he closed the door behind them.

'What's going on?' She asked.

'I don't know.' Said Luke joining her. He sat on the floor, beneath the window. The fever of the orange flame reached over them like a watchful eye. Luke's hair was ruffled, and he had a cut on his cheek. He was panting for air, but he looked scared. 'Is this what you meant about hard times?'

Temina shook her head. 'Not like this.' She said. She looked at the bouquet. 'Wait, where's Celestine?' Luke looked ashamed but equally terrified and he began to cry.

'He's out there fighting. The soldiers came in and they talked to us at first then when more came things got bad. There was this old man who just came out to see what the fuss was about. A…and they stabbed him. They didn't even care, they just walked over him like he wasn't even a person. Celestine lost it and they attacked us. When he finally stopped one of them beating me, he sent me to find you.' Luke wheezed then a succession of snivelling coughs broke him down to weeping into his arms. He hadn't seen death before and he was not cut out for it.

'He can't stay out fighting, there's a whole army out there.' Said Temina.

'I know! But he said he had to defend the people. It's reckless and stupid.' Temina looked out of the window above where they sat on the floor.

'Where is he now?' She asked. Luke turned to look and pointed him out.

'There.' He said.

Celestine ducked under a horizontal swing of a steel short sword. He slammed his bleeding knuckles into the soldier's face before stealing his weapon. He parried an incoming attack from behind then rolled through to slice the attacker's thigh. He dropped immediately. Celestine was getting tired and the waves of enemies kept coming. He paused for breath and checked back to the florists. He saw two soldiers running towards it and Temina unaware in the window. What he didn't notice was the hooded figure standing behind the building, their green eyes fixed upon him. He charged and caught the soldiers very quickly. He slammed both men to the ground knocking them out and checked on Temina who watched him from the behind the window.

A light flickered from his fingers again. He was stirred and filled with adrenaline, but, seeing Temina could even silence the warzone behind him. Her eyes rich and beautiful and her pink lips tightly pressed in tension. Then, the image of Finn kissing those lips burnt in his mind. The mixture of emotions, betrayal, heartbreak, and intense disappointment. He knew he shouldn't feel like that, but he did. It made him angry. A sudden pop in his palms and they orbed with a bright star-like light. He examined them in shock before the heat built within him. It slowed his body and made it borderline impossible to move. Temina's face blurred as he became more and more light-headed. Before his vision completely faded, he was tackled to the ground and stabbed in the stomach.

Luke ran out and tackled the soldier and whaled on him with as many blows as he could muster. Temina rushed to Celestine's side as he futilely held the blood in his wound. His hand trembled and the glow had dissipated. A river of blood flowed from him and now he was starting to lose consciousness again. He fought it before he eventually accepted his fate. He knew going into this fight, that he wasn't likely to come out alive. Temina's face was a perfect last sight to behold. He blinked. In the background, the hooded figure stood watching over Temina's shoulder. Their piercing green eyes, glowing in the shadow. As Luke threw his punches, in his fit of rage he did not see that every blow had been blocked. He was exhausted. Then, the soldier flipped him onto his back and rained down punches on his round face. These were not blocked. Luke screamed in pain and fear.

'Help! Please stop! Please! Please!' Celestine tensed trying to answer his friends call but everything was darkening. He was losing too much blood; he could not move, and his body was going into shock. Temina looked up to see two soldiers grab a handful of her hair and drag her from Celestine into her shop. The second soldier closed the door behind them.

A succession of thumps and cries were the last thing Celestine heard before he drifted away.

22 BEHIND CLOSED DOORS

Celestine was in a pure white void laying face up once again. He could only assume he was face up because he couldn't be confident what up was. He exhaled slowly and controlled. Breathing always helped when he suffered through pain. He had pushed through his limits so often as a child, the pain was a comfort. Pain was progress. He understood that when the pain went away things weren't working anymore. Numbness worried him.

His initial worry came when he couldn't feel the breath pass through his nostrils or lips. It wasn't like the air was thin, it did not exist. That sensation, or lack thereof, brought his attention to the absence of agony induced by the stabbing he suffered. He reached for the wound. To his surprise, it was easy. There was no blood; there was no wound. He got up and he was clean. No ash, no blood, no scars on him whatsoever. He turned to see the very same door that he saw earlier that day. It was freestanding. It looked a lot more damaged and worn than before, but it was smaller this time. No longer was it the size of the wall of Zorrodon, although still big. It eerily resembled the door to the outhouse where he and Staphros trained. He grabbed the handle without thinking and yanked hard. It was locked. His instincts told him to get this door open and he continued to wrestle with the handle but, it wouldn't move.

'It won't open like that.' A soft voice said. Out stepped from behind the door was the hooded figure wrapping dark brown delicate fingers around the hinge. 'It's locked.' They were dressed in a large monk's robe, even though they appeared small. It was hard to see their face because there were no distinguishing tones or features under the hood.

'Am I having another seizure?' Asked Celestine. He'd be shocked if he hadn't already done this earlier that day and not remembered, but he was starting to remember exactly what happened before and the many times before. He just had questions, and this person looked like they had answers.

The figure stood a good distance away, about the span of two people. He couldn't see their features, and their voice gave no clue either.

'No. You've just passed out.' They said. 'Blood loss I believe.' It was coming back to him and the events leading up to his loss of consciousness played in his head until the last seconds. Luke was being beaten and Temina had been dragged into her shop then the door closed. The last he heard was her scream and a large smacking thud. He knew the sound. It was a punch and a hard one at that. His eyes flashed with anger and the door banged. Another crack appeared on the wood. Celestine stepped back examining it.

'What just happened?' He asked. The hooded figure was looking at the door and a flash of sharp white teeth flickered in the shadow under the hood.

'I have no earthly idea.' They said almost to themselves.

'Hey!' Said Celestine getting the figure's attention once more. 'I need to help Temina and Luke. Is there any way you can help me do that?'

'How do you propose I do that?' Asked the figure.

'Well, I did this thing today, where I took this guy's hand and he said yes, and I took over his body and fought for him. Could you do that for me? I can tell you're strong.'

The hooded figure laughed under their cloak, 'So you did that.'

'This isn't a joke!'

'I know, but I cannot help you that way.'

'Then tell me what you can do.' Celestine was getting impatient. The figure waved a hand and manifested a looking glass through which Celestine could see Temina.

'I can show you what is happening behind the door to Temina's shop. I know it's killing you not knowing.' Celestine couldn't see it, but he imagined a thick sickening grin carved on the figures face. They lingered on each of their words like they savoured each syllable. 'I can also tell you that, the means to help your friends lies behind that door.' They said. Celestine reached for the looking glass and his hand went through it. He swung back and watched on helplessly. Temina's face was swollen and bloody, she was screaming and weeping red tears. She was on her knees holding out her hands trying to protect herself. One of the soldiers slammed an armoured fist against her face sending her to the ground with a clap against the wood. Celestine flew into a frenzy and grabbed the door handle once more. He pulled with all his might, but the lock was tight. The CHUCK-CHUCK of the lock catch sounded like the door laughing at the irony of it all.

'Let me through! Let me thorough!' Yelled Celestine. The door would not budge deaf to his desperate pleas. He whirled towards the figure and pointed to them. Temina's screams echoed in the background, reverberating endlessly in the emptiness. 'A key! I... is... is there a key somewhere? Where is it?'

The hooded figure shook their head. 'There is no key. It remains locked because no living man could withstand what lies within.'

'What's that mean?! I can't open it? Why tell me I could then?'

'I didn't say that.' The figure said. 'I said that the means to help your friends was behind that door. You just can't access it while the door is locked.' The thuds and screams compounded in their echoes and with every repetition, it got more frantic and frightened. Celestine was trapped in this infinite loop of helplessness as he heard the woman he loved be slowly tortured to death. In a fit of rage, he slammed the door with his fist. The door shook and the door felt real. The wood was solid and thick, but organic. It was cold to the touch and rough around the edges. He noticed the damage on the door, and it was damp on the particularly worn areas. When his hand touched the damp spots on the door, he felt a power surge through him. It was invigorating. It heightened everything within him, his perception, his strength, his emotions. Whatever was behind the door, that was it. This was a normal door albeit locked, but locks couldn't seal cracks.

He closed his fist and took a deep breath. He fired the first punch and the door gave no quarter. The shock travelled up to his shoulder, but he did it again. He felt a crunch in his fist but still carried on. He started to alternate from left to right, accurately hitting the same spot. He aimed for the centre of a large crack at his eye level. It hurt, but every time he slammed his fist against the wood of the door, he felt the moisture on his skin energise him.

'The door is quite unbreakable.' Said The figure mockingly.

'So am I.' Said Celestine.

Temina's door kicked open. Luke's attacker dragged Luke on the floor by the arm grunting with each pull. That was the biggest fight he posed against the trained soldier. He was barely conscious and brought a trail of blood behind him like a gutted serpent that refused to die. Temina was lying face down on the floor whimpering. She looked up and sought out Luke mustering what little strength she had to reach for him. She had only met him today but right now he was her only friend in the world. She was fully conscious but battered beyond belief. Blood trickled out of her mouth as she wheezed for life. When she had curled up into a ball on the floor, they had kicked her in the sides a few times. Her ribs were broken, one of which stuck into her lung. She couldn't feel it yet, but the men had already killed her with that. Luke's attacker pulled him to his feet and seized an immobilising chokehold on him. Luke didn't stop fighting, even though at this point his fighting was laboured flailing and babbling murmurs.

'We need to finish them off. We're moving on.' He said sniggering. The soldier closest to Temina dragged her to her feet by the hair. She didn't have the energy to scream or fight, she just hung like a doll that had been worn out. She had a million-mile stare coming from her milky, bloodshot eyes. Her head was fuzzy, and sounds were muffled like underwater. Her wheezing was worse now she was upright, and blood flowed down in many streams on her cheeks, mouth, and nose, to form an ocean on her chin. She saw Celestine's body still convulsing on the floor outside. It gave her hope that he was still alive but hurt her to know he was suffering still. He started murmuring and groaning outside. She cried more bloody tears, this time for him, but it steadied her. He got into that position defending her and showing strength now would honour him. She thought of her mother and how she had honoured her in that very way every day.

They gripped her in a chokehold as well. She wasn't going to fight, and she couldn't run away. Restraining her was purely for their satisfaction. The third man was free to do the deed. He had his green uniform on with sooty black hair thinner than a rice noodle. He pulled the blade from his waist and admired the way it glistened in the firelight.

Celestine's convulsions became more violent, blood gushed from him again. It came from his fists. His arms shook, jerking in a rhythmic pattern. The skin started peeling back more and more. White bone started to poking through flesh and the torn tissue peeled onto the ground. The bones chipped like rocks facing a relentless tide, and he started to shriek unconsciously and gasp for air.

Luke's attacker, standing by the door, kicked the door closed behind him.

'I might put that little shit out of his misery when we're done here. I'm amazed he's still alive, I sort of respect him for it.' He said. Now that the door was closed, it revealed the coat hanger. Temina saw Celestine's blue and white coat hanging there. It took her away from this situation temporarily, to the day the two met.

She closed her eyes and reminisced over the game the two played, the long pauses and every voice within her telling her to just kiss him. There was no place she would rather be than in that moment again with him. There was nothing but the truth now that Temina faced her death. In her last moments, she thought of Celestine, and her one regret in life was not listening to that instinct and just kissing him when she had the chance. It was her denial that caused doubt. Now, it was too late, but in her last seconds she finally allowed herself to love him and it was wonderful. Just as she imagined it would be.

Breakthrough.

The cold steel blade caressed Temina's cheek and neck causing her to flinch away. The blade was so sharp that she didn't feel it slice her cheek as it slipped across her face. It just bled.

'Open your eyes love. I want you to see this coming.' Said the third man. The voice sounded as close to a human snake as could be. He enjoyed this more than he should. He dealt most of her injuries and he was going to finish her off. Inclined to obey, she did it without thinking. She saw his corrupt grin sprayed across his face. His eyes bulged and he looked hungry like a predator, a demon who would live on. She saw the blade inches from her face. Behind him was Luke now conscious silently crying for her. He fought but, he was too weak to break the grip which choked him. Her vision was hazy and blurred, but she noticed that she couldn't see it anymore. She couldn't see the coat on the hanger. She blinked and focussed on the corner and then her vision cleared for a second. The wooden arms of the hanger were bare.

Celestine's coat was missing.

The soldier with the knife pulled his knife back and Temina closed her eyes. She heard Luke howl. 'No!!!'

She heard a crack, then a bang, and a boom. Suddenly the grip around her neck was let go and she dropped to her knees. She opened her eyes slowly as blinding starlight shone in the room. The third man was gone and in his place was an actual star glowing in front of her. When the light dimmed, the features of the blue flame on the white coat appeared. The dance of his high ponytail and flowing locks beneath it. He retracted his punch and his coat flapped at the influx of hot hair that swooped in through the new hole in the wall. His golden hair danced at his back and the intense glow settled into a cloak of starlight pulsing around him. He looked back with his shining blue eyes and smiled.

'Are you okay?' Said Celestine.

The man that held Temina wasted no time in trying to attack Celestine. He waved his sword slamming it into his shoulder. Celestine didn't move, at least to the perspection of his onlookers. The blade went right through him. His giveaway was the flapping of his coat coming from above. He appeared to hang in the air as he rotated arching his leg back. The man panicked holding his arms up as Celestine volleyed him in the face sending him through a second hole in the wall. As soon as Celestine landed, he walked towards Luke's attacker. The man trembled and tried to run. He pushed Luke at Celestine and bolted to the hole nearest to him. Celestine snapped his fingers and he stopped. Luke's attacker felt paralysing electricity through his nerves. He froze in an uncomfortable standing contort. Celestine caught Luke in his arms and held him there. Luke looked up at him. His face was bloodied, and he couldn't speak very well through the swelling and lacerations.

'Celestine, I'm sorry I let you down.' He said blubbering in muffled tones. His top lip was swollen to underneath the row of teeth. 'I should have…'

'Luke, you're alright.' Said Celestine.

Luke pushed him away. 'No! I couldn't do what you asked me to do. I failed you.' A clear tear fell from his cheek to the floor.

'No Luke.' Said Celestine. 'You're alright.' As if he spoke it into existence. Luke felt no pain. He felt the skin on his face and examined his hands. There was no swelling, there were no cuts. Luke laughed and cried at the same time. It came in short bursts, one after the other. He didn't know what to do. He couldn't believe it, but then again his best friend was shining in front of him. He didn't know what he could believe anymore. Luke continued to look at himself and test everywhere that hurt just seconds ago. Celestine went to Temina. He knelt by her watching her stunned expression.

'Wh… wha…wha…' Celestine grabbed her by the hands as she babbled and brought her to her feet. He hadn't healed her yet, but it was easier for her to stand now. Likely to be because there was no imminent threat of death anymore. 'What just happened?' She managed to ask when she got to her feet.

'Hold that thought.' Said Celestine. Then he kissed her.

Temina could feel Life rush through her like she had never felt before. It didn't feel like invigoration, but like the essence of Life itself. The feeling was euphoria, vigour, and power. She grabbed onto him and pulled him close with increasing strength. Her heart beat faster, and she felt no pain she felt immortal, invulnerable. She saw what he saw and felt what he felt, she understood now. He was speaking to her through his kiss. He couldn't use words for what he felt about her. The times as a child, watching her grow from afar into the woman of his dreams. The nights he felt like crying because he wanted to be with her, and how almost every day he dreamt of her. The cloak of light intensified brighter and brighter, engulfing the two of them. They were one at this moment, no games, they were in love.

He pulled back first reluctantly, but he didn't have much time and he had much to do. She peered up at him like she missed him already. Her injuries were healed, and she had never felt better. Celestine smirked.

'I'm sorry, you were saying?' He asked her.

Temina blushed in reply.

He turned to Luke. 'I need a favour.' He said. Luke stood bolt upright now even more determined to do right by his friend. Celestine had even cheated death to come back and get Luke out of a tight spot. At this point, it didn't matter what the favour was.

'Anything.' Said Luke immediately.

'Take Temina to The Hideaway and give Staphros this.' Celestine held out an orb of pure light in his palm. 'It's alright. You can hold it.' Luke reluctantly took it, but it was warm and surprisingly pleasant. It had a funny tingle to it.

'Staphros right? What about Talion?' Asked Luke.

'Tell him what's happened, but that message is for Staphros alone.' Said Celestine pointing to the orb in Luke's hand.

Luke nodded. Celestine snapped his fingers and Luke's attacker was freed.

'I'm going to need you to go now.' He said. 'Go tell your friends what's coming.'

Luke's attacker nodded and sprinted away down the street.

'Wait. What will you do?' Asked Luke. Celestine's face turned very hard and cold. His eyes still shined but they lacked the light of compassion he had always had before. His voice went deep, and he spat in anger and violent revulsion.

'I'm going to kill that army.' He said. Then, he disappeared.

23 BETWEEN BROTHERS

The White Wall of Zorrodon was the tallest structure in all Anglonia. It didn't surpass the clouds into the heavens like the onlookers at the bottom thought, but it did kiss the clouds. Celestine retreated from the Temina's shop in an instant without any trace and he landed at the top of the wall. He walked the wall above the black clouds of smog and beneath the clouds of grey that were getting heavier by the second. He had to remove himself from the ground; he had to think clearly to do what he needed to do. He remembered his last words to Luke. "I'm going to kill that army." Celestine hadn't killed a man in his life, and he had no intentions to. That intent came from the people around him, and he didn't blame them. He always had a vague sense that allowed him to feel what others felt, but the awakening of these abilities amplified it tenfold. He could now fully feel what those felt around him, he could also hear their deepest fears and desires. Some begged for a saviour, others wished for salvation for their families, most pleaded for death to come either for them or the army that besieged them. With his glowing blue eyes, Celestine could see the manifestation of everybody's feelings in a red mist. There was anger here and hurt. He felt it when he was down there and could not endure it, even with the divine gifts he had at his hands.

It was a little quieter up where he was. He knew what was to come but he didn't know how he should act. His time was limited. He had reserved himself to die the moment he started punching the door in the white void, as the figure said *"No living man could withstand what was behind the door."* He understood that his body would fail soon, and his life would be forfeit. He only wanted to save Luke and Temina selfishly, but hearing and feeling the pain of the city he could not turn them away. A true hero, in which he always tried to be, was willing to give his life to a cause. This was what he believed Kastielle to do, despite the rumour that surrounded him.

If Kastielle felt anything like he felt now, he understood why his fabled mood swings were so violent. Mood swing, although accurate from an outsider's perspective, could not be further from the truth. A mood swing would connote that they could come back, and that was not the case. It took everything in Celestine's power to maintain some psychological equilibrium. Even away from the emotional pollution at ground level, the effort was still great.

Fighting against this private army would surely overcome him. Even without the resentment and hatred of the people around him, Celestine could not help but picture what those men did to Luke and Temina and hold onto it. Revenge had never been in Celestine's heart until now. For the first time, he felt it so intensely that he wanted blood. When confronted with it, the opportunity to exact the same horror and pain his friends felt, he would take it and he wouldn't be able to stop.

On the ground, Magnus climbed into his carriage with Fredrickson at his back. He sat opposite his second with manic contentment on his face. The glow of the firelight glistened against his sharp grinning teeth. Fredrickson sweated profusely on the opposite side. He trembled while he fidgeted with his fingers. On his way to the carriage, he saw the lifeless face of a boy dead on the floor. The lightless eyes tracked his path, watching him even in the privacy of the locked carriage. Magnus stepped over the boy like he was not there. He did not avoid the countless dead and injured that lay on the streets, nor did he seek them out. He did not care; he saw what he saw like it was normal. The dead eyes of the boy were nothing compared to Magnus's.

'Stop that!' Said Magnus staring out of the window.

'Sorry, sir.' Fredrickson immediately stopped fidgeting with his fingers. The trembling got worse now his hands were idle.

'Calm yourself!' Snapped Magnus. 'Did you not think it would go this way? This is the correction the people deserved for challenging my authority. A mistake I will make sure they will not do again.'

Fredrickson clenched his fists and slowed his panic. 'Where are we going sir?'

'To the root of it all.'

Celestine sat cross-legged on the wall and meditated. He had to reach a state of complete calm before confronting the invading military and he had to be decisive. For that, he had a failsafe, Staphros. The orb that he had given to Luke was a piece of himself. He had no idea how he did it, but he needed a means of talking to Staphros and the orb appeared, the same way it occurred to him to fight for Finn. He had to centre himself away from all of the noise at ground level. If he could concentrate, he could tell Staphros what he needed to tell him.

'Come on Luke! Hurry up!'

Luke had been inspired. He sprinted for his life to the King's Hideaway. Temina kept up with every step. They had not thought of running into trouble although they should have. Luckily, they did not. Luke had one singular goal, make it to the Hideaway and deliver this orb to Staphros. There was a lot to talk about, but neither Luke nor Temina could put it into words. At least for now, they ran in silence.

They crossed into the threshold to the city. It was more of the same orange flame and the city burning. Magnus had gone too far. His wrath had destroyed the city he ruled. Luke began to weave through alleys and ginnels with dancer-like agility until he made it to the King's Hideaway quicker than he thought he could.

He busted through the door without thinking. Staphros roared wielding a Claymore sword. Luke dropped to the ground on his bottom. After all he had been through, he was still nervy. Behind Staphros, Talion was aiming an arrow at the door with a drawn bow.

'Hey! Calm down, it's just us!' Said Luke. Temina waved shyly, flustered and out of breath. Staphros relaxed but eagerly looked around.

'Where is Celestine?' He asked.

'He's out there but...'

'You left him out there?' Talion interjected. 'It's a warzone!'

'Yes but...'

'How did he get out in the first place?' Staphros jumped in.

'We snuck out, but...'

'You snuck out!'

'After all, he had been through! How could you be so irresponsible!?' Said Talion jumping out of his seat and yelling at the young Celtishman.

'I know, but really...'

'No, you don't know, all you do is, not know. You're ignorant!' Staphros ranted.

'Enough!' Temina screamed and the room fell silent. 'You have no idea what the two of us have been through tonight and I will not have you sit there and judge things you don't even know! I would be dead if it were not for Luke! If you listened to him for once maybe you'd find that out!' Temina didn't know where that came from. She was beginning to understand why Luke was so close to Celestine; he was the only one who listened to him. Staphros looked down apologetically, while Talion did not.

'Well that's you told then.' Said Elias. He looked around the room for a reaction, but nobody gave any it was like he was invisible. Luke nodded to Temina to show his mouthing "thank you" that nobody was to hear. She could tell some of those words hurt him, but he would never show it. He'd hide it with a smile, as he did everything else.

'I have a message I think, from Celestine.' His voice was breaking as he choked back the emotion. 'I'm supposed to tell you what's going on, and then give this to Staphros.' He said. He presented the orb of light and handed it to a perplexed Staphros. Talion gasped fell back into his seat. It looked like he knew what it was. He looked petrified and he started quaking uncontrollably. Staphros checked the orb all over.

'What am I meant to do with it?' He asked.

'I dunno, he didn't tell me. Anyway, so Celestine and I...'

Staphros could feel the orb get heavier and hotter. It floated a few inches above his palm, but he could feel the changes in its temperature and density. It floated to rest on his skin and it was strangely cool to the touch. He could feel gentle hands guide him down as heavy tiredness brought him to his knees. He couldn't hear Luke or anything else. He fought the sleep until he couldn't anymore and he drifted off as the ball was absorbed into this skin.

The orb that Celestine left wasn't much of a message at all. It was a portal into the white void within himself. Staphros couldn't see the door or the stream of power that crushed him, but he saw Celestine and what he had become. His silver starlight cloak was magnificent. He was standing and looking to a non-existent distance, possibly looking for him in the emptiness. Staphros grabbed him by the shoulder and turned him around. When Celestine looked at him, he did not greet him as a friend or brother. He did not greet him at all. He looked up to the giant and simply crumbled into tears. Staphros grabbed him tight, holding him as best he could. He remembered the struggles and the glimpses to what he had become, and it was not an easy road. Celestine could put on a brave face for the others, but he had to be honest with Staphros. He was scared, and he was hurting.

'I'm so glad you came.' Said Celestine hugging Staphros tightly. Celestine shook in Staphros's arms burying his head into his shoulder as a weeping child does to his big brother. Staphros held him as any brother should, letting him get it all out. They let go and Celestine wiped his eyes. Even at the best of times, Staphros could always see through his brave face, and shatter through it. All it took normally was a look, or him simply being there.

Celestine needed someone who knew who he was at heart in order to listen to what he had to do. Talion knew him well, but he was also too protective over him. He needed somebody that loved him like a brother to do what needed to be done. Loving him like a son would only serve to hinder his plan.

'Luke said you had a message for me.' Said Staphros.

'Yeah.' Celestine's face turned grim. 'I'll cut to it, I made a choice getting into this state and I'm going to die because of it.' Staphros's face reddened and his cheeks quivered. He was very tense, Staphros wasn't one to show emotions. He couldn't bite these down so easily.

'Why?' He said as quiet as a whisper. His voice was strained as he fought his feelings back.

'I was told that no living man could withstand this degree of power and they were not lying. I had my reasons and I have accepted that fate.' Celestine drew back his coat to reveal his neck which had veins bulging the size of garden snakes. They pulsed like the movements of a caterpillar at a pace that was all to fast. It was a wonder he was still alive at this point. The burst blood vessels were spreading like a rash on his skin.

'Then why didn't you come to The Hideaway with Luke and Temina?'

'The city is under attack and the people need a defender. I can feel their fear and pain. I can stop this, you know I couldn't stand by.' Said Celestine. Staphros struggled to come to terms with it, and Celestine noticed. 'Please Staph, I need you to understand that this isn't a choice for me. The things I can do with these powers are unreal. I can help the city...'

Staphros stopped him. 'I know. It's in your nature, you're a hero you always have been. Even if the situations to show that haven't come up, I knew you were one at heart.' His words hit Celestine hard. Staphros's opinion was as important to him if not more so than Talion's. He looked up to Talion for who he was in Anara and had become in Anglonia. Celestine idolised Staphros as a big brother. Staphros was the standard he had to live up to. Celestine wanted more than anything to be just like Talion. Talion raised Celestine to be the best parts of himself, the perfect reflection of Talion. Staphros raised Celestine to be the person that he could be. He taught him it was okay to be himself. Nobody would ever know that that was the relationship Celestine had with him, not even Staphros himself.

'Thank you.' Celestine bowed his head like he was in the presence of a king. Staphros rested his large hand on his shoulder.

'I hope you didn't bring me here to get my blessing, because you don't have it. I understand why but I don't like it.'

Celestine shook his head sadly.

'What is this a goodbye?' Said Staphros in a rare display of angst and animation. 'I'm supposed to tell the others goodbye for you?'

'No. The others can't know what's going to happen. I came to you because you would understand why I made this choice, and you are the strongest man I know.'

'Then what is it?' Asked Staphros.

'Do you remember when I was a child that I could always tell how you were feeling? How everyone was feeling?'

Staphros nodded.

'Well, that wasn't in my head after all. I feel it now more than ever. I feed off the emotions around me. My own alone are heightened to a point I can barely stand it, but I can feel everyone else's. The trauma, anger, despair, the need for revenge!' Celestine gasped as he clenched his fists white. 'It's like it's happening to me. It feels like I've lost a thousand parents and twice as many children. I've suffered a million mortal wounds but I'm still alive feeling them over and over, but this isn't the torture. The torture is all I want to do is get them back and I can't. I'm stuck. If I go and face them to defend the people, I will kill them and I will lose control and if I spare my soul everyone could die tonight. If I am to die tonight, I don't want to die as one of them.'

'You're not going to die.' Screamed Staphros. The outburst made Celestine jump back. 'You aren't going to die, and you will not become like them.'

'Staph, I don't just feel the emotions of the people being killed, I feel the killer's too. They are enjoying themselves. They have this inexplicable hatred within them for the men, women, and children they're killing. The hate is spreading like the flames over the city, corrupting the souls of everyone in it and only leaving ash. I feel all of it.' Celestine placed his hand on Staphros's shoulder.

Staphros said nothing. He hadn't comprehended the reason he was there yet, but subconsciously he was figuring it out and refusing it.

'I saw them heading south to the docks, I think they're going after him. I'm going to meet them there and put an end to it if I can. Please get there before I lose control. You're the only person strong enough.' A flash of tears tumbled from Celestine's shining eyes.

'Strong enough to do what?' Asked Staphros shaking his head. The reality was setting in.

'Strong enough to kill me before I kill anybody else.'

Staphros blinked his eyes open and sat bolt upright with the suddenness of a catapult, headbutting Luke on the way up. Luke had his head over Staphros's examining the big man and was surprised to see him move so suddenly. Luke barely had time to curse before Staphros was up and making for the door. Staphros hadn't registered the collision and had one sole focus. He picked up a table and examined it, ignoring the calls from Elias, Luke, and Temina asking what he was doing. The table was thick and sturdy. The legs were cast iron, and the surface was seven inches thick Akolese Ebony wood. He then wrapped the thick iron legs around his arm like a shield. He picked up the Claymore and suddenly stopped. Talion was standing in front of the door, arms folded.

'Staphros! What on Earth do you think you're doing?' He asked.

'Sir, I will be back soon, but I can't tell you.' Said Staphros.

'I know this has something to do with Celestine, Luke told me what happened. What did Celestine say in his message?'

'I have to go, sir. Please let me go.' Staphros was now pleading as he dropped to one knee. Talion was irritated and snatched a firm grip on the giant's shoulder. Staphros lifted his head and Talion backed away immediately. He nodded solemnly and stepped aside.

Staphros sprinted out of the door. Talion saw something in Staphros that he had never seen before. Through a life of anguish and pain, Staphros remained composed and grounded. When he looked up at Talion, Talion was compelled not to resist him.

Staphros was openly weeping for the first time in his life.

24 THE ROAR OF A WARRIOR

The red and black sky loomed over the docks of Zorrodon like storm clouds ready to rain blood. It was not until the screaming and fires started in the village that the people of the docks had become aware of the imminent threat. None of them were invited to the arena. They had to tend to the ships of the incoming guests. As busy as it was coming in, it was near destitute coming out. The guests that arrived via ship were not returning to claim their vessel. Hendry and his men were none the wiser until the army arrived to update them and in a rare show of kindness relieved them of their duty. The border was now closed.

Lion was asleep in his bed. He had a woman in his arms sleeping on his chest. This was the first time he managed to get some decent sleep since Kojo disappeared. He didn't remember the woman's name. She was young, an adult but still filled with an optimism that saw Lion as more than he was. That brought peace to him. She brought him some food from Olive, who had almost taken sole responsibility of making sure Lion ate. The weight of Kojo's disappearance bore down on him almost as much as Olive herself. She could see it and wanted to ensure he took care of himself as much as he did others. The young woman brought over the bowl of ground food and fish, then one thing led to another and they ended up in bed together. Lion was known for doing this a lot. Lion much like Talion was perceived as a paragon, though he had his flaws. The temptations of the flesh had a very high success rate when confronted with his willpower. A vice that addled many a great man. He loved every woman in their own unique way. He couldn't find it within himself to love just one, and he respected them too much to lie to them. Every time they were to lay in bed, he'd warn them of the man he was, but they already knew. The man that he was, was more than his infidelity.

Lion's door clattered open with Cyrus panting in the doorway. Lion and the young woman jumped out of their skin covering up as much as they could. Cyrus did not move; now was not a time for modesty.

Cyrus was out late at night as he had heard of the riots in the city and wanted to see if he could get some additional information on what went on. Cyrus had blooded Kojo into the Hondos. He felt just and culpable for Kojo's disappearance as Lion did, but he couldn't rest. His gut told him the worst had happened to the youth. This mission was in search of confirmation and closure for both Olive and Lion.

While he was in the village the struggle could be heard over the wall. The inrush of heavily armed soldiers, in the green garb of the army, meant a swift retaliation was to follow. There was no new news on Kojo, but the word of a riot at the arena dominated the conversation. As the afternoon turned to evening, the word was arrests and executions were to come.

The evening turned to night and the sounds of the struggle stopped. There were, no screams, no shattering glass, there was only eerie quiet. Cyrus could hear his breath and footsteps as he walked the dusty streets. The wind whispered in muted tones and everything slowed in the village. Cyrus could not let this day end without learning something. He stayed out to get information. He could no longer hear his footsteps anymore after midnight. He heard the march of an army raiding the homes in the city and the battered screams of the citizens. He knew the village was next and he knew where was last. He learned a lesson that he had been taught for many years being an Ebony of the dock. He was only visible when he was a threat, but he was also visible when a victim was needed.

The lesson was, *"If it is ever the latter… Run."*

Lion sprung to his feet and got dressed. He was confused by Cyrus's intrusion, but he knew that his actions were sure to be justified.

'Wha gwarn dred!' Asked Lion. The fog of his clouded mind was yet to dissipate.

'De city a burn sah!' Cyrus was wheezing and sweating buckets. 'Magnus a gaan mad and mash up de place to Babylon!'

'How yuh mean?' Lion cocked his head to the side trying to understand.

'Magnus tun bad. Him call inna de army and him want fi tun Zorrodon to ash. Dem say it because of a riot at de arena. Look sah!' Cyrus turned to point to the red sky and the clouds of black smoke. 'Sky tun red, cloud gaan black. Dis him reckoning! Me no know what we can do… so mi haff fi turn to you bredrin.' Misty tears filled Cyrus's bloodshot eyes. Lion could now hear the faint screams from the distance. He could smell the smoke tainted with blood. It awakened him. It told a clearer story than any word could, better than anything Cyrus could have said. He knew within his heart that not only was this Magnus's doing, but that he was heading here. They were two sides of one, each side of equal power and significance, children of Mother Nature. They were connected and the only way this would stop was if that connection was severed.

'Breddah!' Said Lion. 'Tell de man dem fi gaddar everybody at the dock shore. Tell every man fi bring a weapon and be ready to fight. Magnus want a slaughter, we gaan gib war!' Lion didn't want to do things this way, but this had to end definitively. Only one of them were walking out of the docks tonight.

Cyrus got on it right away, as did Lion. They went to knock on every door and gather the masses. They didn't have long. If Lion had remained quiet, they may have left them alone, but he had to push back and now not only were they visible, but they were also a target, or at least he was.

With the effort of the Hondos faction and others willing to help, the Ebonies of Zorrodon Docks had assembled in the dock shore. Their numbers were plenty, close to fifteen thousand, but most of them were women and children. As far as capable men, the numbers were much less. Lion hoped that their united front may deter the invading party from attacking the Docks, but he knew that if this was their strategy they had to be prepared to fight. He looked around, and the people were scared, but they weren't weak. Their unity gave them strength *"We are We"*. They were willing to fight, not for themselves but each other. Magnus was a tyrant, but his army would have a fight on their hands if they wanted it. Their pride and heritage meant that if they were to fight, they would fight to the death. Magnus had to be prepared to do that to all fifteen thousand of them.

As Lion made his way through the crowd, he saw familiar faces strong, Hendry, Olive, Cyrus, Roy, and every other heart he had touched. He was aware that all of them knew him, but ironically now faced with them, he didn't know that he knew them all too. He classed them as friends, as his family even. The pulsing of the flames permeated in the sky painting it a richer red every minute they drew closer. It was like it was alive and the light was its heartbeat.

Up ahead, the sound of marching clapped in the distance getting closer to the courtyard. The chatter and speculation stopped, and the people stared terrified at the long road that led to them from the village. They could see them approaching. At first, their torches appearing like a swarm of fireflies and steadily the faces of their invaders becoming clearer. Amid this swarm, was a plush carriage pulled by two horses. The people of the docks watched helplessly as fate came for them.

The army had combined to invade the docks. Magnus had come for Lion. The carriage stopped, as did the soldiers. The crowd split into an honour guard leading to Magnus's carriage door. His door opened and out he stepped. He sneered at the dusty ground and muggy setting. He looked to the people as a nest of rats that he had found, burrowed beneath the panels of his floor. Although the power to exterminate them was at his disposal, he only wanted one.

'People of the docks!' he said caricature-like. 'I see that you are aware of the swift correction that I have beset on this city.' The people of the docks had a distinct disdain for Magnus. He was one of them, dark-skinned and far from home, but he had betrayed his heritage. He was out only for himself. *"He was He"*

Magnus stood with his army behind him as if he bore gifts for them all.

'This correction comes to remind you people of your place. You all have been guilty of forgetting that, but I'm willing to forgive that if you give me something in return.' A manic grin cracked and curved across his face. 'The man called, Lion.'

There was an uproar of objections and inner discussions. The people had reserved themselves for a fight and they were not going to give up one of their own. Magnus waited patiently but that would not last long. He still had that sickening fake grin on his face that nobody believed, not even himself. One by one, Lion's Hondos bredrin stepped forward with fierce looks on their faces. They would not allow their leader to be surrendered, not without a fight. They wanted to stand as leaders in front of the crowd. They were, outnumbered, outmatched, and at every disadvantage imaginable, but they would not give up one of their own for the world. Magnus spread his arms wide just like someone would when getting ready to hug someone. He still smiled, trying to look friendly, but he was giddy. He got off on this destruction, he loved the people fearing him. The red sky, the black clouds, and a cavalcade of the most dangerous people in the land at his command, he was the most feared man in the city. These Ebonies stood against him, but his mood was tamed because he could smell the fear coming from them.

'Gentlemen, you do not want to do this.' He said.

'You're right! We don't!' Lion's voice shouted as he emerged from the crowd. 'But we will if we have to.' The Hondos men galvanised the people, Lion gave them strength. Collectively they raised what weapons they had or could find, most of them just had their fists. Lion looked back at every face that was willing to fight for him, every one of them he classed as a family and he shook his head. 'And I cannot let that happen!' Lion stepped forward to the middle of the space between both parties and dropped to his knees with his hands behind his head.

Screams and cries of disbelief bellowed from the crowd as the people were understanding what Lion was doing. The more he resisted the more it would escalate. He saw Magnus before him for who he truly was, and he finally saw his reflection, a perfect opposite. Magnus was Nature's son, Injustice, and he was his brother, Justice. They were destined to fight until the end. This was only going to end if it was definitive; only one of them was leaving the docks tonight. Only one of them would allow that to happen without a bloodbath.

Magnus directed two of his men to seize Lion and bring him to him. As the men grabbed him, Cyrus and Roy attempted to charge with the dock folk at his back. The unit or archers drew their bows aimed for each of them.

'Stay where you are!' Lion barked it as an order. He sounded like a parent to an unruly child. A parent that was providing protection that the child wouldn't understand. Sacrifice was never at the feet of the sacrificed. It landed at the feet of those sacrificed for. The men stopped and it dawned on them how powerless they were. They were trapped behind a glass barrier and the penalty was death if they broke it. Every person was willing to die to save one of their own, but the only way to save most of their own was to let one die.

The soldiers threw Lion to Magnus's feet. He stood immediately with the pride that his name was synonymous with. He looked into the pits of Magnus's eyes trying to find his soul, to see the humanity in there, to possibly see if he could understand. What soul he had, was buried too far beneath his corruption. Lion didn't hate him for it; he pitied him. Magnus's smile went and the soldiers slammed the broadside of their swords against the back of Lion's knees dropping him once more.

'So nice to see you again.' Said Magnus. Lion looked up smiling and defiant.

'I know it feels like I know you so well.' He said. Magnus crouched and stared into Lion's eyes.

'Likewise.' He said in hushed anger. He stood back up with his smile and his arms spread. 'This calls for a drink. Fetch me my bottle of the Canewine, the good stuff.'

'I don't feel like drinking.' Said Lion coyly. Magnus glared down with the features of his face covered in shadow.

'You will.' He spat.

The large bottle arrived, and Magnus admired it before handing it over to one of the guards at his disposal. The bottle looked more like a tankard, it was huge. The clay had seven Xs carved into it. The X symbol was to rate the strength and alcohol content. Usually, the rating would be one to five, anything above would be, what the industry would call, "Overproof". The guard popped the bottle and smelt the fumes from the fermented liquid derived from sugarcane. He whipped his face away like he had been punched. This was overproof alright. The other guard that brought him over seized Lion's neck and turned him to face the people of the docks. Once again, his men tried to charge, but Lion raised a staying hand. It was always going to be this bad. As a precaution, Magnus signalled for every man in the army to pull his sword from his sheath. The people were emboldened but there is no more fear-inducing and demoralising sound than that of a drawn sword. The sound of hundreds would make them stay put for what was to come.

Magnus patted the guard with the bottle with no fake façade, there was no need anymore. He hated Lion and now it was oozing out of him like he had sprung a leak. He enjoyed watching him struggle against the chokehold.

'Give the man a drink.' Magnus whispered into his man's ear before retreating into the crowd momentarily.

The soldier tilted the tankard and poured the rich alcoholic liquid into Lion's gasping mouth. He started carefully but then as Lion coughed and spluttered for air the aim didn't matter so much. The guard paused and let Lion breathe; he was conscious he might drown. Then he started again. The smell was so potent that people at the back of both groups could smell it. The echoes of Lion's gasps and coughs reverberated like the haunting cries of a desperate apparition. The liquid flowed again and the soldier that held him let go. Lion dropped to all fours and the Canewine was now being poured on his head. He was drenched in it.

Magnus returned from the crowd. He had a torch in his hand and a look of bad intentions on his face. He tapped the guard to stop him.

'That's enough.' He said quietly. Magnus appeared a man that was serving a duty, embracing the role of executioner. He hated Lion, but there were rules to this. He looked down at the choking rebel. In unison, the army took several steps back to clear the zone. He was waiting to see Lion look up and realise what was to come. One last look of fear that could satisfy him. Lion looked up and blinked unfazed. His eyes stung, he was choking and wheezing, his throat hurt, and he knew he was going to die. He feared death, but Magnus wouldn't get the satisfaction of knowing that.

'Mi have something fi say.' He coughed while looking up with blood-red eyes. As much as Lion was hated by Magnus, he was respected just as much. Magnus had never granted last words to any of his other victims that night or otherwise, but Lion had earned that right no matter how much Magnus begrudged it.

'Mi name is Cleon of Strawberry Wess Akoku. Mi fada was a poet, and mi mudda was a horse breeder. Mi family a come h'over to Anglonia fi h'offer support h'after de Civil war. Mi fada was den murder. Mi mudda was sold inna slavery. Mi naa seen her since. Since den, mi grew up pon the docks of Zorrodon. Mi no have no family, but I av neva been alone. Mi want all a unuh fi know there is nuttin special bout I and I. A you all a part of me. You can carry on the work dat WE have done together. Lion a not juss one man. We are a pride! We are strong! We are we, and whoever com after we, are weeble! So tonight, Mi beg you fi survive de night so unuh can show this city what "Pride" can do.' Lion looked back at Magnus with a stoic gaze. He was ready.

There were quiet whimpers from the dock folk as the members of the populous started to mourn before the death had occurred. There was nothing they could do and that pained them more than anything else. Lion's words resonated with them and they would do him the justice of obeying his last request. Justice was his spirit, the child of Nature that marked him at birth.

He lived by a code but was never sure of his purpose. Now he knew, inspire his people as he was by the divines.

Magnus stepped back and lit the fire.

There was a second or two when the flames lit and engulfed Lion's body, where he tried to stay strong. He was wrapped in bright orange and yellow living light but, he didn't scream, not for that moment. His skin dried and cracked and his lips tightened to contain the groans of pain that rumbled in muted tones beneath the surface. Magnus looked on as his adversary burned before him wondering for that split second if Lion was even human. It was when his dry skin cracked, and the surface of his flesh was touched by the raw brilliant heat that he cried out. Magnus wanted to make Lion look weak, but even in his last moments, he maintained his pride. Although he yelled in pain, it sounded like the final roar of the king of the savannah. The roar of a warrior. It boomed into the heavens and through the black clouds and even made Magnus jump back. Though nobody noticed, Magnus would carry that with him. Even in death Lion showed the difference between them. He was strong and Magnus was weak, he was loved and Magnus was hated, he was dying with Pride and Magnus would live on in shame. Balance was Nature's will and Magnus's curse.

Lion's cry wasn't exactly what he had in mind, but Magnus was satisfied that he inflicted such horrible pain on the rebellious thorn in his side. As Lion burned, he decided his work was done and he would do no more to the people of the docks. The army marched down the street lit by their torches and the one man bonfire at their backs. The flame was still going but black smoke swirled and twisted like a mangled spirit leaving the body. The dreadful reality was that Lion was cooking and his people could smell it. Some of them clamoured to find water and others watched in disbelief. As his Hondos bredrin got closer they could hear his faint murmurs dying along with the fire that cloaked him. He was still alive. The Hondos, the pillar of strength in the community, all broke down in tears of rage against Magnus. They couldn't do anything but watch as Magnus tore from them the one thing that kept them going. Their hope.

Magnus could hear them sobbing behind him and he smirked. He was tempted to laugh and even gloat. He was way down the street and almost to his carriage when a much different sound hit his ears. First, there was a boom then a crack followed by the distinct sound of silence as the sobbing stopped. Then he heard his name being shouted.

'Magnus!' A voice said. Magnus turned around and was hit by the sudden and blinding light of a star standing in front of the dock folk, Celestine. 'You don't get to leave yet!' he said.

The flame that covered Lion was extinguished when Celestine landed, but he could feel that he was too late. His empathic ability could pick up the emotions and prayers of everybody around him. Lion's prayers were now

silent. He heard them so clearly as he rushed to the scene.
But now, Lion was dead.

25 THE HEAD OF THE SNAKE

When Celestine was in the void and punching the door, he could feel the breakthrough coming. He knew what was on the other side, a flood of water. Within those waters, was the power of the universe, the power that King Kastielle himself was bestowed with. He knew it, studied it, he had read the stories a thousand times. That was what the hooded figure meant by the means to save his friends. He could feel the power surge through him as the droplets of water soaked into the bone-deep gashes on his knuckles. As the indentations and cracks intensified, more droplets seeped through. The sensation he felt when he had seizures, began then too. This time, he could control it. He understood it when before, he didn't.

He felt stronger and not only could he see what was happening to Temina and Luke, but he could feel their emotions. Instead of fear or lamentation, Temina thought of him and how she loved him. There was no greater inspiration than that. With the water on his fist, his knuckles shone in starlight and he launched one last punch into the wooden door.

Breakthrough.

The hole he punched was two or three times the size of his fist. The inrush of water was immense, it was like the door punched back with the force of all of Celestine's combined. It sent him to the floor and the intensity pinned him there. The water rushed out of the door like white rapids entwined with the power of all the Children of Nature and the souls of the millions around him. This was unlimited power.

'You did it.' The figure said in shock. Celestine fought against the current that beat him down and stood back up.

'That I did.' He said.

The feelings that Celestine felt as he landed next to Lion was that of pure rich rage. They mourned for Lion, but the only thing they wanted was for Magnus to die. Hate was an infection and it was nesting in Celestine's heart. He started walking forward with a confident irate swagger pointing at the tyrant leader.

'I sent one of your men to tell you I was coming.' He said still walking forward. Magnus turned around with his army.

'Oh, you were the one he was talking about. Well at least we know he wasn't delusional or drunk.' Said Magnus. He turned back to his army. 'Knock' he said. The archery unit drew their bows aiming for Celestine.

'You and your men are going to pay for what you did to these people.' Said Celestine. He then pointed back to Lion. 'To that man!' He continued walking.

'I would stop where you are if I were you, these men will not hesitate to kill you.' Said Magnus. He was unnerved by the arrogance Celestine approached him with. His aura was like he had never seen before. The light made Celestine's features clear in the night and they grimaced with nothing but hate in his eyes.

'Not if I kill them first.' He said. He blinked taking a deep breath. He had to fight the urge.

'You know what, I've had enough of this. Loose'. The archery unit unleashed a volley of arrows towards their encroaching target. Celestine took in a deep breath and bellowed a sky shattering cry. The arrows dropped. Some snapped against a formless shield in the air, while others just ricocheted away. Magnus's face dropped. He realised now that this was no illusion and Celestine wasn't your typical type man. He ran as fast as he could to his carriage. The dock folk cheered to encourage Celestine, but they were driven by bloodthirst. Celestine ran after him. The army ranks closed to block his way, but he was undeterred.

As soon as Celestine got close the men could feel the change in air pressure. There was a weight pulling them down. It slowed them down as Celestine only sped up. The first man thought he had hit Celestine with a strike but, once again his coat gave him away when it flapped in the air. He hung there and twirled horizontally cocking a volley. He launched the kick and sent the man deep into the company. The base of Celestine's foot connected and those nearby could hear the crack of his nose against the impact. Celestine was relieved and disappointed that the soldier was still alive but, his absence of doubt, his lack of remorse, and the unflappable sense of superiority were all gone. He could feel the other people too and he wanted them out of his head. He did not care for their prayers or whether they had families and children. He had seen many a broken family on the way to the docks, many a dead child. The flood of sorrow coursed through him. It was his lifeblood now. Still, the images of every soldier's family invaded his mind. Images of the innocence behind such malice. It made him sick that they did what they did despite having families of their own. They believed the children of the village, the families, were lesser than them. They were like game, free to hunt and destroy.

The weight in the air strengthened. Celestine went deeper into his and everyone else's rage.

Magnus pulled ahead and was almost to his carriage. Celestine burst through the crowd with his singular focus. He was surrounded now and one by one the soldiers blocked his routes of exit. They attacked. In all directions, Celestine launched a cyclone of elbows, knees and sidekicks keeping the attackers at bay. Every shot that he threw had malicious intent and devastating effects. The increase in the air pressure, slowed them down making the soldiers easy targets. Although this power increased his physical capabilities, his technique was forfeit. The mist of corruption in his head hindered his form. He could almost spectate this fight and analyse it from inside the void. If he hadn't been endowed with divine gifts, he would have some serious criticisms about his technique. It was sloppy and erratic. He realised that as time went on, he was becoming more of a spectator to his actions and less in control. He could not let that happen. He fought against himself from the inside to pull his punches. Full power hits would easily kill a man and to have that power at his hands was frightening.

The numbers were too great for him to have split focus even in this enhanced state. No matter how strong he was, he needed presence and clarity to engage multiple foes. A soldier jumped on his back while another punched him in the gut winding him and putting him on one knee. A third man sprinted and lifted his knee into his cheek and then he was swarmed. It rained with a shower of stamping feet and weapons. The men were attacking out of duty and survival. Heels landed on his face, and body the most. Luckily, he remembered how to cover up and that provided some protection. This was the first time that he had been hit in this state and he was surprised that he felt the pain just as much as he would normally. As the boots crunched against him fracturing the most vulnerable bones first, he learned was not invulnerable, although he thought he was. The attack went on as the men clamoured to get a hit in, reaching over each other with sheathed swords, weary not to injure their comrades to land a blow. The scene was eerily similar to the rioters attacking Axrotalus. Hate looked the same on everybody. Celestine lifted his head from his tuck position to see a punt come his way and land flush against his nose and brow.

In the void, Celestine fought against the current. It seemed to intensify the more disquiet his mind was. When he saved Temina and Luke it was a coursing river, and when he meditated to talk to Staphros it was a dribble. Now his legs were weakening, and he was losing his grip. He knew that once he let go, he would lose himself and there would be no coming back from it. He had to hold on.

There was no way to get out of where he was now. He was on the floor being beaten to death. He didn't have full control nor the full capacity to focus on the situation to devise an escape. His body was getting beaten and it was only a matter of time until it gave out. If that happened, he knew the repercussions. He had angered Magnus, made him afraid and exposed him for a coward in front of the people of the docks. He wouldn't let that go and those people wouldn't survive. His time was limited, but he had to save the people before that time ran out. He fought against the current to maintain his composure, but he was weakening himself and he was feeling the strain of holding back. Maybe the only way to beat them would be to give himself away. He felt what was in that stream, what was feeding the power, motivating it. If he gave himself to that, it had dangerous potential. The risk was too great.

As the barrage continued, Celestine's body was mangled. It had been beaten to a point where he could no longer cover up. That was when the sadistic nature of the soldiers came out. They grabbed his limbs one by one and stomped on them, bathing in his screams of agony. Celestine could feel everything. They snapped his joints, broke his bones, and slowly pushed six swords into his chest. As a blade penetrated his lung his screams were scorched to a whisper. The river of blood reddened his white coat, and the starlight aura ebbed to a faint twinkle.

The people of the docks gasped as they watched another hero fall in front of them. Their fear was realised when the army's attention was turned to them. They were visible, they were a target, but they could not run. The Hondos formed in front of the people ready to defend themselves. They weren't going without a fight no matter what. The army set their formation and began to march towards the people, leaving Celestine to suffer.

The two parties faced off, people of the dock having the advantage in sheer numbers, but the army having training, experience, and weaponry, this would be no contest for them. The people of the dock yelled and postured, raising their adrenaline. They cried to the heavens to give them strength, called upon Lion's spirit to enter them. The noise was palpable, louder than anything. It shrouded the area in a cloak of volume. Although having a clear advantage, some soldiers were intimidated.

The constraints of agony plagued Celestine's immobile body. As long as he held onto his soul he would be as powerless as he was outside Temina's shop. This time the door was open, the means to end this were in his hands, he just had to allow it to be. He sensed fear from the dock folk and something unspeakable was coming. Slaughter was inevitable.

Disquiet was rife in his mind, but the flow of water was still slowing. The power was waning, and he was being pulled into the next world, the Willow of Souls where all dead reside. The broken bones, snapped joints, and six swords in his chest, were destroying his body, but his soul could not withstand the internal struggle much longer either. The power wouldn't flow when he died, he could embrace the sweet relief, but he would leave the people to die if he did. He knew the only way to save them would be to use the full extent of his power, and the only way to use that power was to give himself to it. He fought the temptation and prayed for salvation. With his prayer, he heard one back.

"Please let me get there on time!" Once again Staphros was coming to his rescue. Celestine couldn't trust himself with this power, but he could trust Staphros to stop it.

Release.

Cyrus stepped forward and snapped a fist which silenced his people. He crouched like a pouncing jaguar. As the quiet lingered the faint sound of clicking and crunching was coming from behind the invading force. Everybody looked back to watch in amazement as Celestine's body jerked and snapped itself back together. Every laceration burning bright, twisted and mangled limbs spinning back to normalcy with a grind and a crunch. The swelling levelled, the cuts healed, and, one by one, he pulled out the six swords as slowly as they went in. He didn't feel a thing. What was left was a blank expression. Not angry, or sad, or scared, just nothing. The blue in Celestine's eyes had disappeared to pure white.

He stepped forward jerking suddenly and unpredictably as the last of his joints fit back into place. His walk quickened as his body recovered. The soldiers reacted. They had no time to think, they had to finish him off this time. They all sprinted with drawn swords ready to kill Celestine immediately. Celestine roared with his arms to the sky as the armed attackers got closer. He slammed his hands down suddenly. The air pressure hit harder than ever, like a giant boot crushing them and the ground quaked with an audible rumble. They all fell face-first on the ground before struggling back to their feet. The first up was Commander Simmonds. He appeared to be the leader of this group. Celestine stepped over the bodies struggling against the floor like they weren't there.

'He's going after Simmonds!' One of them shouted. Celestine could feel that he was the heart of this group and the most effective way to end them was to kill him.

Celestine grabbed in incoming strike crushing the arm at the wrist. He felt them fighting for one and other to get up. Inspired to protect each other. The hypocrisy. He lifted the pressure and waited for them in the midst of them all. They all stood. They looked at the screaming husk Celestine left lying and the brutal way that he had done it, now they felt the same as the dock folk when they burnt Lion. Almost, but not yet.

With an inspired battle cry, they launched their final attack to end this threat. When the first of them had reached Celestine, he once again disappeared, but they anticipated the move from above. They were well trained and could not be fooled twice. They thrust their swords in the air but, Celestine wasn't there. He had Simmonds by the throat hanging in grasp. Now they felt like the dock folk, now they would know. He wanted so much to rip his throat out, or crush his skull, or even rip his heart out. That was what the dock folk willed him to do. That wouldn't even match the pain that they had to endure. Celestine was still fighting inside although faintly. He screamed blankly and threw Simmonds into deep water uncaring if he sank or swam. That was the only mercy Celestine could muster. Then he was gone again.

He could feel the swell of helplessness in the army as they rushed to save their leader. Simmonds coughed and spluttered as his army rushed to row to rescue him, forgetting about the man who paid them. Celestine however, didn't.

Celestine landed on the plush carriage where Magnus hid. He punched through the top and pulled the cowering mayor out throwing him to the dirt floor. He scuttled back like a wounded spider, covering his flawless white robe in the dirt of the common people. Tears streamed down his face and he was leaving a trail on the floor. A snake shedding its skin of pretence and fakery while pissing himself in fear of real power. The army watched in disbelief as subconsciously they knew there was nothing they could do. They were close to being beaten, now Celestine just needed to cut the head off this snake. He grabbed Magnus's expensive robe and pulled him close.

He placed his palm on his forehead. Celestine had been experiencing all of the people's fear, their hatred, their loss, but most of all their pain physical and psychological. Through the palm of his hand, he gave it all to the tyrant mayor. Magnus's body went stiff as a board and seized on the floor as he dealt with the pain and anguish of over two million oppressed peoples. Celestine summoned strength in his fist burning bright, fierce and white-hot. He drew it back.

'Celestine stop!' Staphros grabbed his hand. 'Listen to me brother, this isn't you.'

Without warning, Staphros was launched across the street into the wall.

Celestine had truly lost himself.

The blow hit suddenly and ferociously. Celestine had surrendered his grip on Magnus's robe and thrust an open palm into Staphros's chest, holding the pose.

Staphros crashed into the wall cracking the concrete structure, before unceremoniously falling face-first onto the floor. This was the first time Staphros had ever been taken from his feet in this way. He had been floored before. Celestine was a tremendous wrestler and grappler, more than often putting Staphros on the ground with guile and timing. This was one single blow that sent him flying. That was what he was in for; that was the calibre of opponent his surrogate brother had become.

He pushed himself to his feet, using the table that he had fashioned into a shield to help himself up. His sword clattered again the wall and slid along the ground. Staphros looked at it and contemplated whether to use it, given how dangerous this situation was. Celestine still hadn't moved. His head twitched like the wings of a housefly, but his body was stationary. The glowing aura around him pulsed, the waves of a rising tide waiting to form a tsunami.

Celestine's head snapped up with the jerky immediacy of his bones snapping into place. His pure white eyes fixed upon the giant. The world blackened and he could only see Staphros standing there, the constant. He had always been there, he pushed Celestine when he couldn't go on, encouraged his success and redeemed his failures.

Staphros eyed his sword and shook his head. He unwrapped the cast iron legs of the table from his arm like they were leather straps and threw it to the ground. The tabletop landed flat with a clap against the dusty floor.

'Let's have one last spar my brother. If you win, I will leave you to do as you wish. But if you want to beat me...' Staphros raised his fists wishing he didn't have to. 'You will have to kill me.'

26 CELESTINE VS STAPHROS

Staphros was a truly prolific genius in combat. For how brilliant Celestine was a fighter, he had never beaten Staphros in a sparring match through the decades of them facing off. Staphros was the greatest warrior he had ever heard of, fact or fiction. Talion was a proud man above all else and was protective of his glory years as the champion of Anara, but even he said he would not have been champion long if Staphros was around back then.

Celestine charged without warning, no telegraph, or acknowledgement of Staphros's challenge. He was right in front of Staphros before he could even get his fists up. There was no time as Celestine volleyed his fist at Staphros's chest. His fist cut the wind causing it to whistle like a songbird before the crash against the stone wall behind his opponent. Staphros narrowly evaded it by rolling to the side.

'I take it you accept then.' He said.

Celestine said nothing. It was shocking to see the extent of Celestine's ability before his eyes. His speed was beyond the capability of any human or beast alike. Staphros was confident in his assumption that his strength matched, seeing that Celestine was elbow deep into a stone wall. Even if he had blocked that strike, it would have meant his life. Celestine was shooting to kill; he was gone. He pulled his fist from the crumbled stone unscathed and unfazed. His soulless eyes shone pure white, absent remorse.

Celestine set off in pursuit of Staphros again. He wanted to end it quickly, remove this obstacle from his way so he could kill Magnus properly. Magnus was presently suffering every pain that he had put the people of Zorrodon through, but there was more to come. Any less would be an undue mercy. Staphros had to be put down for that to happen. He put everything into every punch or kick, loading up and telegraphing his movements. Staphros was quick on his feet and elusive in his movements. Celestine was unnaturally fast now but Staphros was able to evade the incoming barrage because of Celestine's lack of technique. Technique would always beat speed. Staphros still had to move as quickly as possible, but he was confident in his evasive capabilities, although one small mistake would be fatal.

He could see in Celestine's movements a time that he thought he had forgotten. It was like when they first trained when Celestine was a toddler. All Staphros could do then was evasive manoeuvres too, however, the consequences were not injuries to his opponent this time. Three-years-old and erratic fighting with a rage within him that he didn't understand. They trained so he could control it, so the seizures wouldn't come. Staphros had seen Celestine's skin shine many times before, but it didn't grant him power back them. Back then, it tore him apart. Thinking about it, everything that Celestine did now was identical to his infant self and Staphros found himself anticipating the movements before they happened. This was why Celestine picked him, nobody knew him that well.

As raw as Celestine was, he was learning, leveraging the memory in his muscles to age his technique through infancy. His techniques were getting sharper and Staphros had to rely on his anticipation more and more. The gap was narrowing. He grazed Staphros's cheek and Staphros countered with a left hook and a right hook back at him. Celestine knew this was not Staphros's full strength, he sacrificed his full strength to be quick enough to hit his opponent. He remembered the day he learned that. As Staphros countered another hit, Celestine caught it and flung the giant into the wooden dockside stalls.

Staphros struggled to his feet knowing that he had grown. His face had changed, he was stepping into his formative years where he was grasping his techniques. Celestine's face was a blank canvass where Staphros's mind's eyes painted a preteen Celestine. In these years, sparring became challenging, because now Celestine had adequate enough technique to hit him on occasion, but now, Staphros could hit back. He spat a coppery crimson glob into the wooden carnage and this time he would lead in the attack.

He threw a jab cross and hook combination. Boxing was Staphros's favourite style by a very long way. He mastered it quickly and there was not a man alive that could match his skill in the art. Celestine was quick to evade each strike like he had time to spare; he was learning from Staphros. As he ducked underneath the hook, he slammed a low kick into the giant's calf. The impact was blunt and soundless, but it cut like a knife into the solid muscle. A dull ache pulsated in Staphros's leg and he knew a few more of those kicks would come at the forfeit of his ability to stand. Celestine chased him as he hobbled to a nearby house to lean on. He fired a knee into Celestine's sternum, using his speed and momentum against him, he then hit a straight right punch that connected with Celestine on the jaw hard.

Celestine dropped and his glow dimmed. That punch that he landed was square on the jaw and hard enough to knock any man out, maybe even stun a bull. Staphros felt that it landed clean, the satisfying slap of knuckle on the cheek. Before Staphros could allow himself to think he had won, Celestine burnt bright once more. He rose to his feet and Staphros knew the face that was opposing him was the arrogance of a teenage prodigy.

Celestine closed the distance and Staphros stepped into line. He blocked Celestine's roundhouse to his body by dropping his elbow. Unbelievable amounts of damage travelled through the guard. He followed with a hook from the same side which landed. His speed advantage wouldn't allow Staphros time to raise his guard. He slammed another three hooks with the same hand. This time they were blocked. Staphros swung a wild haymaker to create space, and Celestine danced back. Those hits were too fast for Staphros to block or dodge, but they were stinging strikes rather than mortal ones. Celestine was finding what strength was optimal. Staphros shook the cobwebs away and Celestine resumed the attack. He was slightly slower, but still too fast to dodge consistently. Staphros resorted to blocks and parries. He was being pushed back as he slapped away rapid-fire attacks.

Suddenly an opening, uppercut, then hook, Celestine was stunned. Staphros slipped a hazy counter to dig blow after blow into Celestine's body. Blood spurt and erupted from Celestine's mouth to the floor as he wheezed and coughed.

Smack!

Staphros was now looking at the stars; Celestine's desperate knee came out of nowhere. His forehead was split and gushing blood. As the blood rushed out of his head, so did the wind from his mouth. The impact of the sole of Celestine's foot made Staphros's body almost wrap around his ankle as he thrust a side kick into his stomach. Staphros soared like an arrow loosed at a ranged foe, through Magnus's carriage and crashing into a fishing shop. He landed with a crash and shatter of, glass, clay, and wood. There were no signs of movement.

It was silent to the ears that were deaf to the sounds they had become accustomed to, the crackling of the burning village, the washing of the shore, and the settling of the dust. The red sky grew richer reflecting the blood that had been shed this night. The black clouds snowed the ashes of a dead Zorrodon that had not a grave to be buried. The stars were gone, the moon could not be seen. The only star that remained was the brilliant light of Celestine's shining cloak. He was fixated on the fishing shop where Staphros remained motionless.

All the onlookers were stunned at the sights they were witnessing, the dock folk gasped as the soldiers cowered. They were all spectators now, no longer participators in their own fight anymore. Cyrus kept a wondering eye on both Magnus and the shoreline, a helpful lesson from Lion taught him to always looks where others weren't. Magnus was twitching and writing silently on the floor. Whatever this shining man did to him was indeed a punishment worse than death. He hated Magnus but understood why Lion pitied him. Shed of his garbs and status, he was not like the rest of them he was pathetic. It was clear that this man wanted Magnus dead in the same way that he wanted him dead too, but he was unsure whether Lion would want that. In his last words he did not spit hatred to Magnus, but love to his people. Revenge went both ways and perpetuated the hatred. Staphros had a stake in preventing that, and his reasons did not appear to be in service to protect the mayor. It looked like he was protecting the man whom he fought.

Cyrus's wondering eyes caught the incoming of Simmonds fished from the deep waters of the sea. Three of his men carried him and several others flanked with drawn swords. He emerged onto the street, seeing Magnus on the floor, the carriage destroyed, and the man who flung him into the ocean standing above them both. He grimaced.

'Men!' He shouted. 'Get that man!' Simmonds coughed as he barked his command and the army drew their swords to follow the order. Until this point, Celestine had remained stationary, but now his focus was on Simmonds again.

Simmonds pushed his men away and drew his sword on wobbly feet. The dock folk were frozen to their posts, still only spectators. Simmonds limped to the front of his men and led the charge. At the first step, Celestine pointed his fist towards them, and the army stopped in their tracks. They were unable to move; Celestine's will was too strong. The air got thin and one by one they gasped for air like they were choking. They dropped to their knees. Celestine smirked.

Smack!

Celestine didn't see Staphros's knee coming. Once again Celestine's shining cloak dimmed as he lay on the floor.

'If you want to live, LEAVE!' Shouted Staphros to the army. The army gasped for air and studied the giant for a second. Once Celestine stirred to get back up, they scurried away like a colony of ants, leaving Simmonds alone.

Simmonds stood defiantly and Staphros looked back at him coldly.

'I won't stop him next time.' He said. Celestine was back to one knee. Simmonds retreated, leaving Magnus prone and defenceless on the battlefield.

Celestine rose to his feet, angered and technically sound. He wasn't fully himself, but enough to be mortally dangerous. Staphros, however, discovered something in this battle. Celestine was a prodigious fighter because he needed to control the seizures that were brought on by this glow. A glow and seizure that was tempered by a sedative. He was under no illusions that they were way past sedatives, but he noticed that although Celestine didn't feel the pain, he was still vulnerable to concussive blows. Celestine's glow dimmed when Staphros landed hard to his head, but what would happen if he hit as hard as he could. Could he be knocked out, and if so, could he be saved?

'Celestine you are my brother and I love you, but I must do right by you. So, for that.' Staphros picked the splinters and glass shards from his body, then grabbed his shirt and tore it from his chest. The tattered shards of fabric waved in the hot smoky air. 'I'm not going to hold back anymore.'

Temina was across from Talion in the carriage with pale shock and tiredness on both their faces. She had gotten up this morning thinking she was going to make a decent profit selling roses at the fight. Her biggest worry then was not selling enough to cover the overhead cost. So far today, she had fought off an unwanted sexual advance, survived almost certain death, and had fallen in love with what appeared to be a living star. Her day was not going to plan, but the sunrise was coming, and tomorrow was a new day.

Talion sat tapping his cane while swaying in the motion. He had a ponderous look on his face that could have been mistaken for a scowl. Aside from seeing the orb, Talion didn't react to the rather unbelievable news as she expected. He looked like he knew what was going on and was on board with everything she and Luke were saying. Frankly, it worked in their benefit, as they had to do a lot less explaining than they thought. Elias just had to play along like he knew what was going on too, but nobody could know for sure what this insanity was. Talion hadn't said anything during the ride and said very little before; he was just adamant that they needed to find Celestine immediately because the whole country would be in danger if they didn't. Although he claimed to know nothing more than the others, it seemed he was speaking from experience.

Luke was driving Talion's illustrious carriage once again. He had never been trusted with the reigns before today, now he had the reigns twice already. Elias was sat at the top along for the ride next to Luke; he could navigate wherever they needed to go. Though he knew the streets well, Zorrodon was unrecognisable. The city still burnt, there was a slew of the dead, dying, or grieving people on its streets, sodden with the ash of their destroyed homes. Elias had never witnessed anything like this and was forced to bear more with each turn, as the destruction got worse.

'This is bad. This is so bad!' Said Elias gripping his hair with horrified fingers.

'I know mate! I would show it more but I'm coming to grips with not being dead at the moment.' Said Luke. He had told Talion and Elias about what happened, how he was beaten to less than an inch of his life and how Celestine spoke, and he was healed. Nothing made sense about this whole thing. He was hoping that this was a boozy dream, that he would wake up from and it would be the day of the fight again, but that wasn't how things were going to play out. Everything felt too real. Besides, as strange as it sounded, things were too crazy for it to be a dream. No subconscious could invent this scenario.

'What do you think Staphros is doing out here?' Asked Elias.

'My guess, he's stopping Celestine.' Said Luke.

'I'm not sure I follow, you said that he saved your life and stopped those soldiers by the gate. Doesn't seem like the one that needs stopping.'

'There was something in that message I know it, Celestine had to know what was coming. When he spoke to me after he saved Temina and me, he seemed off, like he wasn't himself.'

'Well, from your account wasn't he was shining like a star and mega-powerful. That's not anybody.'

'You're not getting it! I know Celestine well, I know when he isn't himself. No matter what Celestine has always been the kindest man I know. He immobilised the man who attacked me when he saved me and Temina. With a snap of his fingers, it was like lightning was coursing through his body and he was in agony.'

'Rightly so.' Elias interrupted.

'Aye mate, but Celestine looked like enjoyed seeing him like that like he enjoyed being the one to do it.'

'He just stopped him and his comrades from killing his best friend. I'm sure his emotions just bested him at the time, understandably.'

'Possibly, but that just isn't him. Celestine does what he has to do to protect people, he's never enjoyed in anybody's pain no matter how bad they were.' Said Luke. 'He also said he was going to kill that army before he disappeared. I thought at first it was the anger talking, but I saw that he smiled just before he went. I know my friend and I know something is corrupting him.'

'So, you think Celestine is where the army is?'

Luke nodded.

'Well, then he's probably at the docks. If Magnus has gone balls out like this, he's coming for Lion if he hasn't gotten to him already.'

'Which way?'

'Just down that road. If you follow that, it should take you to the centre.' Elias pointed to a street veering right up ahead. Luke steered the horses that way. 'Look, I know he's big and all, but Staphros is still just a man. What can he do against your friend with this immense power?' Asked Elias. Very briefly, Luke felt a confident assurance and a flicker of a smile brightened his face. The smile was not one of happiness or smugness but the kind of smile when true hope appeared in a hopeless situation.

'Staphros is just a man in the way that a shark is just a fish. He's special and he's much different to us. If there is one man in the world that can handle this, it's him.'

'But what can he do against that kind of power?'

'More than you know.' Said Luke.

Staphros had thrown four attempts at the knockout punch and each of them failed. The left and right hook, right uppercut and right cross all either missed or did not connect cleanly enough. Celestine had matured into his optimal self, and Staphros saw a man before him. His techniques were sharp, and he had found the right amount of power to wouldn't sacrifice his speed. Celestine was as good as he ever was, and Staphros was physically outmatched in every way. Celestine was not going to put Staphros away with a single blow, but he was going to hurt him much more than he was going to get hurt, and Staphros was already hurt. His face was covered in crimson as the blood oozed from the gash on his forehead. It coagulated into clumps around his eyes and cheeks where the dirt gathered from Celestine pounding his face into the ground. His eyes were swelling but he could still see for now, but luckily his nose was not broken. Breathing was enough of a chore.

As they faced off, Staphros was breathing heavily. The smoke in the ashy air choked him on inhalation and the ware of battle was tiring him out. When the revelation hit him that it was possible to save Celestine by knocking him out, he went on the attack ignorant to Celestine's rapid learning. Celestine managed to dodge his barrage with ease, but he chased and chased as Celestine evaded and countered. The last counter had put his face in the mud. He knew now that he was not going to hit Celestine with a technique he had used before. He was unsure he had the energy to execute the knockout anyway. His muscles felt like lead, and the blood loss was now beginning to slow him significantly. He had to figure something out quickly because Celestine didn't look fatigued at all, nor was there a blemish on his skin. If this didn't end soon, everything he had done today would be for nothing. Staphros tried to hide his respiratory troubles, but Celestine's eye's saw all.

Celestine closed the distance, he too wanted this to end soon. He leaned away from the defensive swat from the giant. *Smack.* One hit to the body. Staphros fired a straight punch instinctively. *Smack.* The second hit, same spot. Staphros threw an uppercut and missed, but he followed with a spinning back-fist which Celestine ducked. *Smack and Snap.* Celestine had broken his rib.

Staphros dropped to one knee heaving mouthfuls of blood and bile. Breathing was now not only a chore, but it hurt. Celestine didn't relent and flew into a jumping knee to Staphros's face. The giant caught the air bound Celestine and slammed him to the ground. This was his chance! One, two, three, four, five, consecutive punches to the face in quick succession. Celestine's glow dimmed but it wasn't enough; it wasn't gone. Cumulative damage would not put him out; without a devastating final blow. Staphros couldn't generate enough force from this ground position.

Celestine smiled a bloody smile and pushed up with ease before flinging Staphros away. Staphros landed with a smack against the wall, lifting his head to see the bent legs of the table he discarded earlier. They were back where this battle began, the wall, the sword, the shield, and Celestine across from him, absent feeling, remorse, and thought.

Thought.

That was it. Celestine was brilliant physically, almost perfect technically, but his greatest attribute was his mind, as was Staphros's. Maybe it wasn't a technique that was going to facilitate his win, maybe it was a well-placed strategy. Luckily, in his desperation, one came to mind. He stood and dropped his left hand from his chin down by his hip. He bounced on the balls of his feet and used his forward shoulder to cover what his left hand did no longer. His stance was narrow and very defensive, commonly known as "Shelling Up". All he had to do was not be there when Celestine attacked.

Talion's carriage screeched to a halt behind the mass of thousands of dock folk on the shore. The group bundled out; there was no doubt in their mind that they were in the right place. They could hear the screams of exertion, see the flashes of Celestine's light, and feel each impact that landed. They pushed through the crowd to get to the front. Elias's incredulous eyes widened as they witnessed the shining cloak around Celestine.

'By Earth and Sun, you were telling the truth.' He said.

'Aye, course I was!' Said Luke. Talion gasped as he watched his two boys fighting in the street. He didn't know why, but he knew that this fight was for Celestine's soul and Staphros was the only man equipped for this battle. Still, he couldn't just stand by. Staphros was badly injured and narrowly evading the onslaught by Celestine. Talion made his move.

Celestine chased Staphros and tried to hit him, much like he did when the battle began. His failure in doing so was frustrating him and the battle was remarkably similar to the start. The frustration was making him sloppy again. Staphros moved like a boxing veteran taking a gifted youngster to school in the ring and was nigh on untouchable. He stayed as close to the wall as possible with his back to it most of the time. It gave a false sense of security that he was cornered. A real strategist knew that unless you knew what you were doing, you couldn't corner a man at a wall. Staphros's heel caught an extruded stone and tripped. He slammed against the wall and was vulnerable. Celestine launched in, to land the final blow.

'Boys!' Shouted Talion. He was walking towards them slowly. Celestine froze mid punch and saw his uncle approaching. His head twitched and his cloak flickered.

'Talion?' Said Staphros.

Celestine screamed at the name and retreated ripping at his hair. 'He's in the way… He's in the way… He's in the way…' He repeated quicker each time. The blue in his eyes flickered back as inner conflict tore him apart.

Talion stopped in his tracks.

'Celestine. My boy.' He said. Celestine's face hardened and focussed on Talion. Temina and Luke sprinted to Talion's side, but Celestine only saw Talion. Talion was the obstacle. He pounced. Staphros grabbed a rock and launched it at Celestine's head and it connected straight on his ear. Now the focus was back on Staphros.

'Finished with me already brother? Or do you just give up?' he said. He dropped his fist again and bounced on his toes. He nodded to Talion; he had a plan.

Celestine charged and Staphros knew it was now or never to execute the strategy. Step one: Change stance to make all techniques appear different. Step two: Lull Celestine into a previous routine so he becomes the reactive one. Three: Regain energy for the final attack. He could only do this once. Finally: Get Celestine to charge at him and counter with an attack he's seen before.

The inrush came and Staphros launched a counter knee to use Celestine's momentum against him. Celestine saw it coming and dodged it by pulling his body back from the hit, but he didn't see the simultaneous check hook that hit him on the cheek. Staphros pivoted out of the way and directed Celestine headfirst into the wall behind him. Celestine's glow dimmed as he turned around stunned, but Staphros was not done. *Smack.* Punch to the liver. Staphros dragged his left foot back. *Thud.* Kick to the liver. Celestine hunched over as his body seized. *Crack.* A quick kick to the face. Celestine's body shot upright and nose bleeding, but he was starting to heal. Staphros planted his left foot on the ground firmly; he only had one shot to finish this. The intense shining cloak was intensifying as the cumulative damage was waning. This had to work. He put every pain or tiredness away in the back of his mind, numbed himself to execute, for Talion, for Zorrodon, for Celestine.

With pinpoint precision and breakneck speed, Staphros span and slammed a spinning kick, one Celestine would be proud of.

Smack... Lights out.

27 FIVE STAGES

Vida- Narce- 16- 1827

Celestine's shining cloak was extinguished with an explosion that blinded all who saw it. The bright flash engulfed the shore and knocked all spectators back. The whirring squeal in their ears deafened them as their eyes recovered from the flare. They saw Staphros and Celestine lying motionless on the floor, both appeared dead, but they were just supremely tired. Staphros dropped to the floor face first as soon as the kick landed. A man of his experience always knew when an opponent was finished, and Celestine was finished. Now the adrenaline dumped, and the pain set in. His muscles felt like they had each been pulled out of place. There wasn't a part of him that was not shaking; the world was spinning around him. This was his limit. He faded in and out of consciousness, looking over to Celestine who was still. His aura was gone; Celestine had to count on his own strength to survive.

Staphros was content knowing that his brother would not fail in doing that. Rain fell as the giant rested, and the sun started to rise.

Talion, Luke and Temina rushed down the street towards them. In the distance and darkness, a figure stood over Celestine's body, lingering over it, they didn't even acknowledge Staphros was there. At first, Luke thought it was the one that was at the arena, even then that person had a keen interest in Celestine. The black trail led to the space where the tyrant mayor used to be. The rain had blackened the fallen ash to shroud all in dark. The glimmer of the steel dagger in his hand was now the only ominous shine on the dock shore.

'Magnus! Stop!' Screamed Temina. Magnus shot a manic glare at the incoming trio. Then he quickly checked to see if Staphros was moving, he was not. He dropped to his knees and stabbed the dagger in red rage through Celestine's heart. Celestine opened his eyes and jerked as the blade entered. His eyes were blue again, the brilliant blue absent their divine shine. He was

206

himself again; Staphros saved him from himself. He reached out confused trembling as the world blackened around him. The knife in his heart brought ease to the pain of his ravaged body, as he was guided to the next world. The last thing he saw was Magnus's inhuman black smile.

Luke dropped to his knees screaming, as did Temina, but Talion he was possessed with the speed and strength of his youth. He charged at Magnus. Magnus was consumed with the satisfaction of what he did, he didn't see him coming. Talion tackled him to the ground. Magnus fought but could not get free; Talion overpowered him. His tears flowed like rapids over harsh rocks of wrinkles. The tracks of his tears were prominent on his ash darkened face. His eyes were blood red and wide. His breathing was frantic, as he hissed and gritted his teeth like a rabid wolverine. He strangled Magnus with both hands shaking in horror. He clamped his teeth down tight, and saliva escaped his mouth, falling with the tears. He pushed. The life was fading in his nephew's killer's eyes, and he smiled inside then he stopped suddenly.

Talion regained his honour and got off of him. Magnus gasped for air, and rolled to his knees, shocked at the old man's strength. Talion thought of his redemption. He hadn't killed since he left Anara. His war was over; he wasn't a soldier anymore. He wasn't the champion or sworn protector. That was behind him and he felt he had been redeemed for the sake of those who loved him, those who were sacrificed for him. Magnus cowered hoping that he had managed to slither out of another fatal situation. He wanted to escape and hide, get as far away from the Thiago's and Zorrodon as possible. Talion picked up his cane.

'Kastielle I am sorry' he said. Magnus looked on in horror as Talion pulled the handle, revealing a rapier blade. The sunlight beamed against the metal and he pointed it to Magnus's throat. Magnus once again scuttled on the floor like a wounded spider. Luke watched on like a child while Talion stalked the downed Magnus. Talion studied his hidden blade with admiration and fear. Celestine, his boy, the very embodiment of his redemption, if he went through with this, he would lose all the honour that he had worked to salvage. The rain fell harder, large droplets chimed against the steel of the blade. They washed away the dark ash mask on Talion's face revealing his sorrow and shame. He had failed to protect his last connection to home and his honour. He prayed his morning prayer, as he did every day at sunrise. He didn't pray to his beloved alone this day. Today he had to beg for forgiveness for all of those he loved.

'Eros, I am sorry' Said Talion.

Magnus held up his hands begging. 'I am sorry, I was wrong.' He said.

'Isobelle, I am sorry'

'Please!' Magnus wept in stuttering terror.

'Sakura...' Talion heard the cries of Temina and Luke, who's loss was almost as great as his. His resolve hardened. 'Gomen Nasai.' he said in an apology to his beloved. He swiped the blade across Magnus's throat. Magnus's mouth filled with blood his neck gushed violently. He coughed and grimaced as he wrestled for life. He held on helplessly using his fingers to seal the wound, digging his fingers into the folds of his lacerated skin to try and pinch wound together. He gasped, coughed, and spluttered on the ground.

Talion stood there and watched him die.

It was coming into the evening on Sakura Farm when Talion's carriage pulled in through the dirt track. The soil was damp with the morning rain and the grass still had the wet smell on it. Elias drove the carriage with Cyrus of the Hondos sat on the passenger side. The carriage was also being flanked by four of the Hondos on horseback. They all had grave expressions on their face. Samantha and Hana both recognised the carriage and ran to it whilst it was stopping. Samantha looked up at Elias,

'Where's Talion?' She asked. Elias nodded back to the cabin with red eyes. One of the Hondos men dismounted and opened the door. From the cottage, Mac bounded towards the forming group panting hand half barking in excitement. Samantha's eyes lit up to see his face. His eager face reminded her of the pups, they had started to stand up.

'Celestine!' she called. 'Celestine come out here. Mac has something to show you.' There was no answer, not from anybody. She was met with silence and blank expressions from all. She looked to Hana for answers and she had none. Mac circled Samantha in excitement until she rubbed his head and he sat. Finally, Luke stepped out of the carriage. He was white as a sheet and his expression was eerily lost, dead behind the eyes.

'Sam?' he said to his sister in disbelief. He huffed in choked breaths as an infant does when yearning for comfort from a parent. He grabbed his sister and pulled her into the tightest embrace he had ever given her.

'Luke are you okay?' She asked. She hadn't seen him cry like this since their parents died.

Luke didn't answer. He shuddered in her arms before breaking down. He felt like he had been shattered, he was beyond weak.

'Luke, what happened? Where's Celestine?' Asked Hanabi. Mac stood with his head low and crept to the carriage. He sniffed out and froze on the spot. Luke hugged Samantha tighter as she followed Mac's line of sight. She couldn't make it out at first, but there was no mistaking it. Celestine was lying dead on the carriage seats. She gasped at first and shook second.

'He saved the city.' Said Cyrus from atop the carriage. 'They both did.'

'No, no, no, no, Celestine. Not Celestine! Please, not him!' Cried Samantha. Now the balance of support was shifting to Luke, who saved some strength for his sister for this exact moment. She screamed into the sky.

Hana approached the cabin which revealed, Staphros motionless and

Talion in a catatonic state holding his nephews head in his arms, and Temina sat beside Staphros with bandages and medicine at the ready. Hana stepped back in absolute stunned amazement.

'What on Earth happened?'

The Hondos men carried Celestine's body to the medical building behind the Big House. They tried to help Staphros, but he refused and limped into the outhouse. The large door slammed and a noteworthy chuck of the bolt locking the door behind him. Talion bore down the steep step off the carriage and made for the Big House without a word. It was quiet with only the wind telling the story of the day. Hanabi reached for his arm, but he didn't even register her presence. He looked through her, through everything and ambled to his home where he would isolate himself in his bedroom and say his prayers. Temina, Luke, Samantha, and Hana were the only ones left. Luke held his sobbing sister nodded up towards Temina.

'Umm, this is Temina. She uhh, was Celestine's…' He paused. He didn't have a word for what they were, nobody did. It was like they were a day late to it becoming something more than it was. It was Temina's last regret when she faced her death and would remain so forever. When Celestine saved her, it gave her hope that she could put that right, but she couldn't. One kiss was not enough. Samantha turned around, trying to hold it together and took Temina's hand. She helped her out of the cabin.

'I know you. Celestine spoke of you a lot.' She said. Temina's eyes filled with both happiness and deep regret simultaneously. The conflict drew tears, but they did not fall as she fought them back with a smile. Samantha looked up at her smiling. The setting sun revealed the gentle cream of Temina's skin and the rounded curve of her cheeks. Her eyes were full of pain, but they were somehow more enchanting like a tree frozen by winters cold.

'You're just as beautiful as he said.' Said Samantha. Temina took a deep breath and nodded.

'Thank you…' she said almost inaudibly. Her voice came back to her as her composure betrayed her. Samantha took her in her arms and all the love she had for Celestine she poured into Temina. Temina understood why Luke was the way he was, why he was beholden to Celestine and loved him so much. His sister was a carer, a lover, kind, and sweet in ways that Luke tried to hide but he was deep down. Samantha just knew how to show it.

'If you would like a place to stay, I can prepare you a room in the Big House.' Said Hanabi. She was just as affected as the others, but her culture had ingrained in her to hide such flagrant emotions.

'No.' Luke interjected. 'She'll stay in the cottage, in Celestine's room.' He said. He knew all that she wanted was more time with him, time to get to know him. She was unique amongst every other person on this patch of land, she did not have the luxury of Celestine's memory but grieved all the same.

Temina nodded, as did everybody else. Samantha got Elias's attention from atop the cart.

'Thank you for looking after my brother and everyone. If you park the carriage by the barn, I will have someone get that for you. I also have some food left from dinner. Meet me in the Big House and I'll fix you a plate. Tell the other fellas, too.' She said. She was occupying herself now. She always coped with these things by caring for others. She coped with the death of her parents by caring for Luke and she had not stopped caring since.

The group separated knowing each needed their own space. Luke, however, went with Temina, he had memories to spare of his best friend and Temina was in desperate need of some.

Deaths in the family usually came with unwelcome questions, especially the unexpected untimely ones. People were naturally curious and would ask questions like, "What happened?" or "Were you there?". Then there would come the barrage of unwanted but practical questions about funeral arrangements and so on. All who were there wished they weren't, and the residents of Sakura Farm didn't ask any of those questions though they were curious. They just did what they could themselves to ease the burden.

They were floored just hearing of Celestine's death. They could only imagine what it would have been like to see it happen. Unfortunately, the question that was bound to be asked was the worst of all.

'Are you okay?' Asked Hanabi as she stepped through Talion's bedroom door. Talion was at his study staring at a blank page on the table. He had no idea what the page was for. He did not have the means to write or draw, he just had the page. He tapped it with his finger frustrated at its blankness, but incapable of scribing anything, unsure of what to scribe. He didn't notice that Hanabi had come in. She cleared her throat and bowed.

'Sumimasen Talion san.' She said. Talion looked up at her with stone-like features.

'Yes, Hanabi.' He said. He would usually answer in Nihongo, her native tongue. He left the words to hang out in the dulling darkness of the twilight sky. He sounded calm, too calm. It was a kind of calm that was so obviously forced it was more threatening than a primal scream. Hana did not shy away; she trusted Talion, but she approached with caution like entering a lion's den.

'I wanted to ask if you were okay.' She said.

'Then ask away.' Said Talion. Hana was unnerved by his reply, but more so by the look on his face. Even in the shadow of sunset, he looked pale and drawn.

'Are you okay?' She asked.

'No, I am not. Thanks for asking now go away.' He was cold and dismissive, like he was both on the offensive and defensive, not of himself but her. He was trying to spare her but could not muster the words to communicate that. He was so enthralled in his grief and shame he couldn't think. Every part of him wanted a target to let it all out on.

'Okay Talion, but you know if you want to talk about it…'

'Talk about what? What is this "It" that I'd want to talk about?' Asked Talion, losing the calmness he once so vehemently forced.

Hanabi said nothing

'Please tell me. Is it that I watched my nephew, my boy, die in front of me today! Or is "It" the fact that I killed the man who did it.' Said Talion.

Hanabi gasped at the revelation.

'Oh, you didn't know that? Want to talk about it? How I took my first life since leaving the bastard King of Anara!? A man who forced me to kill hundreds upon hundreds of people. Fight in wars I didn't want to fight. Shackled me with loyalty and friendship to ensure I did his bidding. Do you want to know about the mile-long list of disgusting violence that I have committed? Do you?' Talion picked up his cane from the other side of his seat and revealed the rapier sword inside. 'Want to know how I did it today? How I took the hidden blade from my cane and sliced open the Mayor of Zorrodon's throat!? Is that the "It" you want to talk about?' he wasn't yet shouting, but everything about his demeanour showed that he wanted to.

'Talion San, I am trying to help.'

'Can you bring Celestine back?' Said Talion screwing the paper under his hand.

Hanabi said nothing.

'Go on answer me!' Said Talion.

Hanabi shook her head.

'Then you can't help me, so leave me alone.' Said Talion, once again for her good. Hana bowed her head and backed out of the room but stopped just before the door and saw the pain on his face break through. It was a pain so deep; she couldn't leave him. His was a life of pain and it was showing on his face, every year, every month, every day, etched on his face in that one second.

'I know you have lost a lot and you feel alone right now. With Celestine, Kastielle and your country with it, and your wife Sakura…' Talion grabbed the vase in the middle of the table and hurled it at the wall. The pranging sound of the glass, porcelain, and marble, shattering was painful to hear. Hanabi screamed and dropped to her knees cowering. Talion stormed over stabbing his cane with more force with each step.

'Don't you dare evoke her name!' Talion yelled. 'Don't you ever!' Hanabi bowed as if praying and holding her hands together begging. She cried tears of panic, fear, empathy, and sadness. No cultural constraints could contain this emotion.

'Go…Gomen ne!' She pleaded. 'Gomen nasai!' The words hung in the darkness but Talion could hear them over and over. It was her voice but, they were his words. The sin of wrath had taken over him again and he was standing over Hanabi as he did with Magnus. He wished that that lapse in his judgement was a by-product of the wrong that Magnus had committed. Yet, there he was again standing over someone who begged him for mercy and Hana and Magnus were not the only ones that had begged for mercy from him. This wasn't an emotional reaction to his circumstance; this monster had been there for decades. The monster was breaking from the weakened chains. It shook him from his trance, and he gave pause to his anger.

'Hana… I'm sorry.' He said in confused bewilderment. He reached for her to help her to her feet. Hana quivered on her knees when she saw the hand coming and she ran out of the room as quick as she could. She had heard Talion speak of the sin that plagued him, but she didn't believe it until that moment. The look in his eyes showed a man capable of irredeemable acts.

Hana ran to her room and locked the door. Talion stared at his palms as the blood from his past sins resurfaced to stain them red again. He could do nothing to stop it. Hana had left the door open on her way out. He closed it behind her falling against it to sit on the floor.

'I am so sorry.' He said sobbing into his folded arms.

On the far end of Sakura Farm's acreage, the medical facility overlooked the ocean coast at the foot of the white cliffs they sat on top of. It was an elongated rectangular building made of Anglonian red brick. The sun was almost set, sparing the last of its light to shine on the building that housed Celestine. This evening the medical staff, that worked day and night, were not there. The midwives, nurses, and doctors were sent home. The only one that remained was the one who managed the facility day to day, Sandra Doctor, also known as Doc.

Doc had been at Sakura Farm from the beginning. She had come a long way since then, becoming incredibly accomplished in medicine. She, like most others, came to work on Sakura Farm as a slave. The tragedy of her past extended beyond the confines of servitude and that pain would never leave her, no matter how far she had come. She was a house slave to a lord in the north, a lord that had lost his heir fighting in the Anglonian Civil War. In his grief, he sought comfort in the arms of his favourite slave that he called, Sandy. Night after night, she would be snuck into a different chamber in the manor each time and the lord would lay with her, cursing his wife calling her, frigid and barron. When she fell pregnant and eventually birthed a son to the lord, he was ripped away before she could even look at him. She would never get to see him, as the lord sent her to Leeburn Valley to make the trip down south.

On sale and on display as a voluptuous twenty-something that was proven to be fertile and served well as a comfort girl. Slavery was an ugly affair always, but it was on display at her lowest when she met a handsome older man, accompanied by a giant holding a baby in his arms. Talion had heard her story and offered her freedom and requested she works for him. Talion never asked any other slave to work for him, just her. She was to be a wet-nurse for baby Celestine.

As a professional, she knew that Celestine was Talion's boy and was not the boy she had given birth to, but he was hers in the eyes of the mother she never got to be. He clung to her, slept in her bed, and grew in her arms. She watched him learn to walk, learn to speak, and eventually learn to not need her as much. He left her nest forgetting he was ever part of it in the first place. That lesson was much harder for her to learn than him. Once Celestine flew from her nest, she had inherited a duty of care that inspired her to do more. She still watched Celestine from afar, but she would study and become better, become excellent. Her excellence granted her the name Doctor, and she could shed the past away. Discarding the name Sandy once and for all, she was Doc from then on.

Doc stood over Celestine's body numb. She wanted privacy. She wanted a moment to once again be the mother she never had the opportunity to be and for him to be her boy again. Although as each year went by and their connection faded, it never fully disappeared. He always looked at her with reverence and love that only a son could have, she hoped that was so, at least. She wished that her connection with him would be re-established as it was before, and it would invigorate him to live once more. A mother's touch could fix anything. As a woman of science, she knew that that wasn't the case. Her faith remembered how special Celestine was. He could do things that nobody else could, even as a boy. She looked upon his cold and pale face, begging for one more miracle.

She stroked his hair away from his face and he looked at peace. The doubt that ravaged his mind, the need to prove himself was gone. There was nothing left to prove, and he was still, so very still. His skin was soft to the touch yet cold. Scissors sliced though the blood-soaked fabric of his top to reveal the mortal wound. The hole was deep going through his still heart. She cursed in anguish the man capable of doing this to him.

When the Hondos brought him in, they had recounted what they witnessed. Some of it sounded fantastic like they had drunk too much strongwine whilst reading one of Kastielle's fantastic stories. Those details were to be deduced later, what was true, was the outcome. Celestine had died and he did so by fighting for the people who could not. If there was one thing that would force an untimely death upon Celestine it would be in defending others. That just was the man he was. Doc and Talion was wax lyrical like proud parents about Celestine, saying that he was a hero in waiting. They didn't understand that hero, by most other metrics in history, was just another word for martyr.

Half compelled by her duty as a doctor and her instinct as a mother,

Doc cleaned the stab wound and began the stitching. As she threaded the needle, she couldn't help but think she could have done more. She took a step back when Celestine grew up and she watched him from afar. Their connection was strong then and if she acted upon that connection, those instincts, she would have given the boy a mother. Talion was a great man, but a very hard man. It was an inevitability that Celestine would run into battle when he saw others in danger. Even though Talion taught him not to do that, the son would always follow the father's actions and disobey his words. A mother would have lent her knowledge of another way to help. She could have given him an incentive to come home. Give him the love that he lacked from Talion and make him less eager to make him proud by jumping into a war without thought. Of course, she would never blame Talion. She just felt she could have done more.

She could have stopped this.

Doc pulled the thread tight and closed the wound. She took a cloth and wetted it wiping away any dirt she saw on Celestine's body. She was as meticulous as Celestine would have been about himself. She combed his hair and washed it, leaving it to dry in the cold open air.

When Temina first came into the cottage, Luke intended to give her a tour of the place. She walked through the beautifully decorated hallway. The place had a smell that she couldn't define. It was just him, a smell of Celestine. They reached the sitting room without a word. Neither of them knew what to say and there was a very long silence.

Then they cried.

The next few hours were instances of them trading idioms that meant nothing. They knew they were obvious and painful to say and hear, but it was something. Something was always better than the silence or the sound of tears. During one of the longer periods of quiet, the tiredness finally caught up with Temina and she fell asleep. Luke couldn't bring himself to think about sleeping. He was tired but he had gone much longer without sleep with a much greater desire to do so. He wanted to keep busy. He shuffled into the kitchen quietly and cooked a simple meal for him and Temina: eggs, with spinach, and cheese in a stone pot and placed on thick slices of bread. The smell brought Temina from her dreams and into the kitchen.

'Did you make this?' She asked.

Luke nodded. Temina examined what was on the plate and was impressed to see that it looked as good as it smelled.

'It looks delicious thank you.' She sat on the table and lifted her knife and fork. The smell took her out of the moment for a second. As she sliced and had the first mouthful, the flavours made her forget.

'I know it's not much. It's really Samantha that's the chef in the family, but I try from time to time.' Said Luke almost apologetically. He was thinking of her and wanted to take care of her. Temina smiled and shook her head.

'I really appreciate this. Thank you.'

The sun was setting. The cast of shimmering green grass dancing in the breeze was dimming. The reach of the orange overcast pawed its light fingers over the land of Anglonia. Sakura Farm was no exception. The day seemed slow, but now that it was coming to an end it had gone all too soon. When the sun was up, it was like time stopped. Now it was going down the reality was, it had passed everybody by while they were frozen in stasis. Time stopped for no one. The hours passed in a matter of minutes and the minutes felt like days to endure. Everybody dwelled on what may have been, or what could have been. Most of all, they dwelled on what was. Temina could not dwell on what was, because it was never there.

Celestine's bedroom was immaculate on the most part. He took as much care of his environment as he did himself. For a man that combed each strand of hair on his head at least one-hundred times, it meant there was not much mess. Luke was stood in the doorway reluctant to go in. He didn't want to disturb the aura the room had. The bed was neatly made, the rug on the floor and had nary a crease in sight. The wardrobe was left ajar to let his clothes air. This was the room where Temina was going to stay. It was only right because that was what Celestine would have wanted. Luke had retreated up the creaky wooden stairs to "sort things out" in his own words. He knew Celestine. He knew how clean the man was, and he knew there wouldn't be much for him to do, but this was a way for him to be with his friend while still being there for Temina. A Chef, in reference to the siblings not the occupation, never left anybody unattended. Finally, he took a step in and soaked in the presence of his best friend for the first time in this way. The room was heavy like it was filled with water that he couldn't drown in, but he felt like he was floating in it. The desk by the window stood out conspicuously in the immaculate image. It was a bit of a mess. It wasn't terrible, but it was cluttered with papers and parchments. Inkblots and smudges of charcoal on the soft wooden base. Luke hadn't noticed it before, likely because Celestine cleared it when he knew people were coming. That desk always had a white cloth on top of it, with a vase and flowers much like the one that lay shattered on Talion's bedroom floor. It was all about the image, even in the comfort of his bedroom. He had to hide his imperfections always, but he didn't get that opportunity this time. Luke was glad of it though. It gave him something new about his friend to keep for himself.

With the care he imagined his friend would take, he sorted the mess of papers. He never knew Celestine drew, but with every piece of paper he flipped and placed, a new picture was there. Every picture was better than the last, telling the story of the two-hundred-six-day trip around the world between two companions closer than family. Every landscape painted or scratched with graphite or charcoal revealed every detail of where they were.

Luke felt like he was right where the picture was with Celestine at his side. He challenged himself to order the images into piles in order of where they went, last to first. It took him a little longer than he had planned but it occupied him.

The sun climbed down its twilight ladder as the day got darker. With the last slivvers of daylight the sky had to offer, he glimpsed a picture that was unlike the others. Whereas every other picture on the table was an in-depth landscape of where he had been, this final drawing was a portrait. A still of the only muse that would inspire him to capture the human form. Temina.

The picture of her was of her picking the flowers in her garden, for the very special bouquet. Luke could see what went into this picture, what it was crafted with, without flaw. Celestine detailed everything he could. A flawless memory of the woman he loved. Luke placed the picture atop the pile and slid it into the drawer under the desk.

He would tell Temina about the image, just not yet.

When Luke made his way down the stairs, Temina was admiring the impressive collection of books in the sitting room. The room was lit modestly by a few candles as twilight turned to night. Even as basic a fact as Celestine loved to read, was not afforded to her. Everything was new to her. She had the "Quest for the Spiritual Court" book in her hand. That was one of Luke's more recent memories but one of his most cherished ones. The bookshelf was one of Celestine's most prized possessions. It was tall, thick, and sturdy. Most importantly, it was filled with books. Celestine loved to read; he was an adventurer in his mind as well as in body.

'Are you a fan?' Asked Luke. Temina turned around startled almost dropping the book.

'I haven't read them, to be honest, but I have a feeling he liked them.' she said referring to the collection of twenty-four books in the series. She looked at the book in her hands like it was something precious and it was in many ways to many people.

'It was his favourite book.' Luke approached Temina to share her stare at the precious object.

'Have you read it?' She asked.

Luke nodded choking on his words initially. 'I hadn't until recently. Then when I was bored once, then he gave it to me to read. I teased him for reading that stuff, but when I picked it up myself, I understood. He let me keep it after that.' Luke tapped the cover of the book. 'That was the last thing he gave me…' He struggled to get the last words out. He covered his eyes and shuffled into the kitchen to hide his sadness. He wiped his face clear and cleared his throat.

'Luke?' Said Temina to check on him.

'Oh aye!' Luke answered.

'You okay?'

'O'course. Would you like another tea? I'll do us another brew.' Temina stood at the kitchen entrance watching Luke scramble to make the tea. She stopped him.

'It's okay Luke, I'm fine but I think you need time.'

'I'm fine lass.' Luke protested, but he was struggling to hide it.

Temina said nothing, watching him.

'I just want you to be okay.' He hugged her tightly in his arms as he wept into her shoulder. All he wanted to do was to do right by her. His best friend's girl.

'I know Celestine would've wanted the same for you.' She said.

Luke nodded. He knew she was right. He was motivated to take care of her, but part of him was petrified to confront his feelings. He didn't want to go home, to bed, then it would be real. Today would officially be the day his best friend died.

Temina kissed him on the cheek and saw him to the door. She watched him make the long walk across the field to the Big House waving him home. Then she turned to head back in. When that door closed, she was alone and now she had to confront feelings of her own.

She lingered with the door at her back for a while. There was an absence of thought within her, the feeling of drifting that Luke had in Celestine's bedroom. Now that she was cut loose from the safety of Luke's company, the current had washed her into the sitting room. She stared at the bookshelf now realising that she still had the book in her hand. The book felt heavy, like returning it would be a great ordeal. The weight pulled her down to slump against the wall and sit on the floor beside the chair that she had sat on not but minutes ago.

She fixated on the bookshelf piecing the limited time she had to see Celestine's face to create a memory she did not have. The memory was Celestine giving Luke the book. She couldn't explain why she wanted that memory, that image of Celestine, but she did. It meant something more to her, like that moment encapsulated his entire character in a snapshot. A character she hadn't had the chance to see. She closed her eyes and drew the scene in her mind. When the scene was set, ghosts of Celestine and Luke stood before her in the sitting room in the warm candlelight.

She shed a tear of joy and replayed the memory over and over until she was content.

She didn't realise she had fallen asleep until she woke back up. Last she remembered the apparition of Celestine was handing Luke the book in the candlelight. Now the candle had burnt out and the room was pitch black. She couldn't see the bookshelf anymore. The star and moonlight barely revealed the outlines of her fingers. The silver light streamed in through the glass pane of the front door. It shed little light through the sitting room window. Temina rushed to patch together the synthetic memory again but it had been and gone. That was hers and hers alone. She had nothing of his that belonged to her, nothing but the sadness that he was gone. The darkness cloaked his features and now for all her might and imagination, she couldn't even remember his face.

She slammed her head against the side of the chair. Then she did the same with her fists, first at the chair then the wall. She was frustrated with herself more than anything. She hated herself for being so naive and loving a man she didn't know, allowing herself to do this. Now she was stuck here in this extremely unique pain that nobody could understand. She loved a man she did not know and mourned him as if she were his widow.

Love made no sense. Grief took no prisoners.

Temina placed her open palms over her face, bringing on a darkness of her design, and bawled hopelessly into them. Alone, nobody could hear her despair. She didn't know if that was a good or bad thing.

There was a warm but heavy mass that landed on her lap. She removed her hand and there was Porsche, laying on Temina as she did on Celestine when she needed him. It was like this was her way of paying him back. To be there for the woman Celestine loved as he was there for her. Temina looked at the doorway. Mac stood there with a moonlight backdrop flanked by his litter of pups. He bowed his head showing Temina the respect he gave Celestine. Porsche hooked Temina's wrist with her paw and brought it from her face. Even in the dark, Temina could see her features. They were wise and stern. Porsche's eyes told her that she missed him too. The litter of puppies clumsily ambled towards Temina, climbing on their mother to get to her.

Animals had a way of loving more than any human could comprehend, but they also knew how to move on. They loved their master, but he was gone and as hard as it was, they had to accept it and move on. Porsche was trying to get that across to Temina in the only way she knew how. Temina knew that nothing was going to replace Celestine, and there was no way to bring him back, but his dogs needed him, and now they have her. Holding onto forced fake memories was not the way to keep him with her. He'd stay with her no matter what, if she allowed it.

She just had to accept the truth that he was gone.

28 CHAMPION OF ZORRODON - ANGEL OF ANGLONIA

It had been four days since Talion, Staphros, and Luke returned form Zorrodon. In that time, the residents of Sakura Farm got on with what they needed to do. Even without the management or authority, they didn't relent in their duties, in fact, they worked harder. Talion was seldom seen in the Big House, some would catch a glimpse of him whilst delivering food. Most could hear the sombre shuffles of his feet at night as he wandered the halls in the dark. Nobody heard him sleep where his snores were normally audible from rooms away; there was now conspicuous silence. Staphros was completely out of sight. As soon as he locked himself in the outhouse he stayed there. Nobody heard from him at all. He didn't even leave for his morning run anymore, a routine he hadn't missed willingly for eighteen years. Luke, on the other hand, stayed busy.

He took ownership of arranging the funeral himself. The other residents helped as much as they could in their downtime. He visited with Temina often, to see if she was okay. Every day got a little easier for her. She had grown to love her new pack of dogs and often talked about them when Luke visited with her. Porsche and Mac bonded with her and their relationship was getting stronger each day. In the end, relationships were nothing but bonds built upon the foundations of shared endeavour. There was no greater endeavour to be shared than loss.

After the recommended revisions suggested by Staphros, Archie went from an eager youth rushing his project to the consummate perfectionist. He tooled away adding finite details that far exceeded the brief the giant had set. His only hope was to make him proud. When Luke approached him with a new project, it was bittersweet. He was honoured to be trusted with the task, but never in his wildest dreams did he ever think he would be forging Celestine's burial slab. He knew his heart had to go into it and Luke knew that too, but four days was awfully quick. Still, Archie accepted knowing he had to try for Celestine.

It was on the table under a black cloth. The constant slapping of his jittering heel against the floor resembled the erraticism of his heartbeat. He was nervous. Luke wasn't the type of person to get nervous about, but for this reason, this cause, he was. Archie looked up to Celestine, as did many of the children on the farm. He was like everybody's big brother and a lot of those children wanted to be like him.

The forge was hot and in the summer heat Archie was sweating buckets, but he didn't care. Luke had trusted him with this, but Luke hadn't seen it once yet. He had been too busy with the other arrangements. He had taken on the burden alone, Staphros and Talion were locked away in their grief. The furnace was off, the doors were open, but it wasn't getting cooler in there. Archie refused to leave, not even for a drink. He didn't care if that meant that his funeral clothes were sweat through. Celestine deserved his best, his integrity.

Luke walked in he was dressed all in black and his hair was combed to a slick consistency. Archie stood bolt upright.

'Is it ready?' Asked Luke. Archie swallowed hard, unsure of how to answer that. It was ultimately a matter of his choice if it was ready. Even if it wasn't, the funeral was going to begin in an hour, so it had to be. In the end, Archie settled with a nod.

He grabbed the black cloth and revealed the tablet. Archie had poured his heart and soul into this design and it showed. The craftsmanship that went into the shaping of it, the calligraphic golden engravings, and the polished finish, if Luke had the power to give Archie the Smith name, he would have there and then. The boy was good. He nodded in approval and gave the young man a firm handshake.

'It's beautiful.' He said patting Archie on the back of the head. 'Could you run that over to Doc and the others, they will put that on the pyre.' He continued. Archie smiled proud of what he'd done and took the tablet where Luke requested. The golden engraved letters glistened in the new sunlight against their polished stone backdrop. The words etched into Luke's heart; Archie had chosen them well.

"Celestine
Champion of Zorrodon.
Angel of Anglonia.
Vida- Narce- 16- 1827
Aged 27"

The words were simple but, Luke could not think of a better way to describe him. An Angel in western and northern folklore was an individual with a soul of pure good.

The beach was filled with the residents of the farm, Elias of the Hideaway, and The Hondos led by Cyrus now. They saw what Celestine did for them and they appreciated it more than anything. The mass formed an honour guard leading to the ocean bay for a sea burial befitting an adventurer. Everybody was dressed in black and the sun was highest in the sky. The tide rolled in and out darkening what sand it touched. The guests closest to the ocean had their shoes wetted, but that was of little consequence.

Temina came down the path with Luke beside her. She had a black gown that hung loose on her body. She and Luke could feel the atmosphere. There were regrets and pain in such abundance, there was no clear path back to the way things were. That was the case in most funerals. There was never a way back to the way things were. They walked to the end and faced each other. Luke stayed strong and Samantha took his hand, proud that her little brother had organised this. To an outside eye, they would say it was a shame it took Celestine dying for him to be capable of growing up. Samantha saw it a different way. It took Celestine living for him to realise that he was able to. Temina stood alone, next to a sea of people that did not know her, burying the only man she loved.

Talion marched out to the chorus of subdued clapping. This was his first appearance since the death. They were clapping in his honour, but also in appreciation for this first big step to his recovery. He did not walk to the end but stopped just short. He stood upright trying to compose himself, but the applause was unnerving to his resolve. His hand trembled atop his cane and he winced as the sadness overpowered him. He lowered his head and let it wash over him. A teardrop rolled from his nose onto the sea-soaked sand. Hanabi took his hand and held it. She hadn't forgiven him for what happened the other day. In her mind, there was nothing to forgive. Pain was a disease that at times was contagious. Then he heard the clapping and the applause, reading between the lines. Hanabi's hand told him that he wasn't alone in his pain. He was very much a part of something. He still cried, but his tears held a much different meaning.

Porsche and Mac took the lead as Staphros marched down the footpath carrying the boat destined to take Celestine to the beyond. Even after five days, Staphros's face was bruised and his body still visibly ailed him. He still insisted on carrying Celestine alone. He could only trust himself with the job. He marched through the crowd, who applauded for the fallen howling in sorrow. He stopped at Talion and the two rottweilers paused to stare back at him. He and Talion hadn't seen each other since that day. He looked down at him and Talion looked up. Staphros holding the bond between them on his shoulders.

'I'm sor…'

'I know son. I know.' Said Talion.

Staphros marched on.

When they got to the seabed, the dogs stopped and sat as Staphros marched through the space between them. He went far enough in, so the water was waist-deep then he rested the boat on the water. Porsche plodded over to Temina's side rubbing her head against her leg. Mac stayed put. He was sniffing the air, trying to take one last piece of his master before he was gone forever. He sat still mostly though. He knew rationally that there was nothing to take, as rationally as the mind of a dog could be. Mac understood death, he knew its permanence.

Staphros took one last look at his brother. The rocking of the ocean acted as if it was rocking Celestine like a sleeping baby. The seamstresses had designed him a new coat, this time the main body was blue and had golden flames as its trim. It couldn't be seen, but it had the sun surrounded by a ring of stars embroidered on the back also in gold. His hair was perfectly combed a hundred strokes on each part. His face was radiant in the onlooking warming sunlight. Staphros leaned forward and kissed Celestine goodbye.

'Farewell.' He said.

The rocking intensified all of a sudden, as two very large ships sailed towards the beach. The water splashed in intense waves and the tide rushed deeper into the onlooking masses. The sails were lowered on both ships and they coasted along with the current until they were close enough. There was a fever on both ships that blared into the clear sky. The crews were chanting something, but it wasn't until they had gotten much closer that it became clear that they were chanting Celestine's name.

The ship to the left was unrecognisable to all but Luke, The Aduantas. Alec hung from the edge alongside his merry band of travellers. He waved and Luke nodded back raising his fist. The other ship was grand white and royal, The Liusaidh, King Lochlyn II's ship. The King stood at the edge with Finn at his side. Luke had invited Finn to the funeral, not knowing of his misdeeds with Temina. That was a secret she wanted hidden. In his invite, he implored him to tell King Lochlyn II of what Celestine did for him. It appeared that he did one better and convinced him to accompany The Aduantas in guiding Celestine's passage into the afterlife.

The two ships dropped anchor and the ocean rested. The honour guard now extended into the deeper reaches of the ocean. A battalion of king's guards marched to the edge of the ship holding an array of instruments: drums, bagpipes, strings. As the crew assembled on the opposite ship, King Lochlyn II signalled for them to begin. The king's guard played an orchestral composition, that had Celtish heritage and charm. The opposing traveller's crew slammed the side chanting Celestine's name. Staphros turned and bowed to the Celtish king, humbled that he travelled for this.

When news reached Finn about Celestine's death he was devastated.

The two of them had developed a bond of which only allied soldiers could share. Champions nowadays were seen as show ponies, spectacles that the public could cheer for. Finn didn't see it that way and neither did Celestine. They understood the old ways. Talion represented the old way as much as Finn's father did. Champions were there to fight the wars so that it could spare the lives of thousands. That was why Finn couldn't refuse the fight in Zorrodon; it was his war. When that became clear to Celestine, he joined him in whatever way he could, and the burden was shared. His war was won; the Celtish's war was won because of the aid that he provided. Finn told King Lochlyn II of Celestine's deeds and the aid that Talion and the others gave. He told the king that Celestine gave his life protecting him, to preserve the honour of Celtish Anglonia and the king was compelled to come.

Luke released his sister's hand and marched into the water, washing away what everybody thought of him, what he thought of himself. He was supposed to be a joker and now the secret was out that he could be serious. He was supposed to always smile and now the secret was out that he could also cry. Now, under the great eye of Time himself and all whom he loved, he had one more secret to tell. A secret that only Celestine knew when watching him in a pub in Elgin. He took the other side of Celestine, opposite Staphros. Amid the great ships that roared in honour of his friend, and his family that watching him on the sandy shore, Luke realised he was surrounded by love. Resolved to tell the secret only one other knew, The Aduantas stopped banging, the instruments silenced, and Luke told his secret.

He sang.

"There was a man called Celestine,
who travelled round adventuring,
and they called him, an Angel.
He was brave and strong and very kind
and if you met him, I'd bet you'd find
that you'd call him, and Angel."

Luke took a deep breath looking to Finn on The Liusaidh and Alec on The Aduantas for strength. They nodded giving it to him and accompanied by every voice and instrument on each ship they sang "The Angel of Anglonia" Celestine's Song.

"He was an example of good.
He did everything he could.
To keep us safe from harm.
On the docks of Zorrodon.
Cause he was a saint, he was a hero, but before all that.
He was a friend, he was a brother,
He was loved.

Then one day, young Celestine'

Stood up and took on an army.
So we called him, a Legend.
He took men down with a single punch.
He beat their arse, the dirty cunts.
So we called him, a Legend.

But then they, stabbed him in the heart.
When his life's about to start.
I wish this was not his end,
Because he was by best friend.
Cause, he was a saint, he was a hero, but before all that.
He was a friend, he was a brother.
He was loved.

The instruments quieted, and the crews stopped singing, awaiting Luke to close the song. His gentle voice carried to every ear that listened.

That was the story of Celestine.
His goodness matched by only him.
And we call him… An Angel.

Luke stopped and wiped the tears that soaked his face. The crews on both ships continued to sing reprising the song with intent to serenade the spirit to the beyond, per gipsy custom. Luke rested his head on the side of Celestine's boat, knowing what had to come, but unable to let go. Staphros reached across, with steely determination in his glassy eyes.

'Prochnost, comrade.' He said. 'Strength, for him my brother!'

Luke nodded and together they let him go.

29 THE NATURAL ORDER

Those who believed in Mother Nature and her children knew that Nature's will was always carried out. It was the natural order. There was no such thing as a coincidence to those people and nothing was random. If something great happened, it was Nature's will and if tragedy struck, that too was Nature's will. That belief system which grounded many and gave near all hope in times of need was built on the presumption that Mother Nature cared about people. They were wrong; she didn't. Nearly every death, tragedy, or disaster, was purely random and ultimately meaningless, at least in her eyes. However, when Celestine's death was explained in consolation as Nature's will, people didn't know how right they were. His death was a consequence that dated back to the beginning of all.

The Beginning

According to the collection of fantastic tales that detailed Kastielle's incredible life, there existed only Time in the beginning and Time stopped for nothing.

Time existed in a void of emptiness with one sole purpose, keep moving forward. He did not desire to have this purpose, nor did he oppose it. He was not given this purpose from above; nothing was above Time. Moving forward simply qualified his existence. If Time stopped, he would cease to be that what he was. So, in perpetuity, he ran, executing his purpose without straying.

Soon the isolation proved that his purpose was as empty as the void in which he ran. There was no point, no motivation. He needed meaning if he were to carry on, so he took a piece of himself and cradled it as he ran. The piece was formless in his grasp at first, nothing but an idea, a mesh of his hopes and desires. The further that Time ran, the form grew with each of his strides. The form took shape and before long the idea was beginning to...

Begin. There would be something that existed in this vastness other than himself, something that he would be responsible for. The piece of himself grew, matured, and blossomed into someone beautiful, someone meaningful. He named her Nature, his daughter. She called him, Father.

Nature loved her Father Time with all of her heart and wanted nothing more than to gain his approval, but he left her behind as soon as he made her. She did not give up there however, with her unique ability bestowed upon her, she would create a great vessel for Time in the centre of all existence, The Sun. Expecting gratitude, Nature presented this gift to her father only to have it received as he passed her by, without even stopping to acknowledge her.

If she could not instil gratitude within her father, she would summon pride within him.

She gave herself a vessel, not like her fathers, but intricate and magnificent. She set herself to work, designing and discarding. She would settle for no less than perfection. Over and over changes were made, this creation was to be the undeniable display of her value.

The worlds she created were imbalanced, too heavily weighted to one side or another. Her first vessel was created with all of her love, another with frustration, then with woe, ambition, hatred, anger, admiration, jealousy, and pride. She came upon a breakthrough when life in the form of green moss grew on a small patch that she put all of herself in. The love with the hate, the pride with humility, her admiration with disdain, she discovered balance. Her canvas was wiped clean and she had to start from the beginning, placing these combinations in equal value and significance to shape her perfect world. She designed the oceans and the mountains, the rainforests and arid deserts, the peaks and the valleys, the heat and the cold, the land and the seas. These opposites would work in tandem to create harmony, the prefect vessel, Earth.

She presented the perfect vessel to her father Time weary and desperate, even blocking his path with it. She thought that it was sure to get his attention, but she was mistaken. Time breezed through her and The Earth like they were not there, knocking them out of his path like pathetic nuisances. Heartbroken by her father's abject dismissal of her, she now knew that there was nothing that she could do that would get him to acknowledge her. In all of her lustre and omnipotence, the best thing that she could ever produce didn't even get him to stop.

If she could not have his gratitude or his pride, she would have his envy.

With the lessons that she had learned in creating The Earth, she would bear children of her own. They would be pieces of her like she was to Time. Each born with a twin of equal power and significance, so it would mimic The Earth's perfection and balance. They would love her as she did Time and she would reciprocate their affection so their love would grow. She would also strip her love away from her father and scorn him each time he passed her by, filling the void with their vessels to remind Time of the love he had lost. The romance of Nature and Time was over. The reign of Mother Nature began.

As life grew on the Earth, Nature's children became interested in the lifeforms that resided on their mother. This life was not created by Mother Nature, just a by-product of the world that she had created. She had little care of the dwellings of those which lived on her vessel, letting her children intervene with them as often as they liked. That was until dominion over the lifeforms caused conflict amongst her children, causing most unnatural consequences to the life on her vessel. No more were the Children of Nature to intervene with the life on Earth unless called upon. Her children agreed, forming The Spiritual Court on the Arrow Island just if they were ever so needed.

Mother Nature was alone. She had her children, but unlike her father, she had ensured her children would never feel isolated. They would forever be tethered to their sibling that matched them in every way, forever destined to live in harmony. Mother Nature would not know harmony, not know an equal she would be alone with her thoughts. Alone in her love of her children and hatred of her father.

She was an island atop a mountain cursed with solitude, until the dawn of Kastielle Neriah. When Kastielle beseeched The Spiritual Court to save all life on Earth and protect it they denied him. It was only when he fought and earned his request that he got more than what he asked for. His mortal body, imbued with the powers of all Nature's children, making him Nature is equal. She fell in love immediately. It was a different kind of romance that she had for Kastielle, but with the same outcome. Kastielle would fall in love with a mortal woman and reject Nature's advances until his dying day.

Twenty-seven years after Kastielle's death, Mother Nature heard word of a man whose skin was shining, in a private stand in Zorrodon. A stand which was owned by a man she knew very well, Talion Ulrich Schultz, blood brother of her beloved Kastielle. Talion had a history with the world. She watched the man they called Celestine and witnessed the same shine in his skin that Kastielle had. There was no doubt of who he was after that, now her focus could be on the treacherous Talion.

On the docks of Zorrodon, she watched as Celestine and Staphros fought. He fought like Kastielle. Her sharp teeth shining and her leaf green eyes leering, the flames revealing her earth coloured skin. At the conclusion of the fight, there she was behind Magnus. She whispered into his ear and stared directly into Talion's eyes. The vines of her dreadlocks slithering like black vipers down his knife-wielding arm, to guide it true to its target. When the knife penetrated, she cackled and watched on as Talion lost control. The moment Talion unsheathed the blade from his cane, she drew close to him.

He could feel her presence now, her breath on his neck. She had a kindred familiarity that he couldn't shake, the aura of a loving mother. She leaned close wrapping her long black fingers around him. Now he could feel her touch, as he did many times in his youth.

'Do it. Show me you are still the boy I knew.' She said.

'Eros, I am sorry' Said Talion.

'You brave boy.' she said sinking her claws deep into him.

'Isobelle, I am sorry' Said Talion.

'You strong boy.' She said.

'Sakura…' Said Talion. 'Gomen Nasai' When Talion sliced Magnus's neck, she slithered from Talion's side and rested her head against Celestine's chest. Talion watched in disbelief as she heard the final trinity of beats of Celestine's heart. At the last beat, she lifted her head and peeled off her hood.

She stared at him from the corner of his bedroom and then moved like the gentle spread of smoke to the side of the bed. She perched on the headboard. Talion was dreaming of the docks again, lamenting everything he didn't do to save his nephew. She crouched over to hang her face inches above his face. He thick locked hair collapsed to form a curtain of pitch black around them. Talion opened his eyes. He knew exactly who she was, remembered her face. There were no other eyes as green, no skin quite as dark, no face quite as beautiful. Mother Nature brushed her hair back and stroked Talion's face.

'You clever boy!' She said.

Talion screamed in panic covered in a cold sweat and sat up. He passed through the image of Mother Nature above him and she was gone from her perch. He panted examining the room now empty room. The moonlight was shining silver beneath the curtains. The dark corners were empty. He picked up a handkerchief from his bedside table and wiped his head dry. He exhaled as he leaned back. Nothing was in the room; it was just a bad dream. He relaxed. His shoulders went limp as all the tension eased out of him.

'My… Poor… Talion.' Said Mother Nature. Her dark hand and long nails appeared in his eye line rubbing his shoulders. Talion rolled out of his bed in a panic, thudding against the floor. He grabbed his cane and waved it, forgetting to unsheathe it. She was on the headboard, once again perching like a raven. The dark of the room hid her features and body. She looked up to him, revealing her striking green eyes shining in the dark. They pierced through the shadows, appearing in her silhouette as green flames. She arose on his headboard ready for ascent, her cloak was her wings. Talion stuttered garbled nonsense watching her. He trembled and cowered, clawing in a scramble to hide behind his wardrobe. He was pinned in a corner. She dropped off the bed and approached the cowering man before her. She shed her cloak, revealing her dress of leaves and dark brown skin the colour of Earth. Her dark face and light features were a marvel to inspire love, a love that someone would do anything for. Love that Talion did anything for.

'Mo... Mo...Moth...' he stuttered again. She crouched and grabbed his jabbering jaw. She was close, her face in perfect view, entrancing all who beheld it. Her eyes, greener than any leaf or blade of grass, retold Talion's tragic tale thousands of times over. She made him relive his shame. His eyes rolled back as he convulsed in her arms. She rested her palm over his eyes, covering the unsightly pure white of his eyeballs then pulled him close.

'Shhh, my child. You lied to me and now Kastielle's son is dead.' She said. Talion looked up from her bosom like a child in his mother's embrace. His eyes pleaded forgiveness in the face of pure fear.

'Please.' He wept.

Mother Nature tutted. 'You broke my heart. My Talion deceiving me for so long, it is an unforgivable sin in a very long list of unforgivable sins. You know that you need to be punished now.' She cradled him in her arms.

'A...are you going to kill me?' Said Talion. Talion half hoped that she would but she knew that too.

'Oh Talion, I couldn't kill you. It would be too easy on you, but too hard on me. Could you have killed Celestine? Of course not, but you surely did punish him when he was out of line. I've seen his mind, I know what you did to him.' She said. She let go of him and he shuffled further into the corner. 'No, I shall determine your punishment after a brief review. For now, wait on my return; I have a business to attend to. You, on the other hand, should be expecting visitors.' She said.

In a flash of starlight, she disappeared and Talion was back in bed, afraid and broken.

Talion had a history with the world, and he was not always kind to her, nor was she always kind to him.

30 THE BALLAD OF TALION 2: CASE STUDY

Vida- Chrono- 21- 1827

Talion managed to get some sleep before sundown after a torrid night's sleep the night before. The cold slipped through the window and wrapped itself around him once more. It seemed to linger and Talion hadn't the sheet to shield himself from it. He rested on a stone slab, now drifting back and forth between sleeping and waking. Mother Nature had transformed his room into a prison, stripping his luxuries away, at least in his mind. His mattress was stone, his bedsheets bore no warmth. She punished him in her absence, and he was powerless to do anything. As the cold hit him, he could feel the pull of consciousness keep him awake. He fought it until he could feel a cold arm lay heavily on his chest. It was motionless and hung limply at the wrist on the other side. Talion opened his eyes.

Blinking himself into seeing in his low-lit room, the image of the arm came through the haze. It was pale and haggard. The fingers were long and thin. Talion daren't move, his heartbeat quickening until it was painful. He trembled and sweat trickled in waves down his frail body. He closed his eyes, hoping to return to the ignorant bliss he was in mere seconds ago. The darkness of his closed eyes brought very little comfort, but little was better than none. He couldn't see it, but he knew it was there. He could smell it. Not just the arm but her. He knew it was a woman because of the smell, it was perfume. The smell was cherry blossom, a particular smell that he only associated with one girl. The Jilted Bride, Sakura Neriah.

Gentle breath caressed the hairs on the back of Talion's neck.

Talion rolled off of the bed, slapping his hands on the stone floor and scurrying away. He stood and crept forward. He quivered down to his toes. He saw her. Her eyes were closed. She wore her wedding dress, her veil draped over her still angelic face. She was motionless on her back, holding her bouquet, cherry blossoms, lilies, and daffodils. Her pink-tinted silver hair long, loose, and gracious. Talion leaned in closer; he had not seen her in a very long time. Nearly forty years.

The story, Talion and the Broken-Hearted Princess detailed what happened leading up to, and after that day, albeit a romanticised version of events. Nobody knew what truly happened. His intrigue turned into longing. He missed her lips, her smell, her touch. He lifted her veil and leaned in closing his eyes. He had to know those lips once more. He was entranced. His lips brushed hers,

'A little too late for this aren't we?' Said Sakura. Talion jumped back. She remained still as her veil floated down over her face like a curtain of snow. Talion observed her again. She didn't move. The room was silent. He took a deep breath, wiping the sweat from his head. Gingerly, he took a step towards her.

She sat up like rising from the grave.

She moved suddenly yet slow. The look on her face was vacant as she studied the room. As if magnetised, her eyes fixed upon the old man. She smiled pleasantly at first, then it descended into mania. She gritted her teeth and her eyes widened. Her eyes bulged near to popping out of their sockets, glowing in the dark room. Blood seeped from her gums as she clenched her teeth harder and harder.

Snap

One tooth chipped and skipped against the stone floor. Then another and another. The blood gushed from her grinning mouth and down her chin. She looked like a ravenous predator that had just made its kill. Talion lost feeling in his legs and fell. He scrambled to get to his feet. When he looked to find her still on the bed, she was mere inches from his face. Her broken teeth and illuminated eyes were very much alive in this apparition's form. Her hair framed her face like a window, which seemed to enclose him within the panes of her pain.

Her hypnotic stare paralysed him. She had haunted him before, but no times were so real. In this trance, he saw what he wished that he never would, as Sakura decomposed before his eyes.

'It's your fault.' She cursed at him as her skin split and oozed the rotting congealed blood and flesh. The gorgeous pink tint in her hair darkened into a soulless black 'It's your fault.' She coughed blood contaminated with other gelatinous secretions of yellow and green onto his face. 'It's! All! Your! FAULT!' The windows shook, his furniture crashed. Her scream was piercing to his ears; it felt like they were bleeding.

'Stop!' Talion screamed falling to his knees. Sakura disappeared into smoke as Talion panted his way back into sanity. He sat under the window, against the wall.

'You stand on trial for the murder of Sakura Neriah.' Said Sakura. She was restored, her teeth, her hair, and her skin. 'How do you plea?'

This case was built upon the foundation of Sakura's relationship with her brother, the last king of Anara, Kastielle Neriah. Talion and Sakura had, what could be called, a forbidden love. Kastielle did not approve of their relationship in the slightest. Kastielle was very protective of his sister and made his feelings known from the beginning. Kastielle felt responsible for Sakura, due to the unfortunate circumstances in which they had met.

Kastielle served in the Anara military in his late teens and very early twenties. Throughout his tenure, he had become a specialist much like his grandfather Eros, who was, of course, a former champion of Anara. Kastielle was being groomed for that position himself however, Kastielle had no taste for the horrors of war. The mission that he met Sakura was his last. He immediately resigned from his duty in the military upon his return to Anara. Some speculated that this mission forced that decision and was the catalyst for his decision to venture to the Spiritual Court.

It was a time that predated the unification of the nations under Wukong but did not predate the conflict. Kastielle's mission was to do reconnaissance in Yunjia, in the Zhongguo state. He was there on behalf of the state of Nippon. He was tasked with observing a slavers ring and reporting back. It was believed that Zhongguo was trading Nippon nationals as slaves, which violated the tenuous terms of their peace.

He first saw Sakura as a slave girl. She was three years old and completely innocent. She was being led out of a decimated camp of sorts crying. Her face was bruised and her hair was covered in muck, Kastielle couldn't yet see the beautiful pink tint that hid underneath. He snuck through the shrubbery which surrounded the area. He found a close position, so he could hear clearly.

'Okasan! Okasan!' Said Sakura in high pitched cries. Kastielle would later realise she was shouting for her mother. The man who led the infant Sakura through the camp had a large stick in his hand. He was yelling at her. Kastielle could see the spit flying from his bared teeth. The man's eyes reddened with anger. Sakura stopped shouting for her mother. She looked up at him quaking in fear and quelling the sobs into muffled snivels. She understood her life was at risk. Kastielle gripped tightly onto his sword. The man did not stop yelling though, he was lost in his anger. He went on and on looming over her. He appeared a giant in her eyes. She cowered backwards looking up and falling to the ground. He stepped forward and raised his stick and the little girl screamed. Her scream seemed to stop time; it was sharp. Sakura's scream had real fear in it, the full cognisance that she was in real danger and facing death. Kastielle knew of that fear intimately, because he had felt it too as a child. In his experience, he was the only other child that had experienced that. Now they shared endeavour, and their relationship had formed before they had met.

Before the man could lower his arm Kastielle sprang from cover and sliced it off. It landed with a thud and rolled on the floor. The stick clanged against the stone as the severed hand lost its grip. With arrowhead precision, he sliced the man's throat. He could not make a sound as he fell in a heap. Sakura stopped, looked and, screamed again. Kastielle knelt and offered his hand. She trusted him instantly, staying her cries. It was clear then that Sakura, although scared by such sights, had seen them enough to get over them quickly. It was a sad reality. Kastielle wanted to help her and that was so outwardly apparent it granted Kastielle Sakura's immediate trust. This little girl had been through so much but still trusted a stranger in this dark time, only a testament to the connection they had. He led her through the covert route that he took to get to her. It was the safest way back.

On the way, they passed a couple of bodies sprawled on the ground. Sakura stopped suddenly. Her tiny hand quivered as it raised and pointed.

'Okasan! Otosan!' She screamed crying. Kastielle did not speak the language, but he knew what she meant. Grief was a universal language. No child her age should see their parents dead. She sped to their side before Kastielle could stop her. Her screams echoed in the open landscape. The doors busted open and an outpouring of foot soldiers emerged. Kastielle pulled her to her feet hastily.

'Get behind me.' He said animatedly trying to make it easy to understand. 'And don't look.' He said drawing his sword. Sakura looked at the shining silver and shielded her eyes and retreated behind him.

'Hai.' She said. Kastielle turned to face the nine men in front of him. Eros had faced worse odds, however without a toddler at his back.

'Alright then, game on!' He shouted.

The consensus report of that day is that Kastielle engaged nine men in battle and killed them all to protect this girl. Within minutes of meeting her, he wanted to risk his life for her. He abandoned his reconnaissance mission to save her. Kastielle, a man of unwavering duty, neglected his clear instruction for this little girl. Those close to Kastielle would say that he was a hero and would do that for anyone, however, nine men? Bearing in mind that he had not yet been blessed with the gifts of the divine. The second point was his tactics or lack thereof. Kastielle was known for his calculated combat style. Against nine adversaries, he would certainly need to use that talent. However, he drew his sword and engaged them head-on, resulting in a massacre, emotion. He was emotionally invested in Sakura from the beginning.

Following that, he decided to retire from duty immediately and strongly suggested that his grandfather adopt Sakura. Talion was already Eros's ward at the time, but he never made the step to adopt him. Therefore, it was clear that Eros did not adopt lightly, especially given the circumstances, he adopted Kastielle. A popular theory amongst those close to Kastielle and researchers that biographed Kastielle's life, was that Kastielle wished to adopt Sakura himself, but he did not have the means. He needed a house to adopt a child, and he still lived with his grandfather. He convinced Eros to adopt her as his granddaughter which in turn made Sakura, Kastielle's sister, technically. Anybody with eyes could see that their relationship was more, father-daughter than brother-sister.

Kastielle did everything in his power to ensure that Sakura maintained her chastity. This originally had an end in sight: being when she married a man that Kastielle deemed worthy. The end extended indefinitely once Kastielle learned the spell for immortality.

Sakura was the first person he granted immortality to. There was unlimited time to find the perfect man for her now and Kastielle's standards raised to impossible heights. Sakura remained a virgin until the day that she unfortunately died. She had never kissed a man when Kastielle became king nor centuries after. Kastielle's wrath could be fierce if he was in that mood. There was no telling what mood he would be in either. He was known as the "Lunatic King" in the latter years of his royal tenure because of those most violent mood swings.

Sakura was loyal to her big brother who had saved her life. The father-daughter relationship was not one way, she too saw Kastielle as a father figure, even though she called him "Oniisan" which meant brother in her native tongue. She saw him as a father and a guardian and gladly maintained her chastity until Kastielle deemed a man worthy.

Talion was well known as a bit of a lothario. He had his fair share of women, be it on adventures with Kastielle, or meeting an admirer of his champion status. He was indiscriminate and unashamed of his sexual exploration. He was likened to the late former champion Eros in that regard, whose name became synonymous with sexuality. Being immortal taught him not to get attached to women. Kastielle saw Talion as his best friend and a good man, but his sexual exploits were careless and devoid of true feeling. This was Kastielle's suspicion when Talion broached the subject of having feelings for Sakura. Talion's past transgressions had come back to haunt him and he understood why, although his feelings were real. Princess Sakura had caught his eye and never let it go. He pursued her, at first having to convince her that he was genuine. It took years. She knew Talion from childhood, he was always arrogant. Her brother was also very confident, but it was a matter of fact. It was more believing himself rather than convincing himself. That was the difference in Kastielle and Talion. Sakura believed, at first, Talion used sex to affirm his value, but over time he convinced her otherwise.

They talked about their feelings at first. They got to know each other, learning from each other and learning about themselves. Then their conversations became more intimate and often they would embrace and hold each other longer each time. Then when he could, Talion would steal a kiss, and Sakura would steal it back.

This affair lasted many decades in this form, stealing away to an isolated field in Wildberry and getting lost in each other. Talion respected her chastity, knowing that if he betrayed that the trust would be gone. Being with her was enough until it wasn't anymore. Forbidden love, the most intoxicating of aphrodisiacs. It was more potent than power, more liberating than freedom, it conquered everything. That was what Talion was feeling. Sakura was feeling something even more potent. First love. Sakura had lived with guards up, guards that had stayed up for centuries. She had never known romantic love, had never known what to do with it. It hurt when she didn't see Talion, it healed her when she did. She thought about him every morning and dreamt of him every night. To also factor in the life which she had, and the loss she faced early on. It must have affected her mental state. Talion, as the most experienced party in this most sensitive scenario, should have exercised more caution. His selfishness made him reckless.

Talion and Sakura had devised a plan to marry. They had to make sure that they did it first before telling Kastielle. Talion believed that he could prove himself to his friend by marrying Sakura. The sanctity of marriage was a serious commitment, especially to those who were immortal. They both believed it was worth it. Talion knew the risk, Kastielle was losing grip of the man he was, growing up in the forests of Wildberry. He was flitting between two absolutes, pure good or pure evil. His soul, the humanity within him was fading, if not already faded. If this failed, he knew the forfeit would be his life. Having lived for so long, he had learnt to fear death. The reward was worth the forfeit, but that did not scare him any less.

They had made their plans, and everything was set. They found a secluded area in Eagle's Stay, a cliffside overlooking the desert coast to the northeast in Sengham. They had a holy man, a date, and most importantly nobody else knew but those they trusted most. Sakura arrived first dressed in a beautiful white dress, which reflected the satin pink hair that flowed down the back. She had a tiara that her veil was attached to; It blew in the wind. She was a picture of beauty that Talion never got to see.

Sakura waited for the happiest day of her life but, Talion never came. At the dusty peaks of Eagle's Stay, she left her lilies, cherry blossoms, and daffodils, to die on the floor. Her heart lay next to them cursed to beat forever.

Kastielle felt a mixture of betrayal and disgust when faced with Talion. He found him staying at the Cold Brew Inn at the foot of Eagles Stay. Talion was dressed to be married in his champion's uniform when Kastielle found him.

The bedroom door opened and Kastielle appeared. Talion's heart stopped. There was no use lying to him, even before he was divine Kastielle could see though deception very well. His eyes burned with a white-hot fire and his fist glowed its Supernatural glow. Kastielle said no words as he came in. His eyes flashed green and Talion was slammed to the ground. The weight in the room was too much the bear, and Talion felt like a foot on digging into his chest. Determined, Talion crawled for the door against the immense weight upon him. Kastielle grabbed him by the scruff of his neck and flung him against the wall. With a flick of his hand, Kastielle directed the pressure horizontally and pin Talion to the wall. He was suspended off the ground now. Kastielle approached; The Lunatic King approached. He wore a white and gold gown befitting his regal stature. He pressed his open palm against Talion's heart. Talion braced himself for his forfeit, his death. Kastielle instead pulled his hand backwards, holding a white orb.

'You can live. Just without my sister and not forever.' He said low and sinister as he stripped the immortality from his heart. 'Talion Schultz, you are banished.' Kastielle directed a force through Talion which sent him through the wall. Talion got up, blood trickling out the corner of his mouth. He knew pleading would not get through to him, he knew that Kastielle was lost. Talion blinked hazily, coughing up a glop of blood and collapsing once again. Kastielle dragged an unconscious Talion to Sengham's port and threw him on the ship headed to Nippon. He stripped him of his championship status and belt, intended to be worn at his wedding. Talion wanted to wear it to honour his friend, but he had been dishonoured and they were friends no more.

Sakura was found by Kastielle crying on the cliffside. To protect her, Kastielle told her that Talion loved her no more. He intended to show her that their love meant little to him. Kastielle believed that genuinely. Some would say he was blinded by his arrogance, others said he was rightfully protective of his sister from a known womaniser. She didn't believe that Talion didn't love her anymore. She could not believe it. Nevertheless, she returned with Kastielle back to Anara City although, she did not eat, she did not sleep, she suffered. She suffered pain unimaginable, the pain of starvation, the pain of thirst, all the pain that she felt as a slave, all pain that she could understand, to distract from the pain that she could not fathom, a broken heart. She loved Talion and she knew Talion, but she also knew Kastielle. He was a great man, but he could be a tyrant. She knew that if they were discovered there would be a heavy forfeit, and that forfeit may have been paid. She didn't believe Talion did not love her, but she did believe he was dead.

Sakura had not eaten or drank for the entirety of Talion's banishment, twenty years. The immortality spell that Kastielle cast on his sister kept her from dying but did not keep her healthy. Sakura's condition was the closest thing to death any living thing could get. Kastielle called for Talion's immediate return to save his sister.

Talion returned as per Kastielle's request, however, some terms had to be set. Kastielle stopped Talion at Sakura's door; there was still tension between the two of them. Talion harboured anger for him for his banishment and upon news that his banishment had made Sakura fall ill. It made him sick with rage.

'Listen' Said Kastielle. 'You are not here to rekindle your love with my sister. You're here to corroborate my story and that is it.'

'And what story may that be?' Said Talion.

'That you never loved her.' Said Kastielle. Talion tensed and his gaze intensified. He knew he could not do anything to him, but he wanted to try in this moment.

'I'm not doing that.' He said. He turned to walk away, but Kastielle put out a hand. It was like walking into a steel bar. It immediately stopped Talion in his tracks.

'This isn't an option. You do this or you die.' Said Kastielle. Talion curved his lips downwards tightly and shook his head nonchalantly.

'Kill me.' He said ducking below Kastielle's arm like it was a barrier he should not cross.

'Alright.' Kastielle called after him. 'If you do this, I will make you immortal again.'

Talion stopped. In the last twenty years, he had lived with not being immortal, but the idea of death scared him greatly still. Being killed was easy, dying was harder.

'What do you say?' Said Kastielle. Kastielle knew Talion's fears of through their private conversations as brethren. He had no problem with doing that. It was the perfect leverage. Talion turned around and walked back silently. They exchanged glares, Kastielle's green eyes flashing with his smile.

'Fine.' Said Talion shaking his former friend's hand.

Talion entered. She looked like she was withering. Her skin had wrinkled dry and her breathing was like dust. She lost the pink shimmer in her hair and it darkened to a flat lifeless black. The once beautiful princess was ravaged by the illness of a broken heart. Her eyes widened and she reached pathetically towards Talion. Her eyes still had the beautiful Sakura behind them. He took her hand and sat on the chair beside her bed.

'I'm so sorry.' Said Talion kissing her hand. He felt the tears fill his eyes as he rested his head on her bony fingers.

Sakura wheezed, she was too parched and weak to speak. The sound broke Talion's heart. He wanted to make it better and he could. He was at a crossroads at this moment. He had a choice to save the one that he loved at the cost of his life and as he was about to make his decision, the door opened and closed.

'Sakura' Said Kastielle. 'Talion has something he's dying to tell you.' The pressure in the room changed and fear rose within Talion. He could feel

Kastielle's gaze. It was death incarnate inside him. He faced death, but he could die knowing he saved her from the agony she endured, but he didn't want to die, ever.

He lifted his head, dry-eyed. 'I'm sorry, but I don't love you. I never did.' He said. 'I did it to compete with Kastielle. He got himself a princess so why can't I. Foolishly I was going to marry you to get it. You were ripe for the picking, immortal so I had all the time in the world to come up with the perfect lie to get you to trust me. Your brother stopped me just as I was about to bag myself a princess. The King's sister. I think now I have had the time to think about it, it would have been a mistake anyway. He wanted to protect you, but I just wanted to use you.'

Sakura shook her head in disbelief.

Kastielle smirked; he had the control once again.

'You were nothing to me.' Said Talion. He left the room before he could see the tears that had long since run dry return to Sakura's eyes.

'You did the right thing.' Said Kastielle quietly as Talion walked past. He patted him and flashed his majestic green eyes. Talion was once again immortal. At that moment, something snapped inside Talion. He had made many a selfish decision in his life but this one extracted a great cost.

'Fuck you and your damned immortality.' Talion interrupted.

'Have care dear friend. You're speaking to the only man in the world that is capable of killing you. One day, you may beg me to do it, but for today be a good coward and run.' Talion didn't want to live forever with the guilt, but he feared death too much to reject Kastielle's gift. He heeded Kastielle and left never looking back.

He returned to Nippon without saying a word. Town criers were making the rounds when he made port with breaking news.

'Princess Sakura of Anara dies after long illness!' Talion froze in his tracks and a mass exodus heaved from his mouth onto the deck. He fell onto the ground in pieces quaking and sobbing. He had lost his beloved.

Nobody knew how Sakura had died while still gifted with the immortality Kastielle cast upon her. Nami's death could be explained, human physiology could not handle the rigours of delivering a divine child. Sakura's case was harder to understand. Sakura seemed to have died of a broken heart, at least that was what was later determined once all the facts were released. In later studies from Kastielle himself, it came to pass that the laws of life and death, although could be bent, could not be broken and in the case of immortality. There were loopholes. The body, in a completely functional standpoint, could be immortalised. However, the soul could not be changed. Immortality was predicated on the condition of the soul, which in itself is a near-indestructible force. Sakura's case was the first case of that the soul breaking. The soul was supposed to outlast the body and live on in the afterlife, Sakura's body was made unbreakable, and her soul found it's limit.

Ultimately, the opinion that Sakura died of a broken heart was quite inaccurate. Sakura Neriah died of a broken soul, something only Talion was equipped to do given the evidence. The murder weapon was his love, his motive was ingrained in the innate selfishness of his character.

Sakura's apparition rested her case and stood in the incurring moonlight from the window. The figure of her in her wedding dress. Despite the circumstances, Talion cherished that sight. Then, he realised his fault in it all. He faced many crossroads, and every time he chose what was best for him. His selfish choices lead to that end. He knew Sakura would not have made the same choice if the roles were reversed.

'I killed her.' Said Talion crying by the wall. 'I'm guilty.'

Mother Nature smiled watching Talion lay broken on the floor. She would make him pay for every sin, sending him visitors night by night.

31 TRUTH

Outside of Time

It was a gentle easing into the complete darkness for Celestine. He was faced with a bright light at the end of a black tunnel, however, contrary to folklore tales, he was being pulled away from it. The light in front of him was getting further and further away. Life was the light and Death was the dark. Unable to move, he drifted away not even thinking to fight. Temina, Talion, and the others would feel unspeakable grief and Celestine wept for them. He knew his fate; his death was a more vivid memory than any other in his mind and was at peace with the consequences. Those who had to live with it faced the much graver challenge.

He had so many questions, but he was ok without the answers. There was only one that mattered. What next? The light was completely gone, and he was suspended on a pendulum swinging. It was similar to being rocked to sleep, the feeling of comfort reminiscent of the cradle of a mother's bosom. On one side was life and he could still feel the pain of what he went through, he could feel the knife in his heart and the blood choking him. On the other side was the promise of peace in death, there was no more struggle, everything washed away. He was not only stripped of the recent pains, he felt freed of the comparisons to Talion, the shadow of Staphros, and the pressures of those who loved him; he was truly free. The choice was made, and the pendulum stopped. The darkness washed away, and freedom won the battle for Celestine's soul. It was time to rest.

There was a willow tree in the middle of a great lake before him. It was neither hot nor cold, but it was dewy and wet. It was the middle of the night, and the sky was almost completely covered by the overhanging branches and leaves from the looming woods. The faint twinkle of stars crept from above through the small gaps of the leaves, peering like squinted eyelids. The area was lit mostly by the light emanating from the tree in the lake. It was a mesmerising sight, shining and silver, not dissimilar to the shining cloak he donned in Zorrodon. He could hear it speak to him in a language that he didn't know but he understood. The words sunk in and he was overcome. He remembered his family and friends, and the life that he had lived before. For them to move on with their lives, he had to do so with his death. He walked ahead, understanding that the glistening waters and hanging shining leaves were his fate. It would be where his soul would rest.

The blades of the short grass tickled his bare feet reaching between his exposed toes. The lake got bigger and bigger with each step he took, and the height of the tree came into perspective. The tree dwarfed mountains littered with glimmering leaves and was formed with dark jagged bark. The trunk was wider than the Wall of Zorrodon by a dozen times. Celestine reached the edge of the lake. The lake looked like a small ocean, Celestine could not see the other edges nor could he see the bottom. It was the throat of the world, where souls all were swallowed.

He leaned over curiously, staring at the flow of the still bank. He could see bodies floating in the water. Celestine longed to join them, unsure as to why. He knelt on the grass and peered even closer to it. Then what was below rose to the top. Faces of young and old, man and woman drifted by silently decomposing. It was hideous, with their swollen flesh, peeling from the cracking bones. Their eyes, saturated until implosion, leaving some with gaping holes in their skulls and others with jellified secretion trailing their cheeks. Celestine couldn't stand to look but couldn't turn away. There was a force pulling him towards it. Celestine trembled on his hands and knees fighting against it, terrified.

It stopped. Everything stopped, the force that pulled him to the water freed him from the grip and the faces disappeared. From the very depths, an enchanting woman with long flowing red hair rose to the surface. Her skin was pale, and her eyes were strikingly purple. As she drew closer, Celestine was drawn to her, not by a force but by his heart. She reached the surface and he realised it was like looking in a mirror, she looked just like him. His heart knew who she was, but his eyes didn't know her face. There was a magnetic energy between them, that he didn't notice until his nose was wet. The water rippled but the waves were coming towards him. There was a faint sound of the water being tapped, over and over, like shoes on a puddle. He looked up to be blinded by shining starlight. He shielded his eyes and looked back to find the woman had gone. The light swarmed and engulfed him. He stayed where he was. It came closer and closer until it was all around him.

When he lowered his hands and blinked his way back into seeing again clearly, a young man was standing before him, naked and beautiful. He could not distinguish his features. He was a sight to behold. He placed his open palm against Celestine's chest, just by where the bolt had pierced his heart. His hand was soft and radiated with familiar warmth. Celestine examined the light coming from him.

'You're like me?' He said.

'You do not belong here.' Said the man before him. Celestine's chest thudded. It was painful, then it happened again and again. The light disappeared. The hand on his chest grew cold and brittle. The points of his bony fingers dug into Celestine's chest piercing his skin. The pain was fresh and torturous. Celestine investigated the man's face terrified, finding a hood covering it. The shadow hid his features however, the silence revealed the sound of dripping from directly below it. The man turned his head upward and revealed his true face. His face was rotting. The flesh on his right cheek had completely gone. It left streaks of skin and clotted blood as its frame. His mouth was turned into a frantic grin, with parts of his lips gone, revealing the rabid teeth that lie behind. His nose was dripping cartilage, and a river of blood coursed down his face from his head. He pulled his hand from Celestine's chest. It was just bone. It clicked as he formed a fist. Then, he struck Celestine's heart with a sudden force that was greater than any which he had ever felt. Celestine was frozen in fear. For the first time since he was a very small child, another man struck terror into him. Although, was he a man? Somewhere deep in Celestine's heart, he knew that he had just met Death incarnate and he had banished him from his realm. His soul was not welcome.

Celestine fell through the black emptiness until he landed on a sandy floor. The ground rocked and trembled under his feet. Pillars extruded from the ground and statues of legends of man and beast alike were erected. Celestine had no idea what was happening, but some images looked familiar to his mind's eye. There was an arena being formed. The stars fell from all around him like shining raindrops, gracefully landing at a seat to watch. When they landed, they all assumed a physical form. Some were human, others decided to be animals or hybrids. The especially creative ones assumed the form of something never seen before. Still, the cascade of stars fell like the most magnificent and terrifying sight one could imagine. Celestine saw the visage of Death land in the stands. He was on the opposite side with nowhere to hide on the flat sand and a wall behind him, but Death didn't acknowledge him.

The trembling had stopped, and the grandest arena Celestine had ever seen was left. Only the spectators that filled the arena matched its magnificence. There were only a few stars left in the infinity of the sky. It was bare with only hundreds of stars remaining in the stead of millions. They formed an eye-shaped circle with Father Time's Sun in the centre. Much like the embroidery on the back of Celestine's coat, also what would become the symbol of the Kastellian faith when he became king.

The gaze of Father Time was directed to the sands that Celestine found himself on, but not Celestine himself. Now that he thought of it, none of the spectators had acknowledged his presence at all. Their focus was solely on the man in the middle of the sands. The image in Celestine's mind's eye aggregated with what he was witnessing before him. He couldn't believe it. He hadn't seen this place before, but he had read about it over a dozen times. This was the site of the climax to his favourite story, Quest for the Spiritual Court. Which meant, the man in the middle of the sands was, Kastielle Neriah.

'We do keep meeting in the most unlikely of places.' A voice said from behind. Celestine turned to follow the unfamiliar voice to see a familiar sight, the hooded figure that helped him unlock his powers in Zorrodon. Celestine could see more of their features this time, their green eyes, dark skin, and the locks of hair that dangled from the shadow of their cowl. Their voice was softer than before, more comforting, and motherly.

'Where am I?'

'You are at the birthplace of your gifts. Where it all began.' The figure said. The figure placed their soft hands on Celestine and turned him around to watch the event as Kastielle reshaped the world as they knew it.

Kastielle picked up his staff and awaited the opponent he was to fight against for the world's salvation. Celestine had read of the creature Kastielle fought and comprised an image of the hideous figure. He was not prepared for what stepped out to face the future king of Anara.

Screams of agony and horror came from the opposite side of the large arena, as Kastielle's opponent emerged bound in chains. It was coming from an entryway across from him. The sound was concentrated by the acoustics of the stone which surrounded it. The screams made Kastielle and Celestine cold upon hearing them, they grew pale and scared. Kastielle's hands clammed up around his staff while he shivered. He calmed his nerves and anticipated what was to come.

What emerged to face him was not man, or beast, or hybrid, but a grotesque concoction of biology. This thing was far worse than imagination. It had no soul or had too many. It was troubled, tortured, and in constant blatant pain. It was ginormous, with rippling folds of skin, hide, and tissue flapping from the poorly patched chunks of meat on its body. It had over twenty eyes, all pitch black and bleeding. Its mouth reached behind its ears, bearing broken teeth and sharpened fangs. Blood trickled and spurted sporadically from the torn flesh all over its body. This was what The Children of Nature wanted Kastielle to fight. It was their pet monster, Necronomicon.

Celestine expected a valiant fight where Kastielle would combine guile and skill to overthrow the abomination. The story told of Kastielle wielding his trusty staff in a hard-fought battle and in the end, putting the tortured beast out of its misery. As the true events went on before his eyes, the battle wasn't much of a battle at all. It was a massacre.

Kastielle had taken a beating he could not imagine, now he was there face down and refusing to die. His bones were broken, and he was bleeding as much internally as externally. Necronomicon was more than a monster; it was an unnatural abomination. It did not seem to enjoy doing what it did, nor did it hate it. Dealing pain seemed to be as natural as breathing to it, as natural as perpetually screaming in its agony. The screams haunted Kastielle as each of his bones broke, every fibre of tissue tore, every organ ruptured. He could hear the screams. He could see the tears flowing down its many eyes. Kastielle's fingers outstretched, the only part of his body able to move, still trying to fight. His hair was soaked red from the bone-deep gash on his head. As badly as he was beaten, he still knew he had not known pain like the thing that faced him.

Necronomicon was a concoction of creation which embodied the sadism of the Spiritual Court. Whoever tried to face the trials of the Arrow Island and failed, were trapped in the blending of soul and physiology. Badly stitched together, it oozed a trail of blood and puss from its secreting folds of infected flesh. Its skin was burnt as if melted. Thirty souls were trapped in the Necronomicon body, each one of their voices could be heard in its screams.

As Kastielle lay face down in the arena in which the Spiritual Court had created, Celestine could feel what he felt. He could see every trial in which Kastielle embarked upon to get to the very place where he faced his death. His lungs drawing in evermore shallow breaths as the ruptured organs overworked themselves to barely draw enough air to keep him alive. His arms heavy as boulders and the task of moving them was equivalent to moving a mountain.

Kastielle turned his head to see the void of the heavens formed into the watchful eye of stars that hung above. He was not meant to get this far. His destiny was to meet the same fate as every other who tried to embark of the Trials of the Spiritual Court. Abject failure and damnation in the form of his opponent was the plan, not an overachieving mortal that had the audacity to challenge them. It was a personal affront to the divines that he had passed the trials alone, but Kastielle went one step too far.

The rules were simple, pass the trials and you can make any request of the Divines. Kastielle had passed twelve trials and scaled the mountain to gain access to The Spiritual Court. There were things that he had to endure that nobody else could have endured. Kastielle however, had something within him that only his grandfather could see. Eros made no secret that the reason that he adopted Kastielle as his grandchild was because Kastielle refused the clutches of death. After all, he would die on his terms. A boy of eight years old had the resolve of a soldier several times his age. Eros was by his side in that infirmary the entire time and saw his conversation with death with his own eyes. Kastielle had a sheer force of will that could not be denied.

That same will drove him to lose control and confront the Court on their dishonesty.

Necronomicon hobbled towards Kastielle, grimacing whilst holding its bludgeoning hammer. The hammer was Kastielle's size and twice his weight. Kastielle knew his fate was sealed but did not accept it. Hope was lost, but his will never died. Kastielle's fingers scratched Necronomicon's toes, fighting to his end. Necronomicon kicked them away. The look on his face, still defiant but it had something else. It was selfless, respectful, and honest. He didn't mind dying for his people, despite being the greatest example of them in almost every way. He had his faults and his virtues, he was perfect in his imperfections. He was everything The Children of Nature were not. His emerald eyes met with the eye of stars above him. Somehow, he sensed that they did not have the same look on their faces as the spectators who assumed a physical form, who now had so much satisfaction on their face it was bordering on erotic. They had broken another, and this one was probably the best yet. Kastielle had no concern with his opponent, had no concern with the audience, but he maintained eye contact with the eye in the sky. He was at peace with dying for his cause. Celestine knew the sacrifice that Kastielle was willing to make. He was filled with pride that he and his hero were so alike.

Kastielle wished only for his world to have someone or someones to care for it and to love it. He wanted the world to be nurtured by an all-powerful, all-loving, hand. He made peace with that he had failed. Unable to muster the words from his failing voice. He prayed that one day his world would have such a person.

Necronomicon's hammer swung downwards.

'I leave it to you, whoever you are.' Said Kastielle closing his prayer. He closed his eyes and smiled, as the impact of the hammer crashed through his chest. Everything went black and he felt nothing.

Everything in the arena stopped, Kastielle, Necronomicon, and every spectator in the stands including the hooded figure. Celestine looked around at the queerness of this circumstance. Darkness shrouded the arena with a *Thum* as the sun vanished. A man descended from the empty void where the sun used to be and landed softly beside Kastielle. He looked exactly like what Celestine imagined an all-powerful being would look like. So rich in his beauty, and strength, and grandeur. His steely eyes looked to Celestine for a prolonged moment like he was expecting him later, or had seen him before, or seeing him for the millionth time that very second. All Time was in his hands.

Celestine didn't move as Father Time knelt and cradled Kastielle's head in his arms. His prone dead body was still pinned by Necronomicon's hammer. Father Time smiled as he turned to Kastielle and whispered into his ear.

'Your prayer is granted.'

The light blinded Celestine as the sun returned to the sky above and the arena was unfrozen. Starlight filled the area and emanated from the one point the divines were not expecting. Kastielle was imbued with all of their power, and his cloak shined with the same light as theirs.

Suddenly, it was completely dark again.

Celestine was surrounded by stars and suspended in the void of the infinite universe. The arena was gone, Kastielle was gone, everything. Celestine wanted to see how things ended, but he knew the outcome.

'What happened?' Asked Celestine.

'You now know the origin of your powers; they come from Kastielle.' Said the hooded figure.

'But how?'

'Did your uncle ever tell you of your parents?'

'He spoke of my father rarely, he said they fought for Anara together and he didn't know my mother.' Celestine scratched his head confused.

'Talion, ever the clever one.' The figure's full lips curved into a smile as they chuckled.

'Wait, who are you and how do you know my uncle?' Asked Celestine, now confused beyond belief. This figure spoke of Talion as though they knew him very well, like old friends. Celestine knew Talion only kept friends in King Kastielle, Queen Nami, Princess Sakura, and Isobelle and this person was none of them. If they weren't a friend, could they be...

'Well, my father called me Nature, but most people call me Mother Nature.' She let down her hood and revealed her face.

'Oh my!' Celestine was astounded in her presence. He dropped to his knees and bowed at her feet. She rolled her eyes and pulled him back to standing.

'Let's not do that. Things get a little weird after all the bowing.' She said. Celestine thought back to what Luke would say and fought the urge to reply, only if I get a stiffy. He was in the presence of the creator of the universe after all.

He dropped his head. 'Am I dead then?' He asked.

She nodded her head.

'Is there any way you can bring me back?'

She shook her head. 'The soul leaves the body once it dies. I created a great many things, but the living soul was not one of them. We divines cannot even touch them. Once it's gone, we cannot put it back.'

'Oh.' Said Celestine deflated.

She took his hand and stroked it with her thumb to comfort him. 'Do you remember when you were at the door?'

Celestine nodded.

'It was locked, correct?'

Celestine nodded.

'Try it now.' She said.

Celestine concentrated and brought his consciousness to the white void. The door was fully intact without a scratch or chip on it. Mother Nature was at Celestine's back as he edged towards the door. Celestine remembered the pain that the power within caused him. Not only the strain in Zorrodon but the seizures as a child. He remembered them all stood before this door, this great looming wooden door that haunted him. He knew he was different, that he carried something that isolated himself from everybody else.

Mother Nature placed her hand on Celestine's shoulder. 'It's quite alright' She said. Celestine took the round golden doorknob and twisted it. The knob turned fully with ease and the snap and click of the lockset allowed the door to breathe. Celestine pulled and the rush of water crashed out, but this time it ran through him. Celestine was astonished and looked to Mother Nature as the power invigorated him. It wasn't hurting him. For the first time, he felt the beautiful rush of this power and it didn't hurt him. Suddenly, Celestine felt a familiar thud in his chest, but one that he had recently become accustomed to existing without. His heart was beating.

Vida- Labor- 22- 1827

His hands trembled as he examined them, and the white void melted away into a perfect night's sky. The stars reached the horizon on all sides. Celestine could now feel the cold sea breeze, smell the salt in the air, and see the world.

'I couldn't put your soul back into your body, but it appears you can.' Mother Nature said walking by on the water.

'Huh…How?' Asked Celestine.

'Kastielle believed that his soul was somehow integral in unlocking the power behind the door.'

'Like the soul was the key?'

Mother Nature shook her head. 'Like it was the door.'

Celestine thought about the stories he read as a child and how they told how he got the powers but not how he used them. He was stunned to think that he and Kastielle were linked by the same great abilities that made him a fabled hero.

'You said I got these powers from King Kastielle. So, does that mean he was as strong as the books said he was?' He asked.

Mother Nature nodded. 'Stronger in fact. Your uncle was very close to Kastielle.' She said. Talion was always so mysterious about his past, especially when it pertained to King Kastielle. Celestine asked about him several times as a child but Talion's answers were always vague.

'This is a lot to hear right now. I knew Talion and Kastielle, sorry King

Kastielle were friends.' he asked.

'They were much more than friends; their relationship was akin to that of you and Staphros.' Said Mother Nature.

Celestine nodded. 'How did I get my powers from King Kastielle? Was Talion involved, was my father?' he asked.

'It's complicated. I don't think it would be fair of me to tell you plainly, it would be much better if I showed you.' Mother Nature waved her hand and a shining door appeared in the air. She offered her hand do him.

'Seems like every time I see you there's some sort of door involved.' He said smirking.

'Will you come with me?' Asked Mother Nature making her way through the doorway.

'What's in there?' Asked Celestine. She extended her hand out to him.

'Everything you need to know.'

32 THE PRINCE'S BIRTH

Chronus- Natura- 40- 1799

Screams bellowed in the halls of Anara Castle. Nami, Queen of Anara, was giving birth. Nurses and attendants were gathered in her chambers. Nami's cries could be heard in every part of the castle. In her room, the sound echoed off the stone walls. The sound was otherworldly, convulsive, and potent in volume. It was a sound that shouldn't be able to come from a human. Those that remained in the castle, could only freeze in their tracks as their blood was chilled down to the platelets. Net curtains draped from the four pillars which stood at the corners of the Queen's bed. Three sides were closed, and three nurses stood at the end of the bed. An outlier would only be able to see the writhing shadow of a woman in too much in pain with her indignity veiled behind frail curtains.

Nami clawed at her bedsheets as her back arched into an unnatural contour. Her frail bones cracked and popped. Aside from her stomach, her body was diminished down to skin and bones. Her legs trembled down to her toes, and her breath was reducing into drawn dry screeches of her throat. Nami was not simply giving birth; she was exchanging life.

Footsteps pounded the floor at a sprinters pace, as Isobelle burst into the room. Her clothes were in tatters, and her bow, which was held firmly in her hand, was worn. Her cutlass hung at her hip at the beltline of her tight black leggings, in which, her brown blouse was tucked. Isobelle was the sworn protector of the queen, and lifelong friend of the king, Kastielle. Over time, she had developed a relationship with Nami, that rivalled hers and The King's bond. She, much like every other able-bodied resident of Anara, was out fighting against the invasion that besieged her country. She was a soldier at heart, and a good one. Her hair was black very short, and her face was long. She was very tall and slender of frame. Her hips were not shapely, and her breasts were not full. One would have to look closely at her body, to truly determine that she was in fact, a she. In that circumstance, Isobelle would not object; she would take it as a compliment to be mistaken for a man. Although to her dismay that did not happen often. Despite her long face and lack of womanly features of the body, Isobelle was strikingly beautiful in her face. When people eventually looked at her, her large brown eyes, buttoned nose, and colourful lips made it unmistakable that she was a woman. She was a beautiful woman and she hated it.

'Queen Nami! I'm here!' She said.

Nami cried, whimpering at her last contraction. The guttural sound was even more haunting now Isobelle heard it at her side. Isobelle was struck with a sudden chill. She stared wide-eyed and speechless, watching everything unfold behind the curtains. Nami's outline convulsing, banging against the mattress, and gurgling baritone moans as her agony escalated. Isobelle pulled the head nurse back.

'What is happening to her? I have seen lesser women give birth with little trouble.' She said ignorantly.

The head nurse searched for an answer. 'It is difficult to say. Childbirth is a complex ordeal, and it isn't a matter of strength or fortitude. Women just react differently, but regarding this matter, in all my years I have never seen a birth such as this. Her body is losing a life like it is being drained out of her slowly and torturously. We can physically see it happening.' She said.

'Let me see her.' Demanded Isobelle.

The nurse shook her head. 'That isn't the best idea, we have seen her gradual decline into this state, however looking at the portrait on the wall behind you, it's clear how striking her decline truly is.' She said. Isobelle looked back to the wall to see a large picture of her standing next to King Kastielle in his famous armour sitting on the throne. Her hair flowed red and long. It was perfect and straight flicking symmetrically to rest above her chest. Her sand-coloured skin contrasted against the rose of her hair. She was in her green dress, a dress she and Isobelle picked out together in the markets of a forgotten Arabian country. They had been to so many. Her face was regal and beautiful, a beauty that could only be rivalled by beauty itself. Her eyes a unique shade of purple and ever joyful.

Isobelle turned around, dropping her bow and pulling the nurse out of her way. The nurse stumbled to her knees powerlessly, hitting the floor with a yelp. Then, Isobelle stuck her arm in between the crowd of nurses tending to the queen and pushed them out of her way too.

'I need to see her.' She said. All the nurses grabbed her arm and pulled her back with great resistance, all in a desperate attempt to spare her. Isobelle didn't heed their discouragement and yanked her arm back fighting against them, but she was being overwhelmed. She was losing her footing and was being pulled away from the bed. She was weary from battles of the day. Her resolve was fading, and she was beginning to concede. Nami screamed again, this time it was high pitched like an infant girl which faded into cries and whimpers. With a great effort, Isobelle summoned all her strength and pulled free from the nurses.

'Don't!' the nurses all shouted in unison. It was too late; she was already at the bedside. Isobelle was struck with a sudden shower of cold sweat. Her goose fleshed skin grew paler and paler as the strength left her. Her stomach clenched and released again and again; she was barely clinging to her will. Nami was gone, ravaged and deteriorating. What was left of her was a faintly beating heart and an animated corpse in dreadful pain. Her face was drawn in so far Isobelle could see nearly the entirety of her dry bloodshot eyeballs. Blood streamed from her nostrils to her mouth, chin, and neck, now dried and coagulated on her skin. Her eyes were completely rolled backwards, exposing the vascular whites. She hyperventilated scratching wheezing breaths; she was fighting to stay alive. Her gown was soaked with blood and other fluids. She was frail with only bones left under her skin which was mapped with veins and arteries that chartered her dwindling blood supply. Will alone was keeping her alive, her will to ensure her child's survival.

The head nurse grabbed Isobelle and flung her backwards. She was still in shock and went with ease. The force brought her off her feet and straight to her back. The clang of her cutlass against the floor chimed alongside the sound of the thud. She was suddenly struck with the sensation of all the wind escaping her. The image of her friend and queen left her, and she sat back up. The nurses rushed back to Nami's side, and the head nurse pulled Isobelle to her feet.

'That was reckless! We cannot save either of them if you fight us.' She said angrily.

'I needed to see her?'

'You seeing her isn't keeping her alive! We are!'

Isobelle nodded ashamedly.

'As you can see it isn't looking all too well for her, and to be honest we are exhausting every ounce of our capability just to slow her deterioration. Our only option is to try and save the child.' The nurse said. They were surrounded by the echoes of groans, exuding from the veiled nightmare on the bed. Isobelle felt tears fill her eyes and she looked at the picture on the wall. She loved Nami with a love beyond sisterhood that could only be achieved by friends connected through many centuries.

Nami stood tall in her portrait with Kastielle. Kastielle was all-powerful but, she was the strong one much like she was for everybody else. Isobelle could fight better than most men, but Nami had the fortitude and steadfast belief in both herself and those she loved. In that regard, Nami put all to shame. Isobelle let her tears flow. She spent her entire life hiding and fighting against her emotions because that was the manly thing to do. It was Nami who had taught her, that the strength women possessed over men was their ability to deal with their emotions. To cry when needed, to scream when it suited, to swoon when made to, and to laugh when they wanted, women were strong when they allowed themselves to be free within themselves.

'Madam Isobelle.' Said the nurse gently.

'Yes.' she said wiping away her tears.

'There is a way of saving the child, however, it will add to her pain.' She had a grim look on her face, one of those looks that recognised a no-win situation when one presented itself.

'What is it?' Said Isobelle nervously.

'In some cases, we can extract a baby by making an incision in the mother's belly and taking the baby out. In those cases, we would use sedatives or depressants, to dull the pain. However, in this circumstance, Nami has become too weak to withstand such things without her heart failing.'

Isobelle let out a loud gasp; she didn't want to hear it. 'Isn't there another way?' she asked knowing the answer.

'At the moment, both are dying. With this at least we can save one of them.'

'What would happen if you sedated her and her heart stopped? Why does she have to endure the pain of this procedure?'

'We couldn't be certain that we could deliver the baby quick enough before it died too. The risk is too great. It could be attempted, but to ensure the baby has the best chance of survival, sedation is not an option.' The nurse said bluntly.

'I don't know.' Said Isobelle.

'Do it!' Isobelle and the nurse looked at each other confused. Neither of them said what they had heard. 'Do it!' was said again; it came from the bed. It was Nami. Isobelle and the nurse ran to the bedside.

'Your Highness are you sure? It will be a lot of pain you have to endure. With you having regained your senses I hesitate in my conviction.' Said the nurse. The room was overwhelmed with shock. Nami looked like she was straining against more than just the pain. She had regained consciousness, but that feat no longer came easily to her. She looked at both of them.

'Do it! We don't have much time.' Said Nami feeling her will fading. Isobelle grabbed Nami's hand and kissed it. Her tears formed pale tracks down to her pink lips. Their hands clasped; Nami's hands were cold.

'I don't want you to die.' Said Isobelle. Nami beckoned Isobelle closer and she knelt.

'I want you to tell Kastielle that I saw him. Despite everything that he did, I saw him and I will always love him and he will never be alone.' Her hand was trembling and tears flowed down her cheeks, but her eyes were beautiful once again. 'Now go, this won't be something you want to see.'

'No. I need to stay with you. I can't leave you.'

'Isobelle as your friend, no, as your queen I am telling you to leave…

for me'

They held each other's gaze for a while. Heavy silence blanketed the room, it was the only way they could say goodbye. Isobelle got up silently. She stood tall. She stood strong. Her face was still, and she looked high and straight like standing to attention. Her tears fell as heavy as someone stricken with manic grief, yet still, her expression was fierce. Then she marched out of the room, grabbing her bow and closing the door.

Nothing was said and they meant every word of it.

Nateur- Amor- 33- 115

Celestine accompanied Mother Nature and with a sharp drop, he was thrust back to solid ground. He was a long way from home. This was in Anara when it was still whole. Celestine had fantasised about what Anara would have looked like, relegating the opportunity to see it to an impossibility because what was left of it was only The Wasteland. His only opportunity would come by the brushes of artists or the penmanship of authors. He had seen images, paintings by maestros with the details perfect in every way. He had read the great works from authors around the world. Their words described the land to the last fleck of dust caught in the breeze. Celestine was now standing in the planes of Wildberry, the original home of Kastielle himself. He couldn't believe it.

The sound of the songbirds around him, the air, even the smells, everything was different about this place. A thousand pictures and a million words could never equate to a second of experiencing it for himself. It was home in a way.

There was nothing but untouched beautiful fields to the horizon in front of him, framed by hills and hovels. The forest was to his left. The trees were grand and various, with a flock of bushes at their feet. Their bark was rich, and the leaves were plenty, they glossed against the afternoon sunshine.

Celestine heard voices coming from the darkness in the forest. He looked to Mother Nature, who had disappeared. He stopped in his tracks and the voices emerged. Two men, heavily equipped, came from the shadow of the trees. They were familiar faces. The first face didn't take long for Celestine to recognise, even though he looked significantly different, he knew it was Talion. He was younger now. He didn't carry a hidden rapier in his cane but boasted a longsword at his hip and shield on his back. He was wearing thick leather bottoms and a bear pelt around his shoulders. There was something different about him, other than his age and appearance. He didn't carry himself the same way. His chest was puffed out, full of more than youthful bravado, more like absolute confidence. He had a body that rivalled his own, with shapely muscles and strength to match judging by the size of the bag he was carrying. His hair was black and thick, stretching down to his back in a powerful plat. He was a completely different man.

Talion's travel companion was slender and carried a wooden staff that was a little taller than he was. His hair reached his shoulders but sat an unkempt mess atop his head. He wore black with green leather armour over the top. His face was hard but his expression was gentle. At his uncle's side was Kastielle, not yet the king he was destined to be.

Celestine sat in front of the two companions and listened to them talk until day turned to night. He was close to them a few feet at the most, but he daren't move. It was dark and all was still on the planes of Wildberry. Although Celestine was sat in front of them invisible to their eyes, as he was to the spectators in the arena, he was unsure that all eyes couldn't see him.

Talion and Kastielle sat on one side of a campfire and Celestine sat on the other. Fireflies danced in the long grass in the background, the crackles of the firewood clicked a concerto with the crickets. The night was warm and pleasant. The sky was full of stars, watching over Talion and King Kastielle. Their hefty bags had unpacked bedrolls on either side of them.

'There isn't any chance of you bringing the wine is there Kaz?' Said Talion. Kastielle shook his head at first, then he leaned forward and pressed his hand against the dry dirt floor. His glum expression turned into one of sheer smug satisfaction. He elevated his hand slowly which pulsated with starlight. Kastielle had more control over the power now. As though attached to his hand, a bottle of wine extruded from the floor reflecting the gentle glow of Kastielle's palm. It was materialising before their eyes from the cap downwards.

'I don't need to bring wine. Remember?' he said. Talion smirked as he realised to whom he was speaking. Kastielle Neriah, the world's unseen and unappreciated protector.

'I guess you can get away with a bad memory now you have the power of the divines at your fingertips. Although alas dear Kastielle, you forgot the glasses.' Said Talion, sniggering at his friend.

Kastielle winked, 'What's that in your hand?' he asked. Talion looked down to see not only a glass but a full one. He looked back up to see Kastielle with his in the air awaiting the other.

'Cheers,' They both said clanking their glasses together. Kastielle was truly remarkable. To think that he could handle that power with such proficiency. They took hearty gulps of their drinks and savoured the fruity aftertaste they had left behind. Kastielle's face was plastered with a look of troubled thoughts and nerves. Talion hadn't seen such a grim look on his face, not since he returned from the Arrow Island. Even when coming to grips with his new abilities, which was a great task in and of itself, he never looked so troubled. He grew concerned for his friend. That power was more than any human could handle, and Kastielle was displaying signs that it may be the case for him too. He placed his hand on his friend's shoulder.

'Speak brother.' Said Talion seriously.

Kastielle looked to him for support. 'I've met a woman.' He said. Talion was stricken with relief, although still left confused as to why the look was still on his face.

'Then why are you so troubled? This is great news. Well, not so much for me, but don't trouble yourself with that. I do better in the taverns on my own.' He joked. 'Who is this woman then?' Kastielle gulped hard and summoned his courage.

'Princess Nami of Anara.' he said. Talion's face froze in shock. His stunned expression was almost reflected in the campfire flames. It was an image Kastielle nor Celestine were likely to forget.

'Has anybody ever told you, you are an ambitious sod?' Said Talion. Kastielle laughed and nodded in agreement.

'This isn't ambition. This is love. She sees me. She doesn't see my power or potential. I'm not a hero or a threat. I'm Kastielle Neriah that's all.

Talion smiled again 'Well I still fail to understand why you are so troubled. You are lucky to find that in a woman. Most people struggle to find that in anybody, never mind the Princess of Anara.' He said.

'I am troubled because I have been seeing her without her father's knowledge, and we have planned to marry. I'm troubled because this could be treason I'm about to commit.'

'Is she worth it?' Talion refilled his glass.

'She is.'

'Well just let me know when the wedding is.' Said Talion. He rested his cup down and laid down.

Lazè- Innos- 27- 117

Celestine felt the sensation of being pulled backwards. It was like a rope was tied around his waist and he was yanked with the strength of ten Staphroses. He found himself standing in a packed altar. He was surrounded by an army of people, sat in silence in bated breath. They were waiting for the couple to oblige the priest.

'You may now kiss the bride.' The two of them longingly stared at each other. The moment lasted a lifetime. Celestine had only ever thought of King Kastielle, Queen Nami was rarely spoken of. Kastielle's fame was so grand, many forgot she was a factor and Talion never featured her on the very rare occasions he spoke of home. Celestine looked at her for the first time knowing who she was. Her hair was pinned up into a simple bun. It was rich auburn in this light and was elegant in its simplicity. The women of Anara would wear that style for years after. Her eyes were purple and fixed on the tall man in front of her. Her heart was in her stare. Celestine, found her to be familiar looking at her now. There were no pictures of the queen outside Anara, just the faded memories of an ageing generation and words in children's books. She was described accurately enough, but not to the most finite detail and it was those details that were the most compelling. Specifically, it was the shape of her face, eyes, and nose, and the crinkle at her brow when she smiled. She was smiling now at Kastielle and Celestine saw it. He placed his fingers between his eyes, feeling the very slight loose skin which allowed him to do the same thing. Her long eyelashes, and her thinly curved lips. It was like looking in a mirror; he knew he was looking at his mother. He did not know how, but there was no doubt in his mind. That was how he inherited his powers from Kastielle, he was his father.

She closed her eyes. The audience was not in the forefront of her mind anymore. The room was empty. Empty of sound, sight, or feeling. She and Kastielle existed in a vacuum for that second. In her heart. In the perceived darkness, they sealed their marriage with a kiss. Kastielle knew what he could become, and it petrified him. With this kiss, he was king and in the perfect position to become the beacon of hope for his people, however as much as hope was a part of him, so was despair. As much as he wanted to bring about peace, conflict and war would counter. He was more than a man, but being more than a man was a burden he was unsure he could handle. Nami's sweet lips distracted him from the trouble ahead but his hands trembled behind her.

She had seen who he could be, how he could be overwhelmed by the divine part of him. The results were catastrophic and terrifying, yet here she stood beside him. She made a vow without fear, to love him forever. The conversation was clear when she grabbed his hands. They both knew it would get worse in time, Nami just didn't care. That was why she was his salvation. As bad as things could get, she would always provide him with humanity. When he was lost, she would bring him back to his soul, the one part of him that was truly his. What he felt for her, overpowered the almighty influence within him. He loved her too much to let her go, even though she would be safer away from him. He was selfish for that and he knew it, but he feared what he would become if he were to lose her. Celestine could feel that fear.

Mother Nature opened the alter door and beckoned him through. On the other side was the great hall of Anara Castle.

Chronus- Natura- 40- 1799

It was a time of historical significance, The Great Anara Invasion. Celestine felt the anxiety of the country. There was so much pain around him that it terrorised him to the core. This was the reality of war, and this was the war that changed the world. This was the fall of Anara.

The hall had a grand design, with a ceiling as high as the sky. The walls were made of the same white stones as the wall of Zorrodon and were lined with a litany of tapestries telling the story of its great King, The Golden One, King Kastielle. The hall was empty, devoid of furnishings. It was bare aside from the tapestries and Kastielle's throne, upon which he was sat.

Kastielle was in his armour. His crown and his jewels were scattered across the stone floor. He had the same armour which he had on in all the tapestries. He had on green studded leather, over black bottoms. His hair was golden, like Celestine's. The only thing Celestine inherited from him. He had a grim and serious look on his shaven face. The point of his sword was at the floor, and the hilt span in his hand like the world on its axis. The echoing sound of the steel grinding against the floor pierced through Celestine's eardrums. Kastielle was unfazed. His features were young still, but his eyes were world-weary, heavy with responsibility and burdened with the experience of a thousand years. Celestine walked towards him, gingerly at first, until curiosity overcame sensibility. As far as this reality was concerned he did not exist, and he knew that now. So, he approached close, very close. His curiosity made him bold. He was nearly touching noses with the king. He studied his features. The longer he stared at the king, the more real things felt. He rested his hands on the armrests of the throne, intensely staring at the dejected king.

Kastielle looked up, and Celestine froze. At first, he carried on studying his face. Kastielle was now staring back, directly into his eyes. The green in his eyes flickered with light. As a reaction, Celestine's eyes did the same. Kastielle nodded. He didn't say a word when he did. There was still a shadow of a doubt in Celestine that Kastielle could see him and he held the position. They were nose to nose and eye to eye, as still reflections.

Kastielle smirked, got up, and walked through Celestine. He felt the power of the King as his body fazed through him. It was like what he felt from Mother Nature, ten times over. He was dropped to a knee.

Talion entered the great hall. He looked much older than the last time Celestine saw him. It was much easier to recognise the man that walked in the hall compared to the one at the campfire. He was wearing a large leather belt with a gold and diamond plate at the front. It was the belt of Anara's Champion. Celestine had never seen his Uncle Talion with the belt. He was proud. Stories were one thing, seeing it was another. Although he was looking more like the elderly man Celestine knew, he still looked strong as an ox.

'Kastielle, it is bad news' Said Talion. 'It is ever more apparent that Nami will not survive the childbirth. It is like you prophesied; no human can bear the child of a divine.'

Kastielle nodded understanding fully. He stepped back slowly. The sword dropped from his hands and the clatter rang in the emptiness.

'I told her not to bear that child!' He said slamming his fist into the floor, the room shook. 'I don't want an heir! I only ever wanted her!' His cries were frail and genuine. Talion rushed to his knees, not to help him up, as any champion should, but to comfort him as any best friend would. They had their differences but Kastielle was losing the most important person in his life. Talion knew all too well what that was like.

Kastielle gripped Talion's shoulder and screamed. Lightning struck over and over, as a percussion of thunder shook the castle. Celestine's heart could feel Kastielle's loss. It killed him. It killed him because he felt the guilt, the responsibility. It killed him because he was the baby that he never wanted, so his mother died for nothing. A black aura swirled around Kastielle, like flames, which didn't harm Talion yet. His eyes shined bright green against the background of blackened eyeballs. His hair spiked into sharp points and slowly darkened away from the gold. He stood. The ground cracked beneath his feet. With a booming shout, he punched a hole in the thick stone wall revealing the large garden of the castle, Eros Pasture. On the hills beyond, an army of nine thousand strong formed against him.

His pain turned to hatred, hatred directed at the invaders at his gate. The air got heavier, and the pressure was crushing all close by. Celestine resisted with all his might and Talion, cowered away stricken with fear and sadness. Celestine, seeing his uncle cowering on the floor, entered the white void within himself and yanked on the door open without thinking. His shine appeared with a glorious bang and the shine in his eyes glistened against the cosmic glow of his skin. He still had his wits about him as the water flowed through him. Celestine had control now it was time to battle test it. Kastielle looked at him. It was a dark stare. He was smiling maniacally at first, then the expression faded. Celestine could feel shame overcome Kastielle, and he saw the tears trail his cheeks as he began to reach for him. They were connected and Celestine could feel the regret in his heart. Kastielle reached for his son.

Mother Nature grabbed Celestine by the shoulder and wrapped him completely in her cloak.

'I didn't think that he would be able to see you. Kastielle seemed to have had power beyond even me.'

Celestine said nothing. He knew the truth now. She removed her cloak and they emerged into Nami's bedroom. They were met by the cries of a new-born baby. The nurses held him, tiny and vulnerable. The baby's eyes were closed tight, and fists balled tighter. A healthy baby boy. Nami was no longer moving. She was dead. She knew the risks, and the likelihood of this happening. She just wanted Kastielle to have an heir. More importantly, she wanted him to have someone else like him. She didn't need to be divine to know how alone he was. The bridge between two worlds, neither of which he fitted in. That was worth her life to give to him. She was not scared of what he would become without her; she would always be with him through her son.

Her white bedsheets were soaked red with blood. It dripped from the edge of the mattress adding to the pool formed on the floor. It was clear as day to see that the flow was catastrophic. Celestine stared, fascinated at the golden-haired baby. He took a step, then another, leaving Mother Nature to watch him. The baby was so small and fragile. Celestine approached the bed unnoticed by the grieving nurses that saw their queen die. He knew who she was, but he had to see. He stared at the dead expression in her face confirming his fears. She died giving birth to him. He began to cry. Mother Nature comforted him, but he swatted her hands away.

'Why did you bring me here? He asked.

Mother Nature said nothing.

'I know that I am the unwanted child that killed his mother. Is that everything I need to know?' he said turning to face her.

Mother Nature said nothing.

'Well, I didn't want to know! I don't want to be a prince of a fallen kingdom because it means I'm more alone than I thought. My uncle has fed me lies all of my life. He let me suffer with the power of my father nearly every day. I know it was to protect me, but I deserved to know the truth, but not like this.' Celestine slumped against the wall and wept into his arms. 'Why did you have to tell me like this?'

'Every divine being needs a counter of equal value and magnitude; it's the only way to have balance. That was what drove your father mad, he had no equal.' Mother Nature brought Celestine to his feet and pointed to the cot in the corner. 'Celestine you are over there.' Celestine got up and noticed there was a crib sounding the cries of a second child with blue eyes.

'What?' Celestine was in disbelief.

'Now look at him.' Mother Nature said pointing at the other. The baby in the nurse's arms was blinking.

Celestine gulped and was losing his breath. The baby's eyes were red.

'That is your brother Celestine. You are not alone; you never have been.'

33 NEW BONDS

Had- Natura- 20- 1827

It had been one month since Celestine's funeral. Things were on the way to normal, or more accurately a new shade of normal. There was still that hole in everybody's heart. A void that could never be filled, but the choice was to live with it or not live with. The latter would just create a larger void for those who remained. So, everybody bound together chose to and live with it.

Temina decided to take permanent residence in Celestine's cottage. She could not go back to Zorrodon or what was left of it. Between her mother, Lion, and Celestine she had lost too much in that city. She had two jobs on Sakura farm, she worked as a consultant for Doc providing herbal remedies and new ideas and research for medicines. Her more full-time role was a teacher of botanical science. She enjoyed that role very much. The children that she worked with all had their quirks and personalities. She even loved the naughty ones, but she couldn't let them know that. They gave her new life in her new life.

Luke was now a model worker. He was the first up and last to stop. It was such a sudden change in his personality that people were starting to worry about him, but they left it for the time being. Perhaps he was just coping. There was something that happened in Zorrodon before Celestine died that caused the change. When Celestine spoke and said that he was okay, they were connected. He couldn't explain the sensation that he felt but, he felt everything that his best friend knew and thought about him. He never thought of it, but Celestine had just as much if not more admiration for him as he did for Celestine. He knew Celestine thought higher of him than most, but he put him on a pedestal. He saw Luke for what he could be but loved him for who he was. Luke's goal was to honour that view by living up to the potential his friend saw in him.

Just like every other day, Luke was early to rise and already on the farm to find an isolated spot to work. He was making his way to the tool shed when the outhouse door swung open.

'Luke!' Shouted Staphros. 'You work with me today.' Relieved to hear it, Luke ran for the open door.

Staphros was routinely slinging weights around once more in his gymnasium. His veins were pulsing on his arms like a flock of snakes infiltrating his skin. He had visible anger on his face, and he cursed and spat when he lifted his weights. The effect of the fight with Celestine still ran deep. The bruises and swelling were gone, but the internal damage was still prevalent.

Luke had been there an hour or so and he hadn't done any work yet, nor did Staphros ask him to. He retreated into a secluded corner by the stores of food. It was breakfast time and hunger was taking him again. He raided the food store picking out ingredients to a recipe he hadn't decided on yet. His food was not as renowned as his sisters, but he wasn't a slouch in the kitchen. He had, chicken, onion, eggs, tomatoes, and spinach. With the ingredients stacked on top of his folded arms, he shuffled, to the fire stove, and took out some bowls and pans. Staphros didn't notice what was going on at all. He didn't know why he wanted Luke in the outhouse, but he did. Part of him wanted to show his appreciation, but he wasn't sure how to. Staphros made a habit of keeping people out, inviting Luke in was a big step for him. For anybody that knew Staphros well enough, they would understand and take it as a thank you. Luckily, Luke knew Staphros better than he thought.

Luke remembered the look on his face when he was carrying Celestine to the ocean. He hadn't seen Staphros cry, and most likely would never, but, that walk looked like a journey that lasted a decade in seconds. He held Celestine like he would never let him go. He remembered the strength Staphros leant to him when his own strength abandoned him. Prochnost meant strength; Luke never forgot it.

Luke wanted to say thank you too. He cooked the chicken first in the skillet, sprinkling herbs and spices over the top making it dark and charred on the outside. Then he added the onion, spinach, tomatoes and eggs. The spinach reduced, and the tomatoes seeped fruitful juices, and the eggs absorbed the flavours of the chicken. Luke was brought into a trance as he watched the ingredients blend.

Staphros stood with the weight of a horse across his shoulders and squatted to the ground. It was the ninety-eighth time he had repeated that movement. He was rehabilitating the muscle in his legs. The weight on his shoulders was light by his standards, but he had to get functional movement back. He was struggling to build strength in his base. When he pushed back up from the ground, the back of his thigh trembled and gave. The weight on his shoulder tilted to one side. Quickly, Staphros regained his balance shaking on his right leg. He focussed as hard as he could. He shuffled his good leg to a more central position and pushed with a great effort. He didn't scream, curse, or spit; he just breathed hard as he stood back up. He looked down at his leg, and then to the floor. Straightening his bad leg out in front of him, Staphros descended to the floor once more.

'Ninety-nine' he said before nodding off the storm of sweat on his forehead. 'One hundred'. He exclaimed a breath of relief. He hooked the bar onto the rack and dropped to the bench beside him. He massaged his tensed hamstring, to relieve the stress upon it.

Luke approached with a large plate of food. Staphros had forgotten to eat yesterday. His mind was occupied with other things, he didn't seem to be coping as well as Luke. He looked into Luke's face and saw the sweet irony that this pudgy Celtishman had shown a strength that inspired him. Luke was stronger than he thought. Celestine knew that; even from beyond the grave he was teaching him things. The aroma of the meal made his mouth water and remember that he had not eaten for an entire day. It had a variance of flavours that tempted taste. Staphros was seduced, beguiled by hunger. Luke placed the plate on the table and the two sat together and shared a hearty meal.

The sign of a good chef was silence during a meal. Luke couldn't help but watch Staphros's reaction whilst he ate. His stone face crumbled away as he visibly enjoyed the food. Digging in quicker with more on the fork than the last time. Staphros pointed to the plate.

'This is delicious comrade.' He said. Luke couldn't think how to react, and rather clumsily clasped his hands together and bowed. He didn't know why. Staphros continued to eat and it was quiet again.

'I did not get the chance to say this at the funeral but, you did a great job.' Said Staphros.

Luke's face lit up. 'That means a lot coming from you. Honestly.' He said. Staphros reached into his pocket and took out a medal.

'I wanted to give this to you as a token of my appreciation. This is Talion's medal of honour for his service to Anara. He gave it to me when I turned twenty-one. I want you to have it.' Said Staphros.

Luke reached out and then retracted. 'Don't joke around. Really?' He said unsure.

'I never joke!' Staphros snapped seriously.

Luke looked down at his plate hiding within himself and Staphros maintained his glare.

'That, was a joke.' Staphros laughed, as did Luke nervously.

'But… Seriously?' Said Luke. Staphros looped the ribbon around his neck and the medal rested heavily on his chest.

'It's yours.' Said Staphros.

When they finished the food, Luke cleared the plates and washed them.

Staphros got up, opened his cabinet at the wall. It was mounted high, out of reach for most people. It looked out of place against the metal and stone that filled the room. Inside were large clay bottles, Staphros picked one out from an identical row along with two small mugs. When he returned, Luke had finished cleaning the plates. Staphros poured the liquid into the mugs; it was thin and clear. Luke picked his up and smelt it. The smell hit him unexpectedly.

'What is that? It smells like a kind of strongwine, but I've never seen one so clear.' Said Luke. Staphros's eyes lit up.

'This is made in my home country, from root starch. We call it Wudka' he said.

'I'll have to bring you a tankard of Scottsdrink, Celtish strongwine. Ours is brown, cause it's made with malt, barley and tree bark.' Said Luke.

'Sounds, unpleasant.'

'You'd be surprised. So, are we going to drink or are we going to just stare at these?'

Staphros nodded, admiring the cultural directness that was not dissimilar to his own. They both slugged the first drink clean. The clear liquid had a kick that Luke liked. It was thicker and stronger than he thought it would be. Staphros knew the Celtish could drink, but so could his people. He poured another drink for both of them and they clinked their mugs.

'Where are you from, Staphros?' asked Luke.

'I am from, Nurmagastan, Baltic Deutschland.' He replied.

'Ahh, that explains a lot.' Said Luke.

'How so?'

'Those folks tend tae be big. I mean I'm fairly sure they're the biggest people in the world?' Said Luke.

'That we are. I forget that you and Celestine travelled there. Did you like it?' he said.

'Aye.'

'Aye, what does this mean? I hear you say this many times.'

'Oh, aye? It basically means yes where I'm from.'

'But, you are from this country? Anglonia?'

'This is King's Anglonia. Where I'm from is Celtish Anglonia. There's a massive difference.' Said Luke uncharacteristically stern. Staphros also out of character smirked at his rather obvious attempt to wind Luke up. It was one of the few times Staphros saw him serious.

'You should lighten up. I joke comrade.'

'Oh, ha, ha. You're a right funny bastard!' Said Luke sarcastically.

'I said I was joking.'

'Oh, not to worry mate. Bastard is a good thing where I'm from.' Said Luke. 'Sometimes.' Staphros laughed loudly at that one almost choking on his drink. He covered his mouth to try and keep it from flying out. Staphros was just like everyone else Luke thought and it was almost an idiotic notion that he once thought otherwise. He had never noticed before but, Staphros smiled with his eyes and grinned like a child.

For the rest of the day, they enjoyed good food, drink, and company.

34 CRIME AND PUNISHMENT

Staphros sat on his stool troubled. The parchment in his hand was hand-delivered by Cyrus of the Hondos. It was one of their journals. The Hondos thought it would be diminishing to Lion's legacy if they had stopped distributing them. Staphros hadn't purchased one yet; he hadn't gone to back Zorrodon. After learning of the promise that Staphros made to Lion, Cyrus thought it was only right that he knew the events of this past week. Kojo's body had been found on the grounds of the governmental complex, buried in a shallow unmarked grave. The news came directly from the city's new unelected mayor, Adan Thiago. Thiago condemned Magnus for his corruption and the many other crimes he committed. He spoke directly to the killing of Kojo and pardoned him of his crime finding him innocent. The news fell heavily on Staphros. He was raised in squalor, fought in a war, and witnessed countless injustices. The bloodshed had to stop.

He spent the day lamenting the deaths of the many who died, but the greater trouble on his mind was in the form of the newly appointed mayor. Thiago was a name that bore weight all over the world for generations. Staphros studied the sordid history of the family, but his motivation was more personal than the pursuit of knowledge. Before he was deployed to invade Anara as a child, there was a block of time that he couldn't remember. He knew two things after that time, the name Thiago, and that his father arrived with him and didn't leave. It ate at his mind.

The door knocked suddenly, and Luke entered.

'You ready? Everyone's at the cottage now; we're plating up.' He said.

Staphros nodded placing the journal on the table. He grabbed a nice jacket and left with Luke.

Talion's room darkened as evening turned into night. As the sun set and

265

the crickets and owls began their opera, Talion was deaf to the music. The breath of night slithered like vipers of ice around the room, Talion was numb to the chill. The glow of the moon stretched onto his bed shining silver into his face, Talion was blind to the light.

He had become thin and haggard. His beard had grown long and wiry, and his hair was knotted. He was at on the edge of his bed, his legs hanging off of the side. He had on a white gown that hung loosely on his thinning shins. His eyes were red, forever bloodshot. The veins on his hands wrinkled purple and pulsing. He had a grim look on his face like he was looking at something intently or someone.

Talion had faced trial for every single life that he had directly ruined. Each one of them made him watch what he did to them and accept the guilt. Only until he accepted guilt, would he truly know that he was irredeemable, that he deserved the punishment he recieved. The visitors came as apparitions nightly without relent. His mindset shifted and now he did not yearn for death to relieve him of his guilt, he genuinely thought he deserved to die. Mother Nature had won. That was her punishment complete. A parent only punished a child to show them the error of their ways. He was staring at the darkest corner of his room. The part where the moonlight could not reach. There stood a figure in the dark. This one had been present every night since Sakura.

'So are you going to speak this time, or are you here to watch me again?' He asked. It was tall and heroic. It had long dark hair and steely eyes. The figure laughed and stepped out. Talion had seen this figure many a time since locking himself away, this was the first time it did more than just stand.

'I was wondering when you would stop being a coward, old man.' It said. Its voice was deep and familiar. As the moonlight hit it, he was faced with his past, Talion the Torturer, his younger self.

Mother Nature wanted to make Talion see himself and understand the punishment levied against him, now that he understood his wrongdoings. Talion the Torturer was the name given to him by the wronged peoples of Kastielle's tyranny. Talion committed atrocities under that banner and didn't think anything of it until Kastielle turned on him. He had to know that this was his choice; his sins were his alone.

The room was unchanged, and no other accompanied the apparition. Talion had a feeling that this was a guise for Mother Nature, and she had returned from her business. Talion would be relieved to see her but not happy about it. For all the guilt he felt, he believed her just as culpable for the crimes he committed. She was the greatest manipulator in existence.

'Not cowardice, just weariness. You weren't worth my concern, a figment of my loss of sanity or a cruel joke by a pathetic deity.' He was baiting her.

'Oh, you clever boy.' Said The Torturer familiarly. 'I thought facing trial for your sins would leave you more respectful. I was wrong. Clever as you are my boy, you are mistaken. I am not here to prod or punish you but grant you a reprieve for your sins.' Talion got up now aware of his senses. He wrapped on his robe to shield the new cold. He stood examining his younger self.

'I'll pass on the reprieve. You're not qualified to grant me absolution. None of you divines are.' He said.

'Watch your tongue boy.'

Talion stepped closer, inches away from his counterpart. 'Or what? You'll kill me?' The Torturer whipped a backhand across Talion's cheek. Talion looked up and spat blood. The pain was fresh and stinging.

'There are things far worse than death Tal…'

'A fact that I am reminded of every day I wake up wishing I hadn't! What more, Mother Nature!? What more can you take from me?!' Said Talion angrily. He scampered to his feet like a new-born deer. His head was still fuzzy from the back-hand blow. He did not show that it still pained him, except for the wobbling in his knees. The initial rage that appeared on The Torturer's face that was soon controlled.

The Torturer peeled back the curtains and pointed to the outhouse. Talion's blood ran cold.

'That would be just the start. Do not test me again boy.' They said. Talion pressed his hands on the window ledge realising what he had and ultimately what he could lose.

He nodded. Mother Nature shed her guise and stood as herself again.

'Now, are you going to listen like a good boy?' She asked.

Talion nodded.

'You see Talion, I'm not here to take anything away from you. Frankly, I don't have to. Your punishment is coming, and I believe it to be befitting the crime.' Said Mother Nature. She peeled back the other curtain and pointed down to the gate. They were a little march away but he could see incoming torches coming in mass. 'As you already know, you cannot go about killing political figures. You didn't just do that though, you killed a high ranking figure in the Thiago dynasty. So this incoming militia is coming to raid your farm to arrest you, and they're advised to use any means necessary. This is your chance my boy, your chance to show me that you have truly changed. Your chance to make an unselfish decision for once in your life.'

'And do what?' Asked Talion.

'Give yourself up.'

It was a cruel irony. In the weeks he had been trapped in the prison of Mother Nature's making, she hadn't once sent Magnus to put him on trial. Magnus was one of the few kills that he did not regret. He didn't want to go and give them the satisfaction. He stepped away from the window and paced thinking. Mother Nature leaned on the wall by the window.

'Not to rush you, but you don't have much time. That behind me is a company of fifty men, heavily armed and prepared to kill, any women, children, and giants, to get you back to Zorrodon. By the order of Adan Thiago himself.' She said. The name rang in the air like a siren a beacon of the severity of the situation. Talion stopped pacing and gulped hard. 'You already told me I'm not qualified to absolve you, so here's the opportunity to do it yourself. Save the residents of your farm and pay for your sins. Isn't that what you want anyway, or was that just for show? Absolution is not free.'

She got him. The fear ran from his face and he steeled himself to face his punishment. The words that affected people the most were always the true ones. Talion was still the boy that expected the world to provide, and part of him would always be, no matter how many more years he lived. He was hesitant to make this sacrifice, but if he wasn't hesitant it wouldn't be a sacrifice.

'How long do I have?' he asked.

'You have fifteen minutes until they arrive.' Said Mother Nature. She faded into a mist with the diminishing echo of a dying breath. Talion watched it be carried away into the night, knowing it would not be the last time he saw an apparition in his life. She would return to twist the knife before long. The light of torches drew nearer.

Time stopped for no man.

Samantha had arranged for a small group of them to gather this evening to serve as a wake for Celestine. She held it at the cottage where Temina now lived and invited Luke, Hanabi and Staphros; she was insistent on Staphros. The wake was a Celtish tradition where the family of the dead ate and drank in celebration of life. The only rule was that happiness was a must. The wound was too fresh to do it sooner, and still too fresh for some. Talion's exclusion was noted but tactfully recommended by both Staphros and Hanabi. They had spent the most time with him; he was bordering on catatonic. He could barely hold a conversation and never made eye contact. He was a broken man. He was best left to heal, and he would be welcomed when he was ready.

The food was eaten, and the drinks were now being drank. The sitting room was filled with joy in the cottage. Temina had settled in and the others were becoming accustomed to calling the place hers. She on the other hand, always called the cottage Celestine's home; she just had the privilege of living there. The privilege extended beyond being close to him, but the people he called family treated her with a kindness that she could not remember for a long time.

Luke and Staphros stole away into the kitchen while the women talked in the sitting room. Temina was giggling her cheeks red at Samantha who had become quite drunk rather quickly. Samantha was the pride of Celtish

Anglonia for many reasons, but drinking was not one of them. Unlike her kinsmen, she couldn't handle her drink; she was a lightweight among lightweights. She could get tipsy from drinking child's cider, which was the juice of an apple warmed up. Tonight, however, she was on the strongwine, much to her brother's dismay.

Temina, Hanabi, and Samantha clinked the mugs together in a toast to their friendship. Temina and Hanabi were teaching colleagues and often taught lessons together blending botany with philosophy. The children loved it. Hanabi also bonded with Temina because she was a relatively new girl and Hanabi had just learned the ropes. They had shared endeavour. The other thing they shared in their endeavour was how much Samantha helped them. She wasn't just Luke's big sister; she was everyone's. They leaned on her when they needed her, and she was always there to be leaned on. Now they were being asked to respectively return the favour as Samantha physically leaned on them. Samantha's arms spread wide as she elevated on her tiptoes to wrap her arms around Hanabi and Temina. The two were of similar average height, whereas Samantha was every bit of four foot ten and proud of it.

'Ah luhv yuh tooh!' She said smacking a sloppy kiss on each of their cheeks. Temina gently unwrapped Samantha's arm from her. She had been feeling funny lately and didn't want to exacerbate things. Samantha took another sip of her strongwine and hiccupped.

'Don't you think you've had enough?' Asked Hanabi.

Samantha nodded. 'Aye ah have.' Samantha was belligerent, loud, and a little too forward when she was drunk, but strangely she remained sensible. Responsibility was a full-time virtue. She offered the drink to both of them.

Hanabi shook her head and Temina raised the mug in her hand. Samantha was stricken curious.

'Wuh yuh on dere?' she asked. Not waiting for an answer, she bundled over and inspected the contents of the mug. The liquid was amber, and she thought it was ale. Ale wasn't a particularly ladylike drink, but Samantha respected it. When the smell and warmth hit her nose, she knew that it wasn't ale, but child's cider. Temina had been nursing that all evening, like it had been overproof canewine.

'No! Yuh canne drink thah!' Said Samantha thrusting her strongwine in Temina's direction. 'Ave a real drink.'

'I'm fine with this thank you.' Temina said shaking her head. Samantha set her drink down and wandered off without explanation.

'Sam where are you going?' Hanabi asked laughing openly.

Samantha winked and tapped her nose.

Talion wrote two letters. The first was to the people of the farm, a general but heartfelt letter. He detailed why he had to go and how he wished for them to respect any verdict that the Zorrodon judiciary would levy. He talked about how he enjoyed meeting all of them and how he could remember every single face that he passed. He cursed his old age which made him forget their names at times but assured them that he loved them all the same. He thanked them for providing him with life, not a life, but life in its purest form. He finished with saying goodbye and said that he loved them very much because they were his family.

His second letter was addressed to Staphros. He and Staphros had bonded over twenty-seven years. Staphros was a boy who needed a man. He did not need a man to help him, father him, or rub his head and tell him good job. Staphros had learned to live without those things. Staphros needed, a man to teach him how to grow. The irony of it all was he was already six-foot-ten when they met. He seemed pretty adept at growing and even if he wanted it, no man could rub him on the head. Talion detailed in his letter how impressed he was with him, not because of his stature or strength, but how mature he was. He was impressed with how he could teach him every day, even though there was a chasm of years between them.

With a smile on his face he scribed a phrase he repeated over and over to a teenage Staphros, Knowledge is for everyone, wisdom is reserved for the wise. He remembered the look of pride on the young man's face as he realised Talion was speaking about him. Talion held his tears back, as he poured his thanks and gratitude for every brick and pillar of foundation that this farm was built upon. He thanked Staphros for always reminding him of the great man he was, reassuring him that he was still just as great.

The last part of the letter connected well with Staphros's sentiment. It was a seal, a seal of approval, that Talion did not give to many people. He would say how nice they were, how talented or impressive somebody was. He romanticised the past and sometimes the present would pass him by. Staphros received no applause from Talion. He received gratitude for what he had done, but very rarely appreciation for the person he was. It happened, just not often. So, with his final words to him, Talion took his final opportunity:

"With this, I wish to bestow full custody of 'Sakura Farm' in the south-east of King's Anglonia to Staphros of Nurmagastan.

I give this land to you because you are everything you say that I am and more. I have lived a great life among great men, in turn, I became a great man too. You are a great man among Kastielle Neriah, Eros Neriah, and me. You showed me that you are something that I never was nor can ever be. Staphros you are a good man. For that, you deserve my legacy and more.

I love you, my son.

Talion Ulrich Schultz Of Anara"

Ten minutes had passed when Talion sealed both of his letters. He walked the dark hallways of his large home for the last time stopping in the dining hall with the door in front of him. He knew it was time. The closer he got to it the more okay he was with this outcome. This hall where he hosted dinner every evening and held supper every night. The great banquet hall held so many memories. He watched so many children grow into fine adults, some who stayed and some who left. They were all part of these walls. He traipsed through the moonlit room and was thankful for what he had. It didn't make it easier to leave it behind, but having it in the first place was a blessing.

For the last time, Talion walked down the three steps from his porch to the grass and across the field. The farm was best seen under a high bright sun, but the night brought a calmness and serenity. This field bore many a happy memory, such as Celestine and Luke somehow managing to get Staphros to take part in their play "Kastielle and the Cyclops". The boys barely older than infants at the time and young Staphros hadn't yet hardened into the man he was today. Talion remembered it took them close to a week of pestering and a very well thought out pitch of the script by Luke to get him on board. Staphros, of course, played the cyclops, Celestine played Kastielle and Luke played Talion. Talion watched the play and found events hilariously different from the events in the book. Talion remembered himself being a non-factor to the cyclops in this adventure. In the stage adaptation, Talion was the focus of the cyclops's ire, perhaps artistic licence.

Talion favourite part was the song that the boys wrote. It was rather well worded for the writings of children. It later was revealed that Luke took the lead on the songwriting. For the longest time, Talion thought that Celestine was being humble, but after Luke's display at the funeral, Talion was convinced it was the truth. Samantha sang the song; she was seventeen at the time. She sounded like how the sweetest songbirds hoped to sing. Her voice brought tears to his eyes and chills to his fingers.

He reminisced about every conversation he shared with the teachers, gardeners, shepherds, nurses, farmers, chefs, housekeepers and children. Like as if they all appeared as ghosts before him and time slowed down, he heard every word of every conversation as he said goodbye to his land.

He reached the outhouse. Talion rested his hand on the door and hesitated. He wanted to see him one more time, but he knew couldn't. He cursed his grief for shutting him away for so long. He pressed his ear to the door and there he couldn't hear him sleeping. Talion feared the pain that his leaving would cause him, but Staphros had good people around him. He would eventually be okay. He had a duty to the rest of the people, and he knew Staphros would do the same if the roles were reversed. He would do the same because he believed that was what Talion would do. Staphros had an elevated perception of Talion but this time for once, he would live up to that perception. He slipped the letter through the crack where the two doors met, and he sighed.

He looked at the gate, the men were drawing near. They were close enough to be noticed by people soon. With his head held high, he went to meet the incoming force.

Talion got to the gate first. He sat on an overturned barrel twiddling his walking stick. The track was soft and damp. It wasn't quite muddy, but it was getting there. The torches rose from the slope in front, as a company of men spotted him one by one. Talion remained seated.

'Greetings!' He said. They all dressed and looked the same in this light however, there was a spokesperson amongst them, with long black scraggly hair and two buck teeth. He looked like the rat he most certainly based his personality upon.

'We've come to fetch you.' He said in a northern King's Anglo accent. 'So no trouble. If there is, we've been instructed to kill everybody here.' His voice had a hint of excitement. Talion noticed it. His beady eyes, blacker than the deepest hole in the lake of souls. Still, Talion remained calm.

'So, be a good dog…' he said and extended his wrists in surrender. 'and fetch.' A few of the men sniggered deep in the crowd, ignorant to the idea that Talion was talking about them too. The rat-faced spokesman reddened. Talion could only imagine it. The moon and stars could not provide appropriate lighting to show such a minor change in his pigment.

'You think you're funny.' He said looking at Talion, who smiled pleasantly back at him. 'You won't be laughing when the hangman comes.' He smiled a crooked smile, revealing the abundance of missing teeth and the black ones that remained. He clasped the metal bonds on his wrists and neck. Talion looked up, his eyes were steely, and he did not smile. This was the face of his youth, the terrorising face of The Torturer. The rat-faced spokesman looked down and their eyes met. An involuntary chill slithered down his spine and he rushed securing the neck bond.

'How much would you wager on that being true?' Said Talion his voice was deeper and fearsome. 'I have met death himself and smiled in his face. You think your hangman scares me?' His tone was so serious, even if they did not believe him, they could not contest that it was his truth. The spokesman stepped back. The original plan was that he could handle the old man and put him in the cart, but the look in his eye bothered him. He snapped his fingers. Two men broke from the company and grabbed Talion by the shoulders. They hoisted him up and threw him into the cold wood of the cart floor. Talion's bones ached from the impact and chose to remain against the ground.

The cart pulled away and his journey began with no chance of return.

Sitting across from Talion in the dark privacy of his prisoner's carriage, was Mother Nature. He anticipated her return just not so soon.

'Please let me have this moment in peace.' Said Talion shortly. He was tired of the games. Mother Nature could see and feel the anguish he felt leaving his home. She was going to leave him to suffer, but in some twisted way, she still loved her little Talion.

'I honestly didn't think you'd go through with it. I'm proud of you.' She said.

'Leave me alone.' Talion hissed. 'This isn't the time.'

'I know, but I couldn't leave you to your fate without giving you some hope.' She said.

'Hope?'

'Yes, hope.' She said moving to sit next to him. She took his hand. 'Kastielle granted his loved ones immortality with a spell, but his immortality was inherent in his powers. You didn't know that because you never thought to ask.'

'Okay, what are you getting at?' Said Talion.

Mother Nature rolled her eyes. 'You and I both know that Celestine inherited his father's gifts.' She said. Talion blinked as the hazy mind pieced together what she was saying. His eyes brightened.

'Wait, does that mean...'

'Celestine lives and he is returning home.'

Meanwhile, in the cottage, the festivities had ended rather abruptly. Luke sent Samantha to bed after she accosted Staphros with persistent inquiry. Her question was one that had haunted Luke for decades because Samantha was open in her curiosity. When he discovered Samantha in Staphros's ear whispering, the blood drained look on his face told the story. She had asked him about... proportional size. It was a question she often mused to Luke about, and the image was not something Luke wanted to think about, but his sister's eagerness to know utterly mortified him each time it was mentioned. Luke's strong reaction and Samantha repeating the question was typical of the Chef sibling's dynamic. Temina and Hanabi couldn't help but laugh. Hanabi helped Sam to bed and now there only remained Temina, Luke, and Staphros.

Temina sat Luke and Staphros down in the kitchen. She looked like she carried a weight on her shoulders as she sat across from them at the table. They were worried that the wake may have reopened the wound. In reality, she felt the same as they did about it; it was very much needed to move on. Her trouble wasn't so much how she felt, but in how to explain how she felt. She knew her body and she had been feeing strange over the last month and people had started to comment on her glow. The reality was, she was sweating an awful lot more than normal. She nodded with conviction knowing she had to address it.

'I want to talk about Zorrodon.' She said.

Staphros and Luke nodded and leaned forward. This was what troubled her; what troubled everyone.

'Is it about the news?' Said Staphros. Temina looked perplexed. 'Never mind.' That was his trouble to bear.

'I want to talk about that night. I feel I can only talk to the two of you because you witnessed what Celestine could do.' Temina looked at Luke. 'Luke do you remember how it felt to be healed by Celestine.' Luke scratched his head unsure of how to answer. He didn't feel anything in reality, feelings were taken away to be more accurate, but he was compelled to answer.

'I guess, warm?' he said.

'Warm?' Interjected Staphros.

'Aye, warm.' Luke was more assured in his guess now. He got up and poured himself another drink. 'Want one?' He asked while pouring.

Both shook their head.

'How did you feel Temina?' Asked Staphros now very curious.

'Well, it didn't feel warm. Celestine kissed me when he healed me…'

'Lucky you. All I got was…' Staphros shot a stern glare to shut Luke up. It wasn't the time. Temina smiled in thanks as Luke silently returned to his seat.

'Where was I… Yeah, he kissed me and it was like I felt everything he felt for me and everything he wanted with me. He showed me our future, or at least the future he wanted for us.' Temina trailed off and tears rolled down her face.

'It's okay. We're here as long as you need to talk.' Said Staphros.

'Aye! Besides Staph and me knew Celestine a long time. Even before that night, Celestine could sort of project his feelings somehow. We knew how he felt and he knew how we felt.'

'It's not that.' Said Temina wiping her tears away. 'I saw a little boy in the future he showed me and then I started to heal. It was like I was being filled with Life, like the child of Nature, Life. I wanted to check if Luke felt that sensation when Celestine healed him too.'

Luke shook his head. 'I couldn't say. What does Life feel like?'

'You'd know it if you felt it.' Said Temina. Staphros appeared to be decoding a puzzle in his head.

'Why are you asking this?' he asked. Temina looked to the heavens and her tears fell heavier down her cheeks. She couldn't stop as her emotions overflowed. She was afraid, happy, sad, and so determined. The thought brought more tears, the words couldn't leave her. Luke circled the table and sat beside her, wrapping his arm around her shoulders. She rested her head on him thankful for his support, of everyone's support.

'I've been feeling strange since that night. I thought it was the grief but it's only been getting more severe. I'm not sick, I'm surer of that now I know Luke hasn't experienced anything. But I think Celestine did more than just heal me that night.' She said.

'What are you saying?' Asked Staphros.

'I'm saying I think Celestine manifested his future within me. I think I'm pregnant with his child.'

35 ANARA'S FINAL CHAPTER

Chronus- Natura- 40- 1799

It was at the birth of the two Anara princes that marked the day of Anara's fall, the end of The Kastielle Era. Queen Nami was dead; she died giving birth to her two boys. King Kastielle was blinded with grief and abandoned all his sensibilities to go to meet the invading armies who had finally made their way to the grounds of his castle. It was a vast field of seemingly limitless acreage. It had peaks and valleys of shining emerald grass and tall fruitful trees.

On this day, the green grass was covered by a nine-thousand-man garrison in blood-stained armour. The army was the product of the efforts of four different nations and led by four different generals. They banged on their shields confidently. Steel blades clanging against large cast iron. The howl of the whining metal as the swords were pulled from impact reached the castle and beyond. It screamed that there was no escape. The queen was dead and the King was cornered. By the rules of chess, that was checkmate. Anara's royal army was stretched thin across the land, battling widespread skirmishes designed for this one purpose, to isolate the King. It was paramount that Kastielle died at this moment. It was only Kastielle and his two champions, Talion and Isobelle, who were able to fight. After losing the desert to the occupying Arabian Forces, the Anara Royal Army was dealt a tremendous blow losing many good men and women. Those desert troops were the closest to Anara Castle. With them gone, this was the invaders best opportunity to end the war.

Their strategy was sound and collaborative. The soldiers of Akoku formed the cavalry, five hundred black horses mounted by the most skilled riders in the world. The field troops were formed of a collective of Latins and the Norsemen. It was a deadly combination of skill and brute strength that had caused an issue since the war's inception. The field troops were the most abundant in their numbers boasting over seven thousand, their job was to overwhelm the king with sheer numbers. This army was painfully aware of what King Kastielle was capable of. That was why they had to stop him. The archers and infantry of the Wukong nations served as the vanguard. Their plan was set, they awaited the King.

At the last stand, Kastielle was riddled with guilt and anger which had driven him completely into the darkness he fought against for so long. The deeper he stepped into his madness, his anger, the further the power corrupted him. When he emerged from the castle, nobody could believe it was Kastielle at first. The corruption had turned his regal golden locks black. His eyes shone green and the white glow of his mythical power was replaced by a black smog-like aura. It was not until he was close that Kastielle projected his feelings of madness and betrayal upon the encroaching attackers. No matter what, Kastielle was but one man, standing against nine-thousand. The way he walked, arms wide and palms facing upward at a steady consistent pace with swords at his side, he didn't care anymore. His confidence was enough to unnerve hundred-thousand men. Nobody knew the limits of Kastielle's power. Even thirteen hours later, at this battle's conclusion, that threshold remained unclear.

Kastielle ripped and tore through the slurry of foes leaving their dismembered bodies scattered across the field he named in his grandfather's honour. The blood of his enemies covered his arms in layers, dried chipped and coated ten times over. There was no honour here anymore. With half of the men dead, and not even scratching the surface of his powers, his bloodlust became ravenous. Then, he felt the hot burn of the sun on his back. It was like Time, the man who did not stop for his daughter, did not look back to marvel at her gifts to him, not only stopped but personally brought him back to show him the errors of his ways, and, in that eternal split second, Kastielle was subjected to the greatest sadness of his long life. Time proved that although he was worthy and brought all life a shepherd to lead them, he still failed in his journey all those years ago. The selfless orphan found on the streets of Crookston by the greatest of all men, Eros Neriah, was no more. The boy who was destined to become a soldier of not Anara but humankind and all life, was gone. His quest for the Spiritual Court did not end when he got there, and he knew that. That was why he fought the abominable Necronomicon, he died in that arena among every other spirit that wished him dead. Kastielle wanted them to return to not only save but protect the world. Kastielle looked at his former self in shame. Ashamed of what he had become, what his good intentions had turned him into. He was supposed to be the shepherd, not the wolf. The worthy man was worthy no more.

Time showed that in his failure he had taken the lives of many of his countrymen and friends. He showed his part in the death of his sister, Sakura, and what consequences they bore for his friends. The only death that was not his doing was his wife Nami's. She loved him much like the Earth did, because of his faults and his virtues. She saw him even when he could not see himself. He looked at the bodies that he had lay waste, oozing blood from their sliced, torn, and pulverised carcasses all by his hand. He wasn't who he was anymore, but all things return with, Time.

Kastielle exhaled, no longer the Lunatic King not a king at all. He was Kastielle Neriah, the soldier of humanity he was destined to be. The black smog dispersed, and his hair shone gold once more, the beautiful face of the beloved king again. The damage had already been done and the infantry attacked. As the next wave charged, Kastielle could now feel their conflict, their betrayal by his hand. Mostly he could feel fear. This was not what he wanted; these were the people he wanted to protect. He dropped the sword from his hand. The dance of his green eyes shone, and the brilliant white aura returned once more as bright as the sun, stopping all in their tracks. As the light dimmed, Kastielle was washed of his blood and donned his old gi and black staff, gifted to him by his grandfather. He was back.

Three soldiers rushed him with horizontal slashes with their short sword, which Kastielle blocked with his staff. Two others flanked him each side. Kastielle lifted his leg and drove the sole of his foot to the middle soldier's knee dropping him, but not hurting him. He rotated his staff, bringing the other two with the momentum and slipping it to bop them on the head and knock them out. He stopped the right flanker with a front thrust of his staff to the jaw and the one on the left with a hook kick wrapping around his neck. The soldier on his knees rose but was met with a gentle tap that knocked him out too. He lifted the staff and pointed it to the rest of them. Their anxiety and anger rising by the second. Before they could attack again the pressure in the air pinned them.

'I wish I could change. I wish I could feel this way, like myself, forever. But you could never understand the conflict inside me. That is my fault. I was arrogant to think I could control it, that I deserved it and I let you all down. I'm sorry for that, but you won't have to worry anymore. I'm going.' He said knowing that he was the greatest threat to the world and he had to be stopped. To salvage what he had left of his failures he had to go. He had the power of the universe, an infinite power to do anything, including give back the power that was given him. He convulsed as he spat the power from his throat into the sky.

Lightning struck and the winds roared as the heavens swallowed the power Kastielle returned to them. He withered while the thousands of years caught up with him, he smiled content knowing that he would see his wife soon. To his sons, he wished them well.

Kastielle took his last breath before fading into dust.

When he was finally gone, the heavens spat the power back to the ground.

High on her post, a soldier heard Kastielle's scream. Then came the bang. Finally, she saw a shockwave approach quickly from the distance consuming all in its path. It looked like an expanding dome of pure light, like a star was eating Anara itself. Her platoon had occupied Sengham a few days before. Now they were rushing to get away on their ships. She remained to aid in the evacuation efforts. She was from the Wukong Empire. Employed by the occupying forces as a type of scout her people called, Kunoichi. Her name was, Kishi.

The light that reached the sky, rushed like a stampede towards her. Thousands ran for cover in hysterical fever. The sky blackened outside the dome, devoid of stars. The wind swirled into violent tornados and vicious hurricanes. Many were swept away by the storm. Rain shot from the sky accompanied by bolts of lightning. They struck the tall buildings sending rubble raining harshly from above. Some strikes sent a pattering of pebbles and dust, others caused chunks of stone walls to crash to the ground. Now the madness spread to Sengham and the shockwave was close approaching.

Kishi ran for the docks. She led the rest of the city's residents at her tail. She saw mothers carrying their children, running for their lives. Dutiful soldiers like herself ushered the crowd towards the coast. Banners didn't matter at this point, there was only survival. The street was littered with dead. Some of them were from the skirmishes, others were trampled in the panic. Children froze with fear absent their parents, grabbed by passers-by for their safety. The ground trembled. The street narrowed, and the path to the coast was a steep downhill slope. Despite their panic, they had to collectively approach the slope with caution.

Finally, they reached the coast. They had casualties but no time to mourn. The coast was a sandy beach at the inset of a tall crescent-shaped cliff, Eagle's Stay. The beach housed a dock for three ships. Kishi saw ships being boarded by scared citizens at the docks. The city was already burning after a shower of lightning. The shockwave hadn't hit yet but the damage was paramount already. Kishi boarded the ship, after ensuring the most vulnerable boarded safely. They went below deck away from the storm. The evacuation was a success regarding Sengham, but most of Anara suffered the devastation of that blast. The ships rocked heavily as the ocean reacted to the storm above. A siege of lightning bolts harangued the ocean and seashore. The passengers screamed petrified in the dark underbelly of the ship. Kishi scrambled to comfort those she could, unsure of her own reassuring words. The rocking did not settle, and time ran short. A decision had to be made. Either brave the storm or face whatever that shockwave had to give.

Kishi ran onto the deck. The crew was in a frantic rush to set sail. They fought tooth and nail against the beating weather. Kishi rushed out to help but it was too late. She saw the glowing dome-shaped manifest balloon over the edge of the cliff. She had no time to move before it attacked the ships. All three exploded, sending all passengers flying out into the water. The wood and sails set alight. Kishi was hit directly with the blast.

The passengers that were sent to the ocean scurried back to shore if they were able. Kishi drifted back to consciousness after the blast. She saw sights worse than the war. Men, women, and children fell lifelessly with wooden shrapnel lodged in their bodies, gasping for air. Once they hit the ocean, their blood reddened the water as they floated with the tide unable to die without pain.

Screams and cries echoed over the sound of the spattering of rain, rolling of thunder, and the crashing of waves. One by one, the survivors sprinted onto the beach and to a place, they would never recognise. Members of the group looked back to see the oceanic cemetery. There was no mercy or favouritism whoever died, died.

The only way for Kishi to swim through the mass of bodies was to go under the water. She submerged herself. More bodies were drifting down to the sea bed. A dark body pit, a massacre. Kishi searched for a gap to come up for air. When she resurfaced, she was closer to the cliffside than she thought. She was weary and groped for help. Unconsciously, she grabbed a body. She didn't notice until it turned over and the dead stare was in front of her. The face meant nothing to her, it had a long beautiful face and fare skin. Although her beauty was striking, she looked like a proud strong warrior. She pushed her away in horror. They both collided with the bodies around them giving sight to what was beneath the surface. A glint of red light caught her eye. She dived and swam towards it. It was dark under the water with the bodies above coming together and blocking what little light available. Even when the surface was completely covered by the bodies, the red light shone through.

She stopped shocked at the sight. The lights were the eyes of a boy, a baby boy. He was still, pinned against the cliffside. His eyes were open, distant, and shining. His arms hung lifelessly, but the water lifted them to appear like he was asking to be picked up. Kishi reached out to his hanging arms. She grabbed him and rushed to the shore. Kishi ignored everything else around her. She laid the baby on the sand. His eyes were still open, but his body was lifeless. Her heart broke seeing him there. She realised he was so tiny, he had to be only days old if that. This was the horror of war. She never agreed with the Anara invasion, but she was honour bound. Seeing this baby boy laying on the ground, she could see no honour in this.

Her tears fell helplessly down her cheeks. She pressed his chest and patted his back over and over. She could not give up, she would not leave him. His limbs flopped telling the story of his long since passed death. She held him in her arms and kissed him on his head. His eyes were still open and shining red. She pressed sharply on his chest once more. The shine in his eyes disappeared, leaving a rich crimson in its stead. The last sign of life was gone.

Kishi carried him from the beach. She marched away from the hundreds that lay dead in the water or on the sand.

She kept him close to her chest, protecting him from the horror that besieged the land. She walked deeper into the destruction. Anara was truly lost to the world. She passed the boarder of Sengham into the desert, scorched and desolate. Suddenly, the baby coughed. Kishi stopped in her tracks. She examined the baby who didn't move at first then he coughed again. He took a harsh deep breath in and coughed repeatedly. His tiny hands gripped her shirt as he fought the water from his lungs until he cried a powerful cry.

His rich crimson eyes fixed upon her. The burden of realising how alone they were was hers alone to bear. A burden she wished not to share with this baby boy ever, she took his outreaching hand.

'I will name you, Gegan.' She said.

She knew that he was hers to protect until the day she died.

36 THE BALLAD OF TALION 3: THE RED EYED CHILD

Had- Labor- 22- 1827

The destroyed remains of Zorrodon had recovered from the internal siege that Magnus launched. The village was on its way to being restored and the city was on the mend. Talion never really thought about how little he wanted to be there, but the revelation that Celestine was alive made it easier visiting the site of his death. The carriage passed the gates of the governmental complex and into the prison yard. The prison was segmented into three tiers. Tier One was for petty criminals, Tier Two was for the violent criminals, Tier Three was death row. It was where the real villains went, the psychopaths, mass murderers and serial killers. They had never explored this option before, but Tier Three would also be where they kept the killers of political figures. That was where Talion was headed.

Unlike the other two tiers which resembled other traditional buildings, Tier Three was a very tall tower, and unfortunately for Talion, his cell was at the very top. He was handed over to the guards and marched up the stairs. He had to take many rests and fell multiple times because they denied him his cane. After close to an hour of struggle Talion completed his labour of hate up the stairs.

The guard opened the cell door; the room was made of stone. It didn't have a bed or anything else in there. It just had a blanket sprawled on the floor and a bucket in the corner. The place was not designed to be lived in for long. There was a window that looked over the city and let the light in. If the hangman didn't kill him, he was sure that the room would. The guardsman marched Talion in and unlocked his bonds.

'Mr, Thiago will see you tomorrow.' The guardsman said.

Talion nodded. The cell door closed behind him and he sat against a wall. These conditions were far removed from his home, but he had survived worse. He would make do.

Nightfall

Talion wrapped himself in the blanket on the floor and tucked his knees to his chest. It took him a while, but he managed to get to sleep. The slow chill of the night tapped him on the shoulder and pulled him from his slumber. Talion was all too familiar with this sensation. It was that time of night, but he thought he was done with it. He blinked himself awake and stared into the darkest corners of the room.

'Show yourself.' He shouted scuttling back into his corner. There were no games to be played anymore; Mother Nature showed herself immediately. She walked into the moonlight; her footsteps were soundless against the stone flooring. In her hand, she held a dagger with an ivory handle and a black blade. The metal was not of this world.

'Do you remember this?' She asked stroking the sharp edge of the blade without bleeding. 'It was a gift after all, lovingly gifted from me to you. What was it that you named her?' Mother Nature made a pantomime gesture of her thinking. Talion shuffled back as the pale moonlight revealed the runes on the black metal.

'Mo...Mort...' Once again Mother Nature had stricken the former champion of Anara speechless.

'Mortal Maker, the tool of your revenge.' Mother Nature approached Talion and placed the blade in his hands. It was heavy and scorching hot. This was the murder weapon at the scene of his greatest crime.

Nateur- Chrono- 1- 1800

Talion didn't see this coming when he returned to reconcile with his oldest friend before the war. He saw the pain in his eyes when he told Kastielle that Nami had died. That was truly Kastielle, not The Lunatic King. He had to believe that he had confronted this invading force to protect his child and not to satiate bloodlust. Nevertheless, he had to do what he could for everything that their friendship meant, for everything Sakura meant.

He sprinted down the hall and up to Nami's bedroom. Isobelle by Nami's side, the bed looked like the site of a massacre. The blood had dried and left a trail to the cot where Celestine and his twin lay.

'We have to leave now.' Said Talion panting. Isobelle heard and looked up stone-faced.

'I'm not leaving. Not Nami or Kastielle.' She said. She was a woman of duty and she would rather die than desert her post.

'We don't have time. We are in danger Isobelle. Kastielle his fending off an army of thousands on his own. What do you think they will do if they get past him?' He said. Isobelle stood quickly. 'The heirs are not safe here.'

'And you want to run? I knew you were a traitor but a coward as well.' Isobelle spat the words in grief. She needed a target to let her pain out on and Talion was there. Talion had been her friend too long to take it personally; that was just her way. He still needed to get through to her.

'Look out that window. Look what Kastielle is doing out there.' Said Talion. Isobelle went to the window onlooking Eros Pasture. The numbers made her gasp but Kastielle silenced her. There was a rash of bodies in his red wake. 'If you think you can add anything in that battle be my guest, but I'm not getting in his way. I'm taking the children and telling everyone to evacuate immediately.' Talion picked up Celestine who cried in his arms. He waited on Isobelle who fought against her every instinct to help fight to serve the greater purpose. She picked up the other child and they ran for safety.

'Okay, ride to Sengham port and meet me on the cliffside next to it. We can survey the situation from there.'

Isobelle nodded. 'Ride safe brother.' They reached the stables and mounted up. Isobelle has sped ahead. She had the utmost trust in Talion's abilities to protect the child as did he with her. She was always the quicker on a horse and he knew she would get there first. Talion galloped from Anara Castle to Sengham in just over two hours with Celestine in his arms.

When he arrived, the occupying forces had scouts still on the lookout. They didn't know what was coming, but they would soon. Talion had to find his way to the docks while not being detected. He circled the city and onto the crescent shape cliff that overlooked the sea. Isobelle should be waiting there. He reached the peak and was relieved to see her waiting there for him.

He dismounted overjoyed. They hugged each other now infinitely more assured of their and the babies' survival. In their embrace, the two boys grabbed each other's hand. They connected like magnets, two pieces that made one.

'You left me behind.' Talion said stepping back.

'Sorry, I was in a rush. I have never been responsible for a baby before. Did you run into any trouble?'

Talion shook his head. 'You?'

Isobelle shook her head. 'Hey listen, I was thinking if we ditch our armour we may be able to get on one of those. That one down there...' Isobelle pointed to a ship with the Anglonian banner on the sail. 'That one will take us to Anglonia. We can build a life there. I'll raise my kid, you raise yours.' Talion smiled.

'Sounds like a good plan. Let's go then.' He said turning to go.

'Wait, hold on!' Isobelle said. 'I don't want to go through the gates; we might get made. At least in the city, a lot is going on.'

'Don't worry.' Talion said. 'I know this place well; I've sailed from here before. This area is called Eagle's Stay.' Talion unsheathed the black dagger from his waist, lunged, and stabbed it through Isobelle's back and her heart. White light shattered around her, she couldn't scream and went stiff as a board. She dropped the baby. He landed on the grass and cried. Talion withdrew the blade and she turned revealing her petrified face to the score of the cries of a newborn baby boy to be named Gegan.

'Why?' She stammered as the eruption of blood spurted from her wound.

'Because you told him.' Said Talion as he pushed her off the cliffside into the water. Kastielle's spell was broken and she would die for her betrayal.

Had- Labor- 22- 1827

Mother Nature assumed Isobelle's form from that day, stab wound and all. She placed her cold palm on Talion's head. This was the first time seeing this play out, but Talion's memory couldn't lie. Talion snapped from his nightmare to see Isobelle's face, but he heard Mother Nature's voice.

'That was it right? Your revenge over? I remember you begging me once Sakura died for a means to get even. You wanted Kastielle to suffer as you did. You were going to kill Nami with the blade remember? Then you found out she was with child and her fate was sealed. So your revenge spread to whoever was involved, Isobelle. All you needed was an opportunity. Eagle's Stay was a nice touch, but you weren't satisfied were you?'

Talion said nothing.

Mother Nature snagged his throat assuming her normal form again. 'What did you do next Talion!?!'

Talion gasped in hysterical tears refusing to say the words. Mother Nature didn't know what happened, but she had an incredibly good guess.

'Why don't we take a look for ourselves then?' She placed her palm on his face again and brought him back to his nightmare.

Nateur- Chrono- 1- 1800

Talion lifted the baby that would be named Gegan up, cradled him, and looked into the rich crimson of his eyes. Gegan reached for his brother as they both cried for each other. He had the face of his father, the face of his wife's killer. The other child, the one he would name Celestine had his mother's face, the best part of Kastielle. This red-eyed child would grow to be Kastielle, his face would be a constant reminder of the bastard that took Sakura away from him.

'I will not allow you to become the abomination I know you will become! Your father dies here!' He screamed. He would not inflict another Kastielle on the world, not when he could stop it.

He placed baby Celestine on the floor and picked up the Mortal Maker blade. Heavy steps brought him to the edge of the cliff above the water. The spot where he was to marry his love.

He said a prayer to Sakura and stabbed the baby in the heart. He dangled his lifeless body over the water and let go.

Had- Labor- 22- 1827

Mother Nature was not omniscient as many believed; she didn't see all things. She was as interested in the dealing of humans as humans were about the bacteria on their skin. She wasn't aware of all of Talion's sins; she knew of many because Talion either told her or was sent by her directly. He repented for those sins, admitted to the crimes he was ordered to do, but his greatest crime was all his own. Nobody told him to do it, he did it because of his own hate that spread within him.

Mother Nature now knew what she needed to know.

'I have spent an eternity looking for my equal. I think that was why I fell in love with Kastielle the way I did; I loved him more than you could ever know. My father created me as a single omnipotent entity and abandoned me right away. When I had my children, I knew that they all needed a counterpart to balance them. They needed what I never had, and I needed them not to endure the loneliness I had to. Kastielle knew that same loneliness; he felt it too. He was my equal and I was his. We were meant to be, and a mortal woman stole his heart away!' Mother Nature wiped away a tear from her mortal form. 'When he died, I thought I was alone again. Until nine years ago, I came across a man of eighteen years old they called The Demon of the Wasteland, and he looks just like his father. Once again, I found my equal because that boy's immortality wasn't a spell that could be broken. He got that from his dear old daddy.'

'No!' cried Talion as he crawled on the floor to her. 'Please no!'

'You will be executed in Zorrodon, but it will not be by the hangman I assure you.'

Mother Nature faded into dust and darkness leaving Talion alone. In the darkest corner of his isolation, Talion could see the eyes of his final apparition. Their red eyes.

'It will come by the hand of The Demon.'

End.

Angel Of Anglonia

ABOUT THE AUTHOR

I grew up on a council estate in Manchester during the 90s. Growing up I struggled to read for a very long time. I accredit the ability to write and appreciate a book to my mother who spent many an evening, when she wasn't working nights, reading stories with me. I was a weird kid that didn't want children's books, no, I wanted the big boy stories, so she and I read Macbeth together. There, I understood characters and wanted to do that myself from a young age. Another keen influence came from my Dad and Stepmother. My earliest memories of them were sitting in a car on a long trip, and listening to an audiobook. Some Stephen King, or ghost stories, I don't remember anything in the realms of reality. All of my influences came from fantastical places. I could go on, but the gist is, I was bred to love stories.

Now on the other side of 30 and not much wiser than I was as a child, I can honestly say that I embrace my ignorance as a trophy. Learning is the greatest pastime that I've had the privilege to endeavor upon and this book was the greatest education I ever had. I was able to challenge my philosophies and understand the mind of a range of people. Principally, I learned that the story isn't mine when its written. It's yours.

That being said, I'll leave you with this.

The knowledge is the understanding of your life, the ignorance is the opportunity to live it. So, Keep It Simply Stupid.

P.S – The characters of, Porsche and Mac, are a tribute to my dog, Enzo, who had to be put down before writing the Five Stages chapter. If you have read it, you will understand how difficult that was. I bought Enzo with the money I got for my 18th birthday and had him 10 years. He took care of me a lot more than I could possibly take care of him. He was every bit of Porsche in his later years, and Mac X10 in his youth.

Enzo, you were the best dog in the world, and I miss you to this day.

"I love ya, Kid" Your dad, Elston.

Printed in Great Britain
by Amazon

71163928R00175